CORRUPTING CINDERELLA

LOST KINGS MC #2

AUTUMN JONES LAKE

COPYRIGHT

CORRUPTING CINDERELLA

LOST KINGS MC #2

AUTUMN JONES LAKE

ISBN# (Digital) ISBN: 978-0-9907945-2-3

ISBN# (Print) ISBN: 978-0-9907945-3-0
Edited by: Marti Lynch
Formatting: AJ Lake
2018 Cover Designed by: Letitia Hasser, RBA Designs
Photography: Wander Aguiar Photography
Model: Kaz
2nd Edition

REAL LOVE ISN'T A FAIRY TALE.

Although attorney Hope Kendall cares deeply for President of the Lost Kings MC, Rochlan "Rock" North, the truth is they come from completely different worlds. Add to that the fact that they are also both headstrong people, and they have a very rough road ahead of them.

LOVE IS THE ULTIMATE OUTLAW.

For Rock that means introducing Hope to what it really means to be part of his brutal and shady world, where the Lost Kings Motorcycle Club is his main focus. For Hope it means accepting the things she can't change, and understanding that Rock is a man who will do anything to keep her safe.

LOVE DOESN'T FOLLOW any rules.

As Rock continues to draw Hope deeper into his world, painful misunderstandings, past relationships, and opposition from the members of his club will threaten to drive them apart.

HOW DO a lawyer and a badass biker with a heart of gold keep love alive while their opposing worlds collide?

ACKNOWLEDGMENTS

Thank you to my wonderful beta readers who stuck with me for book two!

Allison, Amanda, Angi, Brandy, Elizabeth, Chris, Tamara, Krystal, Clarisse, Rachel, Tammy, Iveta, Robin, Setty, Katie, Maria, Kathrine, and Shelly. Your enthusiasm for the Lost Kings world has been wonderful! I am incredibly lucky to have you for my beta readers.

KA Mitchell, Cara Connelly, Kari W. Cole and Virginia Frost, thank you for all of your valuable feedback, critique, brainstorming, and support. Kari, thank you for the big, green elephant.

Thank you Marti for your patience.

LJ for another gorgeous cover!

I could never name every person individually, but thank you to the readers who reached out to express your love for Slow Burn. I can't tell you how much it meant to have so many people respond so favorably. And I apologize to anyone I scared away with my over-enthusiastic thank yous.

Most of all, I have to thank my husband. For every time I cried about the slowdown of work in my day job this year, and you said "Good. Use the extra time to write," I love you.

LOST KINGS MC SERIES

ULTIMATE SERIES READING ORDER

DEDICATION

For my grandmother, Gloria, who gave me my first romance novel. I wish we'd had more time together, and I hope you're looking down on me with pride.

CHAPTER ONE

ROCK

I HATE BIRTHDAYS.

Well, at least I hate *my* birthday.

Although, this year, I have a lot to celebrate. I'm finally with the person I want to grow old with. Maybe this year's birthday ain't so bad. Given the sort of life I lead, I should be thrilled I even make it to my birthday each year.

It's been a few weeks since Hope and I had our heart-to-heart, subsequent *disagreement,* and the drama at the courthouse. I feel lighter since coming clean with her. Well, sort of. I still have lots of things I'm hiding, but little by little I plan to share everything with her.

We've spent a lot of time together, and I've never been happier. Still there's things I've neglected—nothing important, like weekly church, where we sit down to discuss club business—but I definitely need to show my face at the clubhouse tonight. I've managed to negotiate a few good deals for the MC from my home office, usually with Hope sitting on my lap while I make my cryptic phone calls—so at least I have that to alleviate any guilt over my absence.

As much as I'd like to spend the evening under the covers with

Hope, I can't avoid another Friday night get-together. It's also time I reveal more about this part of my life to her.

"Are you sure you want me there?" she asks for the third time tonight.

She picks at the hem of her shirt as I've noticed she does when she's nervous.

"Of course, doll." Placing a hand on each shoulder, I pull her closer to me. "I haven't been for the last few weeks. I need to put in an appearance, and I want you with me. I need to start introducing you to everyone as my woman."

She rolls her eyes at me. "Your woman. You sound like a caveman."

The corners of my mouth turn up. "You say that like it's an insult."

"I just feel so out of place around your friends."

I sigh and suffer a bit of guilt. I hate making her uncomfortable. And it's quite possible things could get very uncomfortable for my girl tonight. "Your place is with me, doll."

That seems to cheer her up, and she tosses her hands in the air. "Well, what do I wear?"

I thrust my fingers through my hair. Normally, I'd say as little as possible. But I don't want Hope showing those fuckers any more skin than necessary. I wonder if she has a snowsuit?

"Something comfortable. We're riding my bike up."

That gets a smile out of her. My girl has taken to the bike more than I expected she would. She's my perfect blend of sweet and wild.

She dashes into her closet. As I'm standing there, clothes, hangers, and shoes start flying through the air. Some of it lands on the bedroom floor at my feet. I shake my head at the mess she's making. I'm going to need to give my baby an entire room to use as a closet. That way I can just shut the door on the whole thing. If I ever get her to move the fuck in with me.

Fuck. I'm distracted by her bending over, tipping her perfect, denim-covered ass in my direction. I'm so close to skipping the party, except that I know the club will have something planned for my birthday.

We haven't been together long enough that I bother mentioning the day to Hope. It's not as if I'm some little kid expecting a present. Just being with her every second I can get has been enough of a gift. No reason to get greedy.

She's finally ready and proudly shows off her LOKI T-shirt. It's all my favorite things: blue, tight, and tiny—with my club's logo spelled out right over her perfect, perky breasts. Now *that's* a present.

Her lips are quivering with barely concealed glee, and I notice she's got something tucked behind her back.

"Whatcha got there, doll?"

Almost shyly, she swings this box out from behind her. It's wrapped in matte black paper with a silver bow.

"Happy Birthday."

I'm stunned. Completely dumbfounded. How did she even know? I'm standing there like an idiot for so long, worry steals over her face, so I reach out and take the box. It's got some heft to it, and I'm dying to know what my girl got for me. I stagger over to the bed and drop down. She follows and stands over me, running her fingers through my hair.

"I wasn't sure what to get the big, bad biker who has everything…"

It's silly, but when she calls me that, it sends a thrill through me. "Whatever it is, I'll love it," I assure her.

Ripping off the paper leaves my jaw hanging. "My God, Hope. How did you even find this?" I'm holding a box with a bottle of specially aged, sixteen-year-old single malt Scotch. It's in a fancy box because it comes in a wooden frame designed to look like a Viking ship. I know it probably cost quite a bit since only 1,500 bottles were even released in the States. I can't imagine the trouble she went to in order to track it down.

"Do you think you'll like it? I don't know that much about Scotch or liquor in general. The guy I ordered it from told me any serious Scotch drinker would like it." She stops and gives me that shy smile I love so much. "I really liked the ship thingie it comes in, it reminded me of—"

She stops and traces her fingers over my chest. I know she means my pirate ship tattoo, and I don't bother correcting her because I don't care about anything but how generous and lovely my girl is.

"You'll drink it, right?" she says, a bit of worry still clinging to her expression.

"Hell, yes."

Her eyes light up, and she claps her hands together in that way that makes her look so young I feel like a dirty old man next to her.

Having Hope wrapped around me on the way up to the club feels so good, I almost keep driving. The night's cool, but the wind rushing against me brings all my senses alive. Soon enough winter will be here, and I'll be relegated to driving my cage for months on end. I understand why the old-timers relocate to Florida.

The clubhouse is already wild when we arrive. I swear I can hear the thump of music all the way down at the front gate. I drive through carefully because you never know where the party-goers will end up. I back the bike into my spot and say hello to a bunch of people outside. Hope dismounts like a pro and shakes her hair out after handing me her helmet. Random people milling around greet us, and she gives a shy wave in return.

"You're sure you want me here?" she whispers.

I snag her around the waist and pull her close for a searing kiss. She's completely dazed when I'm done with her. Against her ear, I whisper, "If you ask me again, I'm going to give *you* all thirty-eight of my birthday spankings when we get upstairs."

Her eyes go wide and her legs wobble, so I hold her tighter to me. "Are we clear, doll?"

She nods.

"Answer me," I growl in her ear.

"Yes, Rock."

"Good girl." I give her a pat on the ass, but I don't let her go just yet. I've found I have a hard time keeping my hands off of Hope no matter where we are. Makes things awkward when we're out in the "real world" like the grocery store or post office. But this is my club, my world, so I'll be touching her all damn night.

Someone whistles in our direction, and the crunch of gravel reaches my ear. Reluctantly I let go of Hope, but I capture her hand in mine.

"Prez," Wrath greets me. He's made his irritation over my recent absence quite clear at church every weekend. The daily, nagging texts he sends also help get his point across.

With a less than friendly look, he says hello to Hope. He turns back to me, dismissing her, and I can already tell we're going to have issues tonight.

Happy Birthday to me.

Hope

Wrath hates me. I'm not sure what I've done to incur his...well, wrath. But he's definitely not a fan of mine. I try to be as nice as possible, but it doesn't get me anywhere with him. While Rock and Wrath do their death glare thing with each other, I lean over and pull the Scotch out. Rock takes it from me and slips his arm around my waist while tucking the box under his other arm.

"What's in the box, prez?"

"Birthday present from Hope."

Wrath glances at me with a surprised expression. Why is everyone shocked I got my boyfriend a present for his birthday?

Inside is an eye-opener. It's about thirty degrees warmer, and I am way overdressed. The scene makes me appreciate that Rock told me to dress comfortably. The memo the rest of the girls inside got clearly stated "clothing optional." The scent of sex, weed, and alcohol permeates everything.

A crowd forms at the door, and we barely make it inside. Everyone is excited to see Rock. People shout and tug at him. He smiles and acknowledges each person in that easy manner I envy so much.

Turning to me, he bends down. "You okay?"

I nod. Because he can sense how overwhelmed I am, he seats me in a corner of the couch in the back of the room. "I want to go lock this up. I'll be right back. Don't move." As he steps away, he slaps a hand on Wrath's shoulder and whispers something to him. Wrath's gaze flicks in my direction and he nods once.

As Rock moves farther away into the crowd, his big, mean Viking friend pushes his way through the group toward me.

"Didn't think this would be your scene," he shouts over the music.

He drops down next to me on the couch, sending me bouncing into the air a little.

I'm not sure how to respond. Anything I say is bound to be offensive to Wrath or an outright lie. So instead I just smile as if I'm a bit daft.

"How long have you and Rock known each other?" I ask out of curiosity. Rock has explained that Wrath functions as his "enforcer" in the club. I have no clue what that means, but judging from the guy's bulging muscles and scarred knuckles, it's clearer.

"Long damn time."

"Did you meet through the club?"

"No. We knew each other before. Knew Z too." He nods at a tall guy across the room. I recognize the dark hair, simmering blue eyes, and neck tattoo. He took my friend Lilly home the night Rock and I got together. He's surrounded by at least three different barely dressed girls at the moment. I make a mental note to ask Sophie if Lilly and Z have anything going on.

"We all prospected together. Very different time."

I don't know what to say. "Oh."

"You know much about MCs, Hope?"

"No. I mean, only what I've learned from Rock."

He nods, his gaze roaming all over me. He visually gropes me for so long, my skin heats under his scrutiny. "What are you doing here then?" he finally asks.

My brows pull together. What kind of question is that? "I'm here with Rock."

He shakes his head. "What's a woman like you doing with my president? You guys got nothing in common."

Tears sting my eyes, but I'm not going to let this asshole intimidate me. "I like him, and he likes me."

He shakes his head like I'm too dense to get his point. "You're just as clueless as Cinda-fuckin-rella aren't you? He doesn't 'like' you. He's fuckin *in love* with you. As in droppin' responsibilities and getting us into bad shit in love with you. And you're just over there in your little preppy, lawyer world, thinking what exactly? You'll take a walk on the wild side? Throw on some leather and be one of us? You ain't ever gonna be one of us, sweetie."

His words are brutal and they strike their target. He isn't saying anything I haven't already thought of, he's just saying it a lot meaner.

Straightening my spine, I'm determined not to let this asshole get to me. "Are you sure *you're* not in love with him, Wrath? You sound like a jealous boyfriend," I snap back.

My words hit him and his nostrils flare. I'm a little frightened, actually. Suddenly the hard lines of his face diminish, and he lets out a loud chuckle.

"Well, fuck if you aren't a spitfire."

"Well, fuck if you're not a big jerk."

"That I am, sugar." He grins a big, goofy grin at me. The total opposite of the menace he displayed seconds ago—until Rock comes up and kicks him in the calf.

"That did not look like a friendly conversation, asshole. I told you to look after Hope, not terrorize her."

Rock motions for me to stand and then steals my seat. He pulls me onto his lap, and I snuggle up against him, relieved he's returned to save me from his jerkface friend. Wrath cocks his head and takes us in.

"We're solid. Right, Hope?"

I want to say "no, you're an asshole," but I feel like I'm close to passing some sort of test with him. "Yup. Wrath was just giving me the lay of the land."

Rock squeezes the curve of my hip, his hand sneaking under the hem of my T-shirt to brush against my bare skin. I shiver. His other arm is draped over my thighs, holding me tight to him. At last a familiar, friendly face stops by. I sit up straight so I can greet her.

"Hi. Trinity, right?"

She's wearing a lot more makeup than the last time we met, but she's the only other woman here wearing jeans and an entire shirt, so I'm extra happy to see her. "Yeah. Good to see you again, Hope."

My gaze drifts over to Wrath who is watching Trinity with uncomfortable intensity. Trinity completely ignores him, all of her focus on Rock. She taps his shoulder with her fist. "You want a drink, Rock-around-the-clock?"

Underneath me, I feel him chuckle. I remember last time she called him "rock-n-roll," so I guess this is their thing. Geez, how many times has he fucked her? Instantly, I'm insanely jealous.

"Will you bring me a Crown and Coke, please, hon? Hope, what do you want?"

What is this poor girl supposed to be, a waitress for the whole club? That kinda sucks. Wait, why am I feeling bad for her when she's probably fucked my boyfriend sixty ways from Sunday?

"I'm okay. Um, maybe just water with lime?"

Next to me Wrath snickers, and Trinity spares him a glance. It's really more of a glare, and I'm kind of warming up to her now.

Rock traces a finger over my collarbone, pushing my hair behind my shoulder. My eyelids flutter as he presses his lips against my ear. "You still like margaritas, doll?"

I nod because I can't speak with him touching me. "Bring her a margarita, please, Trinny. Not too heavy on the tequila—she's a bit of a lightweight."

Wrath snorts, and Trinity ignores him this time. "Sure. I'll be right back."

Now I feel like a jerk. It's one thing for her to serve Rock in his club, but it's not fair for her to be fetching me drinks. I try to push myself off Rock. "Hold on, Trinity, I'll help you."

She turns back to me with wide eyes and shakes her head. "I got it."

I couldn't follow her if I wanted to anyway, because Rock has banded his arms around me and is keeping me anchored to his lap. "Let Trinny do her job. Your job is to sit here and decorate my lap."

A lick of anger tightens my belly. Rock must sense the shift in my mood because his lips are at my ear again. "Doll, if you get up now, it will be uncomfortable for everyone. You've given me one hell of hard-on from sitting there looking like a virgin in a whorehouse." His deep voice buzzing against my skin does obscene things to my insides.

I turn and whisper in his ear. "You know damn well I'm no virgin." Then I wriggle a bit to confirm his story.

He groans into my ear.

"Careful," he rumbles in that sexy, low, gravelly voice that makes me so weak. The teasing is too much—I need a taste, so I lean in and catch his lips with my own. His hands come up to cup my face, twining in my hair and pulling me tight to him. I hear Wrath muttering and feel the couch shift, but I don't care. High school has to be the last time I made out with someone in a public place like this, but I can't call up a bit of shame. His heart thumps against the hand I have curled on his chest, while the rough prickle of his stubble tickles my other palm. He breaks the kiss, resting his forehead against mine.

"I need to take you upstairs," he says low enough that only I can hear him.

Thank goodness. There's definitely people doing more than making out in this room, and I'm glad Rock doesn't expect that of me. There's a small part of me that's concerned I'm so far under Rock's spell that I'd pretty much do anything he asked.

Before we can escape, the lights dim and people start singing— well, shouting—happy birthday. Trinity and two other girls I haven't met are carrying a huge cake lit with at least thirty-eight candles. Rock's laughter rolls over me and he sits up a little bit as the girls approach, jostling me forward. I attempt to stand so I'm not in the way, but Rock holds me tight.

The girls stop in front of us. One of them is giving me the shifty stink eye. Trinity winks at me. I feel stupid that I didn't help them plan anything for my boyfriend's birthday. Wrath's words about me not fitting in start to mess with my head, and again I try to stand.

Rock pulls my hair into a makeshift ponytail at the base of my neck.

"Help me blow the candles out, sweetheart—there's a fuck lot of them."

I chuckle, because he's a clever bastard. He's not only made sure my hair won't catch fire, he's got me tethered to him with my hair being held hostage. We lean over together and blow the candles out, getting every last one. The girl that's been giving me the *drop dead* glare says in breathy-fake voice, "make a wish."

Rock laughs. "I already got my wish," he says, pulling me tight against him once more.

I angle my head to the side and kiss his cheek. "Aw, thanks."

"We're going to set this at the bar and cut it. I'll come bring you guys a slice. I didn't forget the drinks either," Trinity says with a sheepish smile.

Rock reaches out and catches her hand. "Thanks, Trinny."

"Happy Birthday, Rockstar," she says before taking off.

I want to ask him about her, but I don't know what to say without sounding like a crazy person. Besides, Wrath is still near, and I don't want to give him the satisfaction of my insecurity.

"Okay, now I really need you naked, Hope." This time he says it loud enough that Wrath hears it and responds with an obscene whistle.

Ignoring Wrath, I whip my head around. "We can't leave now. They're bringing you cake."

He shakes his head.

"You'll hurt their feelings if you don't stay," I protest.

"You're such a sweetheart, but you forget I'm the king of this jungle, baby." It's so absurd, I laugh, but I see he's only half joking. A wicked smile lights up his face, and he pulls me so I'm now straddling his lap, shifts his hands under my ass, and lifts us off the couch.

"God, you're strong," I whisper. "It's so fucking sexy."

His mouth twists into that panty-dropping smile of his. "Wrap your legs around me and hold on."

I'm a little embarrassed being carried around like this, but it also turns me on like crazy. He swings by the bar, and Trinity pushes a plate piled high with cake into my hand while giving me a sweet smile. Before we can turn back to the stairs, there's a lot of yelling and commotion at the front door. One of the guys—whose name I don't know—Zero, and two girls walk through the front door. I recognize the tall, skinny blonde right away.

"Happy Birthday, Mr. President!" Inga shouts.

The plate of cake in my hand splatters on the floor.

CHAPTER TWO

ROCK

Fucking hell. Why on earth is Inga here?

In the four or five years I've known her, she's never once come to the clubhouse. I prefer to keep the dancers separate from the MC. Otherwise, lines get blurred, and shit gets complicated.

Like this kind of complicated.

Hope unwraps her legs from me and slides down to the floor. I steady her with an arm around her waist.

Now, Inga is most certainly not the only girl in this room I've fucked. Without even turning my head, I can count at least three others. But Inga is the only one Hope knows for a fact I've fucked, making for one hell of an awkward situation. I don't want her uncomfortable in my clubhouse. I shoot a glare at Zero and Dex. I expect the "what the fuck" is coming through loud and clear in my expression.

"Uh, Inga knew it was your birthday, heard there was a party, and asked if she could follow Dex up," Z gets out before I clock him.

Inga pops a hand on her hip and settles into one of her favorite poses. "Hey, Big Poppa, it's been a minute."

I really hate her fucking nickname for me. She leans in to give me a kiss, but I hold my hand up. Her wounded expression might bother me except I'm so furious, I can't find a single fuck to give. Her eyes shift to Hope and widen in shock.

"Hey, Hope." She swings her gaze back to me, and I can already see the questions forming. "Hope and I just ran into each other not that long—"

"I know. She told me." Actually, because of that run-in, Hope and I had a heart-to-heart that cemented our relationship. Lucky for Inga, the memory of that conversation lessens my fury at her surprise appearance.

She pops her hand back on her hip, and this time my eyes are drawn to her almost non-existent outfit. The only way to describe the black leather and gold shiny stuff is a sort of biker-meets-school-girl-hooker costume.

"Why didn't you tell me you guys were together?" Inga asks Hope.

"It's recent. And none of your business," I answer. Hope still hasn't moved or said a word.

Not at all ruffled, Inga continues as if this falls right into line with her plans. "Well, this here is my friend Peach. She's touring with me, and we wanted to do a special show just for you as a birthday present. Dex said you guys got a private room here."

Like fuck am I going in there alone with her and "Peach."

She leans in closer. "Peach and I just did a film together, and I brought you an advance copy." She reaches into her smart-car-sized purse and pulls out a thick DVD case with a topless Inga on it. Fantastic. Could this night go to shit any faster? Wrath walks up and snatches the movie out of my hand, finally making himself useful.

"Fuckin awesome. We'll toss this in the player out here. Thanks, Inga."

She looks put out but recovers quickly.

"So, where's the private room?"

Z points down the hall. "It's probably full. I'll go clear it out."

"Uh, where's Murphy?" I glance around for my ginger Road Captain. I spot Wrath by the television. "Wrath? Get back here."

Wrath and Murphy lumber up.

"Inga's gonna do a private show."

She frowns at the addition of the other guys. "It's a big room, Ing."

"Peach too," Inga says.

"You know no one here is paying either of you, right?" I remind her.

She laughs, "Poppa, I didn't come here for money."

I wish you hadn't come at all.

"Cookie," Murphy yells, and she comes running.

Wrath picks Trinny up and tosses her over his shoulder before heading down the hall. She playfully slaps his ass, and I wish those two would just get it over with.

People head down the hall, thank fuck, because I am planning to escape upstairs with Hope.

When we're finally not surrounded by ears and eyes, I pick her up and set her on the bar. "Baby doll, I'm so sorry. I had no idea that was going to happen." There's no reason to pretend I don't know why this is awkward.

She runs a hand over my cheek looking so damn sad, I want to wrap my hands around Z's neck and squeeze really hard. "You can go. I'll, uh, wait upstairs."

"Fuck, no."

She hangs her head. "Do you want me to go home?"

Christ.

"Baby. No. I want to go upstairs with you. Fuck, why don't we just leave and go to your house?"

She smiles at me like she doesn't quite believe me.

"Rock! Show's about to start," Wrath shouts.

Fuck me.

"Come on, Hope. Hurry." Trinny yells.

Hope turns and sees Trinity waving at her to join them. Wrath's doing some ridiculous bump and grind dance behind Trinity that I will make fun of him for until the day he fucking dies. Hope giggles and hops off the bar. She holds out her hand to me.

"Let's go, birthday boy."

Z must have realized the error of his ways because his ass is firmly planted in the chair Inga clearly reserved for me. Swan sits in his lap, giggling and whispering in his ear. Inga's frustrated, but she knows better than to mess with Z. Wrath and Trinity are sitting in the middle of the plush bench that runs against the wall. Dex and Cookie are spread out a little farther down from them. Murphy is perched on the bench on the other side of the room. I pull Hope into a corner spot and position her on my lap so I can watch her face. At the first sign of unease across her pretty features, we are gone.

The opening notes of "Rock You All Night Long" come over the speakers, and I groan. Some time ago, the girls at the club decided that should be my theme song, and not a night went by when at least one of them would throw it on. The song brings up a lot of old memories. Not unpleasant ones, but not what I want to think about anymore. Honestly, this is awkward as fuck. That part of my life needs to stay in my rearview so I can move forward with my girl. Instead, the two worlds are colliding violently tonight. Burying my face in Hope's neck, I let her sweet scent relax me. Realizing she's breathing heavy, I lift my head. She's watching the girls intently, lips parted.

Well, fuck me. My girl's into this.

Okay, then.

"You all right?" I ask.

"Never seen anything like this," she answers without taking her eyes off the girls.

That's fine. I've seen enough porn star flesh to last a lifetime. But Hope? This is a brand new vision, and I want to sear it into my memory to take with me when I'm on long rides without her.

I can't take my eyes off her.

The expression that flickers over her face fascinates me. The corner we're in is pretty dark, so I pull her back against my chest and shift my legs so that hers fall open. Holding both her hands in one of mine, I press them between her breasts. I work my other hand between her legs. Rubbing the seam of her jeans. Feeling the heat pouring from her center. Her breath hitches, and she squirms in my grasp. My lips find the pulse point at her neck where I nip and suck at her sensitive skin until she's trembling.

"Rock," she gasps.

At her tone, I glance up and realize a half-dressed Inga is headed our way. Removing my hand from between Hope's legs, I mutter a curse. Inga—she devil that she is—pulls Hope out of my lap and into the middle of the floor. The guys hoot and encourage this insanity.

I'm going to kill every one of them.

Inga and Peach are all over my girl. Hope is being a good sport, trying to dance along with the two pros. Damn, if she isn't sexy as fuck doing it too. Of course, Inga encourages Hope to take her top off.

Oh, fuck, no.

Trinity jumps into the fray, distracting Inga with her wild dance moves. Damn, I love that girl. Wrath yells "take it off" to Hope or Trinny, I'm not sure. Trinity flips him off and starts giving Dex a lap dance.

That's my cue to get my woman. Because…nope. Not happening. What's under Hope's clothes belongs to me alone, and if she's giving anyone a lap dance tonight—it's me. Pulling a page from Wrath's caveman handbook, I toss Hope over my shoulder and head into the hallway. She's giggling and thankfully not at all pissed. The volume in the room detonates after the door closes behind us.

God only knows how far Inga will go. I've never seen her amped up like this.

Upstairs. Please, can I just get my woman upstairs?

No. Of course not.

Teller stops me at the foot of the stairs. So fucking close.

"Prez, can I have a word?"

"Yeah, of course." I motion him to a corner of the room where the least amount of debauchery is going on. Hope takes the detour in stride. Once again she's on my lap. This time she's more engaged with the crowd around her. She nods and smiles at people when they stop over to say hello. I know how shy she is, so I appreciate the effort she's making.

Teller is laying out some personal shit. I feel for the kid. He's only been a full-patched member for a little over seven years, but he stepped up to be treasurer when I needed him to and he's a hard worker. Unfortunately, none of that work gets reported to the government.

"I gotta get custody of Heidi. She's going to end up killing our grandmother. Just two more years 'til she's eighteen. My lawyer says I gotta show I have a steady job. Something on the books."

"Okay. I'd put you on at CB, but I don't think working at a strip club is going to help you get custody of your sixteen-year-old sister."

He snorts.

"My bike shop is official. I could set up payroll or something for that." Not to be a dick, but that's a lot of extra hassle I don't feel like dealing with.

Voices get louder from down the hall—sounds like the party in the champagne room is winding down. Glancing up, I spot Trinity fuming and call her over. "Where's Wrath?"

She practically snarls, "Trying to fuck Inga or Peach."

I lift an eyebrow, and she shrugs. I'm not surprised Wrath would go after a girl he knew I'd been involved with, but that he would do it in front of Trinity tonight does surprise me. A flash of his blond hair catches my attention. Fucker's trying to sneak upstairs with Peach.

My voice easily carries over the crowd. "Wrath! Get over here."

He turns and gives me a face full of pissed off, but strides over. He glances at Trinity, and she ignores him.

"What's doin', prez?"

"I need you to do a brother a solid. Can you put Teller on the books at the gym?"

He glances at Teller. "Yeah, of course. I'll find something. Full time?"

"Yeah, club will cover it."

"No prob. You didn't have to call me over now to do it."

I'm glad he's going to help out. But I'm still pissed at the way he's treated Trinny tonight—time for a lesson.

"I also need you to bring some stuff down to CB. Got a call from them earlier."

His jaw drops. Trinny ducks to the side and stuffs down a giggle.

"Fuck, prez. You serious? Send a prospect."

I arch a brow.

"Fine. Fuck." He shoves his fingers through his hair and tries to locate Peach, who has disappeared into the crowd. I nudge Hope.

"Baby doll, give me a minute, okay?"

"Of course." She scoots off my lap, but before I get up, she swoops in and plants a kiss on my cheek.

"Stay here," I instruct Hope.

I glance at Trinity. "Will you sit with her?" As our longtime club girl, I want Trinity to give Hope some info.

"Of course." She immediately drops next to Hope, and the two of them start chatting.

Satisfied Hope will be okay, I pull Wrath to the door.

"Why you giving me bitch work, Rock? Fuck, man, Peach is a fucking porn star. I wanna hit that." While he's whining about Peach, his eyes are focused behind me where Hope and Trinity are.

Tilting my head into his line of vision, I give it to him straight. "Then don't be making a play for Trinity and two seconds later someone else right in front of her. We fucking talked about this. God damn."

He pulls his stare to me and smirks. "Think she's up for a three-way?"

I shake my head. This asshole never quits.

Suddenly he's all business. "Be serious, prez. You need me to go down to CB or not?"

I've made my point. No reason to make him drive down there and back for nothing. "No. Just tone it down."

"I like Hope, he says out of nowhere.

"Like I give two fucks."

"No, seriously. I gave her shit before, and for a second I thought she was going to cry and you were going to murder me, but then she just dished it right back."

I laugh, although I do kinda want to throat punch him for trying to upset my girl on purpose. Before I get the chance, Z's at my back.

"Yo. Dex wants to nail Inga. You cool with that?"

"Why are you asking?"

Z shrugs. "I may partake as well."

Christ.

"She's fair game. We haven't been a thing for a year and a half."

"Fuck—why didn't you say so sooner?"

"Am I required to update you on where I park my dick now?"

Z gags. Wrath laughs.

Z straightens up and throws Dex a thumbs up. "Hey, I'm sorry Dex and I brought them up. I didn't realize Hope would be here. This asshole said it would be okay." He jerks his thumb at Wrath.

"Surprise, surprise," I grumble.

"What?" Wrath has the nerve to make a "who me" face. Maybe the girls fall for that shit. I don't.

"Go meet me in the conference room."

"Now?"

I ignore him and turn to Z. "Take a run at Peach. Just remember, they're both employees at the dance club. Treat them with respect, even if they don't treat themselves with any."

The corner of Z's mouth lifts in a smile. "Yeah. I got you."

Wrath glares at me while Z flips him off and flees. "Not cool, prez."

I grab him by the back of the neck and aim him in the direction of our war room. "Stop acting like a little bitch. It's my birthday. Come have a drink with someone older and wiser."

I slip my keys out of my pocket and open the door, closing it quietly behind us.

"What up?"

"I wanna show you something."

"Should I be scared?"

Wrath scared of anything is hilarious. "Don't be a dick."

Unlocking my personal cabinet, I pull out the bottle of Scotch Hope gave me and show it to Wrath.

"No shit. Where'd you get that?"

"Birthday present from Hope."

He whistles. "Nice present."

I set out two glasses.

"You're going to open it now?"

"What better time?"

Wrath's hard stare drills into me, and he shakes his head. "I can't believe you brought her here. It's like corrupting fucking Cinderella or something."

My laughter is forced because, while it's an accurate description of the night, I'm not happy about it. I pour the Scotch and hand him one of the glasses. After swirling the caramel-colored liquid around for a bit, he holds up the glass. "May you live to be a hundred years with one extra year to repent."

"Ha. I'll repent nothing." We clink and tip our glasses back.

"Fuck, that's good."

"Smooth and spicy," I agree.

"So, this thing with her is serious?"

His question annoys me for some reason, and it takes me a second to consider how I want to answer. "I feel like we've already had this conversation before, brother."

As usual, nothing fazes him. "Someone like her might be better off as a citizen wife," he suggests.

Wrath is brave for even mentioning such a thing. The idea of keeping Hope away from such a big part of my life leaves me cold. "Too late now."

"You tell her everything?"

"No."

"You gonna?"

I turn this over in my mind before answering. Everything? What's everything?

How we earn? I'm pretty sure she already suspects.

That I've fucked around a lot? I think that's been made more than obvious tonight.

That I preemptively killed two cold-blooded bastards to keep her safe?

I'll keep that one to myself for now.

"Eventually. As a lawyer for the club, she can't spill anything anyway. What we tell her is confidential. She becomes my wife, it will be like double protection."

Wrath nods, looking relieved. Has that been his problem all along?

"Wife. Wow. Okay. Ol' lady status isn't enough?" he asks with an eyebrow lift. When I shake my head, he continues. "You got it bad for this broad, don't ya?"

Unlike some of my brothers, I'm not afraid to express my feelings for the woman I care about. "She's not a broad. And yes."

"No disrespect intended. I like that she can hang. Trin seems to like her too."

"Good. They can be helpful to each other."

Wrath nods, so I guess I don't need to spell it out for him for a change.

I pick up the bottle of Scotch and our glasses. "Go park your ass on the couch and make sure Trinny isn't scaring Hope away."

Hope

"You doing okay with all this?" Trinity asks as soon as the guys are out of earshot. Well, except for Teller, who is so furiously texting someone, I doubt he hears anything we say.

"Yeah."

She shakes her head. "I don't know what the guys were thinking bringing Inga here." She stops and gives me a level stare. "I've never slept with Rock, if you're wondering."

That's a huge relief.

"I can only imagine what you've heard." She flings her hand toward the open room.

"What's your role here?" I'm honestly curious.

"Well, club took me in about eight years ago. I have a room here. Club pays my expenses. I kind of take care of the place, clean up after these pigs. And I make myself available to the guys on an as-needed basis."

I'm not really sure what to say to that. "Why?"

She shrugs and thankfully doesn't seem offended. "I dunno. I grew up around MCs, so I guess I just feel safer around one."

"Safe?" I'm not sure if "safe" is the word I would use for hanging around a bunch of guys who could snap me like a twig.

"Have you seen these guys?" She gestures toward Wrath, who is heading our way with a determined expression. "Wrath is a dick, sure, but he'd never let anyone hurt me."

"I wouldn't let anyone mess with you either, mama," Teller remarks without looking away from his phone.

Trinity giggles and punches his arm. The corner of his mouth twitches, and he winks.

Lowering my voice, now that I know Teller is more alert than I thought, I ask her. "Why aren't you a member? They don't allow women to be members, do they?"

She hesitates. "I don't know if any have ever asked. These types of clubs don't usually have women members."

"What type is that?" I'm so confused with all their specific, odd rules I don't understand.

"Outlaw, outlaw, outlaw..." Teller chants for no discernible reason.

"Giddy-up, brother!" Wrath shouts as he approaches, giving Teller a fist bump. Oh, goody—more grief from the big, blond Viking to look forward to.

Trinity continues educating me. "Look. I grew up around bikers. My dad was in a nasty MC. Got shanked in prison when I was ten, but before that he owned a tattoo shop where all the guys would hang. I saw lots of shit growing up. From what I understand, LOKI was in rough shape when Rock took over. But he and Wrecking Ball," she says, jerking her thumb at Wrath, who blows her a kiss, "and Z whipped the club into shape. Rock's a good guy. He takes care of everyone. He's responsible for the family. Women aren't disrespected here. Rock doesn't allow it. You know, besides the normal antics of the male pig."

For some reason, Wrath takes those words as a cue to squeeze in between Trinity and Teller. Hauling Trinity into his lap, he grins from ear to ear like she just paid him a compliment.

"Ugh, get offa me, you beast." She slaps at his hands, but he wraps himself around her tighter, resting his chin on the crown of her head as if he has no idea what her problem is.

Curious about her story, I ask. "How did you find these guys?"

Trinny waves her hand in the air, then settles it against Wrath's arms encircling her waist. "Club girls know how to find bikers."

"Fuck yeah, baby," Wrath says in a low, rumbling tone that even makes my tummy flutter. As I watch, he takes her ear lobe between his teeth, flicking his tongue back and forth. Her eyes flutter shut for a second and then she elbows him in the chest until he lets go.

She continues as if I hadn't witnessed the intimate moment between them. "But honestly, I was tending bar downtown with this girl." She turns to Wrath. "You remember Stormy?"

"Yup. Poser skank."

She tilts her head as if his assessment is accurate. "She kept telling me about LOKI, and having known bikers since I was a kid, I found her story a little hard to believe."

Wrath pulls his head back, looking indignant. "Cause she made us sound like a bunch of pussies?"

"No." Trinity clarifies. "That you weren't a bunch of pigs. Although she was wrong on you."

"Oink."

"Exactly."

"So where is she now?" I ask.

Wrath shifts his long legs, rolling Trinity in his lap. She wriggles, trying to keep upright, causing Wrath to moan. "Watch it, woman."

"She was not about this life," Teller answers my question after shooting a glare at Trinity and Wrath.

"What? Riding motorcycles?" As usual, I'm having trouble following their jargonized language.

The way the three of them share a look, I know I've just made an ass out of myself. Why, I have no idea, since everyone keeps insisting it's just a "club."

"Thug life," Teller remarks.

I smile because I think it's a joke. "You're not thugs. Well, you probably are," I say pointing at Wrath.

"I definitely am," he says, meeting my stare.

"Anyway," Teller continues, smoothing over the awkward moment. "Stormy-girl found herself a nice citizen husband."

My blank stare is enough that I don't have to voice the "what the heck is that" on the tip of my tongue.

Both Wrath and Teller focus their stony glares on me, but Wrath is the one who delivers the lecture. "She was one of those good girl types lookin' to take a walk on the wild side. You know, spice up her dull, sheltered life? Attaching herself to outlaws made her feel special,"

Wrath says. It's similar to the speech he gave me earlier. Shame—I'd just started to think he might not be a complete asshat.

Trinity seems alarmed by how intense this conversation suddenly turned. "That's not entirely true. She got tired of being passed around. No one was gonna claim her back then, and she really wanted to get married and start a family."

Wrath sneers. "No one was claiming club ass. Back then."

A flash of anger lights up her face, but she doesn't respond. Instead, she leans forward and lowers her voice. "From what I hear, Rock hasn't been with any of the club girls in like a year or something." She straightens up.

I already know this because Rock admitted it to me the afternoon we had our heart-to-heart in his garage. But it still feels good to have confirmation from an inside source.

"All the girls gossip about the guys," she says with a snicker.

Teller chuckles. "Boys compare notes too."

Gross.

Wrath's jaw and his hold on Trinity tightens.

"Anyway, I just wanted you to know. Me and Rock. Never." She makes a slashing motion with her hand.

Wrath's gaze shoots toward the ceiling.

She continues. "He's more like a big brother or father figure—"

"Fuck, Trinny. I am not old enough to be your dad." Rock's back. A smile breaks over my face. I'm so happy to see him. The education I've been getting, while interesting, doesn't have a lot to do with our relationship.

Trinity flushes eight shades of red. "Sorry. You know what I mean."

The party seems to be winding down out here, but there's still a lot of noise going on around us. The music has been lowered, and sex noises can pretty much be heard from every direction. Rock traces his finger over my cheek.

"You okay, doll?"

I nod, enjoying his touch.

Someone comes over, taps his shoulder, and they turn away to talk.

Wrath clears his throat. "Uh…Hope, I'm sorry about Inga coming here tonight. I gave the okay for it. I didn't think Rock would actually bring you to a club party."

Trinity must be as shocked as I am. She twists in his grasp and presses the back of her hand against his forehead. "You feeling okay, Wyatt?"

For a second, the hard lines of his face settle into something softer before he shakes off her hand.

"What? I'm not a total dickhead. I know it's not cool to bring the piece around an ol' lady. Or former piece, as the case may be."

"I have the feeling if I try to decipher that, I'm going to be offended." I'm only half joking.

Trinity lets out a huge laugh, and Wrath opens his mouth. "Well, you're his ol' lady apparently—"

"No. Just stop. Stop talking. Trinity giggles, while covering his mouth with her hand.

"Always good advice, brother." Teller says, looking up from his phone finally. "So, Hope. Rock says you're a lawyer and you do family court work?" Teller asks.

Oh no. I feel it coming. Please don't.

"You heard what I told Rock earlier. I'm trying to get custody—"

"Uh, I was. I haven't practiced law in a while."

Wrath frowns. "Why?"

"Well, um—"

"Because of that thing with Rock?" Wrath prods.

I flush at the reminder of that awful day, remembering that Wrath had been there to witness my humiliation. "No. My husband died last year, and except for helping Winter out, I haven't gone back to work since." I can't bear to tell these people I hardly know that it took me almost ten months to crawl out of bed after Clay's death.

"Oh, shit, Hope. I'm so sorry. I didn't know," Trinity whispers.

Wrath's chin is now resting on Trinity's shoulder, but his eyes are focused on me. "I'm sorry, Hope. I forgot."

"That's okay." I wonder how much of my story Wrath knows. How much do these guys share with each other? And did I just receive another apology from Wrath?

"Sorry, Hope," Teller apologizes. "I just hate the guy that got assigned to me."

Now my curiosity is piqued. "What county?"

"Johnson."

"Oh yeah, they have a small pool of lawyers on the list out there. Who did you get?"

"Lenny Kozak."

It's unprofessional, I know, but my nose wrinkles before I can stop it.

Understanding lights up Teller's eyes. "You've worked with him?"

"Yeah. He's smart but lazy. I hear he used to be a great lawyer, but he does the bare minimum these days. Keep after him."

"I'm back, Baby Doll," Rock says in a voice that makes me melt. He hands me a glass of water. I take a deep sip, realizing I'm parched. We shift places, and I'm in his lap again. I never thought I'd enjoy sitting in someone's lap, like a teenager. But here I am loving every second. Rock's playing with my hair, and I find the movement soothing. Teller's still watching me with bright eyes.

"Did you talk to her?" Rock asks.

"Yeah. She's not working now."

I turn to face Rock, and he arches a brow at me. "You took care of that thing for Winter." One well-muscled shoulder lifts, momentarily distracting me. "Figured you were going back and I'd get you your first new client."

I'm not comfortable discussing my career path in front of an audience. "I'm supposed to go meet with Adam this week about maybe taking over my office again."

His jaw ticks at the mention of my friend's name. Interesting, since he's met Adam.

"Baby doll, that is not an office. It's a closet," he jokes.

I do a little teeth grinding of my own. I'm so pissed he just embarrassed me in front of his friends. As he takes in my reaction, his body tenses underneath me. What does he think I'm going to do— blow up here in front of everyone?

A big, burly red-headed guy walks over and drops next to Teller. "Fuuck, I'm tired." He yawns like a bear.

"Hope, have you met Murphy?" Teller asks.

"Not really."

Murphy sits up and leans over. Since there's three people in our way, he waves at me. "Hi, First Lady," he says with a chuckle.

That makes Rock laugh too.

"First Lady—I like it." And he's swishing my hair off my shoulders, tracing my neck with his fingers, once again chasing my anger away. Dammit. I shiver from his touch.

Another girl I haven't met but I've caught glimpses of all night joins us. She's one of the girls who brought out the cake and gave me the stink eye the whole time she was doing it.

"Geez, why don't you just piss on his leg, girl. Damn. You been in his lap all night. We get it."

As far as greetings go, that's pretty rude.

"Uh, hi. I'm Hope." I don't bother trying to shake her hand—she might stab me.

"Uh, hi. I'm Cookie. I'm you two years ago," she says in a mocking tone.

It takes me a minute to decode that. So she's telling me she's another one of Rock's fuck buddies? Awesome. Girls have been coming up to me all night with fake smiles and hellos while insinuating they've fucked Rock at one time or another. Cookie is the only who's had the balls to be such a nasty bitch about it.

With the exception of Trinity, from now on I'm going to assume Rock has stuck his dick in anyone with a vagina who sets foot in this den of sin.

Wrath snorts. "Hardly."

"Cookie," Rock warns. "You're being rude to my woman."

She takes a step back, the whites of her eyes showing. Apparently the "my woman" thing hits home. But not for long.

"Well, she ain't gotta be so uppity. Bragging about being a lawyer and shit. I saw her leave the champagne room before. Thinks she's too good to hang with us?"

See, now that is hilarious to me, because I am pretty sure I have never once bragged about being a lawyer in my life. One, because the reality of being a lawyer sucks. Two, for this very reason here.

People have unpredictable, asshole-y reactions to hearing that information.

"Are you fucking stupid?" Trinity snarls. "Rock carried his woman outta there. We all saw it. Bitch, go sit down," she finishes with a flick of her wrist.

Why thank you, Trinity.

Wrath's forehead is pressed against Trinity's back, but his entire body vibrates with laughter. Asshat.

"You ain't got nothing to say?" she challenges me. When I don't respond, she continues. "See? Uppity."

"Maybe she's freaked out that you're acting like a psycho-bitch?" Teller offers helpfully.

True, but not helpful, Teller.

Rock is oddly still.

"Cookie, simmer the fuck down," he grits out.

But maybe Cookie is stupid, because she ignores Rock and takes one more jab. "Fuck you too, Trinity. You wanna suck up to this uppity cunt, go ahead, but don't forget you're a whore like the rest of us."

I've never been called a cunt before. At least not to my face. And I'm furious she just called Trinity a whore, when as far as I can tell she's the only one here who doesn't act like a whore.

Apparently that's the last straw for Rock. He shifts me to the couch and towers over Cookie. "You're done."

Her face transforms from rage to disbelief as it sinks in that she may have made a mistake…or ten.

"Rock. I been with the club almost five years. You really gonna pick her over me?"

"Cookie, you were warned multiple times." He reaches back and flicks his hand. "Wrath."

"On it." He pats Trinity's ass, and she slides off his lap onto the couch, clearly unwilling to get too close to Cookie.

"Let's go." He wraps a meaty hand around her toothpick-sized arm. It finally sinks in that the guys mean business.

She starts sobbing. "I'm sorry, Rock."

Now she's sorry.

"You're banned, Cookie. You can see if one of the other charters will take you in, but you ever show your face back here, I'll end you." Rock lays it all out to her with deadly calm as Wrath tugs her to the door.

"Well, that was…" I have no words.

Trinity snorts. "You know how I was telling you about other clubs?"

Teller leans over. "She pulled that shit in another MC, disrespecting an ol' lady, she'd be getting a beatdown or digging her own grave. Not getting a ride home."

CHAPTER THREE

ROCK

IT'S AFTER MIDNIGHT. SO TECHNICALLY BIRTHDAY SEX IS OFF THE TABLE. All I wanted tonight was to take Hope upstairs and bury myself inside her. That's still my plan—it just won't be my birthday when I finally get my wish.

Instead it's been one ugly thing after another, just as I'd feared all along. No wonder it's taken me so long to bring Hope back to the clubhouse.

As I walk back to my girl after sending Cookie home with one of the prospects, I notice Hope's got an uncertain smile stretched across her lips. Trinity and Teller appear to be trying to cheer her up. I could kiss Trinity—in apparently a fatherly way—for sticking up for Hope tonight. Wrath says she stuck up for me too earlier.

When I get closer to Hope, I sense she's angry. I mentally run over the list—and it is a long list—of things that could have pissed her off tonight. I'm impressed she hasn't flipped out at any point this evening —another reason I'm so far gone over her. If I want to remain president, I need an ol' lady who can keep her shit locked down and not throw a tantrum, even when she wants to choke my dumb ass.

The entire trip upstairs, she's silent. I'm concerned when we get on the other side of my bedroom door, she's going to tell me we're through.

As soon as we're alone, I dig into the conversation we need to have. "Let me have it, doll. How you doing?"

"How am I doing?" she answers softly, pronouncing every word very carefully.

Oh yeah, she's pissed.

She lifts her hand and starts ticking off my offenses. "Let's see, you offered my legal services to someone without asking me, again."

Interesting. I didn't expect her to lead with that.

She uncurls a second finger. "You embarrassed me by insulting my office in front of all your friends. That made me feel like a fraud."

Fuck, I hadn't meant to sound so dismissive. "Why didn't you say something?"

"What was I going to say? I'm not going to pick a fight with you in front of your friends. It's rude."

Damn, she's cute. And better ol' lady material than I ever thought.

"Anything else?"

Finished counting, she props her hand on her hip. "What are you fishing for, Rochlan? You want me to comment on the fact that you've apparently stuck your dick in every vagina here? And as if that's not hard enough to swallow, they are complete and utter bitches about it?"

I'll admit, I'm a little turned on by the way she says my full name when she's wound up. "I'm sorry."

She crosses her arms over her chest and glares at me. "You're sorry? You brought me here to let everyone know I was not just a 'piece.' And, by the way, very subtle—making me sit in your lap all night and carrying me around like your favorite chew toy. Maybe next time you can just lift your leg on me instead. But you knew there was a possibility every club girl was going to try to scratch my eyes out, and you didn't have the decency to warn me. Oh, and my personal favorite of the night, the porn star entertainment."

"I did *not* know Inga was going to be here. She's never been here before."

"Yeah, I heard."

"And I have not stuck my dick in every vagina here." Close.

"I heard that too."

"I know how strange all of this must be for you."

"Do you? You don't even like me mentioning the names of my guy friends, but I'm supposed to hang back and act cool when some chick you used to nail gets in my face? I'm supposed to hang out with every woman who has ever sucked your dick like we're all just one big, happy, incestuous little family?"

My woman talking filthy does stuff to me. But this is serious, and we need to work through it. Plus, I'm pretty sure she will knee me in the balls if I try to get sweet with her right now. Just a feeling.

"How would you like to sit around all night making polite chitchat with some guy I used to fuck?"

"I wouldn't." Even the suggestion makes me seethe until I remember her husband is dead. Damn, I've been an asshole. "What do you want me to do, Hope? Should I ban every club girl I've been with?" It's a real possibility. The guys will probably slit my throat, but Hope's right. I can't put her through another night of bullshit. The girls will be taken in by other charters. New ones will always find their way here one way or another. Fuck. I thrust my fingers through my hair. She's got me so damn torqued up again.

"Oh yeah. So everyone can hate me and think I really am a stuck-up bitch? Don't you dare send your little muffler bunny fan club away."

Heh. I'm amused at her use of "muffler bunny" and assume she picked that up from Trinity. Without another word, Hope drops her arms to her side and marches into the bathroom. I use the time to pace because I'm pretty sure when she comes out she's going to ask me to take her home.

Instead, she surprises me by coming out dressed for bed. She shoots me a glare, walks over to her side, and crawls in.

Yeah, definitely no birthday sex. But at least she's staying.

Not sure what else to say, I step into the hallway to clear my head. Catching sight of Z, I lift my chin and he strides over.

"Why aren't you with Hope?"

"Giving her a minute."

"How pissed is she?"

"Very."

"Sorry."

"No. It's on me. Where's Peach?"

He jerks his thumb over his shoulder in the direction of his room. "Not worth the trouble. A little hard to hold a conversation with her."

I snort, because the idea of Z wanting to "hold a conversation" with any woman seems so unlikely.

"Give her a break. It's hard to talk with a dick in your mouth."

"I wouldn't know."

"Very funny, asshole. Since when do you talk to a fuck-and-go?"

He shrugs. "Maybe I want a slice of what you've found."

Hope was right to accuse me of being territorial. "You stay away from what I've found."

He smirks but doesn't respond.

"You know she's going to tell her friend Lilly about this, right?" I ask, just because I feel like being a dick.

His gaze darts to mine like he never considered the possibility, then he tries to act casual. "Nah, that was a one-off. She made that clear."

I raise an eyebrow, encouraging him to continue. Usually Z's the one to explain there would be no repeat performances.

"I could definitely hold a conversation with her. Fucking ah-maazing tits too." Looking down at the ground, he shakes his head. "But, way too smart for me."

I leave Z to work out whatever he's got going through his head. I guess we're all going through our midlife crises a little early. Maybe if we're real lucky, our periods will sync up or some shit.

Hope's curled on her side when I return. Her breathing is steady, but I don't think she's asleep. Even so, I'm careful not to touch her when I slide into bed. I settle on my back and stare up at the ceiling. Party noises still filter in through the thick door.

Suddenly, Hope turns over and curls into my side. Relief grips me so strong I almost don't know how to react. I hook my arm around her, and she snuggles in closer.

"I'm sorry," she whispers.

"You don't have anything to be sorry for. It's my fuck up, Baby Doll."

"I don't know what I'm doing here."

Here could mean many things. In my life. In my bed. In my clubhouse. In this relationship. All those things. I don't know which one she means, so I wait for her continue.

When she finally opens her mouth, she doesn't give me words. A slick, hot trail teases over my chest, circling my nipple. I groan, but don't move. She buries her face in my neck, and I wonder if she's trying to scent another woman on me.

"I was in the hall talking to Z," I reveal.

It's so dark I can't see her expression, but she pulls back. She shifts again and trails her tongue down my chest, then lower, tracing my abs as she goes. Another groan slips out as I sense where she's headed. She pauses at my boxer briefs. Not knowing where we stood, I didn't think crawling into bed without covering my jewels was a great idea. She cups my rapidly growing erection, squeezing me through the material. I bump my hips up and she tugs them off, freeing me.

Without warning, her warm, wet mouth closes over my dick.

"Fuck!"

She takes me deep and quick. Something's not right. Oh, it feels fantastic, but there's a desperate edge to her movements that sets sirens piercing through my thick skull.

"Stop. Stop, Baby Doll." As she moves faster, I suck air in through my teeth. Tunneling my fingers through her hair, I still her movements and pull her up to me. My cock curses at the loss of her sweet mouth. I roll us, pin her down, and kiss her. We're a frantic tumble of lips, tongues, and teeth. Somehow I work her shirt off. Then her shorts get tossed to the floor, and I reach out to grab a condom from the nightstand. She stops me with a hand on my outstretched arm.

"You don't need it."

It would be cruel of her to tease me at this point. "You sure?"

She hums against my neck. "I'm sure. Happy birthday."

Fuck, yes. Happy birthday indeed. All her sweetness belongs to me. As I slide into my luscious girl, we are nothing but slick, hot skin on skin. I have to take a moment to enjoy her fluttering around me. So damn tight. Every bit of her is mine.

"This what I've wanted all night long, Baby Doll."

Warms shivers of pleasure sweep through me as she runs her nails lightly up and down my back, then traces down my arms. "Me too."

"This is all I ever want," I admit. Somehow in the dark it's a lot easier to spill these secrets.

"I know."

Slow strokes. Enjoying every bare inch with nothing between us. Fucking fantastic. I burrow my arms under her, keeping her close. Her legs hug my hips, her heels resting on my ass. Love it. Faster now. Savoring every glide and thrust against her silky heat. I press my lips against her neck, kiss my way to her ear, and gently bite the soft lobe.

"Can you feel that, Baby Doll?" I whisper against her neck.

I feel her face pull into a smile, and her tight little pussy squeezes down on my cock even harder.

"I feel you."

No. She's not getting it. I have to get it out this time. She has to know—now.

"No. Can you feel my heart...I love you so much."

This is why I needed to say it in the dark. If she isn't feeling the same, it's gonna cut through me. A sharp intake of breath. She strokes one hand along my cheek and coos in my ear. "Rochlan—you have no idea—I love you too."

The sweetest words she's ever spoken. I brush my lips back and forth over hers, in a silent thank you.

Best birthday ever.

CHAPTER FOUR

HOPE

THE CLUBHOUSE IS MUCH QUIETER THE NEXT MORNING WHEN ROCK TAKES my hand and leads me downstairs. I'm a little overwhelmed. We fought. We made up. For a while I didn't think I'd be able to get the images of him and other women out of my mind. Picturing him fucking the skanks that hung out in his club or the strippers that worked for him tormented me relentlessly. The irrational and out of control feelings kept me on edge. Worrying about the past served no useful purpose—the logical part of my brain knew that. I also can't deny that Rock has been straight with me all along. He's never hidden his past with the club girls or dancers from me. But knowing and having it thrown in your face were two different things. I couldn't blame him for the actions of others, though—that certainly wasn't fair.

Besides, he loves me. No matter what happens, I'll cherish his words forever. I never, ever thought I would be this lucky to find love again. Shivers work through me when I remember the intensity of his voice as he whispered those words in my ear. His love is a precious gift that I won't allow anyone to tarnish with their ugly words.

Murmurs reach my ears before I actually see anyone. The front door shuts, and everything is quiet until we enter.

"Hey, prez," Wrath says in a hushed tone when he spots us. Trinity is tucked up against him on the couch, using his thigh as a pillow while she sleeps. Rock nods, and I wiggle my fingers as a hello.

Rock throws himself onto the couch next to Wrath and tugs me down with him. He arranges my legs over his lap and leans in, pressing his lips to my ear. "Are you okay with sitting on my lap?"

Shame prickles at me for the words I flung at him last night. I turn and kiss along his jaw until I reach his ear. "Nowhere else I want to be. I'm sorry I said that, I—"

He captures my lips in a kiss, cutting me off. Wrath sighs audibly next to us. Rock presses his forehead to mine for a moment before turning to his friend.

"You're up early."

Wrath's massive shoulders lift in a tight shrug.

"She okay?" He jerks his chin at Trinity. The corner of his mouth tips up in a knowing smile. Wrath's arm is curled around her, resting on her hip.

Snatching his arm away, Wrath stretches it out over the back of the couch and Rock snickers.

"I didn't get any ass last night, thanks to you," he grumbles.

Rock snorts. "Yeah, it's all my fault you're such a prick."

I'm staying out of this one. Although he's nice to look at, Wrath's personality designates him completely unfuckable as far as I'm concerned. Inwardly I cackle that he didn't get any last night.

Z pounds down the stairs next. "Morning, fuckers. Oh, hey, Hope. I'm surprised you're still here."

Rock grunts at him and possibly calls him an asshole under his breath.

Unruffled, Z spins a chair around in front of us. He straddles it, draping his arms over the back. Today he's wearing short sleeves, and I study his inked arms a bit. Rock notices my interest in his friend and pinches my thigh. I had to sit through his ex-whatever doing a special birthday strip show for him and get bitched out by one of his muffler bunnies last night, but I can't look at his friend's arms?

44

Whatever.

I bat my lashes at Z, and he smirks.

"Where's Peach?" Wrath asks.

"Upstairs."

"You nail her?"

I feel Rock shaking his head behind me.

Z shrugs before answering Wrath's question. "She's a shit lay. Mosta them strippers and porn stars are. They act like they're doing ya a favor and just lay there. Fuckin boring."

I snort, then break out into a full-on giggle. "But, you still did her anyway?" I ask.

"Well, yeah. Of course." He flashes another smile at me, and I notice he's got these adorable cheek dimples. "It's my duty to fuck as many women as possible."

Maybe he said it to shock me, but it only makes me laugh harder. "You and Lilly really are kindred spirits."

The silly smile on his face falters. "What?"

"She has a similar theory on dating." His uncertain expression says he wants more information but doesn't want to ask in front of the guys.

Inga joins us next, ending the "strippers are a lousy lay" conversation. Pity.

"Fuuuck." She throws herself on the couch next to Trinity, jostling the poor girl awake. The two sort of glare at each other for a second.

When Trinity realizes she's been using Wrath's thigh as a pillow and that we've all witnessed it, I swear she turns a little green.

"Morning, Trinny," Rock greets her with a slow grin.

She mumbles something that resembles good morning and takes off down the hall. Wrath gets up and follows her. I swing my gaze to Z, silently begging him not to go anywhere and leave us alone with Inga. I get a wink in response. Planting her hands in the couch cushions, Inga does this weird slide/crawl down the couch, giving me an eyeful of cleavage in the process. Rock's playing with my hair, tucking wild strands behind my ear and tracing his fingers down my neck. It tickles, and I giggle.

Something sad passes over Inga's face, which nags at me. After last night, I'm feeling a lot more secure about my position in Rock's life. With that in mind, it's easier to recognize having this PDA moment in front of her might be a little rude, even though she once told me she had no interest in Rock romantically. Last night it seemed she came up here with some sort of expectations, and I ruined that for her. Not my fault, but I still have the twinge of guilt.

Wrath comes back wearing a dejected expression and glares at Inga before sitting back down. Trinity follows and sits on the arm of the couch next to Rock. Basically, she's as far away from Wrath as she can get and still be part of the group conversation. I swivel in Rock's lap so I can see her.

"So, I get how Dex got his nickname now," Inga says out of the blue to no one in particular. I glance at her as she wiggles her fingers in the air. "Real good with his fingers." She winks at Trinity as if she's in on this joke.

Ewww.

Trinity's gaze skips from me to Wrath. "That's what I've heard."

Wrath shakes his head. "That's not how he got his road name."

"So, how did you like our show last night, Hope?" Inga asks in a casual tone, but the hairs on the back of my neck stand up. Any sympathy I might have felt for her a second ago evaporates. The dirty little tramp is up to no good.

I choose to go the diplomatic route with my answer. "You're very talented."

She cocks her head, and a mean-girl grin curls her lips. "Rocky took you away from us before we got to the good stuff. You actually move really well, once you loosen up." While she says "loosen up," it sounds more like "take the stick out of your ass."

"Uh, thanks."

"If you ever want lessons—I mean, you're a little on the old side—I can teach you how to work the pole."

Rock sits up, wrapping his arms around my waist. "Knock it off, Inga."

"Yeah, she knows how to work Rock's pole just fine," Z adds helpfully.

I flick my gaze at him, and he winks again.

Deciding diplomacy is a wasted effort on Inga, I turn and pin her with what I used to think of as my courtroom stare. "Inga, I get that you used to fuck my man, but if I wanted to hang out with a bitch, I'd get a dog. Keep your thinly veiled insults to yourself, you're not fooling anyone." I'm proud of myself for spitting all that out without stumbling over the words. Rock coughs. Wrath and Z whoop and chortle. My brave moment passes as my cheeks heat up, and I imagine I must be furiously blushing but I refuse to lower my gaze. Finally, Rock slides his arms under my knees and stands, lifting me in the air. I gasp, grabbing at his shoulders with the sudden shift.

"You hungry, Baby Doll?"

I trace my fingers over his jaw. He didn't bother shaving this morning, and I like the scruff on him. His eyelids drop at my touch, and I marvel that I have this effect on him.

"Inga, you got a ride home?" he says pointedly.

"I brought my car. Waitin' on Peach."

"She's in my room. I'll go get her," Z says as he pushes out of his chair, clearly eager to get rid of Inga.

She flicks her bony fingers at Z and settles into the couch cushions. "Unless you plan to wake her up with your head between her thighs, I wouldn't bother. She's not a morning person."

"Fuck that shit," Z grumbles and walks off.

Rock sets me down but keeps his arms around me. Behind us Inga huffs, and out of the corner of my eye, I watch her pound up the stairs.

Good riddance.

Trinity slides off the couch. "I'll get breakfast started."

"Hang on, Trinny," Rock says without taking his eyes off me. "After Ing and Peach get the fuck out, round up whoever's awake, and we'll go down to Hog Heaven."

A grin lights up her face. I imagine she's thrilled not to have to cook for a pack of hungover, hungry bikers.

"You want me to call and see if they'll open the back room for us?"

"Yeah. Thanks."

Rock releases me, and I glance up. He leans down and presses his forehead against mine. "Hope," he breathes, his hands cupping my throat, thumbs brushing against my jaw. "Do you have any idea what you do to me?"

Overwhelmed with the tenderness in his voice, my eyes flutter shut.

"I'm so sorry for that scene, baby. But, I'm so proud of you." His lips press against my forehead.

I'm choking on emotions I can't even name. Suddenly I'm acutely aware we're not alone, so I pull away. "Do I have time to fix myself up?"

His gaze travels over my face for a moment. "Sure, Baby Doll." Pulling the keys from his pocket, he hands me the one to his room. "I need to speak with Wrath for a minute. You okay?"

On the verge of tears, I choke out, "I'll be fine."

I run upstairs, praying I won't pass Inga on the way. If I shed one tear in front of that skank, I'll never forgive myself.

Once inside Rock's room, I dump my bag out on the bed and sort through the clothes I brought. Figuring out what to wear helps clear my head. Hog Heaven isn't fancy, but it's the weekend. So, I pull out a frilly, flowy white sleeveless blouse dotted with tiny roses in various shades of blue. Holding up the new pair of jeans I brought, I go back and forth about whether I should wear them. They're skin tight, something I would normally never wear, but they give the illusion that I actually have an ass, and I think Rock will like them.

I hurry through my shower hoping Rock will surprise me, but I have the bathroom to myself. While I'm drying my hair, the door opens, letting some of the steam out. I'm still wrapped in just a towel, and as I meet Rock's hungry gaze in the mirror, I think it's going to be a while before we get to breakfast.

Rock

Fury at Inga's behavior toward Hope has my fist curling and itching to punch through the fucking wall. My girl handled herself well, but she shouldn't have to put up with that shit.

Over the years I've met plenty of guys who got off on a good catfight between an ex and his ol' lady. I've never understood that mindset. There's nothing sexy about having the person you love be tormented because of your past actions. If I could go back in time and toss Inga's job application in the trash, I wouldn't hesitate.

The crazy rituals women put themselves through before going out have never interested me all that much. When I spent my nights holed up at Crystal Ball, I tended to avoid the girls' dressing room like the plague. But, I find myself fascinated as I observe Hope. Some of that is probably because she's standing there in only a towel. But it's cute watching her try to pull and smooth her hair into submission. Her lips twist in annoyance when it doesn't stay where she wants. She looks up and meets my eyes in the mirror.

"I don't know why I'm bothering. It's just going to get messed up. I didn't bring any of my hair stuff with me."

Coming up behind her, I wrap my arms around her waist and kiss the top of her head. "You're beautiful no matter what."

"I love that you see me that way."

I spin her around. "It's not me. You are simply beautiful."

"Thank you."

Maybe I need to show her.

"Baby doll," I breathe against her neck. Kissing my way down her shoulder, I tug the towel from her body. With my hands cupping her hips, I back her onto the bathroom counter.

Three sharp pounds against my bedroom door pull us apart.

"Fuck," I groan.

Z shouts through the door. "Ding dong, bitches be gone! No time for fucking—we want food!" He slams his fist against my door a few more times.

Hope shakes her head and giggles. "I guess we better hurry."

She slides off the counter, whips out an elastic, and quickly twists her hair into a messy braid. Naked—the way I like her—she strides out of the bathroom. I pick up her towel with a shake of my head and follow. She's wriggling her perfect ass into a pair of panties when I find her. I turn away because I'm getting worked up. After a minute, she molds herself against my back, her arms encircling me in a hug. "All set."

I turn and drink her in. Damn, she's so fucking cute, I don't want to take her in public where other people can see what is all mine. I finger the thin straps of her top. "You're going to be cold."

"Oh, yeah." She turns and bends over—

"What the fuck you wearing?"

"Huh?" She straightens and throws on her leather jacket.

"Those jeans."

"Oh, I just bought them. Why? Are they too tight?" She spins and twists, trying to get a glimpse of her own ass.

Fuck, yes, they're too tight. "Yes," I grind out.

She stops trying to turn herself into a pretzel and walks over to the full length mirror on the back of the door. As she bends and poses in the mirror, my fists ball at my sides. She's fucking clueless about what she does to me.

Apparently satisfied, she faces me. "I think they make my butt look nice."

With a twist of the doorknob, she flings the door open and swishes out. It takes a second before I catch up to her.

"You're going to be the death of me."

She flashes a sweet smile at me and takes my hand. Holy fuck, do I love this woman.

"Frank can't give us the back room, so he said no colors, guys," Trinity informs the small group of us who are waiting downstairs.

"Fuck," Z grumbles.

No one else wanted to get their lazy asses up, so only Wrath, Z, and Trinny are out to breakfast with us. The place is packed. Although Frank couldn't give us the back room, he does have a corner table in the back of the joint waiting for us.

Hope orders some frou-frou egg thing I'm surprised to even see on the menu at Hog Heaven.

Wrath is still sulking because Trinny decided to ride here with Z instead of him. Z is, of course, oblivious. Trinity chose to sit next to Hope. The two of them are talking so fast I can't really keep up with their conversation, but I'm thankful they seem to get along so well.

Hope wrinkles her nose at my sausage, biscuits, and gravy when it arrives. Placing a spoon in her hand, I tell her to try it. She hesitates, then digs in. Her eyes light up, and she moans as she licks the gravy from the spoon.

"Holy crap. That is good. I wonder if I could figure out the recipe."

Wrath stares at her like she's nuts.

She licks the spoon again. "What?" Hope asks, genuinely confused.

Z chuckles and resumes shoveling in his food like someone is going to take his plate away any second.

Before Frank brings the check, I wander up to the register to pay the bill. Trinny taps my shoulder while I'm waiting for my change. "Thanks, Rock."

Settling my hand on her shoulder, I give her a quick squeeze. "You're welcome, sweetie. Everything okay?"

She shrugs and nods. I don't press her any further.

I glance at our table and see Z tapping at his cell phone, a feral grin spreading over his face.

"What's he up to?"

Trinity grins and shakes her head. "No idea."

"Hey, the term 'muffler bunny' came out of my girl's mouth last night. You teach her that?" I'm teasing, but Trinity's face twitches with panic.

"It might have slipped out."

"I'm joking, Trinity."

She relaxes a little. "Last night would have been tough to take for anyone, but someone not used to bikers? She handled herself well, Rock. You picked a good one."

Hope and Wrath appear to be having some sort of staring contest. "He giving her shit again?"

"You want me to go check?" Trinny asks.

"Please."

She saunters over with a sway in her hips that takes Wrath's attention away from my girl. Settling her hands on his shoulders relaxes him, and he tips his head up to flash a smile at Trinity. I get my change and head back to our table.

Z looks up and taps Wrath. "Hey, I gotta take off. Give Trinny a lift back?"

Wrath is pleased as fuck. "Yup."

When the four of us hit the parking lot, my brother stretches obscenely and runs a hand over his gut. "It's too nice to be inside. You wanna take the girls for a ride?"

Sounds like a good idea. I hug Hope to my side. "That okay with you?"

A broad grin lights up her face. "Yeah, where?"

Wrath looks around, trying to orient himself. "Fletcher Park isn't far. Should be a nice view on a day like today."

Hope goes rigid next to me, and I remember she has a weird reaction to that place. I want to get her to tell me why. "Why don't you go on ahead and we'll meet you at the overlook?"

"See you in a few." Trinity surprises Hope with a brief hug.

Once they've cleared the parking lot, I sit Hope on my bike. "Are you okay with going up there?"

She tips her head up, squinting at the bright sky. "Yeah."

"Wanna tell me about it?"

She sighs, and I can tell this has something to do with her husband, so I brace myself.

"Clay proposed up there. Not at the overlook, but the area next to it. The one with the gazebo?"

Fuck, that's bad. No wonder the place wigs her out so much. "We don't have to go. I'll text him and tell them we're going to skip it," I say pulling out my cell phone.

Her soft fingers land on my arm. "No, it's okay. I'd like to go there with you."

I search her face for a second. "If you change your mind, just say so, okay? Promise me."

"I promise."

I take my time driving us up there, giving her a chance to back out if she wants. When we reach the overlook, Trinny is standing on the low stone wall snapping pictures with her cell phone. Wrath is standing behind her with his arms wrapped around her legs even though the drop off the cliff is a good five feet away from the wall. At the sound of my bike, she turns. Wrath slips his hands around her waist and sets her on the ground.

"We were wondering if you guys got lost!" She runs over and hugs Hope again.

"You two looked so cute standing there," Hope whispers to Trinny.

Wrath is sitting on the wall facing us now. He lifts his chin at me, and I nod. Out of the corner of my eye, I catch Hope snag Trinny's cell and push her toward Wrath. This should be interesting. But instead of grouching about it, Wrath pulls Trinity between his knees, hugs her close, and allows Hope to snap a bunch of pictures.

Trinny giggles and waves me over. "Your turn! Come on, Rock-steady."

A warm feeling settles over me as I wrap my arms around Hope, and Trinity takes a bunch of pictures. I grab a few shots of just the girls together. Wrath draws the line at them taking pictures of just the two of us. The girls want to walk along the top of the length of the wall, even though technically we could get booted out of the park for it. Every seven feet there's a sign stating no one is to step on or over the stone barrier. I hold Hope's hand as she tightrope walks along the wall. When we reach the end, the girls prance up to the observation deck to look through the viewfinders the park has installed. For a dollar you get enough time to take a quick sweep of the tri-county view. Wrath and I fish out quarters and hand them over.

We take a few steps back. Even though he's staring at the girls' asses, something is bothering him.

"What?" I ask.

He keeps his voice low so we won't be overheard. "We came in the back way. Down at Green Rocks Pavilion there is a horde of Devil's Demons having a barbeque."

That makes no sense. The closest Demon chapter is about four hours from here. Fletcher Park is technically neutral ground. Since we are the dominant MC in this area, normally they would check in with us, even if just to say "hey." We have friendly history with the Demons and maintain a decent relationship. It's a respect thing. "Are you sure? Was it the Kodack chapter?"

"Probably. It was just me and Trin. I didn't exactly stop and play twenty questions."

Shit, yeah. That could have been dangerous. We have no beef with the Demons, but no reason to take a stupid risk either.

"How many?"

"Maybe twenty?"

"Just patch-holders, or did it look like a family event?"

"Family too."

I relax a little. If they're not here to do business, then I'm not going to worry about it. "Who knows, maybe they just needed a place to crash."

"Yeah, but they would need a permit to close down that whole area."

"Call Z and tell him to start making some quiet inquiries. Let's get the girls and go."

Realistically, I doubt this is much of a problem. Like I said, they didn't have to check in with us. It would have been nice since Fletcher Park bumps right up against our territory. It's probably nothing, or it could be a big fucking deal. The president before me would have gone to war over another club stepping foot near our territory without clearing it ahead of time. I prefer a more diplomatic approach that did not end with my brothers injured, dead, or in prison. Call me crazy.

With my VP working his magic, spending the day with Hope doing something normal seems like a good idea. Wrath and Trinity took off for who knows where. Hope and I go to the movies for the first time together. By the time the movie is over, Z has sent me a text that everything is fine. Demons were in the area attending the wedding of a non-patched family member. Z also managed to set up a meeting to discuss a new distribution line through Demon territory while he was at it.

Diplomacy in action, folks.

CHAPTER FIVE

ROCK

BECAUSE THERE CAN NEVER BE A PEACEFUL MOMENT, AS SOON AS HOPE and I return to the clubhouse that evening, I know something is off. Wrath and Trinity are sitting outside talking. He jumps up and strides over as soon as he sees us, Trinity following close behind.

"Inga's back," he announces as soon as I shut my bike down.

"What? Who the fuck brought her back here?"

"Uh, I think Dex has it bad for her." He scratches his head and rolls his eyes skyward. "Or he did."

Shouts can be heard from inside, and Trinny scrunches up her face. Now I'm wishing I had stuck around to talk to Dex this morning.

"What's going on?"

Wrath slides his gaze to Hope and back to me. "She wanted to play choo-choo."

"What are you, five?" I snap.

He's chosen the stupidest time to finally watch his mouth around Hope. She's not going to have any idea what we're talking about anyway. Nor do I want her to.

I point at the house. "Who's in there?"

"Everyone except you, me, Bricks, and maybe Z."

Z chooses that exact moment to step outside. Flushed and sweaty, he shakes his head. "Dude, your girl, Ing, is playing a serious game of Chinese Fingercuffs."

"She's not my girl," I grind out.

"I think she's trying to get you jealous," Trinity offers.

"Yeah, that's not the way to win a guy back," Wrath says with a chuckle.

Hope pulls on my sleeve. "So, your ex-slampiece is in there taking it in every hole from your 'brothers'? Is that what I'm getting out of this conversation?"

I choke at her description. I've never heard that term before, but it doesn't take a genius to figure it out. It's on odd thing to come out of Hope's mouth, and I'm reminded how she can come up with some interesting phrases when she's feeling territorial.

Wrath and Z double over laughing. Hope is not amused. She looks disgusted.

I lift a shoulder. "No one made her."

Now she's really steamed. "What, is she hoping you'll go get in line?"

Wrath is practically pissing his pants with laughter. "Probably," he gasps.

Dick.

"She must have run home and watched one too many Law and Order episodes. They don't make girls pull a train to hang here," Trinity explains to Hope.

"What a relief," Hope snaps.

Z and Wrath straighten up at her tone. Time to diffuse this mess. Settling a hand on Hope's shoulder, I address the guys.

"We're going upstairs."

Wrath snakes an arm around Trinny's waist. Z glances at them and raises an eyebrow.

"Trin and I were going for a walk."

"I'll take care of it," Z says.

"I don't care who does what. Make sure things don't get too out of hand, and make sure she gets home in one piece. Make it clear she's not welcome back. Wipe her GPS if you have to. That bitch can't find her own ass without it."

Next to me, Hope lets out a disgusted snort, probably because I referred to Inga as a bitch, and I find her annoyance unreasonably ironic.

"Oh, some of the guys are filming it," Z adds as an afterthought.

Fucking hell. "End that now. She'll lose her contract if that shit gets out. What the fuck is she thinking?"

Z looks at Hope, then back to me. "Uh, you might want to be the one to take care of that."

"Are you fucking serious? What the fuck are you wearing this for then?" I jab a finger at his VP patch.

"I'm just saying it will be better coming from you."

Motherfucker.

As we go inside, I see at least not all of my officers are degenerate fucktards. Murphy and Teller are relaxing on the couch, chatting with Swan who looks completely freaked out. I turn and put my hands on Hope's shoulders. "Please stay out here."

"Trust me, I don't need to see that."

I smile, and she shoos me away. "Go do your President thing. I'll be right there." She points to the couch.

Love. This. Woman. Thank fuck I finally told her.

I take Wrath to the side. "Stay here with Hope and Trinny. Do not under any circumstances let the girls take a step in that hallway."

"Yeah, sure." He lowers his voice. "Why, you gonna slip in a quick one?"

My hand connects hard with the back of his head before he finishes the last word. "No, fuckface. Just do what I ask," I snap.

"Come on, chickenshit," I yell to Z, and he follows.

"Not cool."

"Fuck you."

He shuts up after that, finally absorbing the fact that I am not finding this situation as funny as he is.

In the last twenty-two years, I've seen just about everything. But the scene in the champagne room even disgusts me. Two more club girls whose names I've not bothered to learn are entertaining the guys not filling Inga. Fuck, even Sparky pried himself away from his plants to partake in the activities.

Someone brought a table from the dining room in. Guess we'll be having a bonfire later, cause I sure as fuck am never eating off it again. A stab of guilt and a prick of pity hit me. If Inga is doing this for my attention, I just don't get it. Since I deliberately avoided the weekends she worked at Crystal Ball, I hadn't seen her for over a year. Did she see some sort of future for us and then lose her mind when she realized I was with Hope?

I shake it off, focusing on what needs to be done. Looking around the room, I spot three cell phone cameras out and operating. A flip of the light switch halts the party. "Listen up, assholes, stop any filming right this fucking second, and everyone in the room hand your cell phones to Z. I count six fuckers in this room and three fuckees. In the next five seconds, Z better be holding nine phones. You can pick them up later."

Groans, mumbling, bitching, and cursing follow the little math problem I just tossed out, but people are zipping up flies and handing over phones. Z gives me a disgusted look as he pockets all the hardware. Wait 'til I tell him he has to go through each one and make sure any videos from tonight are deleted. I spot Dex in a corner looking pretty miserable as I approach.

"I hear this is your doing?"

"Not this situation, prez."

"You know what's going on with her?"

"No idea. Thought she was into me, but then things got out of hand."

"Rocky!" Inga runs over to me without a stitch of clothing or an ounce of shame. She is, however, covered in sweat, cum, and smeared makeup. I shake off the hand she places on my shoulder.

"Did you finally dump that prude and come to join the fun?"

"Inga, this in no way looks like fun to me."

Her face falls. She does that pouty thing I used to find cute even though I knew it was fake as fuck. Now, it just looks cheap and sad.

Keeping my distance and my eyes focused on her face, I ask her, "What the fuck are you trying to prove?"

She shrugs her bony shoulders.

Searching her face, I notice her eyes are glassy, her pupils tiny pinpoints. "Are you high?"

"What do you care?"

"We don't allow drugs up here." I don't consider weed a "drug," so this isn't a lie as far as I'm concerned.

She snorts.

"We don't allow hard drugs," I clarify.

She ignores me and leans over to see Dex. "Hey, where did you go, baby?"

"Just sittin' here, Ing."

"Did you know some of the guys were filming this shit show, Inga? What about your contract?" I don't know why I give a fuck, but I don't want her to lose her income over something that happened in my club.

"Huh?"

Yeah, I'm done with this shit.

"Dex. She's your responsibility. Get her dressed. Get her out of my clubhouse. Take her to your house, wherever she's staying, or a motel, but she is not allowed back here. Got it?"

Inga lets a fist fly at my face. "Fuck you, Rochlan North! You're not fucking God," she screams at me.

I catch her wild fist and hold it tight enough to make an impression on her drug-addled brain. "I am here."

Hope

Although entertaining, the Inga incident depressed the hell out of me. Dex and Z carried her kicking and screaming outside, where she was tossed into the club's van and driven home by a prospect.

Lovely.

Rock hasn't returned yet.

Trinity seems embarrassed or uneasy, and it bothers me because I think that's my doing. Disapproval must be rolling off me in waves, but I can't stop it. She keeps telling me this sort of stuff "almost never" happens here.

It's that "almost" part that bugs me.

Trinity, Teller, and Murphy are laughing and joking around when Rock comes storming down the hall. He throws himself on the couch next to me and scrubs his hands over his face.

"Jesus Christ, that was disgusting."

"Now you know why we were outside, prez," Wrath says, giving Trinity a pointed look. She straightens up and away from Teller.

The front door slams open, and a girl who can't be more than sixteen storms in. Good grief, if this is another "club girl," I'm heading home.

"Marcel!" she howls.

Everyone around me breaks into laughter. Well, except Teller. He's livid. He rockets off the couch and grabs the girl by her shoulders. "What the fuck are you doing here?"

Oh, hell, no. There's no way this girl is legal.

"Grams is driving me nuts! It's barely nine o'clock, and she expects me to be in bed on a Saturday night. What. The. Fuck," she yells dramatically.

Ah, this must be the little sister, Heidi.

Teller leads her over with an arm around her shoulder. She brightens when she sees Rock.

"Hi, Uncle Rock," she says.

"Hey, Heidi-girl. How'd you find your way up here?"

She rolls her eyes. "I'm sixteen, not stupid."

Rock tilts his head, waiting for her to continue. She lets out a dramatic sigh. "My boyfriend, Axel, brought me. He wants to prospect for you guys. He's eighteen. I thought you could talk to him," she adds with a hopeful lilt to her voice.

At the word "boyfriend," Murphy's head snaps up. He shoots an angry glare at Teller, who shrugs his shoulders.

"Hey, Heidi-bug," Murphy calls.

"Don't call me bug, Blake," she snaps back.

Trying to regain control over the situation, Rock snaps his fingers in front of Heidi. "Heidi, we don't allow prospects up here for the first year."

"Oh."

She finally takes in her surroundings. Noticing Rock's hand on my knee, she locks her gaze on me. "Who are you?"

"Heidi, this is my girlfriend, Hope."

"Oh, wow. That's so cool. Uncle Rock's never had a girlfriend before."

I'm kind of charmed by this little hellraiser. "Hi, Heidi. Teller told me all about you last night."

Her angry gaze bores into her brother. Whoops.

"No, honey, all nice things. He was bragging about how smart you are and that you're full of moxie, which I see is totally true."

"What the fuck is that?"

Teller elbows her in the ribs. "Uh, sorry," she apologizes.

I smile. "It's someone spunky. You know, full of energy and courage."

"Oh, I like that. That's a way better road name than bug," she spits at Murphy.

"Love you too, bugaboo," he responds with a grin.

Z comes out of the office looking a little green. He brightens when he spots, Heidi. "Hey, Bug."

"Goddammit," she grumbles under her breath.

Rock motions his VP over. "Hey, do me a favor."

"Gee, prez. I barely finished the last disgusting favor you asked me to do," he says with a healthy dose of irritation.

Rock levels a questioning stare at him, and Z drops the attitude. "What do you need?"

"Heidi brought her boyfriend up. He's interested in becoming a prospect."

"What's his name?"

"Axel," Heidi says while bouncing up and down on her toes.

"At least he won't need a road name," Z jokes.

One corner of Rock's mouth lifts in a wry smile. "Will you go have a chat with him? Make sure he's not a little punk?"

"He's not, Uncle Rock, I swear," Heidi pleads.

She turns and follows Z out. Teller trots behind her, looking up at the ceiling and muttering.

"She's fun," I joke.

"Well, at least in two more years she'll be Murphy's problem," Wrath says with a snort.

"Fuck that, man. I'm just like another big brother to her," Murphy protests.

Rock leans back with a lazy grin. "Please—she's been trying to take that ride since she was twelve."

"Nah. She's like the kid sister I never wanted."

Frankly, I'm a little disgusted at the way they're discussing this girl. "She's a kid," I say.

"Yeah, which is why when she's eighteen, Murphy will sack up and put them both out of each other's misery," Wrath challenges.

I sit up. "Are you serious? Murphy has to be what, ten years older than her?"

"Eight," Murphy says quietly.

"Sorry."

He flashes a grin at me and strokes his chin. "It's the beard."

"Hope, I think you're misunderstanding," Trinity offers.

"What am I missing?"

Trinity looks at the guys. "They're not saying she has to be with Murphy. Or like she's promised to him or anything like that. Is that what you're thinking?"

"Well, yeah." I flick my gaze at Wrath, and he rolls his eyes at me.

"She's had a crush on him forever. You must have had a crush on an older guy when you were a kid, right?" she asks.

I nod even though Rock is watching me with narrowed eyes.

She pats Murphy's knee, which makes Wrath narrow his eyes. "Although Murph will deny it, he's sweet on her too. But he won't do anything about it while she's underage."

"The age of consent is actually seventeen in New York," I say absently.

Wrath snorts in disgust. Trinity shakes her head like I'm dense.

"What if she's still with Axel?" I ask.

Murphy shrugs. "They're more worked up about this than I am. You met her, right? She's a pain in the ass. Not interested."

Wrath reaches over and smacks Murphy on the back of the head. "Keep telling yourself that, buddy."

Shaking my head from this bizarre conversation, I excuse myself to run to the bathroom. With Inga's exit, things seem to have calmed down. There's music coming out of the champagne room, but I don't have to go past it to get to where I want, so I ignore it.

When I return, tense, angry voices hit me as I'm about to turn the corner. I pause to listen, praying no one will come up behind me.

"You can't have your ol' lady questioning the club like that, brother." It's Wrath. What the fuck is his problem with me now?

"Simmer down, asshole." That's Rock, and I smile at his no-bullshit tone.

"It's your fucking fault. Why you always gotta hassle me about Heidi?" Murphy grumbles loud enough for me to catch.

"Wyatt, look at it this way. Heidi is club family. After meeting her for five seconds, Hope was ready to stand up to your scary ass in defense of her. Sounds like perfect ol' lady material to me."

Why, thank you, Trinity.

"Thanks, Trin," Rock says, echoing my thoughts.

Wrath must be considering their words. I wait, holding my breath. I know how close he and Rock are. I shouldn't give a shit about his "seal of approval" but I do.

"I guess. She kept her cool when Cookie got up in her face last night too. And with Inga this morning. I almost pissed myself."

"You should probably talk—"

I choose that moment to walk back into the room, and everyone falls silent for a second.

Rock stands up.

"I've had enough drama for one night. Wrath, tell Z I'll talk to him about Axel in the morning. Someone make sure Heidi gets home. She can't stay here."

Murphy stands and squeezes my shoulder on his way out. "Night, Hope."

Surprised, I turn my head, watching him walk out the door.

At least someone here likes me.

CHAPTER SIX

ROCK

Even though she's pissed about it, Hope agreed to take Teller's case. She's been spending more time at Adam's office, which annoys me less than it used to. I offered to set her up in an office near Crystal Ball, but I don't think she took me seriously, because she laughed in my face.

All this means is that I end up riding downtown more often to take her out to lunch or bring her dinner when she's working late. Lately, I sense she has a bit of the guilts for getting involved in Teller's family drama. With that in mind, I drop by to take her to a late lunch, because I doubt she's bothered to eat yet.

The only person I find in the office is Adam.

"Where's my girl?"

Adam's entire body jerks. "God dammit. Can you make some noise so I know you're here? You scared the shit out of me."

"Christ, I'm not exactly fucking tiny. Maybe you should get your ears checked."

His lips quirk into a brief grin before he ducks his head back down to his computer screen. "She's out. Said she had a client interview."

"Where?"

One shrug later, Hope's buddy is dangerously close to an ass-kicking. I've never liked this idea of her going to her clients' houses. Seems awfully unsafe to me.

I snap my fingers in front of Adam. "Where. Is. She?"

"Dude, chill. I'll pull up her calendar." Adam gets busy tapping his way into her calendar. "We have access to each other's stuff just in case," he tells me as I wait. I guess he's worried I'll think it's weird. But it makes sense, and right now, I'm thankful for it.

He points at the screen. "Here. She's drafting a will and is doing the client intake."

I fight the urge to unhinge his jaw with my fist. "I don't care *what* she's doing. *Where* is she doing it?"

"749 Mason Ave," he answers with a frown.

Fuck me. That's a bad area of Empire. "Jesus. You let her go down there alone?"

Adam looks at me as if I've got a few screws loose. "Uh, she's an independent girl, Rock. One does not tell Hope what to do if one wants to live to see the next day."

We'll see about that.

On my way out, I send her a quick text.

Dropped by to take you to lunch. Where you at?

I don't wait for a response. Just rev up my bike and point it toward Mason Street.

Mason is one of those narrow, one-way streets downtown Empire has in abundance. I find Hope's car easily enough. But no sign of her. I park right next to her car, so there's no way she can leave without me knowing about it.

I scan the street and spot 749 a few doors down from the closed-down shell of the old bar we used to hang out at before we moved the MC out into the wilderness. Still no sign of Hope.

Checking my phone, I see she hasn't responded. A boulder of worry settles in my gut as I stride over to 749 and push open the door.

And run smack into a very frustrated Hope.

Thank fuck.

"Rock! What on earth are you doing here?"

Hope

I'm beyond pissed that I apparently drove down here for nothing. Mrs. Kohn didn't answer her door. The neighborhood is a lot sketchier than I thought it would be, so my nerves are jangling.

Then, bam! There's Rock, looking almost as pissed as I feel. On closer inspection, his pulse is pounding in his neck, body tense, eyes narrowed. Definitely furious and not in a mood to joke around.

He takes me by the elbow and leads me to my car.

"What are you doing down here by yourself?"

A chill settles over me, and a sliver of resentment works into my chest. I'm thirty-fucking-three years old. A professional. I don't need to ask his permission before doing my damn job.

"Listen, I've been doing things on my own for a long damn time, Rock. I've done more client interviews than—"

"You're not alone anymore. You need to interview someone, you tell me and I go with you."

Is he nuts? "That's ridiculous! You have your own things to worry about—"

"I worry about *you*."

"I don't need to be protected like some little kid."

"I'm well aware you're not a kid, Hope. Doesn't mean I want you wandering around the ghetto by yourself."

For a long stretch, we stare at each other in some sort of standoff. Rock is wound tight. Chest heaving, eyes flashing. Why am I questioning him? Oh, right—independence.

"Rock, I'm an independent person. I'm not sure how to handle—"

His expression softens, even as he interrupts me. "Ask me for help, Hope. That's all. Don't put yourself in danger."

"How am I in danger?"

He cocks his head, and I get the feeling he's thinking something rather unkind.

"Did you meet your client?"

"No. No one was home."

"Did it ever occur to you that it could have been a setup? To rob you? Or worse?"

Well, no, that never occurred to me. Stubbornly, I refuse to answer his question.

He nods in his maddeningly knowing way that makes me want to kick him.

Instead, I smooth my hands over the bulging biceps of the big, bad, glowering biker in front of me.

"Okay. But can you accept that I'm a grown woman who can handle things on her own?"

He struggles. I can tell he wants to say no. I'm touched that he manages to rein it in. He nods and traces a finger over my cheek.

"I couldn't stand it if something happened to you, baby."

That melts me, and suddenly I'm acutely aware of how close our bodies are. How much closer I'd like our bodies to be. The heat of his skin radiates through his clothes into me. Adrenaline and emotion swirl between us, lighting a spark of desire. His hand drops to my waist, and he tugs me closer. I lean up to kiss his cheek, inhaling his crisp, raw scent. As I pull back, he turns and catches my lips in a rough kiss. Pressing me against my car door, his hands shackle my wrists against my sides as he takes the kiss even deeper. He swallows every soft moan that leaves my lips.

The blast of a car horn stops us from doing the dirty on the hood of my car. Rock growls against my lips before pulling away. He scowls at the driver, then turns back to me.

"We done here?"

My voice comes out as shaky as the rest of me feels. "Yes."

"Good. Follow me to your office. I want to take you out to lunch."

"Okay."

When we pull into the office parking lot, my stomach clenches. For once, I'm not sure what I want to say. Part of me is still pissed off about his bossy caveman act. The other is floored and not sure how to handle the depth of Rock's emotion for me. I'm proud of my independence, but I can't deny how it feels to have someone worry about me.

I'll never admit it, but his concern was valid. It was weird that the woman wasn't home. Replaying our conversation in my head makes me realize something about the situation had been off from the beginning. What if Rock hadn't shown up and someone else with less than honorable intentions had? Would I have warded them off with my legal pad? Frightened them with the threat of a thousand paper cuts?

Wary of Rock's stiff posture, I don't bother with small talk. I grab the helmet he hands me and get on the bike. He takes us to a quiet Chinese restaurant we've both become fond of, and we grab a table in the back. As we settle next to each other in the curved booth, a thought that reignites my irritation enters my mind.

"You know, it's kind of unfair for you to be so hard on me, when you're always out doing who knows what for the club without telling me."

Rock's stiff jaw tells me maybe it would have been wise to keep that thought to myself.

"That so?" he asks low and deadly.

I straighten up and pin him with a stare. "Yes."

The way he stares right back with no hint of the usual amusement on his face tells me how serious his next words will be. "Well, Baby Doll, I'm a rather big guy who knows how to handle himself, and I'm rarely unarmed. Not a tiny woman with nothing but her briefcase. Besides, on club business I'm usually not alone. I have Wrath or Z for backup. Would you like me to assign one of the prospects to be with you at all times? Because I'll be happy to arrange that."

See, I knew I should have kept my mouth shut.

"Very funny."

"Do I look like I'm joking?"

"I'm not tiny."

Finally a glimmer of a smile at the corners of his mouth. "You are compared to me."

I sigh. "This is hard for me, Rock. I told you how my father died when I was a teenager?"

His face relaxes a little more, and he squeezes my hand under the table. "Yeah."

"Well, my mother kind of fell apart after that. She never held a steady job to begin with, so finding work was next to impossible. We lost our house, then had to move from apartment to apartment. I've been basically taking care of myself since I was thirteen. So as much as I appreciate you wanting to look after me, it's hard for me to accept."

"I need to, Hope." He takes my chin between his thumb and forefinger and forces me to meet his gaze. "Understand where I'm coming from. A real man looks after his woman."

Oh, damn.

The look in his eyes goes distant. "I get it. My father drowned himself in booze and whoring after my mother died. Before that, though, she was the center of his world. I always told myself when I found the right woman, I'd be the kind of man he'd been before she died. Not what he turned into later."

"Okay," I whisper. Because honestly, what else can I say to that?

"Thank you, Baby Doll. I'll try not to overdo it."

I guess that's as much of a concession as I'm going to get.

Deep down, a tiny voice says maybe, just maybe, it's nice to be looked after.

Rock

Fuck me, but Hope makes it hard to take care of her. I love how spirited she is, but it also scares the shit out of me. I can't deny she's clever and smart. Book smart, which I admire. Street smart, not so much. That's fine—I have enough street smarts for both of us. If she'll let me take care of her.

My knuckles glide over the warm, soft skin of her cheek. "Do you have to go back to the office?" At the touch of my hand, her eyes close.

Her eyelids flutter open slowly as she thinks about a response to my question. I love how deeply I can affect her with only a touch.

"No."

"Good."

Our waitress drops off soup for Hope. Watching her sexy fucking lips purse to blow on her spoon gets me in an uncomfortable state fast.

"So, uh, is work picking up at all?" I ask, trying to distract myself.

She shakes her head. "No, that's why I was eager for this appointment today."

"Shit. Sorry, babe. It will happen."

She shrugs. "I'm not worried about it right now."

"Things going okay with Heidi's case?"

She arches an eyebrow at me. "You know I can't talk about that with you."

Yup. My girl takes her shit seriously. Can't pry any information out of her.

She's interrupted by buzzing from her purse and pulls out her cell phone. I lean back against the booth and finish my soda, signaling the waitress for another.

Hope's fingers fly over her phone. "Sophie," she mutters.

Her phone buzzes again. After reading the text, Hope tilts her head to look at me.

"What?"

"Um, Sophie wants to know if we're interested in going to Jonny's show with her this weekend?"

Hope seems so timid as she's asking me this, I feel like an asshole. Why is she afraid to ask me to hang with her friends?

"Yeah, of course, doll."

Her lips roll into a quick grin and she makes a little "squee" noise that I find fucking adorable. She taps out a reply to Sophie, then shoves her phone back in her purse.

"Do you mind if we pick her up?"

"Of course not." I want to question her more about why she's so hesitant, but our food arrives.

She's silent while she arranges everything the way she wants, her pickiness as cute as ever.

"Did Teller's grandmother ever get a lawyer?"

Hope glances up. "Yeah, he's a dick too. We have a trial coming up in two months. I'm hoping we can work something out before then."

"Fuck—by the time the court gets around to sorting it out, she'll be fucking eighteen and it won't matter anyway."

Hope rolls her eyes. "Tell me about it." She goes still for a minute. "Shoot. I forgot, I do need to go back to the office and make some phone calls."

My mouth is full, so I make a disappointed humming noise.

"Sorry, I lose all train of thought when your hands are on me," she says. I think she meant it in a teasing way, but it comes out so serious I'm hard as steel before she finishes speaking.

"Don't ever apologize for that, baby," I manage to get out.

Hope

Lunch with Rock left me happy, but unsettled. At some point, I'm going to need to reflect on what's happening to me, because I don't seem to care about much these days except spending every second with my man. It's dangerous because that is not the type of woman I always aspired to be.

Shaking my head, I sit down behind my desk and flip through Teller's file. I need to call the attorney who has been assigned to represent Heidi in the custody action. I want to get a read on where she's going to land with her recommendation to the court. Ethically, she is supposed to argue whatever her client wants her to argue—even if she disagrees with it. I know for a fact Heidi desperately wants her brother to win this fight, so I'm curious to find out what Heidi's attorney plans to argue.

First, though, I try to call my no-show client from this morning. I get a pre-recorded "the number you have reached has been disconnected…" and hang up.

I stare at Teller's file a little longer, then pull out a legal pad and write down what I want to say to Miss Clark. It's a nervous habit I picked up in law school. I get so flustered speaking on the phone with people, I'm always afraid I'll forget what I want to say.

Once I have it all mapped out, I can't delay any longer, so I dial the other attorney—half hoping I'll just get her voicemail so I can deal with this another day. But she answers the phone herself.

After the introductions, we get down to business.

"Look, Ms. Kendall, I appreciate that you're close to the family—"

Huh?

"What do you mean?"

"Heidi speaks very highly of you."

"Oh, that's nice to hear. She's a good kid."

She blows out a breath, and I brace myself for what's about to come. "I have my reservations about her brother being able to take care of her properly. But on the other hand, I don't think her grandmother is suitable either."

"I hope you're not planning to suggest placement for her."

"No, God, no. Not when she has two relatives who want her. She is a good kid. With the way things are at home, she could easily be out skipping school and doing God only knows what, but she never misses a day and her grades are pretty solid given the turmoil in her life."

I like this attorney. She's clearly done her homework, and she seems to care about Heidi. Considering the pool of lazy attorneys out there that could have been assigned to Heidi, it seems she won the lawyer jackpot. I still want to know what her reservations about my client are, though.

"How can I convince you to give my guy a solid recommendation?"

She snorts into the phone. "You know I have to argue in favor of the brother, since that's what she wants. Doesn't matter what I think. But I'd feel better about it if he had a home of his own and a stable job."

Good point. She really has been thorough. This is something Teller and I have talked about. Repeatedly. He lives at the clubhouse full time. It's about an hour away from Heidi's school and most certainly not the appropriate environment for her. He promised me he was looking into finding an apartment nearby. I also know Rock has been working to get him on the books at one of the Lost Kings legitimate, non-stripper businesses.

"Look, attorney-to-attorney, he is employed full-time, it's just under the table. He's working on getting that straightened out. He's also looking for an apartment near Heidi's school for the two of them. He wants to keep her close to her friends, school, and their grandmother."

"Good. Okay. I feel a lot better about the situation then."

The sound of the front door opening spooks me out of the conversation. Dammit. I forgot to lock the door after Adam left. The basement office has always felt very isolated to me, even though there is a psychiatrist's office right upstairs. When I'm here alone, I almost always keep the front door locked.

It's weird that whoever entered hasn't said anything yet.

I'm so focused on what's going in the waiting area that I miss the last thing Charlotte said.

"Hope? Are you there?"

"Sorry, Charlotte, what was that?"

"I just said we have a pre-trial coming up, I'm hoping we can work things out with Tom, and the grandmother isn't going to dig her heels in. I'm not in the mood for a trial."

That startles a laugh out of me. "Yeah, neither am I. Tom's private pay though, so he might want to ride it all the way through."

She makes a sound between a snort and a chuckle. A snortle. "Yeah."

I hear someone still walking around in the outer office. "Hey, Charlotte, I need to go, but we'll talk soon, okay?"

"Sure."

We say our goodbyes, and I disconnect. Clutching my cell phone in my hand, I make my way out to the waiting area. There's a tall, skinny, shifty-eyed stranger shuffling around. He keeps staring into Adam's darkened office as if my friend might magically appear.

"Can I help you?"

He jumps about three feet in the air before aiming what I can only describe as crazy eyes on me. "Where's Mr. Braydon?"

"He's out. Can I help you?"

"Yeah, he's in charge of my mother's estate, and I need to speak to him."

"Do you have an appointment?"

"Well, no. But I need to talk to him."

This guy has shoved my stranger-danger radar into red alert. Especially since I'm trapped down here with him by myself.

"Let me check his calendar."

He follows me into Adam's office, which makes me even more nervous. Dammit. Why hadn't I asked Rock to come back to the office with me? He'd scare this guy away in two seconds flat. Calling up Adam's calendar takes a few seconds. While I wait, I take a few breaths to calm myself. I have to remind myself to be polite to Adam's client, when I really want to tell him to get the fuck out and come back later.

"What's your name? I'll text Adam and see when he's coming back."

"David Greybell."

I tap out a quick text to Adam, not really expecting a reply since I know he's in court. But at least if I go missing, the police will have an idea of who to question first.

I'm seriously pissed at myself for being so scared. Irrationally, I blame Rock. He got me so flustered after my missed appointment this morning—insinuating that something bad could have happened to me —that I'm seeing threats everywhere.

Finally I get into Adam's calendar and discover he's in Surrogate's Court. Great. He could be there for twenty minutes or two hours— there's no way to tell.

"He hasn't written back yet, so he's probably in court. It looks like he has some time available tomorrow morning. Do you want me to schedule you in?"

"Yes, please."

The reason I suggested that time is because I won't be here. Let Adam deal with his creepy client by himself.

I tap in some information and log off. "Okay, I'll let him know. Thanks."

"Are you an attorney? Maybe you can help me instead?"

"No, that's not my area, and my boyfriend is picking me up any minute."

He looks dejected, and I squelch the impulse to feel bad about brushing him off.

After Mr. Greybell leaves, I lock the door. My hands are shaking. I stare at my cell phone and contemplate calling Rock. After turning it over in my head, I dismiss the idea. He'll just use it as an excuse to be even more hyper-protective. The last thing I need is for him to start sending one of his prospects to work with me.

Hearing the back door slam makes me almost jump out of my skin, even though logically I know it has to be Adam. I stalk down the hall to greet him.

"You just missed your oddball client."

He stops and throws a sarcastic glance at me. "Greybell?"

"Yup."

He waves a hand in the air. "He's a little off, but he's harmless."

"Yeah, well, he made me nervous. I'm so pissed I forgot to lock the front door."

"You can't keep that door locked during business hours. What if a client stops by?"

We've had this discussion before, and I kind of want to clock Adam for being so damn dense. "Uh, when I'm alone down here by myself, I damn well will keep the door locked. Clients will just have to ring the doorbell."

He rolls his eyes at me as if to say "you're such a girl."

"Geez, Hope, there's an office right upstairs."

Crossing my arms over my chest, I give him a hard stare. "I don't care. You're a guy. You don't get it."

His face softens. "You're right. Better to be safe than sorry."

My agitation disappears, and we turn to discussing our current cases. Since I only have the one, my end of the conversation is short. I am able to offer him some advice on a few of his cases, which helps me feel a little less useless.

When we're done with the work talk, Adam's face transforms into a mischievous grin. "Did that big, scary man of yours find you before? He came here all wound up earlier."

"Yeah, he did."

"He's something, Hope. You sure know how to pick 'em."

I know Adam means this as a compliment, and my lips quirk into a smile.

"How about you? When do I get to meet this mystery man you've been seeing?"

He gives me a secret smile. "Soon. I'm thinking of asking him to go to that party of Judge Oak's."

"So, I have to wait until then to meet him? Is he a lawyer?"

Another sly grin. "Sort of."

"What the hell does that mean? Is he out?"

A flash of annoyance crosses his face. "Yes, Hope. Unlike some people we know, I don't deal with guys hiding in the closet."

He's referring to Ross, and I'm thankful I never suggested that because they're both gay lawyers they'd make a perfect couple. Lilly once made that mistake, and Adam still hasn't forgiven her for it.

"Don't start."

He nods. "Are you going to invite your big, scary biker?"

I snort. Then full-out belly laugh. Rock at a political fundraiser? As if that would ever happen. "Uh, no. I don't think he would set foot inside an event like that." In fact, I know he won't—because he told me so—which is why I don't even plan to mention it. What's the point?

"You have to go, Hope. Mara will kill you if you don't."

"Yeah, I am capable of going to things alone, you know."

"I remember." He's referring to Clay.

He didn't do lawyer functions either.

I sure know how to pick them.

CHAPTER SEVEN

HOPE

"Thanks so much for picking me up, guys," Sophie says in a breathless rush as she slides into the backseat of Rock's SUV.

"No problem," Rock answers while reversing out of the driveway. "Thanks for inviting us."

"I'm so happy to have the extra company. I love seeing Jonny's shows, but I always feel weird standing around backstage by myself." Sophie squeezes my shoulder. "It's good to have my partner in crime back."

I chuckle at that. Sophie and I had a lot of fun times in law school. Since I was with Clay, Lilly was her partner in picking up rocker guys, but I appreciate the sentiment.

Sophie lets out this frustrated growling noise. "I hate all the fucking groupies who hang out, trying to grope Jonny when he gets off stage. You can help me kick some skank groupie ass."

Rock chuckles a little uncomfortably.

With a smirk, I turn and face Sophie. "No problem. I've got tons of experience now from dealing with Rock's own personal muffler bunny fan club."

Rock makes a choking sound, and Sophie falls back against the seat in a fit of giggles. "Buttercup, you gotta let me up there one of these days. I'll be happy to take care of those bitches for you." She flashes a glance at Rock.

"You girls done?" he asks with a bemused smile.

Sophie and I burst into another round of giggles while Rock shakes his head.

We're still laughing and carrying on by the time we get to the club. It holds about three thousand people and appears to be sold out tonight. The line down the sidewalk to get in seems miles long. We are able to go right to the front window, give our names, and go right in. The bouncer directs us to the back. We walk through the brightly lit but mostly empty club. Sophie is bouncing up and down with excitement. It's been a few weeks since she and Jonny saw each other, and I fully expect them to disappear into some dark corner when we find him.

Rock and Jonny greet each other like they're long lost brothers, and I really need to find out what the story is there. Jonny isn't talking much because he's preserving his voice for the demanding style of screaming vocals he uses on stage. Sophie brought him a particular type of cough drop, and he thanks her by kissing her long and deep in front of everyone.

Like a king holding court, Rock is busy chatting with the other band members. I'm always amazed at how comfortable he is in any situation. Maybe even a little jealous.

After Jonny and Sophie finish their game of tonsil hockey, she rushes over to me.

"Sorry."

I'm busy watching Rock and Jonny. Rock pulls a package out of his cut and hands it to Jonny, who lights up in a big grin.

"What are they up to?" I ask Sophie.

"No idea. Lots of people bring them shit for the free tix, you know?"

Hmmm.

We mostly stay in the back room during the first couple bands. Rock pulls me into his lap as the rest of the band lights up what

Rock explains to me is a vaporizer. Jonny passes but asks them to save it for later. I arch a brow at Sophie, and she shrugs. She also passes on the weed, but I get the sense she's only doing it so I won't feel weird.

When Rock also passes, one of the guys jokes with him about not sampling his own product. I go absolutely rigid in Rock's lap, and his arms tighten around me.

"I'm good, man," he gets out through clenched teeth.

Lilly joins us, distracting me from the question on the tip of my tongue. She sweeps me into a big hug. The guys in the band are excited to see her, so I assume she's spent a lot of time hanging out with Sophie and Jonny. Rock chuckles when Z walks in the room next. Lilly is sitting on the drummer's lap, and he's dangerously close to motorboating her in front of the entire room. Z takes in the scene and sits down on the arm of the couch next to Rock and me without a word.

"Hey, Z," I greet.

"'Sup, Hope?"

Jonny and Z greet each other with some sort of bro-hug, and I wonder when these two had a chance to meet. Lilly looks up, finally noticing Z, and scrambles out of the drummer's lap. She whispers something in Sophie's ear that makes Sophie tug me out of Rock's lap. The three of us head out into the club and into the ladies' room.

"Wasn't there a bathroom back there?" I ask because we're stuck waiting in a line.

"Trust me, it's more disgusting than this one," Sophie informs us with a shiver.

"Why is Z here?" Lilly asks me.

"I don't know—"

"Jonny put Rock, Hope, and plus two on the list," Sophie answers, clearing up that mystery.

Geez, I hope Wrath isn't going to show up next.

"Shit," Lilly mumbles.

"What are you so freaked out for? I thought you and Z were just fucking around," Sophie asks.

"We are." Lilly sinks her teeth into her bottom lip. "Doesn't mean I want to hang out with him and someone else I'm fucking around with," she says with a nervous chuckle.

I can't stop the eye roll. I love Lilly, but she's non-stop drama.

By the time we make it out of the bathroom, the band is setting up. We reenter the green room where Jonny is busy running through his vocal exercises. Not wanting to make him nervous, I head back to Rock.

"We're probably going to watch the band from the side of the stage," I inform him.

"Okay. You're staying back here, though, right? I don't want you out in the crowd if they start moshing and shit."

I stop and give him a cool look. "Rock, I went to shows long before I knew you. I can handle myself just fine."

His eyebrow quirks at that. Z turns away, shaking with laughter.

The girls and I head into the club.

After the first song, Rock joins us side stage and slips his arms around my waist. I lean into him, and he bends down to kiss my neck. Sophie glances over and breaks into a wide grin. My body is vibrating from being so close to the stage. Having Rock at my back intensifies the sensation.

The show is awesome, and I remember how much I used to enjoy going out with Sophie. Jonny turns into a beast on stage, and I hope he and Sophie manage to make things work. I don't think she realizes it, but he's exactly the kind of guy she's been looking for since I met her. Hot rocker, who has a business with income on the side. Doesn't throw his money away on drugs, and worships the ground she walks on.

After the band finishes what they say is their last song, Jonny paces backstage waiting to go back out for their encore. Looking past Sophie, I realize Lilly has disappeared. Z and Rock are over by the entrance to the back room talking, so she's not with Z. Just as I turn to ask Sophie a question, someone squeezes my ass. Unless Rock has developed some amazing super powers, I know it can't be him, and whirl to confront the ass-grabber. Sophie also squeals. Ass-grabber has an accomplice.

I recognize my perv as the singer of one of the earlier bands.

"Get your hands off me," I order through clenched teeth.

"Come on, baby, you're too hot to be bandwhoring for these old fucks," he breathes in my face. Is it possible to get contact drunk? If so, then his whiskey breath would do the trick.

Sophie pushes the other guy just as the music for the encore starts up.

Suddenly both ass-grabbers are laid out on the floor. Rock has his hand around the throat of mine. "That's my girl you touched, asshole," he shout-growls into the kid's ear.

Jonny has his knee on the chest of the guy who grabbed Sophie and is delivering an equally informative message.

Z hustles us away. "You girls all right?"

I shake him off. "We're fine. We had it covered."

Z cocks his head at me. Security finally shows up and holds on to the two jerks, while Jonny runs out on stage to finish his set. Sophie and I crash into the green room together.

Flopping on the couch side by side, we listen to the band wrap up their set. Rock's still out there somewhere too.

"Man we know how to live it up, buttercup," Sophie giggles.

"Sorry about that."

"What? Our men protecting us? Don't be—"

She's interrupted by Jonny running into the room and scooping her up off the couch. They disappear into another back room that I assume will be off-limits for the rest of the night.

Rock slams through the doors next and heads straight for me. Joining me on the couch, he slips his arm around my shoulders. "You okay?"

"I was fine, Rock. I can take care of myself," I grumble. Looking up, I find Z standing next to the couch. Rock leans over, touching his forehead to mine.

"I see someone grabbin' my girl's ass, I'm gonna to do something about it. It's who I am, Hope. You know this."

He's right. I do know this about him. But still. "You can't go around beating up everyone who looks at me funny."

He chuckles. "Oh yeah—why not?"

I give him an exasperated eye roll.

His expression turns serious. "Babe, that guy didn't just look at you funny. He put his hands on you. That's not okay. You're my girl.

There's no fuckin' way I'm gonna stand by and let that shit happen right in front of me."

I can tell he's pissed that I didn't fall at his feet and thank him for the intervention, because he gets up and walks outside to cool off. Z's still standing there staring at me.

I glare up at him. "You're not going to give me some scary lecture, are you? I get enough of those from Wrath."

Z's face beaks into a warm smile and he sits next to me. "Nah, Hope. You gotta understand, Rock loves how smart and independent you are—"

"Geez, you could've fooled me, the way he's always acting," I scoff.

"I won't get into the other things he likes about you." He gives me a dirty wink that makes me chuckle, then cocks his head at me. "How much has he told you about the club before he took over?"

"Nothing, really."

Z flicks his gaze to where Rock disappeared to. "I can only give you a general outline, you understand?"

I nod so he'll continue. By some silent agreement, the two of us move closer together.

"We lost brothers we were close to because people in control of our club cared more about greed than the brotherhood we're supposed to be about. Not a damn thing Rock could have done to change it. But Rock, he's the type of guy who blames himself for everything bad that happens to the people he cares about."

Oh, wow. That gives me a lot of insight into why he's so goddamn overbearing. I wish I'd been smart enough to piece this together sooner.

"You? I ain't never seen him act about a woman the way he does with you. Knew it the day he met you. Saw it all over his face. I don't think he could stand it if something happened to you."

Heat crawls over my skin.

Z has known Rock a long time. Curiosity makes me blurt out, "What was his ex-wife like?"

Z snorts. "A straight-up useless bitch. Hot, don't get me wrong."

My face must betray some form of jealousy, because Z smirks. "Babe, by the time he realized that wasn't enough, he was already in too deep. But what they had wasn't a marriage. It was an extended hookup. She was only interested in him gettin' that president patch—didn't give a shit about him. Caused him a lot of grief, then deserted him when he needed her most."

I let out a long sigh.

"You love him," Z continues. "We can all see it. Just try to understand he needs his woman to need him, ya know? He's been taking care of the club and everyone under it for years. Keeping his family safe is what matters most to him. He just wants to protect you. It's not a disrespect thing, honey."

"I know."

Z gets up and holds out his hand to pull me off the sinkhole of a couch.

"Ya gotta let him defend his girl. Besides, when shit like that happens, he's doing the world a favor. Guy goes around grabbing women he doesn't know, deserves whatever he gets."

"True. I just…" I think of how to phrase what I want to say so I won't offend Z. "I'm not like those girls that hang out at your club, who thrive on fights and drama. I don't get off on seeing my man 'take care of business,' you know?"

Z studies me carefully. "Hope, I'd never in a million years confuse you with a club whore, trust me. You're all class, babe. And I hear what you're saying. But I gotta ask—did you create the situation?"

"No, of course not."

"Then you're not stirring up trouble just to be a drama queen."

Shit. "Okay. I understand what you're telling me."

He grins. "Glad I could help."

"At least you're not mean."

He grins even bigger. "Baby, I'm a lover, not a fighter."

I shove his shoulder and he wraps an arm around me, giving me a quick hug.

"The fuck, bro? I gotta lay you out too?" Rock growls.

I take a quick step between them, which makes both guys laugh.

"Don't you dare," I warn. "He's been trying to explain to me why you're such a bossy caveman."

"That so?" Rock asks with an eyebrow lift.

Z shrugs and takes a few steps back.

Rock glances down at me. "So your husband used to let you come out to places like this with Sophie all the time?"

Whoa. "Let me? Did you just say 'let me'? Are you serious?"

Rock's mouth twitches, and I can tell he's swallowing whatever he wants to say, and it's not coming easily.

"Didn't he like heavy metal?" Rock asks with his mouth twisted as if he'd been sucking on a lemon. This is his version of being diplomatic.

I'm shaking with laughter at how hard he's trying to control his comments. And after what I've just learned, I understand where he's coming from a lot better, so it's easier to dial down my irritation. "Not so much," I answer.

Rock nods, and I stand up on tiptoes to brush a quick kiss over his lips. Heat flares in his eyes, and we stand there staring at each other.

"Where'd Lilly run off to?" Z asks, snuffing out the fire between us.

Facing Z, I shake my head. "No clue."

He whips out his cell phone with a look on his face that says he's debating calling her.

"You want me to text her?" I ask.

"Naw, that's okay."

I do it anyway because I feel like I owe Z.

Where'd ya go?

At the bar.

Tipping my head up, I catch Z studying me. Rock has wandered over to talk to some of the guys from the band. "She's at the bar out front."

The corners of his mouth curve up, and he taps my shoulder before he walks out.

There's a bit of a commotion at the door. Through the high, square windows, I can see Z in the hallway talking to someone. He finally walks away, and two girls push through the swinging doors. I recognize them from the MC. One of them is the wench who's been giving me shit for a couple weeks now. Her name is Roxy or Foxy, something stupid like that. She a sly little bitch because she always manages to needle me when Rock's not around. She somehow catches me when Trinity's occupied too. Little digs about her relationship with Rock. She insinuates that when he's up there without me she's with him, which I know is bullshit. Me telling her to fuck off hasn't done the trick yet. I think she is angling for a physical confrontation, but that's just not me.

The ugly bitch with her, Cherry, likes to inform me about Rock's past preference for three-ways. They're a charming little duo, even more annoying when joined by their third sidekick, Ginger, who thankfully I don't spot with them tonight. Foxy is short and what I guess guys would refer to as "thick" with bleached-blonde hair, wild tattoos, and piercings. Cherry is also short but skinny as a rail and has clown-colored red hair.

Rock seems to have no one "type" when it comes to the women he fucks.

One of the band guys calls out to Cherry. When she sees Rock, she squeals and is all over him. He politely pushes her away but keeps chatting with her, which pisses me off royally. Foxy spots me and struts over.

Because she's such a classy gal, the first thing out of her mouth is, "What the fuck are you doing here?"

"My friend is dating Jonny Cage. They put us on the list."

Her eyes widen, and I wonder if she was planning to bag Jonny tonight. Inwardly I chuckle, because while I may not have the guts to kick her ass, Sophie most certainly does.

She spins and heads back into the club.

Bye, bitch.

Rock finishes his conversation and heads my way. Cherry follows close behind until she spots me.

"You ready to go, babe?" Rock asks with a big grin on his face. Yeah, I'm ready to go home and crawl into bed. Alone.

Rock

I really can't take my girl anywhere. Christ. I figured she'd be safe backstage—mistake on my part. Seeing that greasy motherfucker groping her almost sent me over the edge. The little bastard is lucky he's still alive.

I might've felt bad for crushing the windpipe of the singer for one of Jonny's support bands if Jonny hadn't broken the guitarist's thumbs.

We make a good pair. We both got stubborn women to take care of, and neither of us has a problem getting our hands dirty.

"You'd make a good King, Jonny." I joke on our way back inside the club.

He grins at me. "This rock star thing doesn't take off, I might take you up on that, man. Fucking bullshit that happening backstage to our girls. I should hire you for security, especially when we play shitholes like this that don't even pretend to search people for weapons."

Yeah, the lack of security in this joint hadn't escaped my notice. I can't believe Hope and Sophie used to hang here a lot when they were in law school.

Unfortunately my big mouth said exactly that when I saw her. From the hurt on her face, I think she took my comment as disrespecting her husband, which wasn't my intention. I'm just all twitchy from seeing her molested right in front of me. I know she thinks she's tough and can handle herself, but I gave it a second and the creepy asshole still didn't remove his hands from her ass.

Fuck.

It's not her I'm mad at, so I try to simmer the fuck down by going back outside.

When I return, Z seems to have imparted some wisdom that's calmed her a bit.

The band liked the green I brought tonight, so I quietly make my way over to discuss future business with them. I don't need Hope overhearing this, but I'd rather not miss this opportunity.

I'm shocked as shit when Roxy and Cherry show up. Had no idea they ran in these circles. But bikers and rockers overlap more than you think, so it shouldn't surprise me. Roxy and I had a thing awhile back. Cherry not so much, although she's never stopped trying. Since Hope came into my life, Roxy has made herself scarce.

Even though the house lights are on and the show ended a while ago, the bar is packed. On our way out, Hope darts over to talk to Lilly for a second. I give Z a shoulder slap.

"Working it out?"

The corner of his mouth twists, and he gives me a subtle head shake.

After the girls hug, Hope marches to the door.

Something is definitely on her mind, but I'm not sure what.

The weed?

The ass-grabbing and subsequent beat-down?

My big, stupid mouth?

Take your pick.

Hope

As we'd planned, Jonny's taking Sophie home. Rock and I leave the club by ourselves. A storm of emotion is brewing through me, brought on by seeing those two skanks from the MC. As he opens the car door for me, he stops to study my face.

"You okay?"

Let it go.

But I can't. My racing thoughts speed away, leaving me out of control and close to tears.

"No."

His startled expression triggers my anger. For someone so in charge and in control, how can he be so fucking clueless? "Why don't you ever pay such close attention to me at the clubhouse?"

"What? None of my brothers would ever harm you, Baby Doll."

"No. Not the guys. Do you have any idea…never mind."

His fingers tighten on my chin, lifting my face to him. "Hope, talk to me."

"The guys treat me well. Except Wrath, but I don't care about him lecturing me and always trying to scare me away—I can handle him. What hurts…" Pain closes my throat, making it impossible to get the words I want to say out.

Tears roll down my cheeks. God, I'm such a coward and a baby. I'm thirty-three years old. My boyfriend is thirty-fucking-eight. Of course he's slept with other women. I've known this all along.

But in a "normal" dating situation, I wouldn't be expected to spend so much time with his past conquests or take shit from them.

My tears alarm him. "Hope, baby, tell me what's wrong. Why are you crying?"

I take several deep breaths, trying to loosen my throat and calm myself.

"You're all worried about me going to clubs and guys hitting on me, but you think nothing of letting those catty bitches at your clubhouse try to rip me apart. Do you have any idea how humiliating it is to be around them, knowing they've been with you and are waiting for the day you finally get bored with me so they can jump you again?"

"Honey, I told you—"

My hurt and sadness suddenly mutates into anger. "No, what pisses me off is I'm expected to cat fight with those bitches and claim you like some piece of territory, right? That's what ol' ladies do? But I can't do that. That's not who I am. You want me to accept your bossy caveman crap, then you've got to accept who I am too."

The confusion on his face is visible. "Why didn't you tell me sooner? Honey, when one got in your face, I got rid of her. I offered to get rid of the rest, and you told me not to."

The hard lump settles back in my throat, but I squeeze out the words anyway. "I didn't realize how horrible it would be week after week. I want to fight my own battles, but I can't deal—I feel like such a coward. I'm too soft for your life, Rock. I settle things with words, not my fists."

"Baby doll, I love you just the way you are. I love how soft and sweet and smart you are. I'm so fucking lucky to have you. I love that you always handle yourself with class. I don't want my woman off starting cat fights and embarrassing me."

"I hate sleeping in that fucking bed, knowing how many skanks have shared it with you," I grit out before I even realize what I'm saying. Panic and sorrow threaten to overwhelm me. I'd feel less exposed if I were standing out here buck naked.

Rock's hands cup my shoulders, and he leans down into my face. "Babe, no one else has ever been in that particular bed but you and me.

I promise you I ended all of those relationships. I've never lied to you. I told you the absolute truth—I haven't been with anyone else since that day I left you at your house." In the middle of his speech, he's managed to maneuver me so I'm sandwiched between his hard chest and the cold metal of the car behind me. Warm lips press against my forehead.

"Please don't punish me for shit I've done in the past, Hope." His low, gravelly voice is unusually strained.

"I'm not." I blink rapidly, trying to stop the tears. "It just hurts."

His rough fingers stroke my cheek. "Baby, I've done everything possible to make it clear to everyone that we're together."

I snort out a humorless laugh. "I know."

"If they're giving you shit, you have to tell me, or Trinit—"

"Don't you dare put this on her. She's been nothing but sweet to me, but she's not supposed to be my babysitter."

"I can't fix it if I don't know. Give me names so I can take care of it."

"Jesus Christ, have you really screwed so many women you can't even remember?"

"Hope—"

"This is stupid. I shouldn't have said anything. Can you take me home now?" I can see he wants to argue, but I push him back. "Please. Take me home. Now."

Rock

Shame isn't an emotion I waste a lot of energy on. At the moment, though, I'm feeling a fuck lot of it crashing over me. For years I told myself I was only fucking around so much until I found the right woman. I wish it had occurred to me how those encounters would affect any future relationship. Deep down I've worried all along Hope and I were not meant to be. We're just too damn different.

She deserves better than me.

But I can't let her go. I love her too fucking much. And I can't stand seeing her hurting. Knowing it's my fault is even worse. She's obviously been holding onto this pain for a while, not wanting to admit any vulnerability. Trying to be strong for me, because she thinks that's what I want her to be.

After she handled herself so well with Cookie and Inga, I figured things were fine. I should have fucking known better. Those catty bitches would mistake Hope's sweet personality for weakness and try to exploit it.

I'm trying not to dwell on the fact that she asked me to take her home.

"Babe, I think we need to talk about this more."

"I can't tonight, Rock. I need some space."

Fuck me. It should have sunk in when she and Sophie were making those jokes earlier. One, Sophie knew exactly what Hope was talking about, so obviously Hope has been distressed enough to talk to Sophie about the situation. Two, Hope's wild laughter seemed a little too out of control and forced. But tonight is the first time we've really hung out with her friends like this, so I assumed I was discovering another side of her.

My knuckles are white from gripping the steering wheel with so much force. With every mile closer to her house, my gut is screaming to ignore her request and take her home with me so we can work this out.

But hounding her isn't going to solve the problem. I should have done something sooner. In my defense, this is the first time in years any of the brothers have had anyone approaching an ol' lady. Bricks hasn't been a patched brother for very long, and he never introduced his ex to the MC. I should have realized it would come as a shock to some of the club girls and they wouldn't behave themselves. Obviously Roxy and Cherry must be two of the culprits, because seeing them tonight seemed to be what triggered Hope. Christ, I've never even fucked Cherry. She started tagging along with Roxy during my self-imposed celibacy thing, so I avoided her. Doesn't mean she hasn't been filling Hope's head with lies, though.

I didn't want to focus on it, but the comment about the bed really got to me. Cause I got rid of my old one the minute I decided to make Hope mine. I don't think the significance of what I revealed to her sunk in.

Most of all, I'm furious with myself. I waited a long time to be her man. My job is to protect her from all threats, and I've failed. Doesn't matter if the threat is the girls who hang around my clubhouse. If I'm going to insist she spend time in my world, it's not fair that she's miserable there. Hope's strengths are in other areas. If I wanted a hair-pulling, face-scratching, brawler for an ol' lady, I could have had my pick. But I love how kindhearted my girl is. I don't want her to change who she is for anything or anyone. Everything in me wants to protect her and keep her safe, so, it's time I step the fuck up and do a better job.

Walking her to her door and saying good night fucking sucks. Her eyes are all red and wet. Words aren't my thing, so the right ones evade me. I'd give anything to see her smile right now.

"Baby, everything will be okay. I'll fix this," I try to reassure her.

"Please just forget I said anything. I don't want to be the cause of trouble in your club." Something dark and uncomfortable spreads through me with her words. She's more composed now, and every calm blink of her eyes stokes my worst fear. That I'll lose the woman I love. I'm so focused on keeping her safe from physical danger I've forgotten that I'm capable of pushing her away all on my own, just because of the people I associate with.

I press my palms to either side of her face. "No, Baby Doll. I've been doing a piss-poor job of taking care of you, and that ends now."

She tries to shake out of my grasp, but I hold her still. Lowering my head by degrees, I seal my mouth over hers. She tastes so fucking sweet, and I desperately want to lick her all over. I relax as her lips open under mine, allowing my tongue to dip inside to stroke over hers. She surges up on her toes, pressing into me. A quiet moan from the back of her throat gets me hard as cement in no time. Slender fingers curl into my leather cut, pulling me closer.

A few seconds later, her hands flatten against my chest and push me back. She chokes on a soft sob.

"Baby, no."

She wriggles out of my embrace and pushes inside. "Text me when you get home," she asks before shutting the door.

I guess it's something.

CHAPTER EIGHT

ROCK

Hope asked me to leave Trinity out of it, but what she doesn't realize is that it's Trinity's unofficial job to make sure the club girls behave themselves. I'm not mad at her. Not at all. I know how sneaky these little bitches can be, but I do want to get some information from her.

Knocking on her door gets me nowhere. Turning around, I see Teller working out in the gym and duck my head inside. "You seen Trin?"

He frowns. "Last I saw, she and Wrath were in the war room watching a movie."

I'm not even sure how to respond to that. The fuck?

Sure enough, I find them coming out of the war room together. I'm not even going to ask.

"Trin, I need to talk to you."

Wrath squeezes her shoulder and whispers something in her ear. As I approach, Wrath gives me a chin lift. "How was the show?"

"Fine. Need to talk to you about some stuff." I made a deal we'll need to hammer out. But Hope's comments about the way my best friend has been treating her have me really pissed off at the moment. "We can discuss it tomorrow, though."

"Hope come back with you?" Trinity asks.

My gaze darts to Wrath, who finally takes a hint and gets lost.

"No, that's kind of what I need to talk to you about." Unlocking the war room, I usher her inside. We pull out the two chairs closest to the door and sit facing each other.

"What's wrong, Rock?"

"You notice any of the girls hassling Hope?"

Trinity thinks it over. "Besides me, she talks to Swan a little bit. She never talks shit about Hope. Same for Envy and Breeze."

All girls I've never slept with, so that doesn't surprise me. But, I seize on another part of what she said. "Who has been talking shit about her?"

Trinity's mouth twists. "Fucking Roxy. She's a cunt."

I can't stop the sharp bark of laughter that escapes me. It's rare to hear Trin use that word. Then I remember after I took myself off the menu, Roxy went at Wrath pretty hard for a while.

"She give you shit too, Trin?"

Trinity shrugs. "Of course, but I can handle it. You think she's been hassling Hope?" My shoulders lift. I have no idea, because Hope won't open up to me. "When? Either you or me is usually with her when she's up here," Trinity finishes.

"I don't know. She wouldn't give me names."

She cocks her head to the side. "Want me to ask her?"

"Nah, she'll know I put you up to it."

Trinity sinks her teeth in her bottom lip as she's thinking over the problem. "If Roxy's giving Hope shit, then Cherry will be in on it too."

Fuck. Trinity and Cherry have a very recent beef, and I'm sure I'm making things worse for Trin right now, but I gotta know. "Anyone else?"

"Ginger," she spits out. Guilt punches me in the gut. Ginger's been causing trouble for years. Her round, rosy ass shoulda been booted from the MC a long time ago.

"They're the toxic twat trio," Trinity tells me with a completely straight face.

"I don't even—"

Trinity shakes her head. "I didn't come up with it."

I hate stirring up bad shit for her, but I have to ask my next question. "Don't get mad, but you know which brothers they're tight with right now?"

Her jaw tightens. "Definitely Stash and Ravage. Probably the prospects. Anyone else you have to ask yourself."

I give her a wry smile and pat her leg. "Thanks, honey. Listen, I told you a long time ago, if we needed to get rid of girls, I'd back you. I don't want you taking shit from any of these bitches. We clear?"

"If we ran off every bitch who gave me lip, there'd be no one left to fuck the guys, Rock," she deadpans.

"Dammit, Trin, I'm serious." But I can't help chuckling a little.

All week long stuff came up that kept us apart. I'm able to take Hope out to lunch twice and we talk every night on the phone, but nothing more than that. She's put up a bit of a wall and talks her way out of spending any nights together. It's killing me, but I'm working hard at trying to give her the space she seems to need.

Besides the sex, I miss waking up next to her, holding her at night, and talking to her in the morning over breakfast. I'm a complete sap and don't give a shit. All I want to do is fix this distance between us because it unnerves me. But I am also trying to tread the line between attentive boyfriend and overbearing asshole. She doesn't bring up the club girl issue again, and neither do I. But it's still hanging in the air every time we talk. Since I haven't had an opportunity to take care of it yet, I don't want to mention it either.

When I ask her what time she wants me to pick her up Friday night —like I have every Friday for the past few weeks—she hesitates.

"I'm going out with a few friends, so I'll drive myself up after."

I don't like this answer at all.

"Will you be drinking?"

"Probably not."

"Hope, I don't want you drinking and driving. You need a ride, call me."

Nothing but dead air. Fuck, I wish I could see her face.

"I will—promise."

"Love you, Baby Doll."

"Me too."

Not good enough. My fist itches to connect with something. If I don't fix this, I'm going to lose her. I can feel it.

The sensible thing to do is call a meeting this week before the rowdiness starts up. This is long overdue. Z gets the word out, and pretty much everyone who has anything to do with the club shows up early tonight.

Hangarounds, club girls, prospects, and patch-holders are seated or standing in the dining room. Trinity and the prospects have taken care of drinks. I notice with a bit of annoyance how none of the other girls, except Swan, have lifted a finger to help Trinity out. That shit ends tonight.

Wrath goes over some new security issues. Nothing top secret, of course, but still important. When he's done, I step up.

I re-iterate a few of the things Wrath touched on before delving into what I really want to talk about.

"I don't think it's a secret that I've taken an ol' lady. Most of you have met Hope." Some of the guys whistle and clap, making my mouth twist up in a grin. "This shouldn't need to be said, but since we've got a few new faces, I'm going to say it anyway. Everyone associated with this club treats her with respect. If you don't, you are directly disrespecting me." I let those words hang in the air so they sink in to a few of the thick skulls I see in the room. "She's a little shy, so I expect all of you to make her feel welcomed in my clubhouse."

Roxy actually has the nerve to raise her hand. My eyes skip to her, and she takes it as permission to open her mouth. "Why ain't she here for this? Ya know, if she's gonna be part of the club."

Some of the guys grumble and shake their heads. "I'll give her the details later," I answer with a hard stare that shuts her the fuck up.

"Next thing I want to talk about…" I curl my finger at Trinity and motion her forward. "Lot of you know Trinity. She's been running the clubhouse and taking care of things for LOKI for a long time." Trinity blushes and ducks her head. A couple of the guys clap and heckle her a little. She giggles, so I let it slide. "Anyone needs supplies for the clubhouse, kitchen stuff, beer—"

One of the guys yells out, "Condoms?"

I shake my head. "Yeah, that too."

"Snugger fit, right, Rav?" Trinity jokes back.

Ravage, is a good sport and laughs along with everyone else.

"Can we get back on track?"

After everyone settles down, I'm able to continue. "Just for clarification, Trinity answers to me. She is in charge of the household stuff. Whether you're a hang-around, prospect, or club girl, if you're spending time in our clubhouse drinking our beer, smoking our weed, enjoying the benefits of the MC, you best pitch the fuck in and help Trin out. Show her respect. She does a lot for the club, and I want to start seeing some fucking gratitude."

Trinity's face flushes bright pink as the guys yell, "Thank you, Trinny!" at her.

I've probably confused things a little by stating that Trinity answers to me. But I have my reasons for phrasing things the way I did, and I don't need to explain myself to anyone.

Clapping my hands, I grab everyone's attention again. "Lecture part's over. Sparky's got some new shit he wants some opinions on—he'll be setting up in the champagne room in a little bit. Pay him a visit if you wanna be his guinea pig."

The volume in the room instantly jumps to ten. Trinity turns to me. "What was that all about?"

"Just what I said. I shouldn't be letting you fend for yourself with these bitches. It's better if it comes from me. And I do appreciate everything you do around here."

Her eyes well up.

"Don't you dare fucking cry on me, Trin," I warn her.

"I'm not," she sniffles. "You've always taken good care of me, Rock. I got no complaints."

"I know."

"I'll do a better job looking out for Hope, promise."

Couple of the girls swarm around Trinity to ask her what she needs help with, and she takes them into the kitchen with her. The toxic trio watches her leave but stays put.

"What's goin' on, prez?" Wrath asks.

"Nothing. Stay close tonight." I nod my head at the three girls. "Keep an eye on them. Their days here are numbered."

Suddenly Wrath's all business. His face locks down into his hard, Enforcer expression. "Rock, if it's a security issue, you gotta tell me."

"Nothing like that."

"They hassling Trin?" he asks with an edge to his voice.

"Possibly."

"Hope?"

I shrug. "Can't get either of them to give me details."

"Rox is trouble, no doubt. You thinking of banning her?"

"Maybe."

"Christ, you're a cryptic fuck tonight."

"We got any brothers coming in from downstate?"

"A few."

"Good. Maybe we can send the toxic trio back with them."

Wrath snorts. "Fine by me."

Hope

Girls' night out is what I need. Rock has consumed my life since the night we got together, and I've been neglecting the few friends I have. Sophie, Mara, and I meet up at Hamilton's. Of course, the only thing I can think about is the first night I came in here after Clay's death. Meeting up with Rock.

Crap. Now I miss him terribly.

Sophie is looking to stir up trouble tonight. She's wearing a black, sparkly crop top and red leather skater skirt that reaches mid-thigh. I'm pretty sure if she twirls around, it will flare up and flash us her underwear. Hopefully she's actually wearing underwear. Her long, curly brown hair is loose, falling halfway down her back.

Mara is married to one of the scariest City Court judges I've ever appeared in front of. I'm surprised he let her out of the house. She is dressed much more conservatively in jeans and a peach-colored, lacy peplum top.

"Who's watching Cora?" I ask when she pulls out her phone for the tenth time. She gives me a strange look.

"Damon."

I melt a little thinking of big, scary Judge Oak home alone with his baby daughter.

"He's picking me up at ten, so let's make those drinks count!"

Sophie orders a pitcher of margaritas, which arrives at the same time Lilly does.

"Seriously, we have got to start meeting half way or something," she grouses as she drops into the chair next to me. "Who's DD?"

I throw my hand up. "I'll do it. I have to drive up to Rock's after anyway."

The later I get there, the better. Hopefully the muffler bunnies will be busy sucking tailpipes and leave me alone.

"How is that going, Hope?" Mara asks.

"Okay."

The corners of Sophie's mouth turn down. "You don't sound so sure. You guys looked pretty tight last week at Jonny's show."

Lilly bristles at the mention of last weekend. Damn, by not being up at the clubhouse all week, I missed out on all the gossip. I wonder what ended up happening with Z.

"I don't know. Some of the same issues kinda came up. That overbearing caveman thing is starting to get on my nerves. Then, two of those bitches from his club showed up there."

"Oh, fuck no, they didn't, babe. Why didn't you point them out to me?" Sophie asks. "I woulda had Jonny kick them out."

"You were preoccupied at the time," I tell her with a pointed look.

She giggles. "Which ones?"

"Uh, Foxy and Cherry."

Mara frowns. "What kind of names are those?"

"Whore names," Lilly declares with a completely straight face, then she turns to me. "Do you mean Roxy?"

"Maybe?" I shrug.

"Definite whore."

Mara taps my shoulder. "Go back to the overbearing caveman thing. That sounded hot."

I half smile. "It is most of the time. Except, you know, where he punches some guy out for grabbing my butt."

Sophie shakes her head at me. "Are you kidding? I was glad Jonny and Rock took care of those two assholes."

"Well, he made a big deal out of chasing me down when I went to a client appointment too."

"Why?" Mara asks.

"Bad neighborhood."

"You went by yourself?"

"Yeah."

Everyone is staring at me now.

"Honey, that man loves you and wants to keep you safe. That's okay. That means he's a keeper," Mara informs me in a very stern tone of voice.

"Mara's a sucker for the strong, dominant type," Sophie says with a giggle.

"Shut the fuck up!" Lilly shouts. "You let that sexy hunk of man meat tie you up and spank you and shit?"

"Jesus Christ, Lilly—inform the whole bar, why don't you," Mara scolds back.

Now we're all staring at Mara, who is bright pink from chest to cheeks.

"We're not hardcore or anything."

"You have a dungeon in your basement," Sophie says with more laughter.

If it's possible, Mara blushes even harder. "Playroom, not dungeon," she corrects.

"I will never look at Judge Oak the same," I mutter to the ceiling.

Mara stares at me in alarm. "You can't say anything. It could really mess up his career if certain people found out."

"Mara, I barely have a clue what's going on, so, we're good there."

Poor Mara is still red in the face as she stands up. "I'm going up to the bar to talk to Brian. Ross wanted me to feel him out while I was here."

"I'll go feel him up," Lilly snickers.

Mara ignores her and heads to the bar.

Sophie's watching me intently. "What else happened after you left the show?"

I sigh, because I've felt bad about this all week. Maybe it will do me good to get it off my chest. "I kind of went off on Rock about the bimbos who keep hassling me at the club."

"Wow. What did he say?"

"I don't know. He seemed surprised, which just pissed me off more, you know? I drive through a bad neighborhood or some guy looks at me funny, and he jumps all over it. But where I feel the most uncomfortable and unsafe, his own clubhouse, he has no clue?"

Sophie reaches across the table and squeezes my hand. "Honey, he's not a mind reader. You told me yourself, those bitches are sneaky."

"I know. That's why I feel bad. I don't know what to say…"

Sophie raises an eyebrow, encouraging me to continue.

"We haven't spent the night together since, kind of at my request."

Lilly and Sophie both looked stunned of course.

"I need a little space. Frankly, I'm shocked he's actually letting me have it. But it also freaks me out."

Sophie chuckles at my inconsistency. "Yeah, must be killing him."

I shake my head, because her words pile on the unease I'm already feeling in my gut over the whole situation. "His best friend there, Wrath, already hates my guts and thinks I don't fit in, so I'm worried about causing trouble."

"Is Wrath the big, hot, hulking blond guy?" Lilly asks. Of course she remembers those details.

"Yeah, he's also mean and scary."

"My favorite kind," Lilly giggles while rubbing her palms together.

"Don't get any ideas," I warn her. "He and Z are really tight."

At that, Lilly shrugs and looks away.

"You're going up there tonight, right?" Sophie asks, steering the conversation back where she wants it.

"Yeah."

"Talk it out with him. I bet you anything he'll be watching out for you like a hawk now that he knows."

I'm not sure if I like that idea or if it makes me feel even more helpless.

Mara returns, shaking her head. "I wish Ross would grow the fuck up and start dating guys in his own damn age range," she grumbles.

Sophie makes a wide-eyed, twisty mouthed face that makes me snort water out my nose. "So, about this dungeon," Lilly prompts as soon as Mara reclaims her seat.

"Oh, jeez," Sophie mutters, rolling her eyes heavenward.

"I need to come stay at your house," Lilly whines.

"We're not swingers," Mara hisses.

Lilly slaps a hand to her chest as if she's offended. "I'll bring my own boy."

We go around and around like this for a while. Even though I haven't had any alcohol, I'm laughing just as hard as my three drunk friends. I've really missed this.

Rock

Hope has ignored every call and every text I've sent her. At first, I figured she was ignoring me to prove a point. She's having fun with her friends. Maybe we've been too fast, too soon and she needs a break. After a couple of hours go by and still no word from my girl, I start to worry.

Of course, there's also the announcement I made earlier. I made a big speech about people showing Hope respect, and now she's not even here…

…Something Roxy comments on as she straddles my lap. "Where's your ol' lady, prez?"

Shoving her off my lap and onto the couch, I ignore her question.

Roxy isn't put off that easily. "Wanna go upstairs? I won't tell goody-two-shoes," she purrs.

Christ. What the fuck did I ever see in this bitch? "Roxy," I warn. "Were you paying attention earlier? Do not talk about my ol' lady that way."

She pushes her lips into a duck-like pout and stomps away.

Trinity takes her place on the couch. "That looked awkward."

Running my fingers through my hair, I nod.

"What's wrong?"

"Haven't heard from Hope all night. She went out with some of her friends, but she's supposed to come up after."

"She probably can't hear her phone if they're out clubbing or something."

"Probably."

"You think she's ignoring you? I'll call her." Trin pulls out her cell phone and dials Hope. I'm surprised. Didn't realize they'd traded numbers.

"Hey, First Lady, it's Trin. Just wondering if I'm gonna see you tonight. Call me back if you get a chance."

My head snapped up when she started talking, then fell back when I realized she was just leaving a message.

"Sorry, Rock. Went straight to voicemail. Maybe she's someplace where they have bad service."

"Yup."

"Do you know where they went?"

"No," I answer with a good amount of cranky asshole in my voice.

Her brows lift, but there's a softness to her expression. "That's not like you."

I let out a sharp exhale. "She's getting fed up with me being so overprotective and shit. I didn't want to push her."

Trinity snickers.

Wrath drops down next to us, ending our conversation.

"How's the training coming?" I ask him.

"Good. You know I don't sweat these fights. Live for that shit."

"Yeah, you just been putting a lot of effort into it lately," I answer with a smirk.

Wrath glares at me.

"What are you so pissed off about?"

He doesn't answer, just keeps giving me the same hard stare, as if that will shut me up.

"Well, boys, seems like you've got things to discuss," Trinity says with a laugh. She pats both of us on the shoulder and hightails it away from the couch.

"Dick," Wrath grumbles at me.

"Asshole," I answer, making him chuckle.

"I'm gonna have Hope come to the fight with us," I tell him.

Wrath lets out a sharp laugh. When I don't join him, he stops and stares. "You're fucking kidding, right?"

"No, why?"

"That's no place for Cinderella. She'll freak the fuck out."

That reminds me. "Listen—whatever you've got against Hope, knock it the fuck off."

Wrath cocks his head at me. "She complaining about me already?" As if that would justify him being a dick to her.

"I know you think you're doing your job. I appreciate that, but don't fuck with me on this. She's going to be part of my life, so stop trying to scare her away. Focus on keeping her safe—that's in your job description too."

"Why the fuck you think I'm trying to scare her away?"

Christ, he's impossible. I just continue to glare at him. He breaks our staring contest first. "Fine. You sure taking her to the fight is safe, though?"

Ignoring his sarcasm, I answer his question. "She'll be fine. Z, Teller, and Murphy will be with us."

Wrath's jaw tightens. "Fine. I'd like to have Trinity there. Maybe it will make her feel more comfortable if Hope comes."

My mouth stretches into a genuine smile. "Good. You want more of the guys to come?"

"Nah. It's bad enough being in Viper territory. We'll have the all clear for us, but we bring too many in, it could get ugly."

He's right about this.

"We'll just have to make sure we keep our girls safe," I say, completely serious.

Wrath's eyes search the room, finally landing on Trinity. "Yeah. Shouldn't be too hard."

CHAPTER NINE

HOPE

AT EXACTLY TEN O'CLOCK, MY THREE DRUNK FRIENDS AND I ARE ON THE sidewalk in front of Hamilton's waiting for Mara's husband. He pulls into a space in front of the restaurant and greets his wife with a big, sweep-her-off-her-feet hug.

I definitely miss Rock.

When they come up for air, Mara reintroduces each of us.

"Hi, Judge Oak," comes out of my mouth automatically, because I'm nerdy that way.

He huffs a laugh. "You can call me Damon, you know."

Through the back window, I spot baby Cora asleep in her car seat.

"Can I take a peek?" I ask Mara.

"Of course." She hits a button, and the back window slides down.

"Oh my goodness, she's so cute. I want to smoosh her little cheeks."

Mara giggles. "Don't. She really hates being woken up."

"Wonder where she gets that from?" Damon teases in a low voice, and suddenly I can't get the image of him tying my friend up out of my head.

He looks each of us over. "You girls okay to drive?"

Lilly chooses that moment to sway on her feet.

His mouth turns down. "I'm guessing that's a no."

Turning away from the baby, I answer, "I'm driving them, Damon. It's okay."

"That's crazy, Hope. Sophie's at least forty-five minutes away. How are they going to get their cars tomorrow?"

I shrug, because we really hadn't thought that far ahead. In the back of my head, I know I'm just looking for any excuse to get to the clubhouse as late as possible.

"You girls can come home with us. I'll bring you back to get your cars in the morning." Damon gestures to the back seat. "Just don't wake Cora."

One look at Sophie and Lilly, and I smell trouble. They're both tight with the effort of holding back laughter. Mara's eyes widen, silently begging them to keep quiet.

"Can we have a tour of your playroom?" Lilly asks with big, innocent eyes.

Damon goes completely rigid next to Mara, who I'm pretty sure is about to kill Lilly. Sophie's doubled over laughing and flashing her ass to all the patrons behind Hamilton's large, plate glass window.

"Someone is getting a trip to the playroom, and it's not your friends," Damon growls into Mara's ear. Since I'm standing right next to them, I hear every word, but shoot my gaze to the sky, pretending to hear nothing.

"I'll go up to the MC with you," Lilly says when she stops laughing.

"Uh, that might not be a good idea. I can't guarantee you won't see something that pisses you off," I say as delicately as possible.

"I'll go with you and kick some muffler bunny ass," Sophie offers.

"Uh, not tonight."

Damon's shrewd gaze takes all of this in. "What are they talking about, Hope?"

Crap. I can see it now. Damon forbidding Mara from hanging out with me because my boyfriend is a criminal. Fantastic.

"Nothing," I answer, hoping it's enough to satisfy his curiosity.

By the time I make it to the clubhouse, it's almost midnight. As I pass the turn-off that will take me home, I contemplate skipping the clubhouse all together, but I miss Rock and I promised to be there. When I pull into the yard, people are everywhere. Music is pumping out of the clubhouse. Front door wide open. I'm a little freaked out, so I pull my phone from my clutch to let Rock know I'm here.

And see he's called and texted me at least ten times tonight.

And gotten Trinity to call me.

Whoops.

I didn't think to look at my phone at all tonight, and guilt descends on me. I bet he's been worried. Deciding to brave the crowd, I dart into the house. A few people stop to say hello, which surprises me. Everyone's being extra nice for some reason.

I can't see Rock anywhere.

Out with my friends downtown, my turquoise dress and lacy knit tights seemed cute and trendy. Here, I feel overdressed and out of place. This is nothing new—I always feel out of place. But tonight I wish I'd stopped home to at least slip into a pair of jeans and a T-shirt.

Screw it. The only opinion that matters to me is Rock's.

Right after that thought, I spot him working his way through the throng of people. Everyone in the room disappears as we stare each other down. His gray eyes are dark with need. It's been a long week apart. Yes, we'd gone to lunch a couple times and we'd spoken on the phone every day, but I'd woken up alone every morning and hated it. After seven days of loneliness, I am desperate for his mouth, his hands, his body.

He stops right in front of me and settles his hands on my waist.

"I've been worried about you. Why didn't you answer any of my calls?"

My mouth turns down, not because he's asking, but because I feel bad for not checking in. I know he worries, and he wasn't asking anything unreasonable.

"I'm sorry—I never heard my phone. I didn't realize you'd tried to call until I was sitting outside, and then I just wanted to come in and find you."

That seems to wipe any remaining bits of anxiety off his face.

"You look gorgeous. How many guys would I have had to beat up tonight if I'd been with you?"

I frown. The answer is none. We hadn't been hit on all night.

"No one."

"I find that hard to believe."

Crisscrossing my forearms behind his neck, I pull him down and, standing on my tiptoes, feather a soft kiss along his lower lip. His arms tighten around me, and I sigh in relief. Our mouths meet again, soft at first as if after our time away from each other we need to ask permission. I hate that feeling. After a few gentle reunion kisses, the light brush of his mouth against mine intensifies, unleashing every bit of passion I'd craved this week. His tongue slicks along my bottom lip, and I open for him. We nip and suck at each other as if we were the only people in the room. Rock's hands slide down to cup my ass, pressing me against him. The proof of how much he wants me pressing into my belly. Breaking our kiss, he touches his forehead to mine.

In a hoarse voice, he whispers, "Baby doll, I've missed you so damn much."

"Me too."

"I've been trying hard to give you the space you seem to need, but it's killing me."

Hot tears fill my eyes from hearing the rawness in his voice as he admits this.

"I'm—"

He shakes his head, cutting off my apology. "I need to take you upstairs. You good with that?"

Before I can answer, the room erupts into whistles and catcalls. Rock groans.

The interruption reminds me of where we're standing. "Let me run to the ladies' room. It was a long drive up."

He flashes a tight smile and lets me go.

Ducking into the bathroom, I quickly take care of business. While I'm at the sink, running a brush through my hair, the door opens and Roxy walks in.

"Oh, you finally decided to show up? Too much of a chicken to sit through the lecture Rock had to give everyone because of your whiny ass?"

I have no clue what she's talking about.

"Everyone here knows what a stuck-up bitch you are. You better watch your fucking back from now on." Then with a nasty smile, she adds, "Don't worry. I kept Rock warmed up for you."

Since I know Rock called me at least ten times, I'm not sure when he would have time to fool around with her skank ass tonight. "I highly doubt that."

"You can't keep a man like him happy for long." She eyes my outfit with a scowl. "You look ridiculous here."

I eye her torn, barely-there denim skirt and midriff-baring tank top with equal scorn. "We can't all shop at Whores "R" Us."

"Bitch."

"Listen up, Roxy. . .or. . .Foxy or whatever the hell your name is. I understand you and Rock have whatever history you have. But that's all it is. History. Stay out of my way, and I'll stay out of yours."

"Fuck you. Who the fuck you think you are?"

Fighting the trembling in my body, I straighten up. "I'm the president's ol' lady." I fix her with my hard lawyer stare. "You don't see Cookie around here anymore, do you?"

Her tiny brain isn't sure how to respond. I use the pause to move around her and head for the door. I should have kept a wider path between us, because she grabs a hank of my hair and yanks. Hard.

I yelp out an unholy shriek and before I know it, Wrath and Rock are pulling her off me. Wrath carries her outside, while she curses and hurls insults at the whole world.

And that's the end of Roxy.

Aw, just as I finally figured out her name.

"Fuck. Are you okay? I got nervous when you were gone so long, and when I saw Roxy come in here after you—"

"I'm fine." I rub the tender spot on my scalp. "Well, I will be fine, especially if I never have to see that skank again."

"Yeah, babe, she's done. Cherry and Ginger too."

I quirk an eyebrow at that cheery news. Rock must have used our week apart to do a little investigating. Those three were the worst of them for sure. No regrets that they're leaving.

"I'm so sorry. This never should have happened."

He ushers me upstairs. Most of the people have gone outside to watch the spectacle of Roxy, Cherry, and Ginger getting the boot.

"Rock, are the other guys, the rest of the club...are they going to blame me for this?"

"Doesn't matter. They broke the rules. Everyone knows what happens."

"Did you say something to them tonight?"

He shifts uncomfortably. "We had a meeting earlier. General club business. Just officially announced your position in my life. Told everyone they need to start showing Trinity more respect too, so it wasn't only about you."

Clever.

"Jeez, I hope the other girls aren't going to turn on Trinity now."

He cocks his head at me as he slides the key in and opens the door.

"You're always worrying about other people aren't you, Baby Doll?"

I'm not sure how to answer that, so I don't.

Rock

Every part of my body sighed in relief the second Hope walked in the clubhouse tonight. I waited until I was calm enough not to give her a hard time for making me worry all night long. I promised I'd try not to be an overbearing dick, so I count to twenty before I approach her. This week without her has been the worst one I've had in a long damn time. I won't risk a repeat.

She's so beautiful. Inside my sinful world, she looks like a character out of some princess movie. I can see her eyes scanning the room looking for me and the nervous way she pulls on her bottom lip. People stop to say hello, and she flashes an anxious smile but responds to everyone with what I know is a kind word.

The blue dress she's wearing flares into a skirt that swirls around her legs just above her knees. The material hugs her curves in all the best places. Curves my hands have missed gripping all week long. She's curled her hair, and it only intensifies the princess thing she's got going on tonight...until my eyes drop to her long legs. I'm not sure what the hell she's wearing, but flashes of her pale, creamy skin peek through the black woven material, teasing the fuck outta me.

Fuck, that's hot.

I want to take her upstairs and find out if they're stockings being held up by some sexy garter getup or pantyhose that I'm going to rip a hole through so I can get to her sweet little pussy.

It's unfortunate if they're expensive, because they're about to get ruined one way or another.

I can barely contain myself as I stop in front of her and grab her hips. By the tone of her voice, I can tell she feels bad for making me worry, so I let it go. She's too damn beautiful, and I want her too much to risk any more fights.

After she trots off, I signal Wrath over. We wait where we have a good view of the hallway and the door to the bathroom.

Sure enough, Roxy stalks in there a few seconds later.

"She's so done, man," Wrath growls.

We hustle over, and as we reach the doorway, their voices come through loud and clear. Hearing my girl stand up for herself and proudly announce, "I'm the president's ol' lady," does something to me. Christ, I fucking love how that sounds coming out of her mouth.

Murder is on my mind when I hear Hope's short scream.

Roxy fights and kicks the whole way out.

Cherry and Ginger come running to her defense. Wrath bans all three of them and tasks Birch with getting them the fuck out of here.

That Hope is worried about Trinity after what just happened to her destroys me. She's so damn sweet. Regret crushes my chest as I think of the pain I've caused her. Hope doesn't deserve the way she's been treated by people associated with my club.

There has to be a way I can make this up to her.

Hope

My eyes immediately go to the corner when we step into Rock's room. What had previously been empty now has a wide, leather chaise lounge chair, reading lamp, and bookshelves set up.

Stopping to stare, I ask, "What's that?"

"For you, Baby Doll. I want you to be more comfortable spending time here."

I'm not sure how to respond. Overwhelming emotions pulse through me. It's just some furniture, but the knowledge that he did all this while I spent most of the week avoiding him stuns me.

Then his hands settle on my hips, the heat of his body sending tingles over my skin. His lips brush against my ear, and a delicious shiver slides through me. "Want to try it out?"

Do I ever.

Approaching it slowly, I slide my fingers over the supple leather, then bend one leg and press it into the seat. My other leg follows, and I fold my arms over the back of the chair, arching my back.

Only a slight creak of the floorboards tells me Rock is now standing behind me. Fingers lightly trail through my hair and down my back.

"How did you know this was what I had in mind?" he asks in a rough voice.

"Great minds and all that," I answer with a soft giggle.

His hand rubs up and down my back. "I like this color on you," he says absently.

My chest tightens. Roxy's ugly words about me looking ridiculous echo in my head, and I sit back on my heels. Rock gives me a questioning look.

"Roxy said I looked ridiculous in your clubhouse."

His face hardens, and he reaches out to tip my chin up. "My first thought when you walked in was how fucking beautiful you were." His fingers skip to my hair, twirling it around. "I like the curls too."

Lowering my eyes, I focus on my hands clasped in my lap. "Thank you."

"No more talking about Roxy. I don't ever want to hear her name pass your lips again. Especially not in here."

A flutter of fury kicks up in my stomach. Ugh, picturing about that little skank in here with my man makes me want to hunt her down and choke her out.

Rock's gentle tugging on the ends of my hair pulls me from my ass-kicking fantasies. I lift my head back up to meet his gaze. "She's never been in here, if that's what you're thinking."

Wow. Okay. Don't want details, but that's good to know. I let out a deep breath and relax my shoulders.

"Can we continue?" Rock asks.

The low rumble of his voice sends heat streaking through me. Too turned on to speak, I nod.

"Good, because I have a mystery to solve."

My forehead wrinkles, and I stare up at him. He taps the back of the chair. "Put your hands here like you were before."

Rising up, I brace myself the way he requested. His big hands slide down my back once more, this time flipping my skirt up. He sucks air in through his teeth.

"Fuck," he groans.

Nervous, I shift to the side a little. "What?"

I'm not sure if he heard me, because he's busy stripping off his clothes. Thud, thud go his boots. Clink of his belt. Rustle of his jeans being shoved to the floor. Each noise heightens my arousal.

"Take your dress off," he orders from behind me.

Straightening up, I pull my hair to the side, revealing the zipper down my back.

Another feral groan from Rock as his warm hand teases the zipper all the way down. He helps me pull the dress up over my head. When I reach to unhook my bra, he stills my hands. "Leave it."

He traces his fingers along the waistband of my tights, sending shivers of anticipation through my belly. "Were these expensive, Baby Doll?" he asks, low and sexy, lips brushing against my ear.

"No," I answer.

"Good."

He nudges me back into place, with my hands braced against the back. The chair dips as he kneels behind me. His hand on my hip steadies me, spreading my knees, pressing my back down, so my ass is angled up. Both of his hands rub and caress my ass through the nylon. A slight pinch and a loud ripping sound fills the air. Cool air kisses my skin.

His palm nuzzles against my now-exposed pussy. More fabric rips, and I let out a long moan.

An excited quiver radiates from my belly down to my clit. One finger pushes inside and I wriggle against him, seeking more.

"Yes," I groan.

His finger pushes deeper. Slow pulses, lulling me into a seductive rhythm. He adds another finger and works me steadily until I'm swaying back and forth.

The harsh rushing through my ears drowns out any sounds for a moment, but I feel him position his cock against me and press inside.

From all the buildup, I'm crazy-close to letting go.

"Not yet, Hope," Rock warns through clenched teeth.

I arch back toward the pounding snap of his hips. His hands tighten around my waist, squeezing hard. Each stroke spirals me higher. Smooth, slick strokes I can't get enough of.

"Please," I beg through moans and gasps.

He curls himself over me, reaching to flick circles over my clit. Hot and wet, he drags his tongue along my neck and nips my earlobe.

His relentless thrusting never stops or slows. He keeps driving into me deeper, working me harder. Everything centers around where we're joined, pleasure drowning me until I can't hold back any longer. My short, erratic screams echo around us.

"Fuck," he gasps behind me. His hips jerk against me a few more times. A low grunt and deep exhalation.

I collapse against the chaise, and he follows me down, rubbing my back, pressing kisses along my spine. Straightening my legs, I shift and turn until I'm facing him. He's on his side, one arm wrapped around my waist, the other propping his head up so he can watch me.

"You owe me a pair of tights," I tease.

He leans down and silences me with a long, deep kiss. After he pulls away, his sexy mouth twists into one of his irresistible smirks.

"Totally worth it."

CHAPTER TEN

ROCK

"Babe, you wanna stay up at the clubhouse or at my house Thursday?"

Since her caseload is still small, Hope's been taking Fridays off, so we normally spend the night together at one of those two places. Now that the clubhouse is free of girls itching to harass her, she seems more comfortable spending time there, which in turn makes my life easier.

She walks into the living room, nervously twisting her hands. "I, uh, have a thing to go to Thursday night."

Her tone puts me on alert, and I sit up. "What kind of thing?"

She waves her hand in the air. "A lawyer thing. For Mara's husband? The judge? I normally wouldn't go—I hate those things—but she asked me to, so…"

"That mean Sophie's going too?"

"Yes…" Something about the way she answers sparks my interest.

"You going together?"

"No, I'm going with Mara's friend, Ross. You've met him. He uh, isn't really 'out' in the legal community. So, Mara used to go to these things as his date, but you know, since she's married now, she asked me if I'd go with him." ·

I have met Ross. I have no problem with all my girl's guy friends being gay. No problem. Still, something about her going as someone else's date, no matter the reason, bothers me.

"You said you don't do those type of things, so that's why I didn't ask," she says hurriedly.

There it is. That's why I feel like shit. She's right. I did make a big point of telling her I would never escort her to something like that. And fuck, I meant it.

But Christ, when I think of the amount of time she's spent with me in my world, all the shit she's put up with from the people in my club, doing that stuff because I needed her to. . .is escorting her to some stupid party really that big a deal? In the entire time we've been together, this is the first time she's gone to one of these things. It's not like she does it all the time.

I've been silent for so long thinking this through that Hope drops her hands and returns to the kitchen where she was preparing dinner. She gives up, just like that.

Maybe she's embarrassed to be seen with me at that type of event? Even with long sleeves and a collared shirt, traces of my ink will be visible.

Well, no, she's introduced me to her friends. By accident mostly. Even the invitation to Jonny's show came unintentionally, because I happened to be sitting next to her when Sophie sent the invite. My girl never asks me to spend time with her friends, but I'm always making her spend time with mine. Fuck, she never demands anything from me.

Except honesty.

Which I haven't completely given her yet.

Pushing off the couch, I find her in the kitchen stirring sauce over the stove.

"Smells good."

Without turning, she answers with a soft, "Thanks."

"Babe, I'll go with you Thursday."

Her shoulders sag, not exactly the reaction I expected. "It's okay.

It'll be boring. Clay never went with me to that type of stuff either. It's not a big deal. I'm used to it."

I'm not crazy enough to think I'm in competition with her dead husband or anything. Still, her admission pushes me forward. Setting my hands on her shoulders, I pull her back from the stove. She drops the wooden spoon she was using on the counter and turns in my arms.

Her deep green eyes stare up at me with concern. "What's wrong, Rochlan?"

She's so serious all of a sudden. Maybe she doesn't want me there.

Truth, give her truth.

"I want to take you."

She lets out a soft sigh. "Why? You can't possibly be jealous of Ross. You've met him."

Cupping her cheeks with my hands, I draw her gaze up to meet mine. "It's not a jealousy thing. You've been so agreeable about spending time doing stuff with me, it's only fair I return the favor."

Confusion clouds her pretty face, and she looks down at the floor.

"That's not our deal. I knew your role as President meant I'd have to spend time at the club. You were upfront with me that you didn't do suits, ties, and schmoozing. I agreed it was okay. I have no right to complain about it now."

Christ, how she's twisting the knife in my heart, and she doesn't even realize it. Throwing my words back at me without any venom. She's completely honest and serious.

"You're not asking me, sweetheart. I'm offering. I should do this for you."

She glances up, and I get a glimpse of cautious optimism that cements my decision.

"It's at this stupid fancy-pants place. You'll hate it."

"Is that your way of asking me if I own a suit?" I tease.

The corners of her mouth twitch up. "No."

"Are you embarrassed to introduce me to your colleagues?"

Tears shimmer in her eyes, and I want to punch myself. She places her hand on my chest. "No. Please don't ever think that."

I should have kept that thought to myself. My girl's not like that. She's proved it over and over again.

"You worried your judge friend won't want me there because of my record?"

She tilts her head as if the thought never occurred to her, and a slight frown darkens her face. "No. It's not like they're going to do a background check at the door."

"You gonna be embarrassed if I can't cover all my ink?"

She tilts her head to the side, and a hint of a naughty smile curves her lips. "No. It's sexy, since I'll be the only one there who gets to see the full picture."

Well, doesn't that answer excite the fuck outta me.

Grasping her hand from my chest, I brush my fingers over her knuckles. "What time should I pick you up?"

The second she opens the door Thursday night, I'm thrilled I offered to do this. Her sharp intake of breath and wide eyes as she takes me in is worth the discomfort I'm feeling in the stiff, preppy getup. I'm equally appreciative of her form-fitting navy dress and classy updo. The high heels accentuate her shapely legs, and I'm ridiculously turned on watching her hips sway as she glides over to my SUV. I relish the contrast between this sexy, elegant woman about to mingle with a bunch of uptight lawyers, and the breathy sex kitten I can turn her into when we're alone.

Although it's sexy as fuck, the tight skirt means she can't quite make it up into my vehicle. Fine with me. It gives me the opportunity to wrap my hands around her waist and give her a boost. She breaks into giggles as she smooths her skirt down. Now that I've had my hands on her, I want to push that skirt up around her thighs and fuck the living fuck out of her.

Instead, like the good escort I plan to be tonight, I fire up the truck and back it down her long driveway.

No matter how obsessed I've been with Hope since the day we met, if you'd told me two years ago I'd be voluntarily throwing on a suit and escorting her to a political fundraiser for a city court judge, I would have knocked you the fuck out. But here I am.

Happy as fuck.

The closer we get to the restaurant, the more nervous she seems.

"Babe, you okay?"

She grasps my hand, holding it tight. "It's not you. Please don't think that. I always get nervous going to these things. I hate them."

Lacing my fingers with hers, we hold hands until I have to put the truck in park. I hand over the keys to the valet and help her down.

"Did I tell you how beautiful you are tonight?"

Her lashes flutter as she drops her gaze. "No."

"Then I'm an asshole. You're gorgeous, and I'm a lucky bastard to have you on my arm."

Mara meets us almost right away, which seems to help Hope relax a notch. I vaguely remember meeting Mara before. Except for her slightly more generous curves and shorter stature, she and Hope could be sisters. Mara has the same fair coloring, although her hair is a few shades lighter.

Squeezing Hope tight, she starts chattering a mile a minute. "I'm so, so happy to see you guys. I hate, hate, hate these things."

Hope's mouth curves into a smile. "I know."

"Tell me the truth, Hope. Does this dress look okay?"

My gaze drifts over the clingy white garment splashed with bright red roses. More than okay. She's quite stunning, actually. But no one asked for my opinion, so I keep it to myself.

"It's beautiful," Hope answers.

Running self-conscious hands over her hips, she asks Hope again, "You're sure it doesn't accentuate my giant, baby-bearing hips?"

I choke on a laugh. A completely inappropriate comment about men liking something to hold on to pops in my head, but I manage to keep my mouth shut.

Hope chuckles. "No, honey. You're gorgeous."

Just then, a tall, authoritative man slips his hand around Mara's waist. "Are you fishing for compliments again, lovely?"

Mara's nose twitches. "No. I was trying to get an honest opinion from Hope. You'll tell me I look hot in a hefty bag."

"That's because it's true."

He tears his gaze from his wife to greet Hope. Then his hawk eyes settle on me. He quirks an eyebrow at Hope.

"Judge Oak, this is my boyfriend, Rochlan North."

He tsks at Hope. "How many times? It's Damon to Mara's friends." We shake hands. "Good to meet you, Mr. North. My wife tells me you take good care of Hope."

Interesting.

"I do my best. She's a stubborn one."

Damon snorts. "I feel your pain," he says with a nod at Mara.

"Hey!" both girls protest. Damon kisses the top of Mara's head. By the possessive way he holds onto her, I get the feeling Mara is the friend who gets the spankings in the group. From what Hope's told me, one of her friends is rather kinky, and I'm mildly amused to find out it's the judge and his wholesome-looking wife.

This party just got a whole lot more interesting.

"Thanks for coming." Damon leans in to Hope. "I appreciate you being here. You know how much Mara hates these things."

Hope grins. "No problem. Go. Mingle. Raise money."

With another thank you, he walks away to socialize with some other guests. Mara stays put. Suddenly her eyes widen as she focuses on something behind us. "Looks like our firecracker is here."

Hope and I turn to see Sophie strutting in with Ross. Firecracker is a good way to describe her. Tight, bright pink dress bordering the edge of classy and...not so classy. Sky-high heels and long curly hair. She fixes her dark blue eyes on us and drags Ross in our direction.

"Where's the champagne?" is the first thing she asks. Mara points her in the right direction, and Sophie stomps over without even saying hello.

Ross shakes my hand. "Hey, date stealer."

I huff out a laugh. "Looks like you made a nice recovery."

"Yeah, going to have my hands full with her for sure."

"What's wrong with her tonight?" Hope asks.

Ross shakes his head. "Got me."

Sophie returns fisting two champagne glasses. She eyes me up and down, then shoots Hope a glare. "I'm so fucking jealous you managed to get your man in a suit and drag him down here."

A flash of guilt crosses Hope's face, and I squeeze her hand. "I offered to join her, Sophie."

Her eyes widen in surprise, but she only answers with, "Looking good, Rock."

"Did you ask Jonny?" Mara asks.

"Fuck, no. He would hate this," she answers, while throwing me another questioning look.

The girls cluster together and start talking in hushed tones. Ross and I make small talk. He's actually kind of funny, so I don't mind being shut out of the girl-talk. Adam and his date join us, and it's a regular sausage fest.

After two glasses of wine, my girl's eyes are glazed, her cheeks flushed, and she's giggling louder than normal. As I slip my hand around her waist, she leans into me. Tipping her head up, a soft smile spreads over her face. "Thank you for this."

"No problem, Baby Doll."

"We can get going soon."

"I'm fine." And I am. I haven't broken out in hives yet. Or wanted to throat punch anyone. Hope's friends are actually down to earth and easy to talk to. We don't mingle much with anyone else, and that suits me just fine.

Our attention is redirected to the middle of the room, where an out-of-control Sophie has taken to the dance floor. She's pulled a mild-looking attorney with her, who seems to be surprised to find himself dancing with such a hot chick.

"Uh, should we do something about that?" Ross asks.

"She'll calm down. If we bug her, it will make it worse," Mara answers, but she doesn't look totally convinced. I can't imagine how awkward this is to have her friend behaving like a drunk sorority girl at her husband's stuffy event.

After a song or two, Sophie does tone it down, although it's still pretty obvious she's drunk off her ass. Hope's invested in her conversation with another young, female attorney who joined their group, so I take the opportunity to duck in the men's room.

As soon as I step out, I spot Sophie holding up the wall across from the bathrooms.

"You okay, Soph?"

She doesn't seem surprised to see me. "You look really good tonight, Rock."

And my danger radar starts pinging like crazy.

"Thanks. You need help getting back to the group?"

She sort of nods, then lurches away from the wall, stumbling against me. She's a slight thing, so the impact barely registers, but I'm not comfortable having one of Hope's best friends plastered to the front of my body either.

Especially when she reaches down and tries to squeeze my dick.

Jerking out of her reach, I grab both her wrists in one hand. "Sophie, you're drunk."

"I know. But you're hot. I'm hot—"

I cut that nonsense off right away. "Sophie, you're one of Hope's best friends."

She makes this mmmmmm noise. "Hope's a good girl, Rock. I'm a dirty girl. I know you like dirty girls better."

Jesus Christ, this is going to shit fast. For the first time in a long time, I don't know what to do. I'm used to drunken scenes like this at the clubhouse. But that's my domain, and I can handle it my way. Here, I don't know what the fuck to do. If it was some random woman, I'd brush her off and walk away. But it's Hope's best friend, so I'm torn. Part of me wants to help her find Ross, and part of me wants to strangle her.

"Come on, let's go find Ross," I say, giving her a tug toward the party. I wish it wasn't so fucking isolated back here. Is it too much to ask for someone to interrupt this cozy little nightmare?

"I don't wanna," she answers, sounding all of five years old. "Kiss me."

Thankfully she's so short, even in her heels she can't reach my face, although she makes a drunken effort to climb my body. Pushing her off me and finally untangling myself, I decide to get the fuck away from Sophie. Yeah, I feel bad about it, but every second I let this go on, the potential for Hope to get hurt increases.

As soon as I reach the guys, I tap Ross. "Sophie's back by the bathroom in a bad way."

"Aw, shit. Thanks, man." He pats me on the shoulder and takes off after Sophie. At least that's taken care of and she's not alone.

Hope spots me and flashes a smile before turning back to her conversation. I don't know what the fuck to do. Do I tell Hope and risk blowing up her friendship with Sophie, who might not even remember what happened tomorrow? I'm not worried about myself—I sure as fuck didn't do anything wrong. What I am worried about is my girl getting hurt. Up until now, Sophie's always been a good friend to Hope. I don't want to be the one who ruins their relationship.

As if she hears my worried thoughts, Hope presses against my side. "How are you?"

Wrapping my arm around her waist, I hug her tight to me. I think she mistakes the gesture for something else. Throaty laughter bubbles out of her and she gives me that look. The one that says she wants to jump my bones but is too shy to make the first move.

Suddenly the last thing I'm thinking about is Sophie's drama.

Hope

The urge to tug Rock into a dark corner and wrap my body around him throbbed through me all evening. Only the fact that we were socializing with my colleagues kept my hands and legs to myself.

Opening my front door earlier to find him in a suit and a smile set my body buzzing. I found Rock hard to resist on a regular basis, but there was something about my big, bad "I don't wear suits" biker decked out in a classic, charcoal gray, wool blend. The crisp, white shirt and royal blue tie emphasized his slate eyes. The simple cut of the jacket stretched across his broad shoulders impeccably, accentuating his powerful build. I wondered where he'd found the time to have something so expertly tailored to him this week.

I'm not sure what I expected him to wear, but this surpasses anything my imagination conjured up. Every inch of him radiates power.

When we finally say our goodbyes, Rock takes my arm to keep me steady. The two small glasses of wine went straight to my head, and he seems to sense it.

As we stand on the sidewalk outside waiting for his SUV, I tug on his sleeve.

Stretching up on my toes so I can whisper in his ear, I ask, "Have I told you how sexy you look tonight?"

I punctuate the compliment by flicking my tongue over his earlobe. I'm close enough to feel the shudder that works through him.

"Careful, counselor." He leans down and brushes his lips against my cheek. A warm shiver works down my neck, stirring up memories of his sinful mouth on other parts of my body.

My arms encircle his neck, fingers lacing together to pull him to me. Then the valet drives up with the car, spoiling my fun.

Amusement sparks in his gray eyes. "Get your sexy ass in the car, Baby Doll. I've got plans for you."

We don't get far before Rock pulls over. Reaching below, he sends his seat all the way back.

"Come here."

I eye his lap, the distance to get over there, and then assess the constraints of my dress.

"I don't think I can."

"Hike that skirt up and haul your sweet little ass over here. Don't make me ask again."

The next moment, he tugs me across his lap. Firm lips on mine, kissing me. Breathing in his scent makes me a little giddy. I kiss him back as if I'll go crazy if I don't get enough. His hands slide over my thighs, pushing my skirt up so I can straddle him.

Weaving his fingers through my hair, he tilts my head back and kisses my neck. His lips move up to my chin and then our mouths slide together.

"What do you want, Rock?"

His lips travel down, soft sucking kisses and licks trailing along my neck and over my collarbone.

"I want my cock in your pussy, fucking you so damn deep, baby."

"Right now?"

"Right fucking now."

I draw back to see his eyes. Even in the dark interior, his hunger for me is obvious. My hands run down his chest, over the dress shirt hiding hard muscles.

His hand catches my wrist. "No time, Baby Doll. Quick and dirty."

My fingers move down to work his belt and slide down his zipper. His hands cup my face, lips press hard against mine. I reach in to free his cock and he groans, a sexy erotic sound that vibrates against my jaw. He's hard and hot in my hands as I slide my fist up and down his length.

"Fuck, Hope. You're killing me."

A devious little laugh I didn't even know I was capable of escapes me.

Rock's hands grip my thighs, sliding under the edges of my dress until his thumbs brush against my panties.

"Soaked, baby," he breathes out.

"Yes. All night. Because you're so fucking sexy, Rochlan."

"Christ," he mutters. Thick fingers tease my panties aside and push inside me. I can't help clenching around him.

Headlights sweep through the tinted glass, illuminating us for a split second. My cheeks heat at the possibility of getting caught like two horny teenagers with no place to fuck but their car.

Rock's thumb caresses my cheek. "You're two seconds from sinking onto my cock, but you're embarrassed that a car drove by? You're too cute."

My panties are wrenched even more to the side as I raise myself over him. Desperate to have him inside me, I place my hands on his broad shoulders for balance. His hands close over my hips, guiding me, lifting his hips to meet me.

"Good fucking girl," he moans as I lower myself. I wait a second. No matter how many times we do this, I need that second to adjust to the exquisite intrusion of being stretched and filled by him.

I suck in a deep breath and take him the rest of the way. "Oh, Rock. That's so good. So good like this." We're so close, cocooned in the confined space of the driver's seat. My legs awkwardly nestled on either side of him. None of it matters. A breathless cry works out of my throat. His hands squeeze my hips and I shift up, then down.

"That's my good girl. Take all of me."

A whimper. Soft wet sounds. Breathy sighs. All of it beautiful music surrounding us. Leaning forward, I tuck myself against the curve of his shoulder, my lips finding his neck. Beneath me, his hips roll. His arms band around my waist, holding me tight as we rock together.

It doesn't take long for me to tighten, shake, tense, and burst apart. Soft waves of pleasure radiate through me until I'm boneless. Rock gives me a second to catch my breath.

"So fucking beautiful. Get ready now."

I tighten my arms around his neck and hold on while he pounds his hips up into me. His arms hold me tight, yanking me down to meet each hard thrust.

He shakes and snarls as his orgasm tears through him. Still clinging to his neck, I brush my lips against his forehead, his cheeks, and finally his lips. We stay close, trading soft kisses for a while.

Rock brushes escaped bits of hair off my forehead, studying my face. Carefully, I lift off him and basically throw myself into the passenger seat. My legs are nothing but jelly, unable to support me for long.

After straightening himself, he reaches over and seatbelts me in, then takes us home.

CHAPTER ELEVEN

HOPE

FOR WEEKS I'VE HEARD WHISPERS AT THE CLUBHOUSE ABOUT THIS FIGHT Wrath is in. It doesn't surprise me that he boxes or wrestles or whatever he does. What surprises me is that Rock asked me if I wanted to go, and I said yes.

I'm curious.

Although, now that we're here, I get the idea that this isn't some nice, neat regulated event we're attending.

Casting a suspicious glance around the run-down parking lot, I dismount from Rock's bike and hand over my helmet.

"Are we even allowed to be here?"

He's too busy chuckling and shaking his head to answer my question.

Why on earth had I agreed to come along?

"You're sure we're not going to get mugged?" Teller, Murphy, and Z pull up next to Rock, drowning out my words.

Rock secures everything and takes my hand. As the only woman in our little group, I'm feeling very out of place.

I'd been informed earlier this was a "no colors" event, so the guys are wearing plain long-sleeved T-shirts. I, however, am wearing a blue shirt with just the Lost Kings design on the front. On the back, conveniently placed just above my ass, Lost Kings MC is spelled out in gray letters.

I'm not sure what to make of it. Part of me is insulted. Part of me is insanely turned on and wants to find a dark corner where I can have Rock to myself for a few minutes.

I tug at the hem of the T-shirt. "You said colors weren't allowed. You sure this is okay? I'm not going to get assaulted or something, am I?"

The guys circle around me. Z pops his sunglasses on top of his head, and with a straight face says, "I'll kill anyone who dares fuck with you, Hope."

The way he says it, I'm not sure if that's comforting or terrifying.

Rock puts his arm around my waist. "Baby, you're repping your man's club and showing your support for Wrath. That's allowed."

Rock pats Z's shoulder as a "thank you," I guess.

"T, you got…?" He rubs his thumb and middle finger together in the universal sign for "cash." Teller pats the chest of his plain, black leather jacket. I assume that's a yes.

"Stick close, Hope. Do not leave my side for any reason. If Z or any of the guys tell you to move, you move."

"Rochlan, you're scaring me."

He smiles at the way I use his full first name. "Baby doll, I'd probably be telling you the same thing if I was taking you to a Patriots game and you were wearing a Giants jersey. No need to be scared."

What the heck does that mean?

Rock takes my left hand. Z walks just a few steps ahead of us. Teller walks to my right, so close he might as well hold my other hand. Murphy is directly behind us as we cross the rundown parking lot.

Saying the old cement factory down by the river has seen better days is an understatement. We walk through weeds and slip through a broken, chain-link fence. With the area cut off by miles of the silver barrier, there is no way anyone could have parked closer. I spot other people appearing out of the dark and trickling into the building.

When we stop and enter the line to get in, I brace myself against Rock and stand on tiptoes. "Is Wrath going to be pissed I'm here?"

Rock stops scanning the crowd long enough to answer my question. "No, Baby Doll. Why would you even think that?"

No other women associated with his club are here. That's why. In fact, looking around, I spot very few women at all. The ones I do see are tarted up in skirts that barely cover their ass cheeks. Most stumble over the uneven ground in their stilettos and have to stop every few seconds to hike up their halter tops. Each one has a logo somewhere on their body that I assume means they are here in support of a rival club. Everything he's told me about their "rivals" scares the pants off me. I shuffle in my Vans slip-ons, relieved Rock warned me to dress comfortably.

His exact words were "for ease of movement," whatever that meant.

We get wanded as we pass through the door. The guy wielding the wand lingers a little too long on my chest, and Rock gives him a hard stare.

The guy doesn't seem very thorough, so I'm not exactly convinced the place is weapons-free.

Once we're inside, the place is an unimpressive, wide-open, concrete space. There are high school gym style bleachers on one side and a crudely constructed ring in the center of the room. No extra pieces of furniture, chairs, nothing.

Rock flicks his wrist, and Teller hurries over to a window and talks into a hole in the glass. With the glare, I can't see who it is. I turn and scan the crowd. A lot of rough-looking guys. No one is smiling. Everyone seems tense and edgy.

I'm completely freaked out.

Everything about this situation is telling me to run. I don't belong. I swear my curiosity will be the death of me.

But I trust Rock to keep me safe.

Z stands rigid, peering into the crowd. I look in the same direction and see Trinity wading through the sea of people to get to us. I'm overjoyed to see her.

I take a step toward her, but Rock pulls me back. He thrusts his chin at Z who launches himself into the crowd to grab Trinity and bring her to us.

I shake off Rock's hand and give her a hug. "You have no idea how happy I am to see you."

Her mouth curves up in a nervous smile. She's dressed almost the same as me, except her club shirt has skinny little straps holding it up instead of actual sleeves. Her breasts are spilling out of the top, and the beautiful ink decorating her shoulder is on display.

"How's our boy?" Z asks her.

"Cold as ice," she answers.

Rock pulls her to his side and puts his arm around her shoulders.

"He'll be fine. He's always like that before a fight. That's why we're out here."

I peer over at her. She's nervous. For Wrath?

Teller jogs over, waving a bunch of slips of paper at us. He hands one to everyone, including me. Not sure what to do with it, I wait. Everyone shoves them in their pockets, so I do the same.

Finally figuring out what we're all doing—yes, I'm slow—I blurt out, "Why would anyone bet against Wrath? He's the scariest guy I've ever met."

Z looks insulted, but everyone else except Trinity laughs.

We take seats at the bottom of the bleachers. The very front row. It doesn't escape my notice that we are positioned next to the closest exit or that Z and Rock have deliberately sandwiched me between them. I have to lean forward and over Z's lap if I want to talk to Trinity. Rock jerks his head, and Z switches places with Trinity so we can talk.

Except she's oddly quiet.

"You okay?"

Her lip quivers. "Yeah, just nervous."

She's absently picking at her nails, sending little chips of polish flying all over the place. I cover her hands with one of mine and squeeze. She wraps her fingers around mine, and we sit holding hands.

Rock leans down and grazes my ear with his lips. "Thanks, Baby Doll."

I turn and catch him for a quick kiss.

With a smile, he explains Wrath's fight will go last. Answering my earlier question about people betting against him, he tells me in a low voice, "People think he's too old to fight. And they always make the mistake of thinking because he's so big, he must be slow."

"Old? Isn't he younger than you?"

That gets a wry smile out of Rock. "Yeah, but for an underground fighter, it's old."

"Okay. Still, though, this seems like a lot of people."

"He hasn't had a fight in a couple of months. Plus, tonight there's more than one fight, so that's why it's so packed and frenzied. People want to see if the big guy is finally going to take a fall."

"Finally?"

"He's never lost an underground fight."

"Yet they still bet against him?"

Rock shrugs.

Z leans over Trinity and taps my leg. "Unlike most of these guys, Wrath has no interest in getting an MMA deal or something. He just enjoys unleashing his fury on people," he jokes like this is all completely normal.

Trinity looks like she's going to be sick. I wrap my arm around her and rub her back for a second.

The first fight is unimpressive. A twenty-nine year-old guy, in reasonably good shape, stomps a pudgy kid in under a minute.

I lean against Rock. "What are the rules?"

He shrugs. "Survival of the fittest?"

Boos and shouts echo in the large space. The crowd is pissed.

Not enough bloodshed, I guess.

The second fight is a little more action-packed. The winner, a short, stocky kid with red hair, wraps things up early by choking his opponent out at the end of the first round. The loser has to be carried out of the ring.

The bloodthirsty crowd roars when the unconscious kid gets taken into a back room.

A sharp, bleating horn cuts through the noise, settling the crowd down.

The man in the center of the ring holds a megaphone up to his lips.

"Five minutes 'til the blood bath you've all been waiting for. Get those bets placed now. Windows close when the opponents reach the ring."

There's a frenzy of pushing and shoving to get over to the windows.

My heart thumps a little faster. The energy level in the place has definitely amped up and twisted into something dangerous. This crowd is intent on two things: blood and money. I'm worried our chances of leaving in one piece are getting worse by the minute.

If Wrath wins, are all the people who lost money going to come after us?

The shouting and shoving has risen to a deadly pitch.

"You sure we're okay?" I ask Rock.

"We're good, Baby Doll."

He looks as still and calm as always. Even so, I can't relax.

I squeeze Trinity's hand, and she gives me a grateful smile.

It doesn't take long for that piercing bleat to silence the room again.

"Tonight we have a meeting of old and young. Our new challenger has been fighting professional MMA for just over seven months. This is his first time in the dirty underground, so let's give the Irish Storm some encouragement, folks!"

I tug on Rock's sleeve. "Why is he going up against a professional?"

"Babe, trust me. It will be fine."

The crowd goes wild when "Irish" enters the ring. Boos, whistles, and cheers fill the room. Our little group remains silent.

Irish Storm wears a serious expression as he bounces up and down, then scans the crowd.

Wrath's opponent has the big and scary thing down pat, but he's nowhere near as terrifying as Wrath.

"Our next fighter scares the shit out of even me. Undefeated in the underground, he doesn't come out of hibernation often, but when he does, it's scary as fuck! Hope you were careful placing your bets because they say the last thing to grow old in a man is Wrath!"

As introductions go, it lacks the fire I expected. But the crowd eats it up. The volume inside the room explodes. I don't think as many people have bet against Wrath as we think.

He's the only one tonight who has music playing when he walks out. I recognize the song as "The Way of the Fist," and I snort with laughter. "That's an appropriate song choice."

Rock looks at me like he's surprised I know it, but he forgets I spent three years of law school chasing Sophie around heavy metal shows on the weekends.

Wrath strolls into the room as if he's stepping into his favorite bar. Casual, like he does this every night of the week. Shirtless, his bulky muscles ripple under his tattooed skin. He's wearing those low slung, shiny athletic shorts I've always found rather sexy, and I see even his legs are covered in ink. As he turns full circle, I spot WRATH tattooed in bold, black, contoured letters across his shoulders. A Lost Kings tattoo, similar to the one that brands Rock's skin, is situated below. I figure he's had the Wrath tat longer than he's been in the MC. As he turns our way, Z leans over and whispers into Trinny's ear. We're sitting close enough that I catch the scowl on Wrath's face.

"Knock it off, Zero," Rock warns.

"What? Just making sure—"

"You're wrong." Trinity cuts him off.

"Yeah, that why you been up in his bed every night for the last two weeks?" In a lower voice that I don't think I was meant to hear, he says to her, "I don't remember you ever spending an entire night with me."

She grits her teeth. "Shut. Up."

"Don't break his concentration, Z," I snap at him, surprising myself.

Z gives me an amused look—thankfully he doesn't seem to be offended. Although he might be trying to rile Wrath, he's also upsetting Trinity. And let's face it, I may not like Wrath all that much, but I don't want to see him get hurt either.

Some sort of bell sounds, and we turn our attention to the ring. The fighters knock knuckles, and then it's game on. I'm not sure what I expected, but it's both stunning and ghastly.

Irish rushes around the ring with an abundance of energy. He shuffles from foot to foot, darts back and forth. After a few exploratory jabs where he catches nothing but air, he backs up. Wrath is surprisingly quick. I also get the impression he's toying with his opponent.

When Wrath finally attacks, I get a visual representation on the true meaning of violence.

The crowd explodes. People rush to get to the ring. We can't see, so Trinity and I hop up on the bleachers.

Wrath is beautifully brutal. He lands punch after punch until blood pours from the kid's nose. Irish ducks and tries for Wrath's legs, to take him to the ground. What a mistake, though, because Wrath rams his knee in his opponent's face and lights into him with his fists again. Last, he crashes his elbow into the center of Irish's nose, and the kid crumples to the ground. There's blood everywhere, and without thinking, a scream tears out of me.

Rock wraps his hands around my waist and plucks me off the bench. "Stop screaming," he shouts.

"Is he dead? Did Wrath kill him?"

"Probably not," Rock answers in a much more normal tone of voice.

"Probably?"

"They know what they're signing up for, Hope."

The fight is called in Wrath's favor, and almost instantly, we're pushed around with the movement of the crowd. People are yelling and rushing toward the window to get their cash.

Teller collects our slips and takes off, Murphy right behind him.

"Prez, we gotta get out of here," Z says in a low, urgent tone. Trinity and I are mashed up between Rock and Z as they keep us protected from the crowd. I peek around Rock and sigh in relief when I see Wrath coming at us. His bare chest is covered in sweat and blood, but he's muscling into a T-shirt as he approaches. His jeans are unbuttoned, shiny gym shorts sticking out, boots unlaced, and a backpack slung over one shoulder.

Trinity wriggles out from under Z and runs right into Wrath. "Whoa, I'm fine." He wraps her up in a hug and kisses the top of her head. Even with all the chaos around, the three of us stop to stare.

"Wrath, we gotta go," Z warns.

He looks up and nods once, then slips a skull cap over his bright blond hair. As a unit, we all move toward one of the side exits. The wash of cold air is a relief. Teller and Murphy are standing tight against the outside wall, waiting for us. Wrath has hold of Trinity's hand now, and she seems to have calmed down.

"I'm in a spot around the back," he informs Rock.

"Fuck. We're in the lot over."

"We'll meet up at the gas station at the bottom of the hill."

Everyone agrees, and we part ways.

"What's wrong, Rock?" I ask as I try to keep up the fast pace the guys have set.

He slides his arm around my shoulders and tugs me close. "Just don't want to be here when things get rowdy. Some people lost a lot of money."

Once we slip through the fence, the five of us break into a sprint across the parking lot. All around us, the sounds of cars and bikes are coming to life. Rock tosses a plain black hoodie at me. After I slip it on, he thrusts my helmet into my hands. We take off at a normal pace with Z in front of us.

Normally, I would rest my head against Rock and close my eyes. But tonight is not a joyride. I feel like I should be alert and aware of what's going on around us, if it's at all possible.

We don't stop at the gas station. Wrath sees us coming and joins us. He takes over the front position, and Z falls behind.

Once we're clear of the Ironworks city limits, I feel better. We're taking the long way back to Empire, and it's all winding, deserted county roads. I start to relax and even slide my hands under Rock's shirt to rest them against his rippling muscles.

Suddenly, Teller appears on our left, wearing a severe expression as he tries to signal to Rock. I turn slightly to see what's got him spooked. A dark SUV is barreling down on us. Z is weaving back and forth to keep the truck away. Murphy is coming up on our other side.

"Rock!"

"Hang on."

He motions Teller and Murphy to get up alongside Wrath.

We're traveling a lot faster than Rock's ever taken me, and as I look at the drop off along the side of the road, I'm terrified we're not going to make it out of this.

The SUV is so close I hear the engine straining. I'm frightened something has happened to Z.

Rock's trying to slow the bike down, but the SUV keeps pace and keeps pushing us to the right. The cliff isn't as steep here, but it's still a fucking hill not meant for two-wheel travel. Which one is more likely to kill us? Being squished by two tons of steel or flying down the slope into a tree?

Neither option appeals to me.

"Hold on as long as you can!" Rock shouts. I guess that means he's considered our options and chosen plan B. As the wheels edge off the pavement, the bike jerks, and I struggle to stay upright. We're bouncing down the hillside a lot faster than feels comfortable. Near the bottom, we collide with a downed tree, throwing us both clear of the bike.

I land hard in the grass. My palms sting from bits of gravel that have migrated down the hill over the years. My right side is in agony. Slowly I inventory my body parts. Legs, feet, arms, hands. Check, check, check. Ouch. My hands are a bloody mess.

And whoever pushed us off the road isn't done with us.

Bullets whiz wildly down the hill. I can just barely see the lights from the SUV stopped on the side of the road. I don't see Rock anywhere. I start crawling on the ground until I reach the bike. On the other side of the log, I spot Rock.

"Hope?"

I hurry to his side in a crouch.

"Are you okay?" My hands fly over his body, checking for injuries.

"Thank God. Are you hurt, baby?" he rasps.

After the spectacular fall we took, I don't think the few scrapes on my palms count as being injured. "No."

Trinity comes out of nowhere. Her face is streaked with mud, and tears are running down her face. Rock is instantly alert.

"Where is he, Trinny?"

"This way." She points behind her. "He's not moving, Rock. It's bad."

Someone above is returning fire, and the bullets have stopped flying our way. For now. Trinity and I rush to follow Rock. He turns and hands me a gun.

A fucking gun.

What the hell am I supposed to do with that?

I slip it into the pocket of my hoodie and pray I don't accidentally shoot my boob off.

When we reach Wrath, he's groaning, and Trinity bursts into tears again.

"Stay quiet, man," Rock says as he puts a hand on Wrath's chest.

Rock has another gun in his hand. Where the fuck has he been hiding this arsenal?

"Hope, what did you do with the gun?"

"It's in my pocket."

He looks about ready to throttle me, and I feel completely useless. "Give it to Trinity."

I hand it over, and she checks it like a badass.

"Stay with him," Rock says to both of us.

Trinity looks down at Wrath once more, and then she's on alert. Wrath starts moaning, and I grab his hand.

"Shh, honey, it's okay," I soothe.

"My leg," he groans.

I run the back of my hand over his cheek and forehead, and it comes away soaked with blood. More gunshots. Trinity is completely still and aware.

"Trin?"

"Right here, Wyatt," she answers without looking down at us.

He struggles to get up, but I stop him with a hand against his chest. "Wrath, don't. You could have something broken. Plus, there's still guys shooting at us."

He croaks out, "Prez?"

"He's okay."

Thankfully, Wrath seems to be coming around. He realizes I'm holding his hand, and he squeezes it tight. "It's going to be okay, Hope." The guy with the broken leg reassures me.

Good grief.

He opens his eyes and looks up at me with concern. "This is why I been tryin' to push you away, Cinderella. So you don't get hurt."

Tears cloud my vision. "Wrath," I sigh. His eyes drift shut.

I check him over for other injuries, and he sucks in a painful breath when I get to his left leg.

"I think it's broken."

He grunts and opens his eyes again. "No shit."

I don't have a lot of light to inspect the damage to his head, but I try to locate the cut. It's not as bad as I feared, but still bleeding a lot.

"Ow, fuck. Watch it," he growls.

He grabs my hand again, holding me still.

"I don't know what to do," I cry miserably.

"Just keep holding my hand. My leg really fucking hurts."

"Okay."

It's quiet up above now. A shiver works over Wrath, and I whip off my sweatshirt, covering as much of his torso as I can with it. I rub my hand over his chest, trying to keep him warm. Tires squeal, and it sounds like the SUV is getting the hell out of there. A few seconds later, two bikes roar to life and take off as well.

The snapping of twigs and crunch of gravel announces someone is coming.

"Trin, it's me and Z—don't shoot," Rock's voice comes out of the darkness.

She makes a clicking noise with the gun and shoves it in the back of her pants. I'm still holding Wrath's hand and running my other hand over him, but I think he passed out.

"You girls okay?" Z asks.

I'm watching to make sure Wrath is still breathing, so I only nod. Rock kneels down beside me and puts his hand on my arm.

"Honey, you're shivering."

"Afraid he's going into shock. He needs an ambulance bad." My voice comes out all quivery.

"A driver stopped. He's calling 911. That's what finally chased those fuckers off."

"His leg, Rock. And his head."

He takes out his cell phone. The shattered screen still provides enough light for Rock to shine it over Wrath's head to check the cut.

"Get that outta my face," Wrath grumbles.

"Well, his personality is fine," Z jokes.

"Fuck off."

Finally, sirens pierce the air.

Z takes off to meet the ambulance and explain where we're located.

Trinity kneels next to Wrath and takes his other hand.

He finally opens an eye. "You okay?"

"Yeah," she answers softly.

His eyes close, and a shiver works over him. "I'm really fucking cold, guys," he grits out.

I shoot a worried glance at Rock, and he shrugs off his jacket, laying it over Wrath's chest. Trinity does the same.

"That better?"

He doesn't answer this time, and tears start dropping down Trinity's cheeks.

Rock

A helicopter had to be called in to lift Wrath out and take him to the nearest hospital. The rest of us got to ride in either an ambulance or cop car.

You can guess which one I ended up in.

No matter how many times I explained to the two useless pigs that we'd been run off the road, they kept insisting something else happened. I had no idea what actually happened or who those fuckers were.

Was I going to tell the cops it probably had to do with the underground fight we just left?

Fuck, no.

But I gave them the rest of the information, so at least it seemed like I wanted to be cooperative. Finally they let me go find Hope.

My girl did amazing.

Atomic rage fills me at the thought that she could have died tonight because of me. She never would have been in this situation otherwise.

People didn't try to run her off the road because she caused them to lose thousands of dollars on an illegal fight. No, that shit is part of my life, and it could have cost her hers. I'm sick with disgust.

But she kept her cool. She didn't panic when we went over the cliff. She listened to me. She did her best to keep Wrath safe and comfortable until we could get him help. I didn't think I could love her more until I saw her kneeling on the ground beside my brother, holding his hand, talking to him softly, her sweatshirt looking like a baby blanket on his big chest.

The hospital doesn't want to let me see her because she's not my wife. I get loud, and next thing I know, she's flying out of one of the emergency room cubicles and into my arms.

"Baby, you okay?"

She winces when I hug her and her hands are bandaged, but other than that, she seems sound. I push all the awful things that could have happened out of my mind.

Trinity is fine. They checked her over. Barely a scratch. Doesn't surprise me. Girl is very resilient.

Wrath is still out cold.

It's hours before they will let us see him, but no one is leaving. The rest of the brothers filter in as the news spreads.

Teller, Murphy, and Dex join me in a huddle.

"What do we know?" Muphy asks.

Teller looks into the hallway. "Z's checking out some leads."

"Can't be fucking Vipers. They would've straight-up shot us, not pulled that cowardly bullshit," I mutter.

"Better not be them. We had the all clear to be there," Murphy reminds me.

Not like it would matter to those honor-less fucks. The stupidity of my decision to bring Hope into this is close to crushing me.

Z bumps my shoulder and pulls me into the hallway.

With a shifty look up and down the open space and a low voice, he explains. "Looks like it was two assholes from Irish's crew."

"Who the fuck is that?"

"The kid Wrath fought? He fucked him up pretty good, so they were looking for payback."

"They could've fucking killed us! Over a goddamn fight their guy signed up for?"

"Fuckin' pussies."

It would have made more sense if it had been one of the other crews who lost money on Wrath. Fuck, it would have made sense if it had been some Vipers since we were in their territory—all clear or not—but this is fucking stupid and senseless.

"Find out who they're connected to. I want to know how much blowback there will be when we handle them."

"Prez—"

"I'm fucking serious, Z. They want to fuck with us? Fine, but Hope and Trinity could have been hurt or killed." I shake my head, still pissed with myself for bringing the girls. "No excuses for bringing the women into our shit."

"I know."

"Payback is a bitch."

"Fuck, yeah."

I give Z a manly slap on the shoulder. "I need you, man. Shit's going bad all around us, and our enforcer is gonna be down for eight or more weeks. You gotta step up."

Z sends me a "fuck you" look, and I feel a little bad for how that came out. "You know what I mean. Membership is tight as it is. With Wrath down, it's gonna be even harder."

We're pulled out of our conversation when Trinity wanders into the hall, looking more lost than I've seen her in years.

I hold out my hand and she drifts over, letting me hug her to my side. "I want you to go home and get some rest, Trin."

"I need to see him first."

Z and I share a glance. "As soon as he's awake, I'll have one of the guys bring you back. Promise."

After some cajoling, Z takes her home, and I go into the waiting room to find Hope standing and staring out the window. I nudge her with my shoulder, and the corners of her mouth lift in a weary smile. She settles down in the chair beside me and takes my hand.

"You all right, Baby Doll?"

"Yeah."

After what seems like many hours, a doctor finally comes in. "Wyatt Ramsey's family?"

I stand up. "I'm his brother." I'm not getting blocked by some bullshit hospital rules again. He's the closest thing I've ever had to a brother anyway, so it's not a lie as far as I'm concerned.

The doctor looks at each of us before pulling me into the hallway. I tug Hope along. Doc looks at her but doesn't say anything.

"Mr. Ramsey has a concussion. The cut on his temple wasn't too severe. We stitched it, but we need to keep him a night or two for observation to make sure there's nothing more serious like a cerebral hemorrhage. Now, his leg is a different story. He suffered a tibial shaft fracture. It's a stable fracture, which is good. With this type of fracture, the bone is barely out of place. The broken ends of the bones basically line up correctly and are aligned."

He rubs his fists together in an imitation of what he's trying to explain. Hope looks ready to barf.

"He's got a cast. It should be completely healed in four to six months if he listens to instructions," the doc continues.

I snort at that.

He nods once as if he suspected Wrath might be an ornery dickhead. "He's in very good shape, a healthy young man, so he should be closer to the four-month end. He's also a large man, so it's crucial he keeps his weight off the leg right now. In a few weeks, I'm going to recommend some sort of physical therapy, and he can probably use a cane or crutches in limited amounts of time. The fracture pain usually stops long before the bone is able to handle the stresses of his everyday activities, so it's going to be important he doesn't overdo it or it could fail to heal properly. Are there a lot of stairs at his house?"

I think about his room at the clubhouse. Upstairs. *Fuck.*

"Yeah." I run through what other options are available. Trinity's room downstairs. Boy, is she going to be pissed. Maybe I'll set him up in my house, although I'd feel safer having him at the clubhouse. Double fuck. Hope's house is a one story. No fucking way.

"We'll get it sorted out, doc. Thanks."

He turns his keen eyes on Hope. "Are you Trinity?"

She blushes before answering. "No."

"Hope?"

An even deeper flush stains her cheeks. "Yes."

"Good—he's been asking for you too. If he's still awake, you both can visit with him for a few minutes."

Hope swings her questioning gaze in my direction, and I shrug. Poor bastard is probably delirious.

I hesitate and wince when I see my brother in the hospital bed. The nurse told me they had to get him a special, larger-sized bed, but he still dwarfs it. We've been through a lot of scrapes and rough times together, but this is definitely the worst I've seen my indestructible best friend.

As soon as he holds his hand out to her, Hope rushes to his side.

I'm not sure how I feel about that.

"Oh my gosh, they shaved all your beautiful hair off," she fusses while gingerly touching his scalp.

Wrath looks her over carefully. "You okay, sweetie?" He frowns at the bandages on her hands.

Sweetie? The letters W, T, and F come to mind.

"Some scrapes. Nothing. How are you?"

"I feel like I got run over."

I step up. "You kinda did, brother."

"Where's Trin? Is she okay?"

"Yeah, I sent her home with one of the guys to get some rest."

His face settles into hard, angry lines. Whether it's from pain or something I said, I'm not sure.

"Who'd you send her home with?"

Something I said. "Easy, brother. She's on her way back now."

Wrath grunts at me and turns his attention to Hope, taking her hand again.

"You sure you're okay? That was some bad shit, sweetheart. Thank you for taking care of me like you did."

Her free hand flutters in the air. "I didn't do anything useful. I froze. Trinity is the one who went all Tomb Raider on us."

Wrath huffs out a laugh, then scrunches up in pain.

"Fuck. How long did doc say I'll be down?"

I don't dick around and just give it to him straight. "Four to six months."

I can see he's already prepared to fight, so I cut him off. "You're going to follow every damn instruction. If you don't, your leg will heal all fucked up and you'll be a gimpy fuck the rest of your life. So six months is nothing to make sure you're not walking in circles from now on."

He chuckles and settles back into the bed. "You gotta take my patch, don't ya?"

"Fuck, man. Why are you worried about that now? It's not going anywhere. Z and the others will take care of shi—"

"Can't ride. You gotta take my cut, prez."

"Knock it off."

Hope seems to have checked out of the conversation, but for some unknown reason, she's still holding the fucker's hand and running her fingers up and down his arm. Mildly disgusted at how jealous I am of my girlfriend comforting my mangled best friend, I wrack my brain for some good news to tell him.

"We know who it was?" he asks before I can come up with a better topic of conversation.

Hope looks at me with the very same question in her eyes.

"Z has a lead on it. We'll discuss it later."

"When they gonna let me out?"

"A day or two. We gotta get you set up on the first floor somewhere—"

"He can stay in my room," Trinity says softly from the doorway.

Wrath's whole face lights the fuck up when he sees her. He holds out his empty hand. Still hanging onto my girl with the other hand, though.

Greedy bastard.

Trinity brushes by me. Except for pulling on her bottom lip with her teeth, she seems calm.

"You're such a big baby. Don't you know how to drive your bike off a cliff by now?"

His face breaks into a wide grin. Hope lets him go and gives him a pat on his uninjured leg before walking to my side.

I tap Wrath's hand once. "We're gonna get going. Trin, you need a ride, call me."

Our departure barely registers for either of them.

I stop in the waiting room to tell everyone else we're leaving. Except we need a damn ride. "Who's got a car?"

Dex jumps up. "Take mine. I'll catch a ride with Swan."

I catch his keys, take Hope's hand, and get the fuck out of there.

Hope is so quiet in the car, I'm worried about how she's processing everything.

"You okay?"

"Just tired. I want to crawl into bed for like a week."

It hits me we haven't discussed where we're going. By some unspoken agreement, we never spend the night at her house together. My plan is to bring her home with me. I need to have her close.

As if she hears my thoughts, she puts her hand over mine. "I'd like to go home. To my house," she clarifies.

Not good. I'm not sure how to frame what I want to say. The thought of having her out of my sight for even a second is unacceptable.

"Do you want to pick up some things and bring them to my house?" I'm not sure why, but I don't think taking her to the MC is a good idea right now, even though it's where she'd be safest. Once again, I find myself trying to tread lightly. Probably because I feel so fucking guilty about what happened. I wish I could see inside her head and know what she's thinking.

After a while, she answers. "No. I'd just like to sleep in my own bed. If you think it's safe." Her words have an edge to them that rattles me. She's implying that I've put her life in danger. It infuriates me because it's true. My temper is not going to help, so I try like hell to simmer down.

"It's safe." I want her to ask me to stay with her. She needs to be the one to break our unspoken agreement. As much as I don't relish the idea of sleeping in the bed she shared with her husband, I need to be with her. I need to wrap my body around hers and reassure myself she's okay.

But she just stares out the window and doesn't say anything.

By the time we reach her house, I'm halfway to a caveman meltdown. Along the way, we discussed superficial things like Wrath's recovery. How long he'll have to wear a cast. If he's really going to be able to sit still for sixteen weeks. She knows a good physical therapist and is going to get me the name. Shit like that.

Nothing about us.

As soon as I pull into the driveway, my phone goes off. Hope sighs and waits for me to take the call. Z has tracked down the two fuckers from last night. My blood goes from simmer to boil in a second.

"I'll be there in half an hour."

I turn and search Hope's eyes but don't see what I'm looking for or what I expect. No love. Not even fear. She's resigned. She's slipping out of my grasp even though she's a mere five inches away.

She leans over and puts her palm against my cheek. Her soft lips press against mine, not nearly long enough.

"Be careful," she whispers.

She lets herself out and stares at me through the open window. Fuck, it's killing me to leave her now. But I don't have a choice.

"Get some rest, I'll call you later."

She nods once, turns, and goes in the house.

This is so fucked.

CHAPTER TWELVE

HOPE

EVERY PART OF MY BODY HURTS. BUT NOTHING COMPARES TO THE PAIN IN my heart when I go in the house by myself. The horror of last night keeps playing over and over in my head. Taking a hot shower doesn't make a dent in my aches, especially since I had to put plastic baggies over my hands to keep my stupid bandages dry.

I crawl into bed, and all I can think about is how much worse things could have been. It's selfish, but I think about what might have happened if I'd broken my leg. What if Rock had broken his back or been killed? So many horrible possibilities. I lost my dad when I was a teenager, and I'm already a thirty-three-year-old widow. I'm well aware of how fragile life is.

Someone deliberately ran us off the road. As a direct result of my involvement with Rock and his club, I'd almost been killed.

What's happened to me? How did I get here?

What am I doing?

It hurts to admit, but I'm not cut out for their life of danger. I couldn't even figure out how to use a stupid gun. It looks so damn easy on television. Trinity had to take it from me. I couldn't remember even basic first aid to do a damn thing for Wrath.

I'm useless. My lack of any practical life skills is probably a huge hindrance to Rock. No wonder his club brothers are so wary about letting me into the fold.

What am I going to do? I've fallen so deep in love with him, so fast. Losing him will kill me, but I need to start preparing myself for the inevitable.

Rock's indifference on the drive here hurt like hellfire. He's probably pissed for getting involved with someone weak like me. I wanted to invite him in, but it was clear he had other places to be.

I roll over and curl into Clay's pillows. His scent is long gone, but it still comforts me knowing he used to sleep on them. I pray like hell he's not watching over me. He'd probably be ashamed of me.

"I'm sorry I'm such a fuck-up. I miss you," I whisper before crying myself to sleep.

Rock

The fuckers who ran us off the road are almost too easy to find. Two punk-ass little bitches, too stupid to realize who they had fucked with.

At first they seem to be under the impression it was nothing more than a prank.

Considering how bad my brother is hurt and how badly the people I care about could have been hurt, I don't share their amusement.

They are not laughing when Z and I leave.

Payback is a bitch indeed.

Whether they make it to the hospital or not doesn't concern me a whip.

Going to see Hope in this condition seems like a bad idea. I stop at my house to clean up, grab a quick nap, and then head back to the hospital. Teller, Murphy, and Heidi are in the waiting room when I get there.

"That big bastard awake?" I ask as I take a seat next to Teller.

Murphy snorts. "Trin's in there with him. It looked a little intense, so we left."

Heidi's tuned into our conversation, so I don't voice the questions I want to ask. Instead, I grunt and pick up a magazine.

"Where's Hope?" Heidi asks.

Goddammit.

"Home." I'm short so the nosy little snot will take a hint.

"Is she coming here?"

Of course, sixteen-year-old girls don't take hints.

"I don't know."

"She's kind of family now, isn't she? Shouldn't she be here?"

"Dammit, Heidi, would you leave him alone?" Murphy scolds her.

His words send her into a snit, and she takes off.

Christ.

Deciding Wrath and Trinity have had enough time to do whatever the fuck they're doing, I stomp into his room.

She's curled up on the bed with him, his arm wrapped around her middle. They're murmuring to each other, and he's playing with her hair. I would have been less surprised to find them actually fucking.

I paste on my favorite shit-stirring grin, enjoying the fuck out of this. "Well, hello, kids!"

"Shit, fuck, damn!" Trinity scrambles out of the bed.

"Ow, fuck, Trin," Wrath growls, leaning down to rub his fucked-up leg.

"Sorry, sorry." She whips her head in my direction, eyes pleading with me not to tease her.

I don't have it in me to mess with Trinity.

"Uh, I'm gonna go." She scurries out of the room, slamming the door behind her.

I just can't keep this shit-eating grin off my face.

"Knock it off, dick," Wrath says as he settles back down into the bed.

"Sorry I interrupted cuddle time."

"Fuck you."

We glare at each other for a few minutes. Wrath rolls his eyes first.

"You come here to tell me anything useful? Maybe bring me something?"

"What the hell do you want, balloons and flowers?"

"A fucking magazine would be nice. I'm bored as fuck."

I jerk my thumb toward the door. "Didn't look bored a minute ago."

Wrath clenches and releases his hands. Is he thinking of hitting me? Wouldn't be the first time.

"Did Hope come with you?"

Well, fuck, if that isn't enough to wipe the smile clean off my face.

"No."

"She okay?"

"I dunno. She's. . ." Do I want to spill all her baggage to him? "You don't realize she lost her dad when she was a teenager. Lost her husband young. I think this rattled her."

"Oh, fuck. I didn't know about her dad. That's rough."

"Yeah, and her mom went to shit after, so she basically got abandoned there."

"Okay. Got it."

I rub the back of my neck. "I'm afraid this brought up bad shit for her." I'm not sure how much I want to share about my concerns. Although, since the accident, Wrath seems sweet on Hope, he wasn't exactly her biggest cheerleader before, and I don't want to dredge that shit back up.

Fuck it.

"I'm worried she's not dealing with it well."

"Not surprising. After getting through that other shit, sounds like she lived a pretty normal life 'til you barged in."

"Thanks."

"I'm not trying to be a dick. I just don't know how you think it's going to work out between the two of you."

"This wasn't exactly normal."

"You know what I mean. Look, I get it, she's a total sweetheart. Treats everyone with respect. She's not stuck up. I like how nice she is to Trinity. Hell, I like her. But I think soon, she's going to start dividing your focus. You can't be half in, half out as our President."

"You want the gavel?"

"Fuck, no, that's not what I'm trying to say. But she doesn't get what we're about—at all. She's too clean for our life. I've tried explaining shit to her, and it goes in one ear and out the other. Don't drag her into it anymore. It's not fair to her."

"What exactly did you try to explain to her?"

"*We are outlaws.* She acts like it's a bedtime story that has nothing to do with you two."

"How many times have I told you to leave that shit to me? I'll tell her things when I think she's ready to hear them."

"Yeah, but by then she'll be so deep in our shit, she'll blow the MC to hell trying to escape."

Fuck.

"Rock. You think she's going to fall so far in love with you she's going to overlook the fact that we're up to our balls in illegal shit?"

Yes. Because I'm so fucking in love with her that I don't care if she fits into my world or not. I'll find a way to make this work, because there is no other option.

My lack of an answer has Wrath shaking his head.

Hope

One day, and no word from Rock.

I've been dumped.

I feel it in my gut.

Except maybe something happened to him? We were, after all, run off the road and shot at the other night.

Somehow, I'd conveniently forgotten that.

I miss him so bad, but I refuse to call him first. I'm too embarrassed.

What I do instead is almost worse. I decide to go visit Wrath. I really do want to see him and make sure he's okay. But I won't lie—a tiny part of me wants to run into Rock.

I hate the idea of visiting anyone in the hospital empty-handed. What the hell does a big scary biker/fighter who's probably bored to death want? Besides a piece of ass. Food? Hospital food is awful and probably not enough for a guy his size.

I stop at Five Guys and grab two cheeseburgers and a large order of their fresh-cut fries. Running into the bookstore, I grab the first magazine I see with a motorcycle and a half-naked chick on the cover.

Even though I secretly hope to run into Rock, I avoid the waiting room and go straight to Wrath's room. After a few taps on the door, I hear him call out for me to enter.

He's alone.

I'm relieved, yet also disappointed.

His face registers a whole lot of surprise when he sees me.

"Hey, sweetheart, what are you doing here? You just missed Rock."

"Oh." I hesitate, feeling a little foolish.

"Whatcha got? You bring me real food?" He holds his hands out, clawing his fists into a gimmie, gimmie gesture that makes me break into a smile.

As I hand him the bag, his eyes widen in delight. "Oh, fuck, yeah."

He spills all the food out onto the wheely tray next to his bed and moans around a mouthful of French fries. "If things don't work out with you and Rock, I may have to claim you myself."

I'm not sure how to respond, so I thrust the magazine at him.

He chuckles at the busty redhead on the cover. "Thank you. I've been bored shitless."

"I figured you might be. Also figured they probably weren't feeding you enough."

"Damn right."

"Shoot, I forgot to grab a drink. You want—"

He shakes his head, cutting me off, and points to a small refrigerator in the corner. "Will you grab me a ginger ale from there, babe?"

"Sure."

When I return to him, he's eyeing me up and down. It dawns on me he probably ogled my ass the entire time I was bent over digging out his soda.

"Pig."

"Oink."

We're standing there, kind of half-smiling at each other, when Rock walks in without knocking.

I've missed him so much. This is ridiculous, but he's fucking beautiful. My breath catches, and I stand there taking all of him in. Just beautiful.

A scowl screws up his face. "Baby doll, what are you doing here?"

His tone stabs me in the chest. But before I can come up with a response, Wrath jabs his index finger at me. "*She* brought me food and reading material." He holds up the magazine and waves it at Rock.

Rock's scowl deepens. "Christ, you're a baby."

"A baby with a full belly. Thank you, Hope." He turns and smiles at me sweetly.

Wow.

If I'd known Wrath's approval could be bought with some cheeseburgers, I would have gone that route a lot sooner.

Rock

Apparently I've wandered into some alternate universe where Hope and Wrath are pals.

Fantastic.

My girl brought him food and reading material. How fucking sweet is that? Especially when you consider he's been a dick to her for about ninety-nine percent of the time they've known each other.

Or did she do it expecting to run into me? God, I hope so.

I'm confused about where we stand. Fuck, she's got me twisted up —and not in the fun way this time. Except for the quick glance when I walked in, she keeps her head down. Her fingers are loosely tangled in Wrath's hand. The fucker is eating up her attention with a shovel. I wish he wasn't lying there all broken, because I'd really like to kick his ass.

Zeroing in on their intertwined fingers sends a jolt of crazy burning through me.

This is awkward as fuck. I hate that Wrath is here to witness it after our earlier talk.

The urge to punch him in the face comes on strong.

Then he surprises me by letting out a yawn worthy of a grizzly bear.

Hope's gaze swings to him, and she blushes.

"Oh my gosh, you must be so tired. I'll let you get some rest."

She leans over and gives him a peck on the cheek.

Wrath flashes a crooked smile at me, and it's a fight not to break his other damn leg.

Jackass.

"Thanks for the food, sweetheart."

"Get better, big guy."

Big guy. The fuck?

Hope stops in front of me, eyes glued to the floor. I brush my hand over her arm, and she finally meets my gaze. Surprise, longing, and doubt play over her beautiful face I love so damn much.

"We need to talk."

Every part of her goes soft, almost scared. "Okay."

We walk out to the parking lot without speaking. I don't know what to say. Where to start. I've fought too hard, waited too long to have her. I'm not losing her or giving her up now.

My bike is parked right against the brick building. Hope gives it a once-over.

"It's okay?"

"Yeah, few scratches. Nothing I can't fix. Will you come home with me?"

"No."

Fuck.

"I mean, I'm not getting on that thing. I can't. Yet. I'm sorry."

I reach out to run one finger gently across her cheek, brushing the hair off her face and over her shoulder. "Baby doll, it's okay. Will you follow me home so we can talk, though?"

"Say what you need to say here. There's no reason to drag it out."

Confused, I stare at her until her meaning sinks in. "Drag what out? What's going on inside your pretty head?"

The little twitch at the corner of her mouth gives her away. Her breath hitches. Shit, is she holding back tears?

I can't stand seeing her so upset. Gathering her in my arms, I press her cheek to my chest and run my hands over her back. "Hope, talk to me."

"I'm so sorry. I'm not..." she drifts off and starts sobbing again. What the hell?

"You're not what, baby?"

"I'm not cut out for this. You must be so disappointed."

Disappointed?

"About what?"

"Me. I had no clue. I was so scared. I couldn't stand it if you got hurt." She sucks in a breath and lets it out slow. "Or if I lost you."

She's not making a lot of sense.

"You're not going to lose me. I'm beyond sorry about what happened. It honestly had nothing to do with the club. But it's still my fault. You know I wouldn't put you in danger on purpose, right? I'd do anything to keep you safe." I have done just about everything a man can do to keep his woman safe.

I'm not sure if she absorbed any of that. She pulls away and wipes her face. "Let's just say goodbye now, okay?"

Fear sends a surge of adrenaline through me. "Say goodbye? What are you talking about?"

"I'm never going to be the type of woman you need. I'm not tough like Trinity."

"Is that what's wrong? Here I thought you were mad at me for dragging you into my shitty, fucked-up world and almost getting you killed. But you're worried you're not tough enough for me?"

With her mouth set in a grim line, she nods. "You just dropped me off, and I didn't hear from you..."

I crush her against me again. "Hope, no."

Fuck. Do I tell her the truth? What the hell—I'm about to lose her anyway.

Lowering my voice, since we're in the hospital parking lot, for fuck's sake, I try to explain. "We got a lead on the guys who ran us off the road. I needed to take care of that. I also thought you were pissed at me, so I wanted to give you a little space."

"Oh, what did the police do?"

Huh? "The police?"

Suddenly I get where she's going. "Honey, I love you, but that is not how I handle things. They could have killed you. All of us, my brothers, Trinity. My best friend is seriously fucked up and out of commission for the next few months. I protect what's mine, and I don't do it by crying to the cops about it."

She takes a minute to absorb that. I watch the recognition flare in her eyes as my words sink in.

"Okay."

Okay? That's it? "Anything else you want to ask me?"

"No. I get it. Going to the police would have been pointless. You would have had to explain where we were coming from, and once they heard that, they would have assumed we were all gangsters or something and not put much effort into the case. See if we all kill each other to make their jobs easier."

What. The. Fuck? Where has *this* girl been hiding all along? Speechless, I just stare at her for a minute.

This mix of offended innocence sweeps over her face. "What? I'm a lawyer, not stupid. I have no love for law enforcement. I've seen how many times they railroad innocent people, and how they use legal extortion to extract what they want. I'm not saying I condone taking matters into your own hands—because you could have gotten hurt— or that I love the idea, but I understand it under these circumstances."

My jaw is working, but nothing comes out of my mouth. She slips her hand over it, silencing me. "I don't want any details about what you guys did, though, okay? If I had to represent you in connection with this…well, it's just better I don't know."

Without releasing my hold on her, I tug my phone out of my pocket.

"What are you doing?"

"Texting one of the guys to bring my bike up to the clubhouse. I'm not letting you out of my sight for a second."

CHAPTER THIRTEEN

ROCK

SOMEHOW, I LOST THE BATTLE TO DRIVE US TO MY HOUSE. I'M NOT SURE how I feel about that. Normally I prefer to be the one in control of the vehicle I'm in. Not that Hope's a bad driver, but she's my woman, and I should be driving her. I'm all sorts of twitchy sitting in the passenger seat, which makes her laugh repeatedly at my expense. I tell myself the only reason she's behind the wheel is when she bent over to clean out the passenger side—cause my girl keeps her car as messy as her closets—she distracted me with thoughts of getting her back to my house and bent over my bed. Thank fuck we're only a few blocks away, although with the traffic and red lights every thirty fucking feet, it seems to take forever.

I'm on her the second we set foot inside. The way I strip her down is almost violent, but she can't seem to get enough. Like a wild man, my gaze darts to every available surface. Bend her over the table? Up on the counter? No. Ultimately, I want her under me for a long damn time, so we're going upstairs.

For some reason, she still has her bra and panties on when we get inside my bedroom. Why her tits aren't filling my palms right now is a mystery. I lost my shirt and boots somewhere downstairs, but she's struggling to get my jeans off, while I'm trying to figure out the tricky little hooks on her bra. Finally I get her free. The bra goes sailing across the room while I fill my mouth with a tasty little nipple. With one arm around her waist and my other hand holding her tit for my greedy fucking mouth, I walk her backwards to the bed. My hand slides down under her panties to cup one little round ass cheek. How could she ever think I would give any of this up?

I turn and take her down to the bed with me so she's straddling my lap. She works her satin-covered pussy over my fly. The sexiest mewling noises are coming out of her mouth. I sit up and cup her face with my hands, pulling her to me for more scorching kisses.

"Panties off, now," I growl against her lips. But I don't give her a chance to lift off me for even a second. Instead, I twine my hands in the thin waistband and snap it in half. Pushing and nudging her down, I fall over her. Her hands are at my jeans, frantically shoving them down over my hips, freeing my cock. My girl is just as crazed as I am. She lifts her legs, spreading wide, and hooks her feet into the waistband to push my pants down my legs. It's sexy as fuck, how nuts she is to get me inside of her. I don't want to disappoint, so the minute the tip of my dick gets near her slick pussy, I slide home.

We both groan at the intensity. In seconds, my furious thrusting is pushing her down the bed. Wrapping my arms around her, I anchor her with hands on her shoulders to keep her still so I can fuck her hard and fast. Once I finally kick my fucking pants off, I sit back on my heels and take it slow. Keeping her legs spread wide, I'm in the perfect position to watch myself slide in and out of her pretty pussy. I place one hand on her mound to keep her still and use my thumb to play with her clit.

Fuck, that's the hottest damn thing.

I fall down over her, licking and sucking at her neck. Her hands are all over me, rubbing and squeezing my back, my arms, my shoulders. I can't stop slamming up inside her. All mine.

"Tell me I own your fucking pussy, Baby Doll."

She stares up at me in big owl-eyed surprise. Damn, that expression only makes the fire roaring through me hotter.

"Say it," I growl against her lips.

"I'm yours."

Not good enough. "Say the actual words. Tell me that pussy belongs to me."

She hesitates. I'm balls deep, fucking her half to death, and she's embarrassed. It would be adorable if I wasn't so desperate.

"You own my pussy, only you," she says so soft and sweet.

Damn right. I take her lips, fucking her mouth with my tongue. My hips pump into her with short, sharp strokes. She breaks our kiss, breathing hard. One hand slides into my hair, nails raking against my scalp. Fuck, I love when she does that. My eyes close, then snap open when she yanks my hair back—hard.

"Tell *me* I own your cock."

I chuckle. Look who's not embarrassed anymore. "Yeah, Baby Doll, you own that cock. Now, come all over it for me."

My filthy words set her off. I watch her face as she rides it out—lips parted, cheeks flushed, eyes closed. Squeezing me so damn tight, I'm about to blow. When she relaxes, I slow my furious thrusting.

"Don't stop. Feels too good." She moans the words, but I get what she's saying.

Primal need wraps its arms around my chest. One minute I'm fucking her, balls tightening, ready to burst, that familiar zip of pleasure shooting down my spine and the next I'm sliding out of her slick heat and spraying her belly with my cum. I can't stop. Don't want to stop. My eyes shut as I ride out one of the most intense orgasms of my life.

Holy fuck.

Afraid of what I'll see, it takes me a minute to open my eyes when I finally finish. There's no anger on her face, though. She's smiling, laughing a little, as she looks from the mess on her stomach to my face.

"I'll be right back. Don't move." I stumble out of the bed and stagger into the bathroom to find something to clean her up with. When I get back, she hasn't moved, except her fingers are busy twisting and pulling at her still-hard nipples.

I'm barely going to have a second to clean her up before I'm back inside her again.

Later, it's dark, and neither of us can move. I think we've screwed ourselves into some sort of coma. My dick actually feels a little raw. I know I need to get up and feed my girl, but I don't think my legs can carry me all the way downstairs. She's fucked everything out of me. I'm drained. Zapped.

Stupid-happy.

She nuzzles closer to me, pressing her soft lips against my hip, snaking her tongue along the v of my obliques. "Mmm, I think this is my favorite part of you," she sighs.

She's so damn close to my cock, he jumps. Good to know he's not dead after all.

Still kissing the area in question, she traces her fingers across the other side.

"That tickles, Baby Doll."

She giggles, the sound vibrating against my skin. Making two finger guns with my hands, I place them at the spots she's busy worshiping.

"When I was younger, I wanted to get a pistol tattooed on each side."

"Oh, baby, you don't need any help finding your cock," she teases.

"Very funny. Come here." With a final kiss in the crease of my thigh, her soft hair brushing right up against my dick, she crawls up and snuggles next to me. Except for her soft, steady breathing, she's quiet, and I figure she's fallen asleep.

"Rochlan, were you mad I went to visit Wrath in the hospital?" she asks suddenly. Her voice is still husky from screaming my name while I plowed into her from behind earlier.

Aw, fuck. My woman knows what's going on in my caveman brain better than I do.

I give her a little squeeze. "No, Baby Doll. Not mad. Not mad at all. That was very sweet of you."

"Okay. I thought…"

"What, honey? Tell me."

"I didn't know if I broke some secret, biker bro code, or something?"

I can't stop laughing. She's so fucking cute. Where does she come up with this shit?

Now she's pissed, and she thumps my chest with her fingers.

"No broken bro code," I reassure her with a teasing grin.

"Shut up," she grumbles before climbing back on top of me.

"Hope—"

"Shhh…"

She shuts me up with soft kisses, and to my surprise, my cock reports for duty immediately.

"You have to do all the work this time, Baby Doll."

She chuckles soft against my ear. Her silky hair all around me, sliding over my cheek smells so fucking good.

"My pleasure." She reaches down and grips me, then lowers herself onto my abused cock.

"Ride me," I urge.

And she does.

CHAPTER FOURTEEN

HOPE

I think Rock and I spent over twenty-four hours in bed. Talking and fucking. Mostly fucking.

My legs are so shaky when we crawl into the bathroom the next morning, I worry I'll slip and kill us both in the shower. He works me over good, and as soon as I finish, he's sliding his thick cock out of me and coming all over my back.

I've created a monster.

But I can't help but smile.

He cleans me up and pulls me to him. My back against his front. I arch and wrap my arms around his neck and he takes full advantage, cupping my breasts and gently tugging my nipples.

When we finally make it downstairs, there's an odd metallic buzzing sound coming from the kitchen. We discover Rock's phone—which he left on the counter last night during our frantic race to fuck each other's brains out—has been ringing so much it vibrated its way into the sink.

"Jesus Christ," he mutters as he grabs the phone. Standing at his side, I see he must have a dozen or more missed calls.

"I better call back before they come looking for me."

As he dials, I start preparing breakfast. I also guzzle about a gallon of water. Who ever heard of sex-dehydration? I set aside a large glass of water for Rock and point to it while he's talking on the phone.

Judging from his end of the conversation, the hospital is releasing Wrath, and the guys have been calling him to coordinate the trip. A sliver of guilt pricks me. I hope we didn't cause Wrath to have to stay in the hospital longer than necessary because we couldn't be reached.

My sore lady bits are relieved we have a distraction.

After hanging up, he stares at what I've made for breakfast for a couple seconds. "Sorry, I didn't mean to be on the phone so long."

"No problem. Everything okay?"

He eats quickly. "I gotta go pick him up. He's being a big baby about taking a wheel chair home. Trinity is up at the clubhouse getting her room ready for him."

I arch a brow, so he'll explain. "Her room is on the first floor. She offered. I figure if he bugs her too much, she can just move into his room upstairs where he can't get to her."

I let out a soft chuckle at that. Trinity and I haven't talked about her relationship much, but I'm curious how this is going to work out. I imagine Wrath is a handful. And by handful, I mean giant pain in the ass.

For some reason, I'm feeling awkward again. "Do you want me to come with you?"

"Yes. But you probably shouldn't. He'll be even more difficult if he thinks he's showing weakness in front of you."

Sounds about right.

"Besides cheeseburgers, what does he like? I'll stop and get some stuff to welcome him home."

"You don't have to do that. Trinity and the other girls got it handled."

"Oh." Here I go feeling useless again.

"Hope, the only person you have to worry about taking care of is *me*."

A sly smile curves my lips. "I think I did a pretty good job of that last night."

He leans over and kisses my forehead. "Yes, you did."

"I guess I'll go home. I haven't really been there much in the last few days."

His face clouds over, troubled. "I didn't say I don't want you to come up to the clubhouse at all. Just don't stress out feeling like you have to do anything extra."

"Okay."

When I arrive, my house feels empty. Why do I even bother any more? I should sell it and move to a smaller apartment. Just thinking about getting rid of the house I shared with Clay sends me into a crying jag. Settling into my bed to let it all out, I end up falling asleep.

It's dark when I finally wake up. After searching all over, I figure I left my cell phone in my car. I'm worried Rock may have tried to reach me, so I hurry up to grab it. I also collect my mail, because I don't think I've bothered to get it in a few days now.

My phone buzzes, startling me. Tucking the mail under my arm, I smile when I see Rock's number and pick up the call.

"Where are you, Baby Doll?" His smooth voice tickles my insides.

"Home."

He makes a displeased humming noise.

"Your home should be with me." His voice comes through clear and certain.

I'm speechless, standing in my driveway like a moron.

"Hope?"

"I'm here. Did you mean that?"

He sighs. "Yes. I've wanted to discuss it with you for a while now."

"Okay."

"Yeah?"

"Okay, we can discuss it. Face to face."

"Fair enough. I miss you."

"I miss you too."

"Come up here tonight. Things are a little nuts with everyone welcoming the big baby home, so I don't want to leave."

"I don't mind driving up. Do you need me to bring anything?"

Another sigh.

"Rock, I pass a grocery store on my way—it's not a big deal."

"If you could bring up some six packs of Coke, that would be great." In the background I hear someone shout "beer!" and then some static. He must have covered the phone because I hear the distinct yell of "shut the fuck up!" to whoever it was.

"Sorry."

"I can bring beer too."

"Just whatever's cheapest for these assholes."

I giggle.

More static, and it sounds like someone is trying to wrestle the phone from Rock. "Let me talk to her."

"Hi, Hope." Sounds like Wrath. "Why aren't you at my welcome home party yet?"

"I'm on my way."

"Will you bring me a bottle of Jack, sweetheart, please?"

I burst out laughing when I hear the definite smack of skin on skin and Wrath yelp.

"Fuck him, Hope. Don't you dare bring that dick anything."

I'm still shaking with laughter when I get in my car.

The Coke is easy enough to find. I buy a bunch of twelve packs. The beer is harder. I know jack-all about beer. I grab a few different cases of cheap stuff. And then because I'm a total girl, I buy a few of the more expensive six packs because I think the bottles are pretty or the names are cute. I figure in a house full of men, someone is bound to drink the stuff. I run through produce to grab oranges, lemons, and some limes for myself.

There's a liquor store right next to the grocery, so of course I run in. Saying I know anything more about liquor than I do about beer is laughable. It's almost closing time, but the owner smiles big when I bring up the largest bottle of Jack Daniels they sell. On impulse, I run back and grab bottles of Crown Royal and Jameson as well.

The owner cards me. Since I'm still feeling pretty haggard from the events of the last few days, that small gesture makes me ridiculously happy.

I send Rock a text to let him know I should be there in twenty minutes.

He's outside waiting for me when I back my car up to the front steps. He jogs over to my window. "What are you doing?"

"Someone needs to unload the trunk. I got it all in there, but I'm not taking it all out."

He snorts and opens my door.

"What am I going to do with you?" One panty-melting kiss later, and I'm wondering why I've been away from this man for so long. Reaching back into the car, I grab the two paper bags from the liquor store and haul them out. I hand Rock the one with the Crown and Jameson and keep the Jack. "Where's the invalid?"

"Inside, soaking up all the attention," he answers with an eye roll.

Peeking in the bag, he lifts his gaze to mine. "You didn't have to do that."

I shrug. He slips his hand around the back of my neck and pulls me to him for another kiss. "You're so sweet, Baby Doll."

The corners of my mouth lift at the soft, sexy tone he uses.

"Prez, you need me?"

Rock pulls away. "Axel, this is my woman. Hope, our newest prospect."

I hold out my hand, and he hesitates before giving it a quick shake. "Heidi's boyfriend, right? She couldn't stop talking about you when we met."

Axel looks extremely pleased and grins at me. He's a handsome kid. If I were sixteen and had his attention, I'd be in serious trouble.

Rock shoves my keys in Axel's chest. "Unload her car. Get Hoot to help. Then park it over there and leave the keys on my desk."

"Sure."

"Thanks, Axel," I say because it doesn't appear Rock is going to do it.

"No problem."

He happily gets to work.

The scene inside doesn't shock me like it might have months ago. Someone brought in a special chair for Wrath and he's sitting in the middle of the room, letting everyone fawn all over him. Trinity is hovering over at the bar, but she squeals and gives me a big hug when I come in.

"Hope! You're finally here," Wrath calls.

I'm shocked he seems so happy to see me. When I approach and he sees the bag in my hand, he looks almost giddy. "Whatcha got?"

Handing him the bottle, I giggle at his excited expression. "Oh, now that's what I'm talking about. Fuck, you're awesome. I didn't expect you to get such a big-ass bottle." He looks up at me with soft eyes. An almost guilty expression clouds his face for a moment. "Thanks, sweetheart, that was real nice of you."

Something strange is going on. Maybe he bumped his head harder than we realize. I reach out and run my fingers over his shoulder.

"And that's enough of that," Rock says from behind me. Before I know what's happening, Rock scoops me up and carries me to the couch. He settles me in his lap, keeping his arms around my waist.

"Jealous much?" I tease.

One corner of his mouth twists up in a sexy smile. I lean in and whisper against his ear, "You already know you own my p—"

"Hello, kids," Wrath interrupts, flinging himself onto the couch. His crutches go clattering to the floor and he kicks them to the side with his good foot.

Rock sighs. "Aren't you supposed to be using a wheelchair?"

"Fuck that shit." He focuses his gaze on me. "What's doin', Cinderella?"

I snort out a laugh. "Stop calling me that. I'm no Cinderella." Glancing at Rock, I run my fingers over his cheek. "Although, you are definitely my Prince Charming." A broad grin curves his lips and he kisses my fingers.

"Christ you two are going to make me hurl," Wrath bitches.

Rock ignores his friend. "This ain't a fairy tale, Baby Doll."

"No kidding," I agree with an exaggerated eye-roll that makes both of them laugh.

We're interrupted by one of the girls—Swan, I think—who comes over and whispers in Wrath's ear. Rock rubs my back and kisses my cheek. My eyes flutter shut at the feel of his lips on my face. When I open them, Wrath's shaking his head and clearly giving Swan a look of dismissal. She shrugs and says hi to me before sauntering away.

Wrath turns on a more serious expression and aims his attention on

Rock. "Anyway, since you were unreachable before—" He gives me a pointed look like it's all my fault Rock kept me horizontal for twenty-four hours straight. "I didn't get to tell you my big news. I got someone to maybe cover my classes down at the gym. But I need your help to oversee stuff until I can get down there."

"You own a gym?" I ask.

Wrath quirks a smile at me. "I didn't get this buff by sitting around on my ass, sweetheart."

I chuckle. "You're impressed with yourself."

His grin widens. "Just know my strengths. All brawn. No brains."

He says it with a smile, but it still bothers me for some reason. Many words come to mind when I think of Wrath: mean, scary, loyal, terrifying, formidable—but not dumb. "That's not true."

"Please. I never would have graduated from high school if this fuck hadn't forced me to," he says with a punch to Rock's bicep. Rock sighs as if he'd rather talk about anything else, but I'm fascinated with their history, so I ignore him.

"Really?"

"Yup. Gave me a roof over my head on the condition that I stay in school."

I glance at Rock. "That was nice. Your dad didn't mind having him around? I imagine he took a lot of care and feeding."

Wrath snorts.

"Already had my own place by then," Rock answers slowly.

"Total shithole," Wrath elaborates. "But better than the street or some chick's basement."

"How old were you?"

Wrath glances around the room before answering. "Sixteen? Seventeen? Was doing small backyard fights and shit for money."

"He was a talented, yet angry little fucker," Rock says without a trace of a smile.

"I doubt he was little, even back then," I tease.

Wrath grins at me. "Very true," he agrees. "Rock wanted me to teach him how to fight. In exchange he let me sleep on his couch. Said he'd start bringing me to the MC when I finished school. He was barely a prospect himself."

"You two must have been something back then."

Rock raises an eyebrow and shakes his head.

"Stayed with him until after the she-devil moved in, then I moved into the old MC."

"She-devil?" I ask.

Rock tenses under me and sighs louder this time.

"His whore of an ex-wife," Wrath explains with a scowl.

Wow. Okay. I'm not sure what to do with that. I've heard some unfavorable things about her from Z, but Wrath has some intense opinions on this subject too.

"Hmm…I guess I should be flattered when you call me Cinderella, then, huh?" I joke to ease some of the tension.

Wrath cocks his head and seems to be considering what he wants to say for a change.

"Can we save the history lessons for another day and get back to the gym?" Rock asks. "I'd like to take Hope upstairs soon," he adds with a dirty wink at me.

Smart move, because now I'm blushing so furiously I've forgotten what we were even discussing.

Wrath snickers at my discomfort. "Yeah okay, you're not going to like this, but—" He stops and glances at me, then gives Rock a look. I grit my teeth because I know what's coming.

Rock thrusts his chin in the direction of the bar. "Babe, can you see if Trinity needs any help, and bring me back a Crown and Coke in a few minutes? Please."

Scooting off his lap and out of his reach, I grumble at him, "You could have just said 'club business, get lost' you know."

Rock' face softens and he gives me an apologetic smile.

Rock

"You gonna pay for that later?" Wrath asks in his uniquely dickish way.

My gaze is glued to Hope's backside as she walks through the crowd to the bar. Already I miss having her body heat against me.

Shaking it off, I turn and focus on my brother. "Speak."

"Christ. You really ain't tired of hittin' that yet, are you?"

I cock an eyebrow at him. "One brush with death wasn't enough for you this week?"

Finally, he wipes the brash grin off. "Sorry. I just never...*never* seen you like this. It's fuckin' weird."

"Get used to it."

He throws a quick glance at Trinity.

"How's that working out?" I ask, because I can be a dick too.

His jaw clenches for a second before answering. "Fine. We can talk about that later."

"Yeah, okay. The gym," I prompt, because I wasn't kidding about taking Hope upstairs.

"Irish visited me in the hospital."

I rocket forward. "What the fuck?"

He holds up a hand in "calm down" gesture. "No, it's all good. He apologized. Heard about the shit his crew pulled. Wanted me to know he had no part of it. He was really upset. They're up at Northern Hospital, by the way."

I grunt at that. I must be getting soft. They should be fucking dead. "You trust this little punk? How do you know he's not trying to worm his way in for some payback?"

"That's why I need you to oversee him. I'll talk to Whisper and Jake too. But I could use his help. And he asked if I'd help train him when I'm better. Guess he was impressed with the way I kicked his ass."

"Up to you, brother. It's your place."

"I got at least a week to think it over. He's pretty fucked up. Not in any shape to be doin' much," he says with a big dose of glee.

I just shake my head.

Hope

Trinity flashes me a warm smile as I approach the bar.

"I've been sent away," I grumble as lean my elbows on the shiny wood counter.

A sympathetic smile turns the corners of her mouth up. "Club business?"

"Something about Wrath's gym."

She seems surprised and hesitates for a second. "Always play dumb when it comes to club business, Hope."

Startled and feeling a little foolish, I straighten up and take a step back from the bar.

Alarm crosses Trinity's face and she reaches for me. "I'm sorry, Hope. I didn't mean to sound like I was scolding you. Just if…you know, we were ever around any other clubs or one of our other charters—always act as if you hear nothing."

I realize Trinity's trying to help me—she wasn't trying to be mean. Also, I need to acknowledge that she knows a hell of a lot more about this stuff than I do, so instead of getting offended, I might want to listen to what she has to say if I plan to stay in Rock's life.

Anywhere else, I wouldn't tolerate being excluded from something because I'm female. How much of myself am I willing to give up to keep Rock?

I'll save that dilemma for another time. I realize I haven't responded and Trinity is about to freak out because she thinks she's offended me. "Sorry, Trinity. I know you're just looking out for me." I resume my position, leaning on the bar counter.

Her shoulders drop and she gives me another faint smile. "I'm used to it, but I can imagine it's weird for you." Her gaze sweeps over me, and her mouth twists into a playful grin. "FYI, I wouldn't keep standing like that in a room full of bikers. You know how they say men think about sex seventy-five percent of the time? With these guys, it's closer to ninety-nine percent."

I turn my head and catch a glimpse of Rock watching me intently from across the room. Very slightly I shift my weight, wiggling my ass at him. He closes his eyes and shakes his head.

"Hey, Hope. Keep standing like that and you're just begging for a spankin'," Z says, startling me into an upright position. I yank my shirt down.

Trinity's giggling. "Told ya."

"You startled me, you perv!" I say, giving him a playful smack on the arm.

I get a roguish smile in return.

"Rock's gonna kill you," Trinity mutters.

"Nah. Hope's like that hot sister-in-law you got inappropriate feelings for, but wouldn't touch on a dare."

A confused, nervous giggle bursts out of me. "Thanks, I think."

Z winks at me, then focuses on Trinity. "Now you—nothing about my feelings for you are brotherly. What are you doing later?"

Poor Trinity blushes and flicks her eyes at me. Suddenly, I wish I was elsewhere.

"Can I get a Crown and Coke to go, please?" I ask.

Ignoring Z, Trinity pours the drink and hands it to me.

I leave them staring at each other because it's awkward and I want no part of it.

Rock glances up as I approach. "Everything okay?" he asks as I hand him his drink.

"Yeah, things were just getting a little too intense up there—" One glance at a tightly coiled Wrath, and I wish I'd kept my mouth shut.

Rock rolls his eyes and pulls me into his lap.

"What are you talkin' about, Hope?" Wrath asks.

Slipping my arms around Rock, I soak in his warmth and burrow my face in his shoulder. "Nothing," I mumble against Rock's neck.

The couch shifts, and I pick my head up to see Wrath pulling himself up pretty gracefully for a big guy with a broken leg. "'Scuse me," he snarls and heads for the bar.

Rock shakes his head.

"Sorry," I whisper.

Under me, Rock's shaking with laughter. After a minute, he leans down and whispers in my ear, "You ready to head upstairs?"

I don't get to answer because Z throws himself on the couch next to us. "That was fun. Thanks, Hope," he says, patting my leg with a chuckle.

"Jerk," I grumble at him.

Rock cocks an eyebrow at Z. "Seriously?"

While I don't feel bad about the guys messing with each other— honestly Wrath has it coming in spades—I can't get Trinity's mortified expression out of my head.

"Z threatened to spank my ass before too," I blurt out.

Rock growls. Z's eyes widen and jumps up off the couch. "That was dirty, Hope," he says with a grin and takes off.

I can't help laughing. Rock gives me a squeeze. "Sorry I chased you away before."

A sigh escapes me before I answer. "I understand."

"Have a good talk with Trinity?"

"Sort of. She always seems so afraid she's going to offend me."

He nods and holds me a little tighter. "You're the president's ol' lady," he says if that explains anything. "I'm glad you two get along," he continues. "She could use a good girl friend."

I glance at the bar, where she's surrounded by guys and working fast to hand out drinks. A glowering Wrath standing next to the bar, seems to be waiting for her to finish.

"Yeah, I guess so," I answer dryly.

Rock plants a soft kiss on my cheek. "I'm about done here, Baby Doll."

Shivering from his touch, I turn and give him a longer kiss.

"Me too," I utter breathlessly when we part.

CHAPTER FIFTEEN

HOPE

Breakfast the next morning is a little weird. Too many questions I'm too chicken to ask float through my head. Z and Wrath sort of glare at each other, but overall they seem to have calmed down.

Trinity walks out of the kitchen, coffee pot in hand, and thinking over Rock's words from last night, I work out a plan in my head. She fills everyone's mug, then turns to head back.

"Trinity?"

She stops, glances back. "You need something, Hope?"

Next to me, Rock is still, but I feel his eyes on me. Across the table, Wrath is also oddly quiet. Only Z, Murphy, and Teller go on talking, taking no notice.

Shit, I shouldn't do this in front of everyone. Throwing on a casual smile, I ask, "Don't you ever eat breakfast?"

She stiffens, but pastes on a smile as she takes a few steps closer to the table. "Sure, in the kitchen while I'm getting everyone else's stuff together."

"Oh, no wonder you stay so skinny," I tease.

"Look who's talking," she jokes back.

Actually, with my grief diet behind me, I've been packing weight back on with frightening speed. Every time I complain about it, Rock either says he doesn't know what I'm talking about or he's glad because he needs more to hold onto. Neither answer comforts me. I make a mental note to start using the gym here soon.

Shaking that off, I continue with my mission. "Well, I'm kind of on testosterone overload. Would you mind eating breakfast out here today?" I ask shyly.

A nervous smile flitters over her lips, and her gaze jumps to Rock. Under the table, I dig my fingers into his leg. If he chases her away, I'm going to be super pissed.

With my head turned, I can't see his face, but whatever unspoken permission he must have given makes her relax.

"Sure, I'll be right back."

Worried it's going to take her forever, I jump up before Rock can stop me and follow her into the kitchen.

"Hope, what are you doing?" she asks when I follow behind her. Birch is by the stove, getting plates ready. Well, at least someone helps her out around here.

"The sooner you get your butt out there, the sooner you can rescue me from all the bro talk," I joke.

"Oh, okay." I can tell I've made her nervous and feel bad about it, so I try to act casual while I dig around in the kitchen for my breakfast. Then I realize I have no idea where everything is kept. Figuring now is as good a time as any to start learning, I wander around the kitchen until I locate the pantry. Sticking my head inside, I find boxes of cereal and pull out two of those tiny single-serve boxes of trusty cornflakes. In the fridge I find a small container of skim milk, so I grab that too.

Birch keeps watching me with interest.

"Bowls?"

He reaches into one of the cabinets and hands me down a bowl, then pulls out the drawer in front of him and gives me a spoon. "Thanks."

My gaze flicks to Trinity. "What are you having, Trin?"

"Probably cereal too," she answers without looking over.

"Cornflakes?"

"Sure."

Grabbing two more little boxes from the pantry, I return and add another bowl and spoon to my armful. Birch helpfully hands me a tray. It occurs to me that while Trinity probably can't boss Birch around, based on what Rock says about me being his ol' lady, I can. I don't mean it in a power trip, bossy-pants sort of way, but a help us out sorta way.

Trin has three trays set up. It's ridiculous for her to make three trips back and forth before she can even sit down.

"Hey, Birch, help us carry these out, okay?" I ask.

"Yeah, of course." I think it's the first time I've ever heard him speak. Trinity glances at me with worried eyes, which I ignore. Jerking my chin to the trays, I ask, "which one is Rock's?"

She points it out, and I transfer my stuff to that tray and pick it up. Ignoring her bugged-out eyes, I bump my hip against the kitchen door. "Hurry up, Trinity. Food is getting cold," I call over my shoulder.

Rock watches me with interest as I set the tray down and hand him his plate. I place everything else on the table as well and set up a spot for Trinity next to me. Wrath's keen gaze is also fixed on me, but I ignore him. When Trinity is done setting plates in front of Wrath and Z, I pat the chair next to me.

"Hey," Murphy grouches, then smiles to cover it up.

"Birch is coming," I explain.

There's tension at the table, but I don't really care. Maybe I've overstepped, and if that's the case, Rock can tell me later. I wasn't kidding about needing female companionship. I can only listen to cryptic club business conversation and gear head talk for so long before I lose my mind.

Under the table, Rock's hand gives my thigh a gentle squeeze. I'm not sure how to interpret it, but I don't think he's mad.

Except for Wrath, everyone else has gone back to their conversations. Dumping both boxes of cereal into my bowl, I glance up. "How do you feel today?"

He continues staring at me for a few moments before answering. "Hung over. Sore. But happy to be home."

A smile tugs at the corners of my mouth. "I think everyone is relieved you're home."

Next to me, Trinity is silent. She hasn't moved a muscle. It dawns on me—perhaps a little too late—that it might be awkward for her to eat breakfast at the same table as Wrath and Z, after last night. Oops. Too late now.

Using it as an excuse, I pick up the milk and push it into her hands. "Sorry, didn't mean to hog up the milk, Trin."

She shakes out of her trance. "Thanks, Hope."

The tension seems to melt. The guys go back to talking. Z is lamenting the "last run of the season" they're all going to miss.

"Fucking go," Wrath growls.

"No fucking way. We all go, or no one goes," Murphy shoots back.

"We'll do up a big one at the start of the next season for you," Teller adds.

The guys all grumble about being stuck in their "cages" through the winter. Their grumbling turns to excitement as they discuss the plans they have to tear down and upgrade their motorcycles in the next few months. I anticipate that means they will be spending a lot of time out in that giant garage, and now I understand why it's heated.

Conversation shifts to a club business run, which I gather is a totally different thing than the other type of run they'd been discussing.

Rock cuts them off. "We'll figure it out later."

They go back to debating bike modifications, and my mind zones out.

After a bit, I nudge Trinity with my elbow. "Don't you ever get tired of all the boy talk?" I mock whisper.

She huffs out a soft laugh. "Not really."

"What do you like to do, Trin?"

She shrugs. "This place keeps me busy. I can't wait for next spring. The guys are going to put in a garden so I can grow some veggies and stuff here."

Wrath glances at us and flashes a smile. "We'll get the prospects started on that early, so it's ready for you."

Inside I'm laughing. Guess the prospects don't get to fix their bikes up over the winter.

Z punches Teller in the arm. "You should let me get one of those compact tractors. I could do all sorts of shit around here with one."

"So, stop whining about it and bring it up at church," Teller answers back.

Z flips him off, and they go back to their guy talk.

"So gardening? Are you the one who keeps the big Buddha guy looking spiffy?" I tease.

I finally get a genuine smile out of Trinity. "Yeah, that's me," she says with a sparkle in her tawny eyes.

"Neat. I've never been able to keep any plants alive for more than a week."

"Sparky helps," Trinity explains.

That confuses me. "Which one is he?"

Rock interrupts by wrapping an arm around my shoulders. "Babe, is that all you're gonna eat?"

"Yes, I'm getting fat enough, thanks to you."

"Oh, geez. You two can go sit over there if you're gonna start talking diets and stuff," Z says, motioning over to the table by the window.

"You need more protein," Wrath interjects, pointing at my now-empty bowl.

"Fuck, here we go. Mr. Clean Eating Fighter," Teller jokes.

Wrath shrugs. "Whatever, welterweight."

The guys start trading insults, and I poke Trinity again. "What else do you do for fun around here?"

She arches a brow at me, and too late I realize she might have interpreted my question as "besides fuck the guys," which was so not what I meant.

"I read a lot," she finally answers.

We discuss some of our favorite books, and I promise to stop by her room later so I can borrow a few from her.

"Hey, I don't know what kind of music you like, but my friend, Sophie, has an extra ticket to see Afterlife on Friday. You think you'd like to go?"

Rock nudges me. "Hey," he huffs in an offended tone.

"Girls' night," I answer without turning my head.

Trinity hesitates.

"Come on. You'll probably need a night off from playing nurse to Wrath, right?" I say, jerking my chin in his direction. A brief smile twists his lips before his gaze slips to Rock.

She flicks a glance at Wrath who gives her an almost imperceptible nod of his head.

"Yeah, I like them a lot. Sounds like fun."

Ignoring their exchange, I clap my hands together. "Cool. You'll like Sophie and Lilly. Hell, they'll probably like you more than me."

Z's watching us now. "Where is the show, Hope? Not the dive we went to last time?"

"No. Downtown at the arena."

He nods, and I get the feeling girls' night is going to include an escort whether we want it or not.

Rock

Seeing my girl working hard to befriend Trinity is a gut punch that emphasizes how perfect Hope is for me. Trinity has had a difficult life, and she's important to me. There's never been anything sexual about our relationship, but every woman I've been with over the years has seen Trinity as a threat and treated her accordingly. Club girls, jealous of her position in the house, usually treat her as competition they can defeat. Trinity has always handled the turmoil well. With the life she's lived, she expects it, I guess.

It's obvious she's not sure what to make of Hope's eagerness to be friends. I figure they'll work it out over time. Hope can be persistent that way.

Even though I'm happy about their budding friendship, it doesn't mean I'm thrilled about them running around downtown Empire together for their girls' night out. Adding Lilly and Sophie to the mix doesn't make me any more confident.

But I didn't run a strip club in Empire for years without making a few friends. One of those friends now manages the company that provides security for the arena the girls are going to for their show. After I make that phone call, it's a lot easier to pretend to be the laid-back boyfriend eager to send his girl off for a night of rowdiness with her friends.

THE GIRLS HAVE BEEN BACK and forth all afternoon getting ready for their evening out. Fed up and chased from Trinity's room, Wrath throws himself onto the couch. "I can't believe you're letting them do this."

Adam's words drift into my head, and I chuckle. "One doesn't *let* Hope do anything, brother. And I don't think you have much say over Trinny, either," I remind him with a pointed look.

"Fuck off," he growls. Pointing to his cast, he grinds out another concern. "It's kinda soon after this bullshit to be letting them run around unprotected."

Okay, he's got a point there.

"Z and I took care of those fucks."

Wrath's jaw ticks, but he nods.

Music drifts out from the back of the house. Wrath rolls his eyes at me. "It's like backstage at a fashion show down there. Why couldn't they do that shit in your room?"

I shrug. "Who's coming up tonight?" I ask to change the subject.

"Fuck if I know," Wrath grumbles, surprising me, since he's usually on top of every person who comes through our gate.

"You worried about something else?"

He glances at me with a pained expression, and understanding dawns on me. Brother's hating this so much, I almost manage not to laugh. "They're not going out to pick up guys."

"I know Hope isn't. But those other two you told me about..." he trails off.

I elbow him in the ribs. "I called Blue. He'll make sure they're protected at the show, and Birch will be on their tail. They'll be fine."

That didn't exactly address his concerns, but he relaxes a little.

"Whatever," he mumbles as he swipes up the remote and flicks the television on.

Sparky wanders up long enough to grab something from the kitchen and head back downstairs to his plants. Shaking my head, I go into the war room to work on some stuff that came up during the week.

Loud giggles pull me back into the main room. "We're almost ready to go," Hope shouts.

"Oh, hey," she says, hurrying over when I come out of the war room.

Fuck me. Nope. Not okay letting her go out at all now.

Wrath gives me a smug look that I interpret as "still cool with this, bro?"

As far as dresses go, I'm sure it's tame compared to what her friends will be wearing. It's black and has a tight top held together with laces all the way up. The swinging skirt stops way too far above her knees for my taste. Her legs are covered in black stockings with some sort of lacy, flowery pattern. I swear my girl has given me some sort of fucking pantyhose fetish, because all I can think about is ripping right through them and fucking her hard. My filthy thoughts must be plastered all over my face because suddenly her cheeks are bright pink.

Clearing my throat, I ask, "Aren't you going to be cold?"

She holds up a bright blue leather jacket that I recognize as Trinity's. My eyes skip down to the black, knee-high boots her legs are encased in, and I stifle a groan.

Soft clicking announces Trinity's arrival. Wrath's smug face turns downright deadly when he gets a look at her. Royal blue, equally tight and short, Trinity's dress makes her blonde hair seem even brighter. She's also wearing black tights and boots. The two of them make quite a pair. Wrath pushes himself off the couch and hobbles over.

"Jacket?" I cough out.

She holds up a black leather jacket that I'm pretty sure is actually Hope's. "Yes, Dad."

"Very funny." Pulling out my phone, I snap a picture. "Just in case you go missing, so I have something to give the police." I meant it as a joke, but it came out kind of strained.

"Very funny," Hope teases me with my own words. Grabbing hold of Trinity's hand, she drags her to the door. "Let's go. I don't like the bossy caveman faces I'm seeing."

Trinity chuckles nervously.

"Hey, wait a sec," I call. Hope turns, and I crook my finger at her. Smiling, she saunters over.

"Have fun, but be careful?"

"Of course."

"Where you going first?"

"We're meeting up at the Red Room for drinks, then walking to the arena. Sophie has parking passes for her firm's garage we can use."

"Okay. Just be careful walking around down there."

She smiles, but I can tell she's fighting the urge to tell me to fuck off. "I will." She tilts her head in Trinity's direction. "I've got the little blonde badass with me. We'll be fine."

I snort at that. My eyes skip to Trinity and Wrath. He's bent over whispering something in her ear. She's blushing and smiling, so at least he's not giving her a hard time. Laughing, she pushes him away and grabs Hope's hand.

"Let's run before they change their minds." Trinity giggles, hauling Hope out the door.

I paste on a smile as I walk the girls out. My gimpy brother doesn't share my lazy grin as we send the girls off in Trinity's jeep.

As soon as they're out of sight, he storms back in the house. "When did we turn into such whipped pussies?" he snaps. "No way should we be letting our women out dressed like that."

Oh boy. I'm laughing so hard, I can't even respond. "Something you want to share?"

Realizing what he's said, he clams up and grabs a bottle of Jack from behind the bar. He points at the couch. "I'll be over there until they get back. You better stay sober in case they need anything. Not like I can drive anywhere."

Christ, this is good. I smile at the distraction, then head back into the war room to finish up what I was working on before the clubhouse gets too noisy.

Hope

I'm not good at being a girly-girl. Never have been. Neither is Trinity, but I think that's why we're having so much fun together. After chasing Wrath out of her room, we rifled through her closet until we found a royal blue dress she had hanging in the back.

Holding it up against her, I smile. "This is it. Makes your eyes pop."

She slides her fingers over the material, almost reverently. "I haven't worn it in years. I hope it still fits."

She ducks into the bathroom to try it on and shyly comes back out. "You think it's okay?"

"Yeah, you look great."

Glancing down at her legs, she lets out a curse. "It's kinda cold for bare legs. I don't have any stockings. I never dress up."

"I've got plenty." After discovering Rock's fascination with my legwear, I've been hoarding tights like a squirrel stocks up on nuts for the winter. I dash upstairs and grab an unopened pair. Thinking she might want to wear boots, I grab both pairs I keep stashed here.

We spend some more time fixing our hair, and Trinity helps me throw on some makeup. By the time we're ready to leave, I'm buzzing with excitement. Sophie has sent me about a half dozen texts telling me to hurry my butt downtown.

Seeing the looks on the guys' faces when we enter the main room is worth all the time we spent getting ready. It takes some effort not to laugh my ass off. Then I get nervous that they might try to stop us from leaving. As much as it offends my independence streak, I recognize it's a possibility.

Trinity and I breathe sighs of relief when we're finally in the jeep, bouncing down the road. Her jeep is badass. Bright, shiny blue with a matching hard top, four doors, and big knobby tires. "This thing is awesome, Trinity."

She glances over at me with a shy smile. "It's really the club's. Rock wanted me to have four-wheel drive when I moved up here. He makes sure I get a new one every couple of years." Then she adds quickly, "Since I do the shopping and stuff for the club."

Turning that over in my head, I'm not sure how I feel about it. Basically, she's saying my boyfriend buys her a new car every couple years. It's a little fucking weird, honestly. I'm not exactly jealous, but once again, I'm reminded of my outsider status. Damn, I didn't want things to be awkward between us, and now we've kind of run out of things to talk about.

"Tell me how you met Sophie and Lilly," Trinity asks.

Smiling at the memory, I tell Trinity about the first week of law school when Sophie and I met.

After a while, I'm afraid I'm boring her, so I wind up.

Glancing in her rear view, Trinity's mouth quirks. "We have an escort."

"What?" I ask, twisting in my seat to look out the back window.

"It's probably Birch or Hoot just making sure we're okay. You didn't honestly think prez would let us wander around downtown by ourselves?"

Well, yeah, I did.

A few months ago I might have been outraged, but I understand Rock's hyper-protectiveness better now. Especially after the epic crash we took. Honestly, given the crap I suspect his club is involved in, I should probably demand an escort everywhere I go. A question forms in my mind. It's not fair to ask Trinity, but it pops out anyway.

"Do you know what kind of stuff the club is involved in?" Even though my voice is soft, the question seems to boom inside the quiet interior.

A pained look flashes over Trinity's face, and I feel like a jerk for putting her in an awkward position. While we might be becoming friends, I know damn well her loyalty is to the club first. They've taken care of her for a long time. Even if she knows something, she's not going to share it with me. By asking, I may have just squelched our budding friendship.

"Club doesn't share stuff like that with me, Hope. You should ask Rock."

I have asked. Indirectly. Here and there.

"Sorry. I shouldn't have asked you."

"It's okay. You're not the typical biker's ol' lady."

"Yeah, I know," I sigh, and want to pinch myself for sounding so pathetic.

She glances at me. "I don't mean it in a bad way. Rock's not the typical MC President. You're good for him."

"Thanks."

We move onto less serious topics for the rest of the drive. I direct Trinity to the parking lot Sophie told us to use right off the highway. As planned, we meet up with Sophie and Lilly on the top level.

"Finally!" Sophie screeches while pulling me into a tight hug. A pang of guilt taps my belly for keeping them waiting.

Lilly gives me a quick hug. Trinity hangs back watching us, so I grab her hand and pull her forward to make the introductions. She seems surprised when I introduce her as my friend.

Lilly takes in Trinity with narrowed eyes but doesn't say anything other than hello. I wonder what that's about, but figure I'll let it go for now. Trin may know how to handle herself at the MC and during a gunfight, but she seems a little out of place here, so I feel protective of her.

No one followed us to the top of the garage, so I wonder where our escort disappeared to. Not wanting to alert Lilly and Sophie, I don't ask Trinity. As we walk, I take out my phone and send Rock a quick text letting him know we made it downtown safe.

When I slip my phone back into my purse, I catch Trinity's eye and she gives me a nod.

The Red Room is packed. People like us, who stopped in before the show. Groupies hoping to run into band members. The way we're dressed, we fit right in.

Sliding into a corner stool at the bar, Sophie orders a round of tequila shots.

"No fucking way. You know what that shit does to me," Lilly grumbles.

After throwing her head back and laughing, Sophie answers. "Who said any of them were for you?"

Oh boy. It's going to be that kind of night.

Trinity is quiet. Assessing my friends, I guess. A table near the back opens up, and we snag it.

"So, how tight are you with Z?" Lilly asks after we place our dinner orders.

Trinity slips on a placid face before answering. "I've known him for a long time."

Lilly narrows her eyes. "You fuck him?"

"Lilly!" I gasp and smack her arm.

Sophie gives her friend the side eye as well.

Trinity's mouth twists down. "Not lately," she finally answers.

Okay, wow. I had not been expecting that at all.

Lilly gives a curt nod. "He fuck around the MC a lot?"

Trinity cocks her head. "Why are you so curious?"

Sitting back in her seat, Lilly fiddles with her napkin before answering. "We hooked up. He keeps calling. I just want to know if he's worth the effort, or if he's full of shit."

Trinity sighs and glances at me. "Besides club girls, I've never seen him with the same chick twice. That's all I can really tell you."

I'm not sure in what world that information is helpful, or positive, but it seems to appease Lilly. For now.

When the crowd starts to thin, we follow the herd down the street to the arena. The cavernous building echoes from thousands of excited voices finding their seats, pumped up for Afterlife.

This show is a lot more subdued and organized because the arena is better staffed. We are thoroughly searched on the way in. Sophie surprises us with box seats. Her company was nice enough to let her use their box for the show. Apparently her firm doesn't have any other metalheads. We even have a stocked minibar, which Sophie violates almost immediately.

The show's good. Although the box seats are nice, it's not as much fun as being up close to the stage, but it is safer. That makes me think of Rock. He'd be happy that we're up here. Away from danger.

I send him a text to let him know.

Good, is all I get in return.

Afterward, one of the band's crew members stops by to invite us backstage. Apparently Sophie knows people everywhere she goes.

Curious, Trinity and I tag along. Sophie greets a tiny redhead after we pass through a second round of security who walks us backstage. I gather from their conversation she's a band member's girlfriend and she and Sophie have met on one of Jonny's tours.

"You okay with this?" I ask Trinity.

She shrugs. "Sure. I wouldn't mind meeting Chase. He's fucking hot."

I giggle at that. While the band members are definitely sexy, young studs, they don't really hold a candle to our big, manly bikers. Not in my mind anyway.

In the green room, Sophie's friend, Sydney, introduces us to the guitar player and lead singer. Trinity is definitely digging the singer, Chase, which I find hilarious. He's tall and well-muscled, but in a lean way, completely the opposite of Wrath. We do our fangirl thing— asking for a photograph—and the band humors us. Sophie seems ready to smack me for not acting cool, but I'm having too much fun to care.

As the atmosphere changes from fun to rowdy, I realize I'm tired and would rather be in my boyfriend's arms than with a bunch of strangers searching for a backstage hook-up.

I tap Sophie on the shoulder. "We're going to get going. You two okay?"

One corner of her mouth turns down. "Party pooper."

"I know. I suck. Forgive me?"

"Yeah, I'd want to rush home too if I had a hunk of man like yours waiting for me."

"Where's Jonny?"

She rolls her eyes. "Texas, I think. I'm taking a few weeks off when his tour is over. Going to see if we can make things work."

"Good. You know he's nuts about you."

"Yeah, I know."

Trinity edges closer and bumps me with her hip. "Ready?"

"Yup."

After a round of hugs, Trinity and I head out of the backstage area.

"Hey, Trinity," a thick, rough voice calls from behind us.

She whirls around. "Oh, shit. Hey, Blue."

A big, round brute of a man ambles up to us. He gives me a thorough visual fondle before turning to Trinity. "Enjoy the show?"

"Oh yeah, it was great. What are you doing here?"

"Working security."

"Cool. Oh, this is Rock's ol' lady, Hope. Hope, Blue used to bounce at CB."

"Oh, hi."

"Where you ladies parked?"

"The garage on Second Street."

He nods and gives the backstage area a once-over. "I'll walk you girls out."

"You don't have to do that," I protest.

He takes each of us by the elbow and leads us outside. Trinity's mouth quirks. "Just go with it, Hope. If I had to guess, Rock called him and asked him to keep an eye on us."

Blue smirks, but doesn't admit or deny.

Sonofabitch. I'll admit, I'm impressed with how far Rock's reach is.

Once we're safely on our way back, Trinity giggles. "Birch is back. Let's outrun him."

"Yeah, I wouldn't mind surprising them at the clubhouse."

She glances over. "You trust Rock, don't you? I swear, Hope, I've known him for a long time now, and I've never seen him crazy about a woman the way he is with you."

"So I keep hearing."

Trinity snorts. "I get it. Believe me."

Punching the gas, we rocket forward, and cut over two lanes to take the next exit. Gripping the "oh shit" handle, I suck air in through my teeth. "Geez, Trinity."

She giggles, but eases off the gas.

After a while we're alone on the long, winding road to the clubhouse. "I meant what I said, Hope."

With the surrounding darkness and the hum of the knobby wheels over the rough country road, I'd been halfway to snoozeville.

"What's that?"

"Rock. He's protective of the whole family, you know. But the girls he used to…" she pauses as I think she searches for a term that won't offend me "… hang with. They were out of sight, out of mind. Not that he's ever been cruel, but unless we had bad shit going down with a rival club or something, he didn't put tails on them. He didn't really give any of them a second thought once he was done with them."

I get that Trinity, in her own sweet way, is trying to make me feel better, but the information actually makes me want to barf.

"I'm making it worse, aren't I?" she asks with a nervous chuckle.

"Kinda."

Once we pull in the gate, the place is alive with people.

Trinity ends up parking down the hill, and we hike up to the clubhouse. We find a nice surprise waiting for us—Rock and Wrath sitting outside talking. Not a club girl in sight.

Hurrying over, I throw myself in Rock's arms before he even realizes we're there. "Holy—"

I cut him off with a fierce kiss. Behind me, Trinity giggles and Wrath groans.

Cradling my face in his palms, Rock traces his tongue along my lower lip, dipping into my mouth with a soft lash of his tongue. Suddenly, I wish we were upstairs instead of standing outside in front of everyone. As our kiss deepens, I hear the front door open and slam shut.

Pulling back a fraction, I notice we're now alone outside.

Rock strokes his fingers over my cheek. "Have fun, Baby Doll?"

"Yes, but I missed you," I say breathlessly while looking up at his handsome face.

A knowing grin curves his sexy lips. "I missed you too."

"You had eyes on us, though, didn't you?" I ask, striving to keep my voice even.

"You mad?" He's wary, but unapologetic.

I sigh and glance down at my hands, which are still covered in healing scrapes from the accident. "No. I appreciate how much you care."

His body relaxes. Even in the garish glow provided by the outdoor floodlights, I get a little lost in his storm-gray eyes, the sharp lines of his jaw, and the sensual curve of his lips. His look is equally hungry, and I never tire of the way he makes me feel. Beautiful, cherished, sexy.

"Take me upstairs, Rochlan. Do filthy things to me."

His eyebrow quirks, and a grin curves his mouth. "You're bossy tonight."

"You love it."

"That I do." Lacing our fingers together, he walks me inside.

Rock

I unglue my gaze from Hope's sexy fucking lips long enough to get us inside and up to my room. Even her scent, crisp autumn air mixed with her natural sweet fragrance, short-circuits my brain tonight. Christ, I'm fucked up if I can't stand being away from this woman for more than a couple hours.

It doesn't bother me in the slightest.

She tosses her jacket on the leather chaise, and I still her with hands on her shoulders.

"Any ass-grabbers tonight?" I ask.

"Not yet," she teases back.

"Babe, you have no idea."

She blushes and bends over to unzip her boots.

"Uh-uh," I scold from behind her. "I can't believe I let you go out of the house dressed in so little."

From here, I see her shoulders tense. She's about to ream me out for the "let you" part. "Can't help it, Hope. You're too fucking sexy."

As I turn her toward me, I see the blush creeping up her neck. I love how shy my woman is. It takes a lot to work her up, but when she finally lets go, it's so fucking beautiful. Eventually she relaxes and the shyness melts away.

Brushing her hair over her shoulder, I lean down to press kisses along her exposed neck.

Someone bangs on our door, interrupting my filthy plans to ruin another pair of her stockings. Stalking to the door, I throw it open to find an anxious Teller. "I'm sorry, prez. I just got a call from Heidi. Our grandmother had a heart attack or something. Ambulance is taking her to the hospital. I had a little too much to drink earlier…" he trails off.

"Yeah, okay."

"I can't find Murph or I wouldn't bug you guys." His mouth twists into a grimace. "And Trinity's busy with…Wrath."

Christ.

"Give me a sec, okay?"

Hope comes up behind me, nudging the door open wider. "You okay, Teller?"

"Yeah, just shaken up. Heidi sounded terrified."

Hope reaches out and squeezes his arm. "I'll come with."

Teller takes a deep breath and flashes a quick smile. "Thanks, Hope. I appreciate it."

Huh. Apparently my brother finds Hope more comforting in a family crisis than me. Go figure.

"I'll, uh, go wait downstairs."

Hope watches him weave down the hall before turning to me. "Just let me change out of this dress."

I groan as my plans for unlacing that sexy-as-fuck dress with my teeth go up in flames.

She's all business as she steps into her closet, quickly works the laces loose, and lifts the dress up, tossing it on the floor. She bends over to unzip her boots, and I groan again at the sight of her in nothing but a black bra and the black pantyhose. I need to get a grip, or we're never going to make it to the hospital.

Turning in the opposite direction, I head to the bathroom, where I splash some cold water over my face and clean up. When I re-enter the bedroom, Hope's dressed in faded jeans, a club sweatshirt and boots. "Ready?" I ask.

"Yup," she chirps back.

I grab my own sweatshirt and we head downstairs. Hope tugs my hand, pulling me to a stop before the staircase.

I turn, a "what" forming on the tip of my tongue, when she reaches up and kisses my cheek. Her lips brush against my ear. "I left the tights on under my jeans."

"Fuuuck," I groan. "What are you trying to do to me?"

She lets out a giggle and races down the stairs ahead of me.

Teller's sitting on the couch alone, head in his hands. He glances up when he hears us. "I'm so sorry, guys."

Hope hurries over and takes his hand. "You know we'd go with you no matter what, Teller."

"Thanks."

The ride to the hospital seems to take forever. There's not a lot to say. Heidi calls with an update, and even up front I hear the panic in her voice.

"Marcel!" she yells and runs to her brother as soon as we get there. He gives her a big, brotherly hug as she breaks into sobs.

"I'm sorry," she cries.

"For what, Bug? It's a good thing you were there to call for help."

She shakes her head and buries herself against his chest again.

Axel strides in next. Poor kid looks completely unsure of what to do. But he's here for Heidi, and I respect that.

A nurse ushers us into the waiting room so we're not jamming up her hallway. Heidi sees Axel and bursts into tears again. He gives her a hug, but is clearly uncomfortable showing her affection in front of her brother and me.

Good.

Heidi finally notices Hope, and her face twists. While I talk to the guys, Heidi edges toward Hope. Eventually, they get up and leave the room together.

Hope

Something is bothering Heidi. But she's not going to spill with her brother and Rock in the same room. As soon as we're out of their eyesight, she bursts into tears again.

"Hope, it's all my fault," she whispers.

"Honey, I'm sure that's not true."

She glances back at the waiting room. "Grandma caught me sneaking in the house, and we had a fight. I went to my room and heard her stomping around and yelling downstairs. Then all of a sudden she was quiet. I figured, good, she finally shut up." Big, fat tears slide down her face. "After a while, it just seemed too quiet, so I went downstairs. Hope, she must have passed out, and I just let her lay there…" She trails off as she breaks into more tears.

Poor Heidi. "Honey, it's not your fault. You did go check on her. And you called the ambulance. She's getting treatment now. It's okay."

"It's my fault, though. If she hadn't caught me—"

"Were you with Axel, honey?"

She slides a guilty look toward the waiting room. "Not exactly."

I have no idea what that's supposed to mean and it's not really important, so I let it go.

"Am I going to get in trouble, Hope?"

I resist the urge to grin at her question. "No, honey. Why would you think that?"

"Cause we had that fight—"

"Did it turn physical?"

Her eyes widen, and she shakes her head violently. "God, no. It's just that…I know she has a heart problem, and I snapped back at her when she called me names."

The picture I'm getting of what life is like with Heidi's grandmother is unpleasant and a little too reminiscent of my own teenage years. My heart goes out to this motherless girl, who while a little wild, is still very sweet.

"No, honey. You're not in trouble. It's normal to fight with family members sometimes."

"Please don't tell my brother. He's going to be so pissed at me. Gram's already furious with him because of the custody thing, and now this…"

Now it's my turn to have a guilty moment. I'm also aware the woman has some health problems. I'm sure the legal dispute hasn't helped.

Murphy stalks into the hospital, coming straight at us.

"I got your message, Heidi-bug. You okay?"

Her nose twitches at the nickname, and I hold back a laugh.

"Yeah, thanks for coming."

"Hey, First Lady." Murphy nods his head at me. "Prez with you?"

I tilt my head toward the waiting room. "He's in there with Teller and Axel."

His eyes narrow at hearing Axel's name, but he doesn't comment.

"Need anything, Bug?"

Heidi shakes her head.

When we're alone again, I give Heidi another hug. "It's not your fault, sweetheart, okay? Why don't we join the others and wait for news?"

"Okay. Thank you, Hope."

"You're welcome, sweetie."

The guys break up their conversation when we reenter the room. Rock holds his hand out, and Heidi accepts a quick squeeze. "Thanks for bringing my brother down, Uncle Rock."

"No problem, Heidi-girl."

She grins when he doesn't add her hated nickname.

"How'd you get here, Bug?" Murphy asks.

Her gaze darts between Axel and Murphy. Finally she settles into the chair next to her boyfriend, and he wraps an arm around her shoulders. "Ambulance."

"I'll give you a lift home later," Murphy says.

"I got her, bro," Axel asserts.

Murphy acts as if Axel hadn't even spoken.

So much for Murphy not being into Heidi. I wonder if he's going to freak out when he discovers she was sneaking around with Axel.

Shaking my head, I decide none of this is my problem.

Rock pats the chair next to him, and I drop into it with a sigh. His hand slides under my hair to massage my neck. "Rough night, Baby Doll."

"Yeah."

We don't have to wait too much longer. A nurse comes in and informs us that Mrs. Whelan is stable. She's going to be out for the night, so the nurse urges everyone to go home and return in the morning.

Teller gets up and gives Rock a fist bump. "I'll catch a ride with Murphy, prez. Thanks for staying."

Rock stands up and pulls Teller in for a quick man-hug. "You need anything, call me. Don't care what time it is."

"Promise."

Rock turns to me. "Mind staying at my house, instead of driving back to the club?"

I mentally run over what I have stashed at Rock's house. "Sure, that's fine."

Rock scans the group. "Anyone need a lift?"

Axel and Heidi are standing apart from the group holding hands. Murphy watches them from his seat and doesn't even glance up at Rock's question. Teller kicks Murphy's leg to grab his attention. "We cool, bro?"

"Yeah, man. You ready to leave?"

"Yeah." He turns to Axel and Heidi. "Axel, you want to follow us? I'm gonna stay at Gram's with bug tonight."

"Yeah, okay. I got her."

"Cool, let's go." Teller punches Murphy's shoulder, and he finally gets up.

Rock and I walk ahead of the group. We reach our car first and say our good nights to everyone.

"Well, that was awkward," I say with a snicker as soon as Rock closes his door.

"What?"

"Murphy. What's his deal with Axel?"

Rock gives me one of his "are you kidding" looks. "Axel's a good kid. I hate to break it to Murphy, but I think Heidi really is over her crush on him."

"Duh. I wanted to marry a Backstreet Boy, when I was twelve."

Laughter echoes through the interior. "I have no words, Hope."

"I aim to entertain."

He starts up the car and points us toward his house.

"What'd you talk about with Heidi?"

"Oh, she was worried this was all her fault because she got into an argument with her grandmother tonight."

"Poor kid. This shit has been rough on her."

"Does anyone know where her mom is?"

"Nah. We tried helping Teller track her down for a long time. Nothing ever came of it."

"That's awful. I know she's a handful sometimes, but she's basically a good kid."

"I know."

We're quiet the rest of the way. Me because my brain is trying to work out how this hospitalization is going to affect my legal case. Terrible, I know. But I can't help it. I also realize there's a possibility their grandmother may need the sort of round-the-clock care that only a nursing home can provide. Custody should automatically go to Teller then—

"We're home, babe," Rock says, breaking into my thoughts. A loud yawn escapes me.

"You okay?"

"Yeah, just trying to work out how this will affect the case."

Rock squints at me, probably thinking I'm an insensitive jerk. Instead of chastising me for my callousness, he squeezes my hand. "Thanks for caring about them so much."

"Of course."

"I mean it. Teller and Heidi are like family."

"I know."

"Known Heidi since she was a little kid."

Goosebumps work over my arms. Rock's such a softy underneath all his hard exterior.

"I'll go in early tomorrow to do a little research and make some phone calls."

"Tomorrow is Saturday, babe." His hand reaches over and squeezes my thigh. "Besides, I think you mentioned something before about what you're wearing underneath these jeans?"

Suddenly legal work is the furthest thing from my mind.

CHAPTER SIXTEEN

HOPE

"Hey, Hope. This yours?" Z asks as he's walking into the clubhouse dining room for breakfast.

I glance at the cell phone he pushes my way.

"Yeah. Where was it?"

A careless lift of his shoulders. "Found it in the couch cushions."

Not surprising. I'm always losing my cell phone. And since I usually keep it on silent so it doesn't go off when I'm in court, it's almost impossible to find it.

"Thanks."

Z throws a smirk at me and heads into the kitchen.

Rock slips his hand over mine and gives it a squeeze.

"What are your plans for today?"

It's Monday, and since he convinced me the stuff with Teller's grandmother could wait until today, he knows damn well I am planning to go into the office.

I slant a look at him, and his mouth quirks.

"What are your plans?" I ask instead of giving him a verbal answer.

I get a side-eye in return. That's right. Rock is always up in my business, but I have no idea about anything he does if it's "for the club."

Whatever.

"Actually, I have to take care of a few things at CB today."

My nose wrinkles, which he catches. He lets out a soft chuckle.

"It's closed today, babe. That's why I'm going."

See, that doesn't make me feel any better. If it was crawling with dancers, he'd have a hard time saying no?

"Hey, what's that face for?" he asks against my ear. His lips brushing over the sensitive skin there sends a shiver through me.

"Nothing," I whisper.

Before this conversation can go any further, we're interrupted by Z and Trinity coming out of the kitchen. They're playfully arguing over something. She's carrying a tray with her and doesn't stop to sit with us.

"Stop fucking babying him, Trin," Rock teases as she goes by.

She laughs but doesn't say anything else.

Z shakes his head as he sits down. "Those two."

Rock snorts in agreement.

"Did Teller stay up here last night?" I ask, hoping one of them will know.

"Nah, he's still staying with Bug."

"Good."

"She's already in lawyer mode," Rock jokes while jerking his head at me.

Z chuckles. "You're a good girl, Hope."

"Thanks, I think."

He laughs even harder. I've found it's difficult to offend Z. He's a regular ray of sunshine compared to Wrath.

"Alright, I need to get going." I push my chair out and grab my dishes. Rock stops me. "Leave it. I'll take care of it."

I arch an eyebrow at him. "You will, or you'll have Trinity do it?"

Z bursts out laughing.

Rock's jaw works, but a smile is hovering at the corners of his mouth. I lean over and brush a kiss against his cheek. His hand locks around my wrist, pulling me closer. "Give me a real kiss," he says.

"Please don't," Z begs, reminding me that we have an audience.

Rock shoots him a dirty look and stands, yanking me against his chest. "You stopping home first?"

"Yes. I need to change." I wave my free hand that isn't trapped between our bodies over my jeans and sweatshirt.

He turns and tucks me against his side to walk me out. "You need to grab anything from upstairs?"

"No, I'm good."

He sighs in disapproval.

"Why are you trying to get me—"

Oh.

The carnal look on his face can't really be ignored. Especially when he pushes me inside the champagne room.

"Hey—" I protest, but it's quickly cut off by his mouth on mine.

Rock

Even though it's indirectly my fault she has to go, I'm not ready for Hope to leave. It's ridiculous because after she got me so worked up Friday night, we spent a large portion of the weekend in bed.

No matter how many times we fuck, I can't seem to get enough of her. Probably because what we have is so much more than fucking.

If she doesn't need to go upstairs, the champagne room is my next best option. It will definitely be empty this early on a Monday morning. Picking Hope up, I pin her to the wall just inside the door.

"What are you doing?" she asks breathlessly against my mouth.

I lean into her neck, inhaling her sweet scent before answering. "Well, I'm not giving you a lap dance." I was aiming for light and teasing, but it comes out tense and strangled.

Hope's eyes go wide, but her mouth curves in a sexy smile. "What if someone walks in?"

"Doll, no one is coming in here." But to make her feel better, I reach over and flip the lock. To do it, I need to pin her to the wall with my hips. Her head falls back against the wall with a soft thump from the extra friction. I take a second to let my eyes travel over her body.

Flushed cheeks, erect nipples—visible even through the heavy fabric of her sweatshirt every time she takes a heaving breath.

Damn.

The sight of how turned on she is already has me harder than steel-reinforced concrete and aching with an almost violent need to fuck her.

First, I need to set her down and strip her pants off.

As I release her, she slides down the wall and her eyes flare in surprise. Gripping her hips, I walk/push her to the couch lining one side of the room. I'm almost frantic trying to figure out which way I want to take her first. Finally, I sit down and pull her to me. My hands go straight for her jeans and begin working them down her legs. She gives me a soft sigh of anticipation and kicks her pants off after I work them past her knees.

"Shirt, baby," I tell her.

It drops to the floor in a soft whoosh of fabric. Her hands immediately go to my shirt next, and my dick jumps. I love that she's just as crazed to see me as I am to see her.

I crook a finger at her and free my aching dick from my jeans. Without a word, she plants one knee next to me and steadies herself on my shoulders. Looking into my eyes, she centers herself. "Rochlan?"

"Yes, doll?" I manage to choke out.

"I love you."

For some reason, her voice breaks and she seems close to tears. Stroking my hands over her back, I guide her to my cock. "Baby, I love you too. So much."

Once she's perfectly lined up, she sinks down slowly. Hot breath hisses out between her clenched teeth and over my cheek. My hand grips her hip, kneading her soft flesh.

Across the way, the mirror gives me a fantastic view. The graceful lines of her back, the cute little dimples above her perfect ass, her long hair swishing against her pale skin.

"You're fucking beautiful." My hand threads into her hair, pulling her down for a kiss. Wrapping my arms around her tight, I slam my cock up into her. A groan tears out of my throat. "I can see you in the mirror, Hope. See everything. Beautiful."

She whimpers against my neck and struggles to turn, but I hold her tight. Now's not the time for my girl to get shy.

Our skin slaps together, quick and furious. Hope's gone. Writhing above me, moaning, squeezing me so fucking tight. She's making little mindless noises as I keep drilling up into her. She stills, a soundless scream on her lips, and I feel my own orgasm boiling through me.

My lips find hers, and her fingers tunnel through my hair, sending shivers up and down my spine.

I'm not thrilled as I watch her dress a few minutes later. She catches the look on my face, and the corner of her mouth kicks up.

"See, if you hadn't interfered in my business and made me take their case, I could spend the day with you."

It's clear she's only teasing, but her words still make me pause.

I may be a lot of things, but I'm not some backwards asshole who's going to take a smart, driven woman like Hope and attempt to turn her into my mindless sex slave—as appealing as that might sound. So no, it's off to work for her.

"I've kept you long enough, doll."

CHAPTER SEVENTEEN

HOPE

FILLING OUT THE ORDER TO SHOW CAUSE, GETTING IT SIGNED BY A JUDGE and filed with the court, takes up most of my morning. I'm feeling very accomplished by the time everything is in place. Teller calls to let me know they are not releasing his grandmother any time soon, so it's a good thing I've gotten the ball rolling.

Adam bounds into my office a little before noon.

"Hey. I got called into court this afternoon. Want to take my place at a CLE?"

I'm woefully short on credits, but the thought of sitting through some boring legal education class all afternoon is very unappealing.

"Come on, your buddy, Judge Oak is one of the lecturers. It's already paid for."

"Oh, okay. I need the credits. How much do I owe you?"

He waves his hand in the air. "I just don't want it to go to waste. Starts at one, so you might want to head down now."

Dammit.

Packing up my stuff, I grab a granola bar and head downtown. Miraculously, I find a parking spot right in front of the building where the class is. The woman in charge of checking us in hassles me a bit as I try to explain I'm taking Adam's place. Judge Oak comes over to say hello and smooths things over for me.

"Thank you, Damon."

"No problem. Good to see you."

"Is Mara coming?" It would be nice to be able to sit with someone I know.

He chuckles and shakes his head. "No. She refuses to come to my lectures any more."

Crap.

Feeling supremely awkward and out of place, I grab a seat near the back of the small classroom. Too late, I realize it's a panel of four lecturers. They've got Judge Oak, a public defender, a district attorney from Empire County, and a criminal defense attorney who is in private practice. My eyes almost bug out of my head when I see who the defense attorney is. Tony Cain. Former Slater County District Attorney. The guy I went up against when I represented Rock in his last drug possession case. The case where he humiliated me in court by asking to have another lawyer represent him.

Before we were together.

Before my husband died.

Horrible, sickening sensations slither through my belly as I remember that day. All of my thoughts and emotions are tangled together with my feelings of grief over Clay's death. My guilt over my inappropriate feelings toward Rock at the time.

I end up not hearing much of the two-hour class.

In a hurry to leave afterward, I don't bother to say goodbye to Damon. He's surrounded by sycophant attorneys peppering him with questions, and I don't have the patience to get in line.

I want to go home and crawl into bed.

To my utter confusion, I find Rock waiting outside for me, casually leaning up against my car. His gaze flicks up and down the street, keeping an eye out for me, I assume.

Is this a coincidence?

Whatever it is, I'm already so rattled from the Tony Cain sighting that the first thing I do is snap at Rock. "What the hell are you doing here?"

A frown settles over his face as he turns to look at me.

"What's wrong, Hope?"

No, I'm not going to be dissuaded by his handsome face or his sexy damn mouth. "Why are you here?"

He cocks his head as if it's an absurd question. "I wanted to see you."

"How did you know I was here?"

He pauses. Something flashes in his eyes, but I can't fathom what it is.

Finally, he reaches out and pulls me to him. "Your calendar," he answers.

My head is aware this can't be true, but my body is distracted by his lips on mine. Before I can question him further, I'm wrapped in his arms, snuggled against him. The lingering bad feelings from the lecture melt away as I take shelter in his arms.

"Rock?"

We're rudely interrupted, and I jump back. It finally dawns on me how embarrassing it is to be making out with my boyfriend when about forty of my colleagues are about to empty out of the building behind me.

Why do I have so little self-control around him?

The unease on Rock's face surprises me. I've never seen him look uneasy in any situation.

I turn to see who interrupted us, and almost fall down when I realize it's Tony Cain. His eyes skip right over me as his mouth breaks into a grin. They perform a manly handshake ritual that suggests a certain familiarity. The kind of handshake people who know each other in a personal, friendly way do, immediately setting off alarm bells in my head.

"Hey, Tony. How are you?" Rock asks evenly.

"Good, man, just got done teaching a class. What the hell are you doing down here?"

Rock jerks his chin in my direction, and Tony finally glances over. He's having trouble placing me. I haven't seen the guy in at least two years, so that's not surprising. The Capital Region is, after all, crawling with attorneys.

Finding some glimmer of professionalism, I stick out my hand. "Hope Kendall. I just took your class, Mr. Cain."

Now he seems to recognize me, and his gaze darts back to Rock.

"Nice to see you again, Ms. Kendall. I hope you got a lot out of the class."

"Oh, absolutely," I answer with a straight face. "It's been quite an education."

CHAPTER EIGHTEEN

ROCK

Tony motherfucking Cain.

Fuck me.

Of all the times to run into my childhood friend, now is the least appropriate. Hope seems ready to murder my ass, and I am not looking forward to the questions she's going to fire at me the second we're alone.

He slaps me on the shoulder. "Call me so we can catch up. Things are good?"

I nod. "Yeah, things are good." Or they were good until this whole situation happened.

We wrap up our conversation, and as he walks away, Hope starts edging toward her car. Away from me. From where I'm standing, I see she's shaking.

This time, it's not from desire. Not even fear.

It's rage. I see it in her wide green eyes that are drilling into me with a million accusations.

"Hope—"

"Don't," she spits out.

I didn't have the good sense to park my bike in front of her car this time. She's inside and gunning the engine within seconds. Deciding this isn't the best place for a scene, I let her go.

But I'm not far behind.

I track her down at her office. Thankfully, it looks like Adam is gone for the day. I don't have a key for the back entrance, so I jog down the front steps and ring the bell. I end up leaning on it for quite a while before Hope's furious face appears on the other side of the glass.

The door swings open, and she lets me in.

Well, really, I push my way in. "Let me explain."

She folds her arms over her chest and takes a step back. "How do you know Tony?" She shoots at me.

"We grew up together. He lived down the street from me."

"You've got to be fucking kidding me." Her voice zips up a few octaves. "Why was he prosecuting your case?"

I shrug, not quite sure how to explain. I've given her a vague outline, that I fired her as my attorney publicly so the Vipers would lose interest in her. I never got into the fact that Tony rigged the case at my request. After everything we've gone through since then, it seemed pointless to go into the whole mess.

"Hope—"

"Tell me something. Did Tony renege on the deal because you asked him to?"

"Yes."

She blows out an irritated breath. "Do you know how many times I used to go over that whole horrible day in my head? Wondering what I did wrong? How I fucked it up so royally bad that you had an excuse to fire me on the spot in front of everyone? You know I stopped practicing criminal law because of that day?"

Shit. "I know, honey. I'm sorry. I told you—"

"Yeah. You told me about the war with your rival and cutting ties with me. I get that part. I didn't realize you were responsible for tanking the deal, though. I didn't realize the whole damn situation was a set up. I still doubt myself all the time because of that. Shit." She focuses her eyes on me, and they're so full of pain I caused, I can't stand it.

"Hope. I asked him to help. Originally, I'd asked him to dismiss the whole thing so it would look good for you and give your practice a little boost."

That was perhaps the very worst thing I could have said, because she goes nuclear. "Do you think my career is some sort of fucking game? Who the fuck do you think you are?"

I thought I'd seen every side of Hope by now. I thought I'd seen her angry before. I was dead wrong.

"My God, all this time, I thought I did something wrong. Missed something big. On top of that, I had all that fucking guilt and shame because of my feelings for you. But it was nothing more than some elaborate game of chess for you and Tony. Holy shit, am I stupid. Did you guys have a good laugh when you were done?"

"Hope, it wasn't like that at all. I hated doing that to you. I—"

"Get out."

"Hope—"

"Get. The. Fuck. Out. I can't even look at you, let alone listen to any more of the bullshit that comes out of your mouth, Rock. Get out."

I hold my hands up in surrender. The last thing I want to do is leave, but she's only getting more enraged and not willing to listen to reason.

"Okay, we'll talk later."

"No. We won't."

She slams the door behind me hard enough to rattle the glass.

Fuck.

Hope

I'm shaking so hard after I finally get Rock to leave that I stumble. Kicking off my heels and hurling them down the hallway doesn't make me feel any better. I manage to stagger into my office before I dissolve into a puddle of tears. Deep, ragged sobs tear out of my chest. I'm so damn hurt and confused. I sink onto the floor and replay that day in my head. The bits I haven't blocked out. Rock giving me shit the day before about the one year of probation. Tony giving me that long lecture about Rock's motorcycle gang.

All of it gimmicks and lies.

I snort at the irony of Tony Cain being just as much of a crook as Rock. I gotta admit, my faith in the criminal justice system and my entire profession has taken a huge hit today.

Give my practice a boost. More like some scheme to get in my pants. Damn, I'm an idiot.

Christ, were those charges even real to begin with? Or was it more manipulation to "help" my career? I remember the day outside of family court when Winter's ex assaulted me. One of the cops knew Rock pretty damn well.

Rock has friends everywhere.

After the tears stop, I realize what's driving my anger is how humiliated and stupid I feel.

That's going to take some time to get over.

It seems like forever before I finally pick myself up off the floor. A quick step in the hallway and I retrieve my shoes. I sit behind my desk and enter in my CLE credits so I don't forget about them when the time comes to renew my license. The sound of the front door opening startles me.

I swear to God if it's fucking Rock, I'm going to choke him out.

Why didn't I remember to lock the damn door?

I was too busy having my pride stomped on by a pair of size thirteen steel-toed boots, that's why.

Since I'm ninety-nine percent sure it's Rock, I don't bother slipping my shoes back on. Instead, I tear ass into the hallway.

"Rock, I can't deal with this now. You need—"

It's Mr. Greybell.

"Oh my gosh! I'm so sorry, Mr. Greybell. I thought you were someone else."

He cocks his head, and his eyes roam over me in a distinctly creepy manner I don't care for. He stops at my bare feet. The intensity of his gaze makes me wiggle my toes into the flat, industrial carpet.

"Uh, Adam isn't here right now."

His eyes finally leave my feet, but travel back up my legs before answering.

"That's okay. I came to see you."

"Me?"

"I wanted to ask you to have dinner with me."

I bite down on the tip of my tongue to stop the "hell fucking no" from escaping. The guy creeps me out something fierce, but I don't want to be rude. "Oh, Mr. Greybell, that's very nice of you to ask, but I think I mentioned I have a boyfriend."

A boyfriend I am dearly wishing I hadn't chased away at the moment. Where is his overbearing, caveman ass when I need it?

Rock

Hope's screams of "get the fuck out" keep echoing in my head, yet here I am, still sitting out in the parking lot. Waiting for her. I tell myself it's only to make sure she gets home okay since she's so upset. Hell, maybe that's even the reason. Who knows?

I do know that the flimsy building did a lousy job of concealing the sounds of her crying after I left. Her gut-wrenching sobs nearly tore me apart as I stood with my back against the wall of the building and listened. Everything in me said to go comfort her, but the small part of my brain that actually functions knew it was a bad idea.

So, I wait. She quieted down after a while, and I went and sat on my bike next to her car. The spot gives me a prime view of the back entrance to the building, so I can spot her as soon as she comes out. Maybe we'll talk when she leaves. Maybe she'll yell at me some more. Maybe I'll just end up following her home to make sure she gets there okay. I don't know.

I should have seen this coming. She's told me plainly that she wants to hear the truth from me. Many times. There's a lot of fucking truths I can't give her. I could have given her this one.

Honestly, it never occurred to me.

Tony and I grew up together, sure. We keep in touch. We have a precise sort of give-and-take relationship. Sometimes we reminisce about the old days. Although we've got history, we're polite, distant friends. He's not someone I'd ever call "brother." That title is reserved for my fellow Kings. When I need to call in a favor with Tony, it definitely costs me.

I don't trust him with my life.

The fact that Hope still wrestles with that day burns me. I had no damn clue. That she's still suffering some guilt and grief about our relationship and her husband's death doesn't surprise me. That she connects all of it together does.

My explanations for my behavior apparently only went so far. I'm really not sure how to fix this.

A short, sharp scream interrupts my thoughts, and my head snaps up. My eyes focus on the building, as if that's going to help me hear what's going on inside any better. A crash and another short scream. Definitely Hope.

The fuck?

I tear ass to the front of the building, where there's a sedan parked right in front, blocking the entire driveway. No fucking way for me to see it from where I'd been waiting. Rushing down the stairs, I muscle through the door, then pause.

Hope

"Mr. Greybell? Did you hear me? I appreciate your invitation, but I have a boyfriend. I actually need to meet him in a few minutes." Somehow my fear makes that lie come out very smooth.

Greybell is freaking me out with his blank stare and stiff posture. He seems to be contemplating something. I'm not sure what. Most likely I'd rather not know. Without tipping him off, I glance at my desk, trying to spot my cell phone. Not there. Did I leave it in my briefcase? I don't have a phone at my desk, and I can't easily make it into Adam's office.

After staring at me for much too long, he slips his hand in his pocket, withdrawing a folded up piece of paper.

"I wanted to give you this," he says with a slightly unhinged laugh.

"What is it?"

He holds it out to me, but I don't really want to get any closer to him. Instead, I edge back into my office. My briefcase is on the floor, propped up against the side of my desk. I'm almost positive that's where my phone is.

Holding up one finger, I say, "Give me one second, David."

I dash into my office, plunging my hand into the outside pocket of my briefcase. Just as my fingers curl around my phone, David wraps his hand around my arm, yanking me to my feet.

"Ow! Get off me!" I screech at the top of my lungs. For once, I'm grateful for the shitty soundproofing in this old building. Someone upstairs should be able to hear me screaming.

"Shh. Shh. I just want to talk to you. I wrote this for you."

Why did I have to be so damn nice to this asshole? I should have thrown him out.

For a slender guy, he's got an iron grip on my arm. He yanks me and then slams me into my desk. The front of my thighs dig painfully into the lip of my desk. My breasts and face are mashed into the hard wooden surface. I wish I kept my desk neater. There is definitely a ballpoint pen poking into my boob. I just know it's going to leave a mark, ruining my shirt.

What the hell is wrong with me?

Greybell slides a piece of paper next to my face. My cheek is pressed so tight against the desk it's hard to form words.

"It's kind of hard to read from this position, Mr. Greybell."

He doesn't seem bothered by my sarcasm.

"It's a poem I wrote for you."

Oh geezus.

I'm not sure what he plans to do with me. I'm not even sure if he has a plan. Despite the obscene position he's forced me into, he hasn't touched me inappropriately.

Who am I kidding? Appropriate left the building a couple minutes ago.

This guy needs psychiatric help. Like, locked up away from society kind of help. Locked up far away from *me* type of help.

Harmless my ass. I'm going to kill Adam when I see him.

I realize I'm making a whining noise. "Please stop, you're hurting me." The begging quality to my voice really ticks me off.

He bends over me, pressing me even more painfully into the desk. I don't even want to contemplate what is prodding my ass. If I ignore it, maybe it will go away.

God dammit. Haven't I been bitching to Rock repeatedly that I can take care of myself? Why am I letting this skinny little wacko do this to me? He doesn't seem to have a weapon. Didn't I take a self-defense class once upon a time? The memory of which body parts to hit is fuzzy. Maybe that's lack of oxygen.

Foot stomp—yeah, that was definitely one of the spots.

Damn, if only I had my shoes on.

I make an attempt to stomp on his instep, but it's futile. I can't get enough leverage to raise my foot and end up banging my knee into the metal side of the desk and hurting my foot. For all my trouble, I don't even think he even noticed.

A noise reaches my ear. Someone's in the office.

Please let it be Rock.

I'm so, so sorry for yelling at him. I hate that if I never see him again, that's how we left things.

No!

"Get off me!" I scream with renewed purpose. At the same time, I throw my elbow back and connect with his soft gut. He jumps back enough for me to wriggle free.

Then Rock is there, throwing Greybell to the floor.

"Rock! Thank God!"

I've never been so happy to see anyone in my life.

Rock

Pulling the pistol out of the holster at my back takes a second. I flip off the safety and hold the gun at my side.

A thump. Sounds like a struggle.

Hope's voice. "Please stop, you're hurting me."

I see motherfucking red.

It takes every ounce of control I possess not to storm down the hallway and murder whoever made my girl say that.

All sorts of thoughts go through me.

Viper? How'd they connect me to Hope? Why here? Why now?

One of the guys from the fight?

Does she have a tarp I can wrap the body in? Because there is no way this motherfucker is walking out of here alive. All these things race through my head as I inch down the hallway. Adam's office is dark, but light pours into the hall from Hope's office. Shadows waver over the carpet.

Whispering that I can't make out reaches my ears. Hope whines.

Fuck caution.

Inside her office, a guy I don't recognize has her bent over and pinned to her desk. White-hot fucking rage slams through me at the sight. Only concern that I'll accidentally shoot Hope makes me tuck the gun back in my pants. From this angle, I can't tell if he has a weapon. I'm worried if I startle the prick, he'll end up seriously injuring her.

"Get off me!" she screams, throwing an elbow back into the guy's gut. He jumps back enough for me to tell he's unarmed, and I hurl myself at him, grabbing him around the neck. Hope shakes free just in time, because the motherfucker is on the floor with my knee in his chest within seconds.

"Rock! Thank God," she gasps.

She's reaching for her cell phone. To call the police, I assume.

"Wait." I glance down at the scrawny fuck beneath me. "Who're you with?"

"What?" he gasps out.

Leaning over so my knee grinds into his chest a little harder, I yank his shirt up to check his ink.

No ink on his front. I push up his sleeves. No ink on his arms. I'm about to turn the sniveling fuck over when Hope's hand clamps down on my shoulder, pulling me back.

"He's one of Adam's clients, Rock. Don't hurt him. I don't think he's well."

No fucking shit he's not well. He's about to be really fucking unwell in a minute.

The guy is sobbing under me now, chanting "I'm sorry" over and over again.

Christ.

I ease up my hold on the little fuck, then stand. "Move and I'll shoot you," I growl down at him.

Hope

With my heart hammering away, blood thundering through my ears, I almost don't hear Rock threaten to shoot poor David.

Poor David, my ass.

My cell phone is still clutched in my hand, and I uncurl my fingers to hand it over to Rock. I'm shaking way too much to make any sense on the phone.

He gives me a tortured look, as if calling the cops offends him on some basic level. A complex mish-mash of emotions forces me into hysterical giggles. Oh boy. He hates when his friends look at me in a way he thinks is inappropriate.

"You okay, baby?" Rock asks as he curves his arm around my waist, pulling me tight to his side.

I bury my face in his shoulder and nod. He shifts his body a bit. "Don't test me, motherfucker," he snarls. Then I hear the distinct sounds of him dialing 911. He gives them a brief, clipped version of the story, the address, and hangs up. I'm sure they loved that.

After a few minutes, he squeezes me a little tighter. "You got any zip ties here?"

"Huh?" I shake myself out of his arms, meeting his questioning eyes. Dropping my gaze, I take in Rock's big-booted foot, pinning David to the floor. The corners of my mouth turn down.

"Don't," he warns.

"Is that really necessary?"

His jaw clenches. "Yes. But my leg's getting tired, so, you got any zip ties?"

I shake my head because I'm not even sure what the hell he's asking for.

It's moot anyway, because the banging at the front door signals Empire's finest has arrived. Rock jerks his chin in the direction of the commotion.

"Let them in."

Scurrying down the hall, I smooth my hands over my clothes, wincing at all the sore spots along my body. I take a few deep breaths and pray I won't burst into tears and make a fool of myself in front of the cops.

Rock

Dealing with the bastards in blue wears down my last bit of patience for this entire day. The fucker questioning Hope at the moment is dangerously close to having my fist rammed down his throat. Especially if he insinuates one more time that she and that whimpering pile of shit were somehow "involved."

"Miss Kendall, maybe we should speak privately," he suggests while throwing me a glance.

Yeah, 'cause I'm the problem.

I honestly don't care if I get carted off to county when I jab my finger in his chest, knocking him back a few steps. "You got a woman?"

Fucker has the nerve to sneer at me. "Yeah, a fiancée."

"What would you have done if you walked in on her bent over a fucking desk, begging some creepy asshole to let her go, 'cause he was hurtin' her?"

The cocky smirk slips off his face, replaced by something a little darker that I recognize and actually respect.

"Thought so. Be fucking grateful my girl calmed me down. The way I wanted to handle this was very different."

He knocks my hand away from his chest. "I'm sure it was, Mr. North."

I can't tell if he thinks he's intimidating me or he actually agrees.

Hope's soft hand against my chest breaks my focus. "Rock, it's okay," she says softly.

It is most certainly not okay. Nothing about this is okay.

She turns her head, and in a stronger voice says, "Officer, I've told you everything I know. I only met Mr. Greybell once before. He's attorney Braydon's client. Adam assured me the guy was a little weird but not dangerous. I have no idea why he attacked me."

A prison psychologist once taught me these breathing exercises to calm myself down when the need to kill someone struck me. I'd never admit it, but they worked well enough to keep me from acting irrationally more than once in my life. I'm employing one of those techniques right this second, because Adam just walked in and I'm pretty sure if I kill Adam, Hope's going to be pissed with me.

"What the fuck is going on?" the cocky shit asks.

Since I'm still busy counting to ten in my head, I let Officer Might-have-some-balls answer Adam's question.

Hope shakes herself free from my hold and storms over to Adam. She's still not wearing shoes so Adam's got a good six inches on her, but it doesn't stop her from smacking his arm. Or yelling at him. "Your harmless client fucking attacked me, that's what's going on!"

The look of worry, alarm, regret, whatever it is that passes over his face is probably the only thing that keeps him off my "people I need to kill" list.

"Jesus Christ, are you okay, Hope?" He pulls her in for a quick hug, then pushes her away to look her over. Officer Dickface quirks an eyebrow at me, and I shrug.

Adam's gaze lands on me, and he groans. "Fuck, you're not going to kill me, are you?"

"Not today."

Hope glares at both of us.

The officers who were in the back with Greybell walk him to the front door. They nod to Officer Dickwad. "Taking him in to process."

"Officer, is jail really appropriate? Maybe he should be sent to a hospital or something?" Hope asks.

Good fucking God, what am I going to do with her?

"Let his lawyer worry about that, Miss Kendall," the officer says gently, then glances at Adam. "That you?"

"No, sir, I'm an estate attorney. David, is there someone you want me to call?" Adam asks the piece of shit who attacked my woman.

Okay, now Adam just earned himself an engraved spot on my list.

The guy must be in shock, because he doesn't answer or even acknowledge Adam. The cops shrug and lead him out the door, steering clear of me for some reason.

"I'm taking her home," I tell Officer Donut Dick.

He opens his mouth to protest, then thinks better of it.

One look at Hope, and it's clear why. Although she was ready to pound the crap out of Adam a minute ago, she's pale everywhere except her cheeks, which are an unhealthy shade of red. There is some slight discoloration forming on her cheek and around her neck, which sends me into rage-y caveman mode all over again. Her glassy eyes meet mine, and she visibly shivers.

"Can you give me a number in case we need to reach her?" Officer Working-my-last-nerve asks.

After wrapping Hope in my arms, I rattle off my number and address to the cop. Hope, thank fuck, doesn't contradict me. I'm sure soon she'll remember we were in the middle of a huge fight, but right now she's not doing so well. Fight or not, she's coming home with me, because I'm not letting her out of my sight.

When I finally get her outside, she sucks in the cool night air in greedy gulps. The sun has long since set.

"I don't feel well," she whispers.

My girl is proud, so she must be feeling pretty damn bad to admit that.

"When's the last time you ate something?"

The fact that she has to stop and think about it is all I need to know. I've got fuck all in the way of food at my house, so once I get her settled in her car, I tap out a few texts to remedy that situation.

I get Hope inside my house and settled on the couch before she conks out. After covering her with a blanket, I walk back into the kitchen. I'm not waiting long before Hoot shows up with a bag of Chinese takeout.

"Axel should be by in a few with groceries," he huffs out after setting the bag on the counter.

"Good. I need one of you to go down to Hope's office, grab my bike, and bring it here." Hoot seems a little shocked I'm willing to let either of them near my bike, but it's the last thing I'm worried about.

"No problem."

Like a good little prospect, he goes outside to wait for Axel.

Kicking off my boots, I contemplate the wisdom of waking Hope. She needs her rest, but she also needs to eat something. As I pad back into the living room, I'm struck by how fucking tiny and fragile she looks burrowed into my couch. All the awful possibilities of what could have happened had I not been there tear through my brain. The irony of the attack having nothing to do with me or the club is something I set aside to examine later.

Hope looks so peaceful, I don't want to startle her. Gently, I brush my fingers over her cheek, pushing her hair behind her ear. "Hope, baby, dinner's here."

"Hmmm," she mumbles. She blinks a few times before looking up at me. A soft smile is the first expression she has when she meets my gaze, and my heart jumps.

I'm almost too choked up to speak. "You want to eat here or in the kitchen?" I ask while nodding at the coffee table.

She throws back the blanket and sits up. "Kitchen. Let me run to the bathroom, and I'll meet you in there." She stands and winces, then rolls her shoulders. "I hurt everywhere."

I'm itching to run my hands over her, but I don't want to add to any of her aches.

She glances down at her rumpled clothes. "Do you have something I can change into?"

"Yeah, of course. Give me a sec."

She runs down to the bathroom, and I dig through some clean laundry in the mudroom. I tap on the bathroom door, and she answers in her underwear. Normally I'd be primed to jump her, but the bruising over the delicate skin of her stomach, thighs and upper arms has me knotted into such a murderous fit I can't even think straight.

"Christ, I'm going to kill that fucker."

Her eyes widen in surprise. "It looks worse than it feels."

I know she's lying because she told me not five minutes ago how bad she was hurting.

I hand over the clothes and press a quick kiss to her cheek. "Hurry, dinner's getting cold," I croak out.

"Okay." She doesn't bother closing the door, just slips into the long T-shirt and shorts I gave her.

She curls her fingers around my hand and tugs me to the kitchen. "I'm so far past hungry, I feel sick. But I know I need to eat something," she says over her shoulder.

Right. Food.

Feed my girl now.

Murder guy later.

CHAPTER NINETEEN

HOPE

MY MIND IS A MESS AS WE SIT DOWN TO EAT. MY STOMACH ROLLS, AND I'M not sure I'll be able to keep anything down. Rock pries the lid off a plastic container of wonton soup and nudges it in front of me. Not really caring what I look like, I pick up the container and suck down a good portion of the broth.

"Stop staring at me, and eat your own dinner," I mutter, which makes Rock chuckle.

We eat in silence. After the day we've had, I'm not sure there's a whole lot to say.

Rock heard me recount my story to the officers over and over, so nothing needs to be said about that.

The whole incident with Tony seems rather insignificant now. Maybe tomorrow when I reflect on it again, I'll feel differently, but at the moment I can't muster up any feelings on the subject.

Rock's entire body is tense as he watches me.

When I finally push my food away, he puts his hand over mine. "Feel better?"

"I do, actually." Well, except for the soreness prickling my stomach and legs.

Fear slams into me, and an image of David grabbing me and throwing me against my desk makes me shudder.

"Hope?"

I open my eyes and meet his concerned, stormy-gray stare. "I'm okay."

Someone bangs on the back door and I rocket out of my seat, slamming my knee into the underside of the table in the process. "Ouch!"

"Shh, calm down. It's one of the prospects."

He shouts "come in," and Axel walks through the door carrying two handfuls of grocery bags. He sets them on the counter and starts quietly putting things away. It amuses me that he seems to know the layout of Rock's kitchen better than I do, and I drop back into my chair.

"Hey, Axel," I call out. He turns and glances at Rock before answering.

"How you doin', Hope?"

I'm not sure what Axel knows, so I just say, "Okay."

When it looks like he's almost finished, I ask, "Is Heidi with you?"

His mouth turns down. "No. She's home."

"Teller with her?"

"I think so."

When all the bags are empty, Rock kicks a chair at Axel. Although he seems surprised, he joins us.

"Teller been up to the clubhouse today?" Rock asks Axel.

"Yeah, but he left so he could meet Heidi at the bus stop." He rolls his eyes.

"I'm sure she loved that," I say with a snort.

Axel cracks a smile. "Uh, she was pretty pissed. Called and gave me an earful."

Now Rock chuckles.

"He brought her to see their grandmother," Axels says with a serious expression, "but I guess that didn't go too well."

I raise an eyebrow for him to continue, but he shrugs.

"She didn't give me any details."

"Are you hungry, Axel?" I ask, gesturing to the table. It seems rude to have all this food laid out and not offer him any.

"No, thanks, Hope. I already had dinner." He glances at Rock. "Hoot said you need us to pick up your bike?"

"Yeah. Leave it here."

Axel nods and stands.

"Give me a second, babe," Rock says and follows Axel outside.

While they're gone, I clean up the kitchen. Peering into the fridge, I find that Axel brought over skim milk and some other things that Rock must have told him I'd want. Such a small thing, but it touches me for some reason.

The door bangs shut, and I hear the snick of the lock. Then Rock is wrapping his arms loosely around me. "Baby, I want you resting, not cleaning up the kitchen."

He steers me into the living room, and we settle on the couch to watch a movie. I barely make it through the opening credits before I'm out. In the distant recesses of my mind, I register the rumble of a motorcycle, Rock speaking softly on the phone, and then nothing.

In the morning, I wake up in Rock's bed. He's curled so tight around me, it takes a second to extract myself so I can run to the bathroom.

When I return, he's sitting up waiting for me. He holds out his hand, and I hurry to wrap myself up in his arms.

"How do you feel today, Baby Doll?" he rasps in his morning-rough voice.

"Better." It's not quite a lie. Almost.

"Do you want to talk about yesterday?" he asks.

My head is resting on his chest, so even when I tip my head up, I can't really see his face. I trace my fingers over the stubble along his jaw.

"Which part? The attack, or the fact that you've been lying to me for a while?"

Whoops. That came out harsher than I meant. Underneath me, Rock's body tightens, and for a second he stops breathing.

"Wherever you want to start, doll," he finally answers.

Propping myself up on one elbow, I move so we're facing each other. "Why didn't you tell me you knew Tony?"

He seems surprised. "When? Back then, or now?"

"Don't be dense. Now."

His jaw ticks, and I think I might have accidentally insulted him.

"Honestly? It never occurred to me."

I turn that over in my head. He seems sincere.

"What if we'd run into him somewhere?"

"Babe, we did run into him somewhere," he answers with a wry twist of his lips.

"What made you think you could manipulate my career? Back then," I add.

He seems puzzled by the question.

"I liked you." He presses a finger against my lips when I go to speak. I sit up so I can see him better. "Let me finish," he requests, "I thought you were smart, and I wanted to do something to help you."

"So, it wasn't a way to get in my pants?"

Now I think I've offended him. It's pretty clear from his expression that had never occurred to him.

"No." He sits up quickly and takes my hand. "Fuck, no, Hope. I told you how bad I wanted you, but I also respected you. You know loyalty means something to me." He taps his fingers against his chest, right below his "Strength from Loyalty" tattoo. "Christ, my ex cheated on me left and right. I knew that day we first kissed you were struggling."

Heat races across my cheeks as I remember that illicit kiss. Guilt rushes through my gut because at the time I had no business wanting Rock the way I did.

He places a finger under my chin, tipping my head up. "You were struggling, but you said no. I respected that. A lot, Hope. You know as well as I do, you can't help being attracted to someone, but you can chose whether you act on it or not."

"God, you're full of yourself," I grouch.

His laughter rumbles between us. "Be honest. If you hadn't been married, would you have come home with me that night if I'd asked?"

A different kind of heat streaks through me, but then another memory of that day squelches that fire. "No."

He quirks an eyebrow.

"I caught you coming out of the closet with Inga. No way would I have wanted to sleep with you a few hours later."

He doesn't laugh at me like I expected. "If you hadn't been strictly off limits, I never would have been in that closet with her," he says with such sincerity I believe every word. After a second, he runs his fingers over my cheek. "I did feel bad about that, you know," he adds, a pained expression settling over his face.

The way he admits that, the raw emotion in his words, loosens the tightness inside my chest. "Why? You were single and free to do whatever you wanted."

"I know. But the look on your face bugged the shit out of me for days."

Wow. That my big, tough, reformed manwhore has no problem admitting this to me erases any leftover doubts from our argument. I'm too choked up to say anything, so I bob my head up and down like a dope.

"That's all my plan with Tony was, Hope. I'm surrounded by all sorts of crap. You were this bright, sweet, genuinely good person. It was just my way of wanting to do something nice for you, the only way I could figure how."

If I twist my mindset a bit and see it from his perspective, it makes perfect sense.

"Okay, but you can't keep sticking your nose in my career, no matter how good your intentions are. Let me figure out what to do on my own." I thump him lightly on the chest to emphasize my point.

He snatches up my hand and kisses my fingers. "Hope, I'm not that guy. I don't want you to give up your career for me if that's what you're thinking."

"What are you talking about? I know that. Is that why you keep pushing me?"

"Well, yeah." A sheepish smile tugs at the corners of his mouth. "Plus, I like the idea of you doing stuff for the club. It's like a small way for you to be a part of it."

"I knew it. You don't allow women members, do you?"

The sheepish smile turns into a smirk.

I need to take a deep breath. In a small amount of time, he's admitted a number of stunning things to me. Each one explains so much. I feel like an absolute bitch for the way I've treated him.

"Rock, listen. I had these misgivings before we ever got together. The day we met, I think I told you I was struggling financially. Being a lawyer isn't what I thought it was going to be. I think you understand how much I withdrew from everything after Clay died. So now, I'm trying to figure out what I want to do with myself. Yes, I like spending all the extra time with you. But trust me, I have no intention of giving up my own life to just sit around and wait on you all day, if that's what you're worried about."

"Well now that you mention it—"

"Please, my vagina needs a break every now and then."

That gets a good, solid laugh out of him.

"Fair enough, doll."

"Good, and don't lie to me anymore."

He takes a deep breath, signaling this conversation is not finished, even though I thought it was. "I didn't lie to you. If you had asked me for some reason, I would have told you about Tony."

"Really?" I ask with a bit more sarcasm than I intended.

"Yes," he answers in his typical, no bullshit way.

I'm not so sure about that, but I nod anyway.

"You still hide other stuff from me, though."

"Hope, you know there is shit I can not tell you."

"Rock—"

"No. Can you tell me stuff about your clients?"

"Of course not."

"Right. You're bound by your confidentiality rules. So am I. Try to see it that way."

"That's ridiculous. I actually took an oath. I lose my license—"

Now Rock's pissed. "Babe, you best believe that I've taken some oaths of my own, and I have a fuck lot more to lose than a license."

"It's not the same," I protest.

"No, it's not." It sounds like he's agreeing with me, but I don't think that's what he's actually doing.

For some stupid reason, the term spousal privilege pops into my lawyer brain. "What if we were married?" I blurt out without thinking. "You'd still—"

I stop because he has this strange look on his face.

Way too late, I realize what I just said.

Crap.

CHAPTER TWENTY

ROCK

"What if we were married?"

Her words punch me in the gut, and any anger I was feeling a minute ago vanishes. "You think about that?"

A deep flush stains her cheeks, and she starts squirming away from me.

Oh, hell, no.

Launching myself on top of her, I pin her underneath me. "Tell me. Do you think about us that way?"

She struggles and won't meet my eyes. "I'm sorry, I shouldn't have said that. I know you don't want—"

I love her, but obviously, my girl knows jack about what I want. There's a fuck ton of things I want from Hope.

The words property patch spring to mind. I need to have that conversation with her soon. It's way more important to me than a wedding ring. I realize it's going to take a lengthy discussion for her to understand and not be offended.

But damn, I want—no, I need—her so fucking bad. In so many ways.

Leaning down, I take her lips in a soft, teasing kiss. "I want all sorts of things from you, Baby Doll."

Her forehead wrinkles with a bunch of unasked questions, so I continue.

"I want you to move in here for one thing." Fuck, it feels good to finally say that to her face.

"You do?" she asks with such surprise my heart clenches.

"Yes, Baby Doll. I hate every night we spend apart."

She looks so uncertain that I'm taken aback. Before I lose my shit, it occurs to me there could be another reason for her hesitance.

"Baby, you not ready to let your house go?"

She sinks her teeth into her bottom lip and nods. "I haven't even been able to pack his things up yet. Selling our house? I don't know."

I shift my weight off her and sit back. A brick to the face would have hit me with less force. She still considers it "their" house.

"I'm sorry," she says.

It takes me a second to remember how to work my mouth. "Don't be. I get it." I want to understand, anyway.

We're interrupted from this painful circle of a conversation by someone banging on the back door.

"Fuck." It better be life or death, or I swear to Buddha someone is going to ground.

Hope twists and checks out the clock. "I should go—"

"No. I want you close today." Actually, after her revelation, spending the day with her is going to be a challenge, but since I'm still worried about her safety, I'll have to suck it up.

She opens her mouth to protest.

"I'm not fucking around, Hope. You got work shit to do, I'll take you." I'm telling her all of this as I jump into a pair of jeans and throw on a T-shirt so I can go slap the shit out of whoever keeps banging on the door downstairs.

She goes to protest again, and I try that honesty thing she wants so much. "Hope, please. Give me this."

Begging works. She nods. "Okay."

Leaning over, I dip down and press a kiss to her forehead. "Thank you."

Downstairs, I find Z at the back door.

"Why didn't you just come in?" I snap.

"Got it locked down tight, brother. Forgot my key."

After leading him into the kitchen, I get some coffee going. I want to get breakfast started for Hope, but I doubt she'll come downstairs if she thinks this is club business. Which, by the way, I would like to find out myself, so I can get in the right frame of mind.

"What's up?"

"Wrath sent me. Said some shit went down, wanted to know what you need."

I snort and shake my head. I'd only spoken to Wrath briefly last night. I hadn't told either prospect what went down, yet somehow, he got some details. Even when he's down, brother is on top of things.

I give Z a brief outline of the attack, completely leaving out the Tony Cain portion of the afternoon. It's not relevant.

Z cracks his knuckles multiple times throughout my rundown. "Where is this motherfucker now?"

"Don't you dare." Hope's voice comes from just outside the kitchen entryway before she comes into view.

T-shirt hanging to her thighs, bare legs, mussed hair, she's fuckin' beautiful. Z runs his gaze over her a little too long for my taste, so I give him a slap.

He shakes it off and glares at me. "What?"

Hope narrows her eyes at me and comes around the corner to grab some coffee. As she stretches up to grab a couple mugs, the hem of her shirt rises, exposing the bruising all over the front of her thighs.

Beside me, Z sucks in a breath. "Holy fuck, Hope." His gaze darts to me, and it's full of murderous intent. "He do that to her?"

"I sure as fuck didn't."

Hope pads over and squeezes Z's shoulder while giving him a peck on the cheek. "Thanks for worrying about me, but I'm really okay."

I allow this because she initiated it, and my brother keeps his hands to himself. Although he does stare at her ass a little too long as she walks away, so this time, I punch him in the arm.

"Fuck, prez," he grumbles, rubbing his arm.

"Rock," Hope warns.

"You staying for breakfast?" I ask Z.

His face says he's surprised I asked. Am I really that much of a dick? Maybe I want the distraction of another person around, so Hope and I don't have to go back to the conversation we were having before he got here.

"Sure, thanks." He slips off his jacket and takes a seat next to Hope.

"You hurt anywhere else, sweetheart?" he asks while I start digging stuff out of the fridge. The question makes me pause as the image of that fuck forcing her over the desk assaults my memory. I can't even think about what could have happened if I hadn't been there, or I really will go track that scumfucker down and kill him.

Between fixing breakfast and fantasizing about gutting Greybell, I didn't hear Hope's answer. I do hear Z trying to pry some info out of her, though. He thinks he's being subtle, but he hasn't dealt with a woman like Hope before.

"Knock it off, Z. I'm not giving you information so you can go track him down and hurt him. I think he's mentally unstable. Hopefully he'll get some treatment in jail or something."

At that, I glance over at the two of them. Z's slack-jawed expression is pretty damn funny.

Her innocent—clueless, as Wrath likes to put it—outlook on the situation doesn't annoy Z the way it would Wrath. Z pats her hand and responds in a gentle tone. "Darlin', what I had in mind would be a lot kinder than the treatment he's going to get in jail."

CHAPTER TWENTY-ONE

HOPE

Rock has been my constant shadow for the past week. Even though he has kept himself very well-informed of Greybell's whereabouts and knows the poor guy is still sitting in the county jail, he is very reluctant to let me out of his sight.

We never got back to our conversation about moving in together, but I've spent every night at his house since, so maybe he thinks we don't need to discuss it. Heck, even I'm not sure if it needs to be discussed. I probably should move in with him and get it over with.

Something keeps stopping me. Every damn time I try to pack up Clay's things, it's so overwhelming I end up taking a nap instead.

Surprisingly, we haven't spent a lot of time up at the MC lately. I think he's trying to make up for the Tony Cain incident, even though I've made my peace with it.

The last few days have been similar to when we first started seeing each other. Just the two of us spending time together at his house.

I imagine Rock's absence is pissing Wrath off something fierce. Since he's still laid up with the broken leg, Z is the one who makes the trips to visit Rock when something comes up that needs his attention.

I'm sure whatever truce Wrath and I may have put in place has been obliterated.

Feeling a bit claustrophobic yesterday, I put my foot down and insisted on going into the office. I really did need to grab some things to prepare for the upcoming hearing in Teller's case. Rock agreed to let me go on the condition he went with me. Although I hate myself for it, I was relieved to have him there, because seeing the scene of the crime again sent me into a panic attack. Bless Rock's heart, he kept his "told you so" to himself.

Today something came up that Rock couldn't put off—although he refused to tell me what, and that is also a conversation we haven't gone back to—so I skipped on out the door to my office by myself.

And found Hoot waiting for me on the front steps.

Seems I'm destined to have a chaperone whether I like it or not.

"Hoot, you must have more important things to do than play babysitter," I scold as I let him in the office.

"Nope. Prez wants me here, I'm staying here. I promise not to get in your way, Hope."

"I know you won't. You want a soda or something?"

"I'll get it. Go ahead and do your thing. Pretend I'm not here."

Yeah, like that's easy with his lanky, six-foot frame taking up the entire waiting area.

But eventually I fall into my work and manage to forget he's out there. He's a good bodyguard. Quiet and thoughtful. Rock's trained him well.

A little after five, I hear someone at the front door. By Hoot's tone, I know it's Rock even before my ears catch the deep, gravelly tones of his voice.

Rock's gaze locks with mine as I walk into the hallway to greet him. "Hey, Baby Doll. Prospect behave himself?" I notice he has this way of not even using the prospect's club nickname when he addresses any of them.

Poor Hoot seems a little tense until I give an affirmative answer. "Absolutely. He's been a perfect bodyguard. Didn't even know he was here."

"Good," Rock jerks his head at the door, giving Hoot the signal that he's free to go.

"Take care, Hope."

I breathe a little easier when I see Rock slip the deadbolt into place. He notices and flashes a tight smile. "You okay?"

I nod. "I'll wrap up, and we can go."

"Okay."

I hear him following me down the hall. When I step into my office, a chill works over me. Before I know it, Rock's arms slide around my waist, pulling me against his chest. He plants a kiss on the top of my head. "I missed you, today."

"Missed you too. Everything go okay?"

"Mmhm," he hums against my ear.

When we make it out to the parking lot, Rock stares at my car for a second. "I'd really like you on the back of my bike, baby," he says softly. Even in the early evening light, the weight of his stormy gaze heats my skin.

On tiptoes, I reach up and give him a kiss. "I'll be right behind you, promise."

I am so not leaving my car here so I can be stranded at his house, no matter how hot he's making me with his I-want-to-fuck-you-right-now eyes. The response I get is not surprising, but it does excite me. He pulls me tight and gives me a kiss to think about on the drive to his house.

When I pull into his driveway, he's at my car door before I even shut the engine off. I get a kiss on the cheek before Rock turns and glances at the garage.

"What?"

He swings his gaze to me. "Nothing. You hungry?"

I wasn't until he mentioned food, then my stomach rumbled.

"Yeah."

Rock takes my briefcase along with all the other items I dragged back to his house and leads me inside. He sets my stuff in the living room and turns to me.

"Babe, what do you think about setting up an office here for yourself?"

I'm a little shocked. We never got back to that whole "moving in together" discussion. This seems like a compromise of sorts. Or maybe Rock is upset I rejected him the first time and doesn't want to risk asking again?

"What do you mean?"

"I mean, you spend a lot of your time here. So maybe you would be more comfortable if you had a space to work in when you don't feel like going to your office."

I cock my head at him. "Where?"

He shrugs and glances down the hallway. "I got a spare room down here that's just being used to store parts and stuff. I can move that stuff out to the garage."

Wow.

"You sure? I don't want to take up space you're using. Honestly, Rock, I don't need it. I can work from my laptop out here if I really need to. It's not like I'm drowning in work anyway."

He stares at me a little longer, then shrugs. "Think about it."

We're interrupted from talking about it by his cell phone going off. Before he gets it out, a second cell phone starts jittering across the table. He answers one and picks up the extra to check the number before flipping it open and closed. I've never realized he uses more than one phone, but it doesn't surprise me for some reason. He holds up one finger at me and stalks into the kitchen while murmuring into the phone. I hear the back door open and shut, so I wander out to the kitchen. I can see him through the glass pacing back and forth in the mudroom, intent on the call.

I figure I'll start dinner while I wait. A prickle of unease curls through my belly. Something is definitely up. I keep busy by rubbing a steak down with olive oil, rosemary and garlic, while heating up a cast iron skillet I find in a cabinet. Potatoes get diced and herbed, then thrown in the oven. I find some salad fixings and put that together in a big bowl. Finally, I'm ready to sear the steaks, but there's still no indication Rock will be returning. I pull out my own cell phone and set it on the counter to use the timer. I'm terrible at judging how long to cook steaks, so I set the timer to sear each side for seven minutes.

While I'm waiting to turn the steaks, I consider Rock's offer of an office in his home. Wandering down the hall, I push open the door to his spare room. It is indeed full of boxes and shiny parts. Even though it's a lot of stuff crammed into the space, everything seems neat and orderly. My cell phone buzzes from the kitchen, and I run out to turn the steaks.

Rock finally returns. "That smells amazing, sweetheart." He kisses my forehead before flashing a pained smile at me. "I really need to head out for a few. Are you okay here?"

My face must fall because he pulls me into a hug. "I'm sorry to run out after you just went to all this trouble. Will you wrap it up for me, and I'll eat when I get back?"

Tears threaten to fall. I hate this. I hate it because he's not going to tell me what's going on or why he needs to leave so suddenly. I mean, at least if he was a doctor or something he could say "honey, I have a patient I need to see," but he's not going to tell me a thing. I can ask, but I know where that will get me.

"Yeah, of course," I finally answer.

He knows. He knows damn well that I'm pissed and hurt, but he ignores it. "I need to run upstairs before I go."

Whatever.

The timer goes off, and I turn the steaks off and plate them so they can rest for a few minutes before I slice into one. Dressed all in black now, Rock thunders back down the stairs while I'm taking the potatoes out of the oven. He's tense and doesn't give me a hug or anything else this time.

He stops at the door. "Either Hoot or Axel will be stopping by to check on you a little later."

"How long are you going to be gone?" I ask. Why I bother, I don't know.

"Not sure. Shouldn't be long."

Yeah, that's real helpful.

Then he's gone, and I eat dinner alone.

By the time I'm done, pissed off is a rather weak description of what I'm feeling. As I'm wrapping everything up, I accidentally knock my cell phone on the floor. I've done this a million times, but for some goddamn reason, this time the screen shatters.

"Frick!"

The phone is basically useless. I guess the phone is still working, but I can't get it to do anything because I can't work the stupid touch screen. I need my phone. I mean, theoretically Teller is my only client right now, and he has multiple ways to get in touch with me if he needs to. But my cell phone is the only number listed on my business cards, so the thought of not having it in working condition really freaks me out. I feel naked and vulnerable without it actually.

I glance at the clock. If I leave now, I have time to make it to the cell store at Stonewell Mall and get a new phone. I was due for a new one anyway, but I hate dealing with the hassle of sales people and all the other bullshit that comes along with it. Although, now I don't have a choice.

There's no sign of Hoot or anyone else, so after scribbling a quick note for Rock, I hurry to my car and head to the mall. Traffic is light, and I make it there in plenty of time before closing.

The girl who helps me is way too bubbly for this time of night. She inspects the screen and shakes her head. "Honestly, since it's not covered by warranty, it will be cheaper to just upgrade."

"I figured."

She shows me all the new phones and I dither back and forth before finally choosing one.

"Normally we charge twenty-five dollars to move your contacts over, but since it's just me tonight, I'll do it for free," she says with a conspiratorial whisper.

While she's working, she frowns, then smiles at me. "Aw, that's sweet. You and your man keep track of each other?"

"What?"

She gestures to the device my shattered phone is hooked up to. "You got that app Pinpoint installed on your phone. My sister and her husband use it. That way, she can call him when he's passing the grocery store and ask him to grab milk," she says with a giggle.

"Wait. What are you talking about?"

Her face falls, and suddenly the bubbly sales girl disappears into someone a little more uncomfortable. "Ah, it's an app, to like, track someone's phone. It's not one that like monitors your texts and emails or stuff like that, though."

Geez, you can do that to people? I shake my head. "But I didn't install that."

"Oh, well, sometimes people secretly install them on their spouse's phone to find out if they're cheating on them."

My eyes fill with tears, and I have to choke back a sob.

Now she looks like she'd like to close up shop early and run home. "Ah, it looks like it was installed recently."

I flash back to the day Rock met me after the CLE. Because of the Tony Cain fiasco and then the Greybell attack, I never did figure out how he'd found me there.

Sonofabitch!

Rock

I felt like shit for ruining the nice dinner Hope made and leaving her to eat alone. When this bullshit is over, I'll think of a way to make it up to her.

I tried to get out of this meet. Spent forever on the fuckin' phone trying to handle it from home. Fucking Green Street Crew. I'm tired of these little bitches jerkin' me around. It's why I've been workin' so damn hard to line up an alternate pipeline so we're not so dependent on these street punks.

Wrath is twisted as fuck that he can't be at this meet. I'm not sure what poor Trinity had to do in order to keep him calm and at the clubhouse, but she's someone else I'm going to have to show some appreciation real soon.

Would I feel better with Wrath there? Absolutely. Do I trust the rest of my guys? No doubt.

There's no time to drive all the way to the MC, so we meet up in the parking lot of Crystal Ball.

Z, Dex, Murphy, and Bricks are waiting for me when I pull up. Teller is still dealing with Heidi drama, so I told him to stay put. Besides, if I bring too many guys, it will give GSC the impression they make me nervous. Z and Dex get in the SUV with me, while Murphy and Bricks will take their bikes. I don't have to ask if everyone is armed. I do ask Z if he's wearing a vest. He answers by yanking up his sweatshirt to show me the Kevlar.

"Who did you talk to, Z?"

"Some punk named Cheeky."

I shake my head. "All to meet up with Gunner?"

"I think so. Jesus Christ, if I wanted to be dragged out of my house at all hours, I woulda been a doctor like my mama wanted," Z snarks.

"I thought your mom wanted you to be a construction worker?" Dex asks from the back seat.

Z turns and flashes a grin. "Yeah, when she realized I wasn't smart enough to be a doctor, she had to adjust."

I knock him back to his side of the truck. "My gain."

Z snorts.

"How pissed is Wrath?" I ask.

Dex chuckles. In my rear view, I spot him shaking his head.

Z's the one to answer, though. "Fuckin' livid, bro. Holy shit. You better go up there when we're done."

"Christ, I gotta check in with him like I'm a little fuckin kid?"

"This shit sucks all around," Z says without any humor.

"I hear that."

I steer the truck into Riverwalk Park, back to our usual meeting spot. Murphy and Bricks are right behind me. I spot a silver Cadillac and a black SUV farther back. I park near the exit facing out. Z gets out first and scans the area. Four GSC kids pop out of the SUV and Z's body goes rigid, his hand moving to his back. Coming up alongside him, I tell him to chill under my breath.

As soon as I got out, one of the kids opened the Cadillac door, and I'm shocked as shit by who steps out.

"Loco, the fuck you doing here?" I call to the GSC street boss, closing the distance between us. His four little soldiers get all twitchy with their weapons, which makes my guys twitchy with theirs.

"Break off," Loco shouts to his crew. I wave a hand at mine. Z comes up along side me.

"The fuck?" he mutters.

Loco is a tall, skinny black kid who doesn't look all that

threatening. But he didn't get that name by accident. Street crews shake in their boots at the sound of his name. I respect the guy as far as we do business together. I don't give a single fuck about him otherwise. He certainly doesn't scare me. Then again, few people do.

I am curious about why the fuck he dragged me out here tonight, though.

"What's goin' on?"

He holds his hand out to give me one of his gangster handshakes. "How you doin' Rock, it's been a minute."

"Yeah."

His gaze slips to Z and he nods. "'Sup VP?"

"Loco," Z answers, with his own nod.

While Loco takes a second to survey my crew, I do the same. I spot Pinky and Kidd, but no Gunner.

Shocking.

Loco snaps his fingers, and a chunky, pasty kid shuffles forward. He's got the gangster swagger down, but other than that, he looks as if he spends too much time sitting around inhaling cheeseburgers.

I'm seriously bored with this whole situation.

"I want you to meet Cheeky. He's takin' the drops from now on."

I raise an eyebrow at that. "Gunner move up?" I ask, even though I'm fairly certain the answer is a big, fat "fuck no."

Loco snorts. "Not exactly. More like what they call," he glances at the shrubbery obscuring our view of the highway, "a lateral move."

In their world, that could mean anything. I don't care enough to press for more details.

I hold out my hand for Cheeky, who seeks Loco's permission before taking it.

"Rock, I had another reason for this meet. I hear you tryin' to move some stuff out West. If your crew got more product, I was hoping you'd offer it to us first before looking for other buyers."

This is completely unwelcome news. Why the fuck Loco is up in my business is very concerning.

I shrug. "Thought you guys were tapped out."

"No."

"Where'd you hear that story?"

He gives me a level stare and cocks his head. "Let's take a walk."

Z bristles next to me. "It's fine," I tell him.

"Play nice," Loco cautions Cheeky.

I nod to Dex, Murphy, and Bricks for them to join Z. "Mingle."

Z shakes his head. "You leave my eyesight, I'm coming after you."

"Got it."

I jam my hands in my pockets and nod at Loco. We take a leisurely walk down to the river. The air has a bite to it, and the gentle rippling of the Hudson is completely at odds with what's going on inside my head.

When we've gone far enough for our voices not to carry back to the rest of our crews, we stop and face each other. Not a lick of fear runs through me. Fuck, nothing is running through me. Mild curiosity mixed with a hint of irritation, maybe.

"Look, Rock, I know you think we're just a bunch of street punks," he starts, then nods when I don't agree or disagree. "That's true for a lot of them. Me, I grew up with a different mindset. I got bigger ambitions."

"Okay."

"I'm telling you this so you understand why I know the shit I know. I ain't fuckin' playin', man. You got access to more product, we want it."

I keep my face completely neutral even though I'm seriously fucking pissed. "No problem. I thought you had all you could handle."

"Yeah, Gunner was fuckin' lazy."

"Kidd and Pinky ain't much more helpful, from where I'm standing."

He narrows his cold eyes at me. "Kidd's my blood, man."

I don't give an inch. "Sometimes blood is the most unfaithful and disloyal relation you'll ever have." I'm not fucking joking either. No one can fuck you over worse than blood relatives.

He takes a step back and looks at me like my words made him shit his pants.

"I got mad respect for you, Rock. Your fuckin' crew is solid. Loyal. I want to understand how you made that happen."

Seriously? I don't even have words for how surreal this

conversation is. Is he telling me he took a run at one of my brothers and came up empty? The thought that he might have tried makes me want to empty my clip in him right this second.

"We've been through a lot of bad shit together. Trust. Like you said, loyalty. Always got each other's backs."

Loco nods at me like there has to be more to the story. It's like he's asking me to explain what makes a good human being and what makes a bad one. I don't fucking know. It depends on your perspective. I'm sure your average citizen thinks I'm a lowlife criminal, while a more hardcore criminal might think I'm a sopping wet pussy.

"You're confident that if I stepped to you right this second your guys would put a bullet in each one of my guys' brains, right?" he asks.

Yeah, I'm not liking this conversation. At all.

"I ain't threatening you, Rock. I've got genuine curiosity."

"Something like that."

"What's your end goal?"

"Family, freedom. I don't give a shit about much more than that, Loco."

"Not money?"

"Got that."

"Not enough that you don't have to roll out to meet me."

I snort at that. "You got me there." I think more about what he's actually saying. "You trying to tell me you wanna be a kingpin, Loco?" There's a sarcastic edge to my voice, but Loco either doesn't catch it or straight up ignores it.

"Yeah, man. And I think you can be a part of that."

Aw, I'm flattered.

"You got a woman, Rock?" When I don't answer, he chuckles. "By that face you makin', you dizzy on some dame enough that you want to slit my throat for even askin' 'bout her. Why just one, when you can have your pick of them fuckin' dancers you got in your club?"

"Are you asking for dating advice?"

That makes Loco laugh pretty fuckin' hard. "No."

If this conversation goes on much longer, no amount of breathing exercises will stop me from killing this fuck. "How much more weight can you handle?"

"All you got."

I stare at him. "You know we're a small operation."

"Not that fuckin' small from where I'm standin'. Best shit in the state. Probably the East Coast."

I don't doubt it. Sparky takes his crops seriously. But I don't like the idea of Loco talking us up to anyone outside of the area.

"I got a few other obligations, but I'll talk to Sparky. We can probably come up with five crates on the same schedule."

"That'll work, man. Why you wanna cart that shit out West, when we be right here?"

"Told you, thought you were at capacity."

"These other obligations?"

This I won't budge on. "MC ties, non-negotiable."

"Even if I could triple what you're getting?"

Fuck. "Yeah, even then."

"See, a man who isn't motivated by money unnerves me, Rock. I don't get that mindset."

There's a lot of shit about Loco I don't "get" nor do I ever want to. "To what end do you want the money, Loco?"

"Dude, I won't rest 'til I'm sittin on a big ol' pile o' cash. You feel me?"

"Sure." Yup, known plenty of guys like that.

"Besides that, it's security for me and my kids. You got kids, Rock?"

"No."

"Ah, maybe that's why you're so content. You got a kid, man, you look in their eyes and want to do better for them than was ever done for you. Make sure they don't struggle."

Holy fuck. All right. He's most definitely some sort of sociopath, but I guess Loco's not a complete soulless fuck. Good to know.

"Everyone's gotta struggle a little bit, Loco, or they never appreciate what they have."

He stops and takes that in. "Yeah, good point."

We walk back up to the guys and work out the logistics of the new arrangements with Cheeky. I'm feeling some serious what-the-fuck coming from Z. I'm assuming he thinks the club should have voted this.

Loco dismisses his guys, and I nod for everyone except Z to hang back.

"You cool working with Cheeky?" Loco asks.

I'm shocked he cares about my opinion. Cheeky seems soft and easy to manipulate so…"Yeah, I'm good."

"Cool."

He gives me another gangster handshake. "Let's not wait so long to meet up again."

Yeah, I can't wait.

Hope

I'm not as fond of the f-word as Rock is. To him, it's a medium he uses to create all sorts of artful expressions.

Fuck, fuck, fuck!

My use of the word tends to be more prosaic.

Rock fucking bugged my phone. Holy frick! Did I suddenly end up in some twisted, made-for-television movie and no one told me?

That Rock thinks I would ever cheat on him and he needs to monitor me makes me completely rage-crazed. Like, I wish to God I had the same app installed on his phone, so I could track him down and choke the life out of his Cro-Magnon, cave-dwelling ass.

There's no way in hell I am driving back to his house. I don't want to go to my house, though, either, because I'm sure it's the first place he'll look when he realizes I didn't come back to his house.

I honestly think this it for me. The last straw. Time to get off this ride of crazy before I end up sequestered away at the MC tied to his fucking bed like a damn hostage.

This shit actually scares me.

After finding out that he tagged me like some damn dog—on top of the fact that he took off to do who-knows-what dangerous mission tonight—I think I've had enough. As I check into the nearest Holiday

Inn, I'm filled with a grim glee that he's going to freak the fuck out when he can't find me.

Rock

Hope hasn't answered my calls or texts, so I assume she gave up waiting for me and went to bed. At least I want that to be true. The more likely scenario is she's pissed at me and not answering on purpose.

She can be cute that way.

My ass is dragging as I drive Z and Dex back to CB. Dex gives me a fist bump before he leaves. Z sticks around.

"Prez, the fuck?"

"I don't like it any more than you, brother."

The more I think of the conversation, the less I like what I heard. My takeaway is this: Loco is a goddamn sociopath. While he might like me or even respect me in his own twisted way, he'd have no problem gutting me if I was standing between him and a slice of his favorite cake. The fact that he basically ascertained the only way to hurt me—through my loved ones—is also not sitting well.

Suddenly any games Hope might be playing don't seem as funny.

I'm consumed with an urgent need to see her.

"Listen, I didn't like some of the shit he was saying. How he knows what feelers we got out there ain't exactly making me happy. I also got the impression he tried to pry some info out of one of us, and since no one has stepped up and said anything, I'm concerned."

Z blows out a long breath

"That's bad."

His phone buzzes in his hand. "It's Wrath." He answers and puts it on speaker phone.

"What the motherfuck, Z? I've been going nuts. Everyone whole?" his voice booms through the car.

Normally, I'd have a good chuckle over his reaction, but I'm not feeling very comical tonight. "We're good, brother," I answer.

"Rock, you dick. You coulda at least let me ride along."

"And do what, watch if Loco decided to blow us up?"

"Fuck you. I'm not an invalid. What are you talking about? Loco came?"

"Yeah. Wanted to introduce Gunner's replacement."

Wrath snorts. "Knew that little shit wouldn't last long."

"Also wanted to let me know he was onto our Western connection and that he wants it."

"Fuuuck."

"Yeah."

"You tell him yes for now?"

"Of course," I answer, throwing a glance at Z.

"I'll call everyone in for church tomorrow," Wrath says.

"I'll do it, brother. It's my job," Z answers.

"We seem to have flipped jobs, bro, if you haven't noticed," Wrath says with a glum laugh.

Catching Z's eye, I shake my head slightly. Let Wrath do this.

"Thanks man," Z says.

"You guys comin' back here?" Wrath asks.

My hesitation says everything. "Fucking bring her with you, Rock. I'm sure Trin wouldn't mind some alternate company."

I choke on a laugh over that. I'm sure she'd be relieved to hang out with someone else.

"Tomorrow, I promise."

We sign off, and Z glances at me. "Is Hope doing okay?"

"Yeah."

He slaps me on the shoulder as he gets out. "Go give her a special wake-up call, prez."

"I plan to."

I do not plan to come home and find Hope's car gone from my driveway. Storming inside, I find the place cleaned up and a note waiting on the counter for me.

Broke phone. Running to mall to get a new one.

Love, Me.

So that explains why she didn't answer any of my texts earlier. Maybe. Since it's almost midnight and she's not back yet, my stomach churns. The mall closes at ten. It's less than five miles from my house. There is no way she shouldn't be back by now.

Maybe she came back and got pissed when she realized I was still out?

Something's wrong.

I got that fucking conversation with Loco messing with my mind. Asking about my woman. Trying to get inside my head. He could have had his crew come here and nab Hope while I was at that bullshit meet and greet. I pull out my personal phone and call up the app that will give me an idea of where to find my girl. When I had Z install it on her phone, I swore I'd only use it when necessary.

Now feels very fucking necessary.

I get nothing. Nothing. No blip. No message saying "unavailable at this time." Nothing.

My eyes drift to the note. Fuckingfuck! The fucking app won't be on her new phone. I try calling her, and it goes straight to a generic voicemail. Jesus Christ, this is the worst possible timing.

I glance at the note and then my phone again. No.

Maybe she needed to go to her house for some reason.

She's not at her house.

I don't have Sophie's number on me, but I do remember where she lives. It's really fucking late by the time I get there. No sign of Hope's car. I struggle with whether I should wake Sophie up, but after that scene at the Judge's fundraiser, I decide it's wiser not to. She's an extra complication I don't have the patience for right now.

God dammit. Instead of tracking Hope's phone, I should have rigged her fuckin' car.

I swing by her office on my way home just in case, but the parking lot is empty. I manage to grab maybe an hour of sleep before I head back to Hope's house and wait.

At ten in the morning, she rolls into the driveway.

Shock, clear as day, is written all over her face when she sees me.

Her body is tight and controlled, even though she's pretending to be carefree.

I amble up to her. "Mind telling me where you've been?"

"Oh, couldn't you track me on your phone?" she questions in that angry-sarcastic way of hers that usually gets me rock hard in two seconds.

Not today.

"No."

She unlocks the door and miraculously lets me inside. Well, I follow her in so close, she doesn't have a choice. I seem to be doing that a lot lately.

As soon as we're inside, she whirls around and starts grilling me. "So you admit you installed an app on my phone to track me?"

"Yes."

I figure honesty will keep her simmering anger from boiling over. She's got me. No point lying.

"How can you think I would ever cheat on you?"

Okay, that's unexpected. "What?"

"I'm with you all the time—"

"Baby, that's not why. I'm worried about you." Doesn't Hope realize by now how much I fucking care about her? I know how loyal my girl is. I'd never spend a second thinking she'd step out on me. "What if Greybell had succeeded in throwing you in his trunk and I needed to find you?"

She cocks her head.

I try to explain it another way. "I worry about something happening to you—"

Her face twists in anger. "This. This right here, Rock, is why I can't move in with you. This scares me."

Thunk—the sensation of my heart free-falling into my stomach. Hope scared of me fucking hurts.

"Baby, how can you say that? I want to make sure you're safe."

"Because it's fucking creepy!" she explodes.

I can't figure this out. "It's not a way for me to spy on you. But if something happened and I needed to find you, that's the only time I would use it."

"You should have asked me, told me, talked to me about it. Not just do it behind my back."

"I got enemies, Hope."

I don't want to scare her, so I stop there. But this shit last night with GSC. Our beef with the Vipers getting stirred up again. The crash after the fight. Hope going out alone all the time to meet her clients. Clients fucking attacking her in her own damn office, for fuck's sake...I need this extra protection on my girl. I can't tell her all of this, though. I don't want to risk her deciding it's too dangerous for us to be together.

"I'm not a fucking dog you can micro-chip, Rock. I'm a human being. It's like you don't respect me at all."

Now I'm pissed. I respect her more than any woman I've ever known. Love her more than any person—ever.

"It's not about respect. You're everything to me, Hope. I don't want anything to happen to you."

She falters, her anger disappearing for a second. "I don't want anything to happen to you, so where's my app? Where's my way to track you down if something bad happens to you—which by the way, is far more likely, Mr. leaves-the-house-all-hours-of-the-night-without-telling-me-why."

What she's suggesting is fucking insane. Holy fuck. That's all I would have needed last night was Hope—lovely, beautiful but reckless Hope—rolling up on Loco and his trigger twitchy crew during our bizarre friendly, but not so friendly, standoff. "That would be a bad idea, Hope," I say as plainly as possible.

"Of course it would be. You'd never want me to know where you are." Her furious face is red but still beautiful, and for a moment I'm distracted. She waggles her fingers in the air between us, drawing my attention to her words. "We're not equals in this."

"Jesus Christ! It's not about that at all, Hope."

"Then explain it to me."

"I can't."

She pauses and considers my refusal before asking her next question. "Would you do something like this to Wrath?"

"What? How is that even relevant?"

"Would you spy on him without telling him?" she persists.

"I wasn't spying on you!"

"Answer me."

"Babe, no one is going to kidnap him. It's not the same thing."

"I can't tell if you're being deliberately obtuse or you really are this dense. Either way, I need you to leave."

She folds her arms over her chest.

"No."

She arches a brow at me. "No?"

"I didn't do anything wrong, Hope."

She strides over and opens the door. "Get out. You went too far this time, Rock. I'm done. I can't do this anymore. Please go."

Words fail me, so I walk out the door.

CHAPTER TWENTY-TWO

HOPE

AFTER ROCK FINALLY, RELUCTANTLY—VERY RELUCTANTLY—LEAVES, I FLOP onto my bed and collapse into tears. I am weak. I am such a girl. It hurts. It feels wrong to even think it, but the pain is uncomfortably close to how I felt after Clay's death.

How do people do this? How do they go on and survive after bigger tragedies than I've been through? I don't know. I don't have it in me, I guess.

After a few hours of wallowing, I snap on the bedside lamp and stare at the bedroom. Clay's side is still intact. I pull on a pair of sweats and a T-shirt and finally do what I should have done months ago. Sifting through Clay's clothes seems like the easiest place to start, but it's not. Most of the things in his closet have a musty tinge to them from sitting so long, untouched. But a few sweaters still have enough of his scent clinging to them that I burst into tears. I set those aside for now and pack the rest into boxes. The criminal defense bar has a program where you can donate 'professional' type clothing for defendants to wear to trial—instead of the prejudice-inducing orange jumpsuits they might otherwise wear. That's where I'm going to send

Clay's business casual clothing and suits. I feel good about myself once I make that decision, and the sorting and packing goes much smoother.

When I run out of boxes and garbage bags, I stop. As I look around at all the bags and boxes, I'm thrilled with the progress I've made.

Rock will—wait. Rock will nothing, because I told him we were over.

It makes sense for me to get rid of these things. This house. Pare it all down to nothing and find an apartment. No other man I might want to date will tolerate the shadow of my dead husband hanging around.

Other man? There are no other men compared to Rock. How can there be another man?

He's it, and I know it.

I've been making him put up with all my grief and guilt. He's done it and not said a word. Been very sweet and understanding, even though it probably kills him. That shows me just how much he does respect me. If I stopped my righteous indignation long enough to grasp it.

Dammit.

We still need to talk about this overwhelming need to protect me and go behind my back to keep track of me. I'm so not okay with that. If he'd just told me, explained it, I probably would have thought it was sweet, like the girl in the cellphone shop did. But by being sneaky, it made it ugly and infuriating.

Still, there were better ways I could have explained it.

Now he's gone.

Rock

I can't stand going back to my house. If I catch Hope's scent on my sheets, I will lose my fucking mind.

Wrath spots me the minute I step in the front door of the clubhouse.

"Where you been, fucker?" is his idea of a greeting.

Through hell is what I want to answer, but I don't.

"Why you waiting around for me like a nervous momma?" I ask instead.

Wrath curves his body to the side in an exaggerated movement. "Where's your girl? Thought she was comin' with."

My jaw clenches, but before I can come up with any reasonable excuse, Z thunders down the stairs.

"'Sup, prez?" He also glances at the empty air behind me. "Where's Hope?"

Shrugging off my cut, I storm into the war room, ignoring both of them. I'm not about to sit down and talk about my feelings with my brothers.

Not fucking happening.

I can hear the two fuckers out in the living room clucking about my dickish behavior.

Fuck.

Both their heads snap up when I bump into the couch. I drop down opposite from where they're sitting. "Hope's a little pissed at me."

And isn't that the understatement of the year?

For the second time in two weeks, she told me to "get out." Shouted it at me, actually.

This time I don't think there's any repairing it. You went too far this time, Rock. I'm done. I can't do this anymore.

"What'd you do now, Rock?" Z asks. He's asking as my friend, not my VP.

I look up, catching his eye. "She found the app I had you install."

"Fuck, man, how? I buried it deep—"

Poor Z's gonna get himself all worked into a fit if he thinks he fucked something up. I wave my hand in the air. "No. The phone broke and she had to take it up to the store—"

Z nods, satisfied it's not his fault.

Wrath has his face screwed into an incredulous expression. "Wait a second. You put a tracking app on Hope's phone and didn't tell her about it?"

Surprised Wrath cares so much, I just nod.

"Whoa. I mean I get why you didn't ask her, but to not even tell her? Bro, that's fucked up." Then he turns away and mutters, "and everyone thinks *I'm* the asshole 'round here," loud enough for me to hear.

"Big help, bro, thanks," I tell him in my most sarcastic if-you-weren't-my-best-friend-I'd-kill-you voice.

"You jacked Trin's phone," Z points out to Wrath.

His face transforms into one that has made lesser men shit their pants. Z is oblivious. "Technically you did, asshole. Besides, that's different," Wrath growls.

"She's club property," Z says with a grin that is about to get his teeth knocked down his throat by the look on Wrath's face.

"It's different because I told her we did it. She wasn't surprised. But she grew up in this life and understands." He swings his glacial gaze back my way. "Hope is citizen, Rock. You keep trying to integrate her into our world, but you're not straight with her. Women like her get offended by that shit."

Anyone who looks at Wrath and assumes he's all brawn and no brain is seriously fucking stupid. Brother is apparently smarter than I am. Well, sometimes.

"How you gonna fix it?" Z asks.

She gave me the way. It's a pretty fucking big gesture. Impossible really.

"I don't know."

CHAPTER TWENTY-THREE

ROCK

I'M TWISTED THE FUCK UP AND EXHAUSTED BY THE SHIT GOING ON BETWEEN Hope and me.

So it's the worst time to get the okay for something I've been waiting on for a while now. The Superintendent of Southaven Supermax has finally determined I am fit to visit the only member of my charter currently inside.

Because my Road Captain and Treasurer have nice, squeaky clean records, they usually make the trip out to Central New York to visit Grinder. But the old goat keeps asking for me, and the right thing to do is honor his request.

My record is not so spotless, so like a good little productive member of society, I sought permission in writing from the Superintendent to visit my former sponsor.

Permission granted.

It's been a few years since we've had a face-to-face. We went into the slightly more pleasant Eastwood Correctional together. I did my damnedest to get the fuck out and never go back inside, while Grinder —well, he sought protection for us from some very expensive sources.

The things they demanded of him are what got him the ticket to Southaven.

So yeah, I've got a bit of guilt about the fact that I'm out free enjoying my life, while Grinder is sitting in one of the shittiest prisons —literally—New York State has to offer. Some of that guilt is offset by the fact that I never should have gone inside for what I ultimately got nailed for.

But not much.

Inside or not, Grinder is still a brother. Forever Kings, Kings Forever. We do what we can for him from outside. We keep his offender account plush so he can get whatever he wants from the commissary. His ol' lady, Rose, has nothing to do with the MC any more. Wants it that way. I still check on her from time to time. Make sure she has whatever she needs. She's not so fond of my face or voice. Any reminder of LOKI really. So she gets a check in the mail. They never get returned.

We have a private attorney working on Grinder's appeals, even though all of us know it's pretty much a dead end. He's done so much bad shit on the inside—hence the extended vacation at Southaven— that his original conviction could be outright overturned—null and void—and he'd still be inside for years to come.

Since I've had a couple near misses in the last few years, maybe this trip to the Supermax will do me some good. Remind me why I work so damn hard to keep myself and my brothers straddling the line between legal and illegal, rather than falling headfirst into bad shit that might bring fucktons of quick, easy cash but also the potential for lots of years spent in places like this shithole.

Christ, my rage-fueled brother Wrath wouldn't last a day inside without beating the fuck out of someone and getting thrown in solitary for an extended vacation of his own.

Since I took control of the Lost Kings, I've worked hard to insulate myself with people in positions that can help me and my brothers avoid Grinder's fate. If New York ever gets its head out of its ass and legalizes weed, I'd sleep a lot easier. I already have things in place to turn us legit as soon the legislature and governor give the green light.

Yeah, it's a long drive out in my comfortable but unfamiliar rental car, so I have lots of time to think over all this shit.

And avoid thinking about where I stand with Hope.

I left my cut at home. I'd like to avoid the hassle of an ass-probing strip search, so I'm in complete compliance with the facility's endless visitor rules and guidelines. Besides my ink, nothing on my body associates me with LOKI. No jewelry. No thinly veiled logos or sayings. Nothing. And it feels fucking weird. Like my identity is somewhere in limbo back in Empire, waiting for me to return. I've got a simple, plain black sweatshirt on and black track pants. No zippers or buttons to attract the attention of the metal detector. No pockets to attract the hands of the guards. I'm even wearing plain black underwear, since the rules specifically stated visitors should be wearing underwear. I don't even want to ponder what incident led them to including that in the official guidelines.

The scene inside is as depressing as I expected. I suffer a bit of guilt over making Teller and Murphy do this trip every month. They barely knew Grinder. But at least maybe it helps them understand why I prefer to avoid the things I do.

I timed my trip so I'd get here right after count, and the waiting area is full of visitors who had the same idea. Voluntarily walking myself inside a prison is not sitting well with me, but I suck it the fuck up and make my way through the metal detectors. The visiting room I'm escorted to is different than I expected. No metal cage separating us. Regular tables and chairs. I guess Grinder's been behaving himself.

I stand up to greet him. We're allowed a quick handshake before the guards gesture for us to sit down.

Time inside has not been kind to my friend. At six-two, he's always been a big guy, but now he's thin and gray.

"Long fucking time, Rock," he greets me in the same slow, rumbling voice I remember.

"Yeah," I agree, because what else am I going to say? He knows why I haven't come to visit.

"I hear the MC is doing well."

"We're solid."

"Thanks for making sure my account is full."

"Of course."

"You seen Rosie lately?"

"No, man. She don't want to see anyone associated with the MC."

"You take care of her?"

"Send her money. She takes it."

He nods. "That's good."

"She come visit?"

"Never. Don't want her to see me here."

I can understand that. That's kind of a dead end conversation topic.

"So what'd you do to get into the fancy visiting room?"

His mouth quirks, and a hint of the guy I remember makes a brief appearance.

"Got myself up to level three now. Comes with all sorts of privileges. Even allowed to wear my own underwear, instead of that state-issued crap."

It feels horrifically inappropriate to laugh, but I chuckle anyway. Grinder seems to appreciate it.

"That's good, man."

"It is. There's talk I might get shipped back to a regular facility to finish out my sentence."

"No shit?"

"Hoping I can transfer down to Pine."

"That would be nice. A lot closer, so more of the guys could come visit."

"Please, they're all too young to even remember me now."

I snort at that. It's not really true. The guys remember Grinder. We just don't talk about him a lot.

"How's Wrath?"

"Ornery as ever."

"Z?"

"Still sticking his dick in anything that moves."

"You?"

I'm not sure how I feel about discussing Hope with Grinder. Part of me doesn't want to rub my happiness in his face. Part of me doesn't want anyone inside these walls even knowing she exists and that she's important to me.

"Been seeing a girl for a little while."

He cocks an eyebrow at me. "Club girl?"

"Nah. Farthest thing from it."

"How's that working out?"

I almost choke on the answer. "Most days, pretty damn good. Sometimes, a little rough."

Real fucking rough.

He nods thoughtfully. "Rosie didn't know shit about MCs before we met."

"I remember you telling me that." Seemed strange to me, even back then. Now it's uncomfortably familiar.

From what I remember, Grinder's ol' lady was in med school when they met. Way he told it, she hopped on the back of his bike and never looked back.

"So fucking smart." He shakes his head, flexes his hands. "Bet she wishes she'd never met my dumb ass, never left med school. She'd probably be a doctor with a nice little private practice like she always wanted, if it hadn't been for me."

"That was her choice."

He gives me a level stare. "Nah. Hated anything that took her away from me. Made her fucking miserable until she quit."

That's some pretty heavy self-realization Grinder's got going on. I guess sitting in a cell for twenty-three hours a day, six days a week by yourself will do that to a guy—if it doesn't drive him insane first. Turning over his words, I can't help but think about my own situation. I'd never do that to Hope. In fact, I keep trying to push her back into her career. Still, this whole conversation is stirring up a storm inside of me.

A big one.

"If I ever get the fuck outta here, you gonna have a place for me?"

"Of course. What kind of question is that?"

He shrugs. "Nice to have something to look forward to."

We talk a while longer. Nothing of any consequence, but I sense he just enjoys the company. Again, I feel like shit for not coming out more often. The guards let me grab a bunch of snacks from the vending machines, so for the rest of the visit we consume a lot of crap that comes out of crinkly wrappers. At three-thirty, all the visitors are kicked out. Grinder promises to keep me up to date on his transfer request. I promise I'll be back out to see him soon.

I intend to keep that promise.

My body feels like it's connected to a live wire the whole ride home. I have never been so fuckin' anxious to get off the road. Everything in me is screaming to go see my girl and fix this fuckery between us before I lose her for good.

Hope doesn't want to see me. She made that damn clear. I can't stand this, though. I have to see her. I just need the right excuse.

The perfect plan comes to me, and I discard it immediately. The guys will slit my throat if they ever find out.

It's a bad fucking idea. But I can't shake it.

I think it's the last play I've got.

Hope

I miss Rock like crazy.

I'm trying so hard to understand him. Why he does the things he does. Our relationship has been so complicated from the very beginning. Even after my husband's death. Rock and I have such differing viewpoints on so many things.

The one thing we certainly agree on is sex. The sex is freaking amazing.

But is that enough?

Almost immediately I'm ready to kick my own butt. We have more than sex. He sees things in me I don't even recognize and loves me for them. Although his life with the club confuses me, I respect his devotion to the people he considers his "family." He cares about something bigger than himself, and over the years I've found that to be a rare quality in people. Anyone can spout off nonsense about how they'd die for their loved ones, but Rock means it right down to his very soul. It's hard not to admire that level of commitment.

His obsession with keeping me safe comes from a good place. A place of protecting me, not controlling me. There's a difference, and I know in my heart he's on the right side of that very thin line.

I'm not sure what to do about it, though. Every day that goes by without a word from him scares me. Maybe I finally pushed him away for good. Maybe he's decided I'm too much work, and he's back to his former ways of screwing dancers and club girls who aren't so complicated and pissy.

The thought makes me sick.

I need something to take my mind off of our situation. A distraction in the form of my crazy friend Lilly would be perfect.

It only makes sense that since we both work downtown, Lilly and I would occasionally get together for lunch. Yet for some reason, we never do. Now that I am down here more frequently but still don't have a lot of clients, I have more free time on my hands, so when she asks me to come meet her, I'm happy to say yes.

Lunch with Lilly should help me take my mind of the situation with Rock. I feel like I'm dangerously close to caving in to every one of his demands, and I don't like what that says about me.

Sophie is traveling again this week, so it will just be the two of us. Or so I think. When I finally make my way through the concourse to the food court where many state workers spend their lunch hour, she's sitting with a straight-laced younger guy I don't recognize.

"Hope! Over here." She stands up and waves frantically. I take a second to adjust to the sight of Professional Lilly. Boobs snuggled down under layers of fabric, hair twisted into a professional knot, skirt an inch below her knees. I glance down at my own pants and blouse and feel a little underdressed next to her, which is pretty hysterical when you think about it.

"Hey, hon." Lilly leans over and gives me a quick hug. She gestures to her companion. "This is Brad. We work together sometimes and ran into each other on the way down, so I invited him." She gives me an I'm-sorry-I-hope-you're-not-mad face. "Brad, this is my friend, Hope."

He actually stands up to greet me and shake my hand. "Nice to meet you."

"You too." My gaze darts around the cafeteria. "Anything here that won't make me want to barf?" I ask Lilly.

She squints and points to the far, back corner. "The deli. They make great sandwiches."

"'Kay. I'll be right back."

I'm anxious because I know Lilly only gets an hour for lunch and it takes forever to place my order.

When I return, they're both talking about someone I don't know. Work stuff, I guess.

"So, what do you do, Hope?"

My mouth is full of turkey sandwich, so Lilly answers for me. "She's a lawyer."

Brad raises an eyebrow. "Nice. What do you practice?"

My nose wrinkles, but I give my standard answer before asking him, "You?"

"I'm a consultant with Empire Canvassing."

"Don't let him fool you—he's a dirty lobbyist," Lilly says with a dramatic head shake.

My lips curve up at the generic sounding name of his firm. "What are you lobbying for?"

He rolls his eyes in obvious delight and gives me a broad grin. "A new tech company that manufactures grow house equipment."

My blank look seems to amuse both of them. "They're lobbying to legalize pot in New York," Lilly explains.

"Why are tech companies interested in that?"

I get the impression Brad is not impressed with my intellect. "Big money to be made in the states that are legalizing. Think about it. You've heard of NORML, right?"

"Sure."

"Well, they've been pushing for marijuana reform for years with no movement. But these investors and lobbyists who are backed by big-money have managed to propel some of the legislation forward in no time."

I think about some of my clients—heck, Rock being one of them— getting dragged through the criminal justice system for stupid, simple pot possession. "I guess if that's what it takes to finally get some sensible laws and stop sending people to prison for something so silly, it's a good thing."

Brad seems surprised. I guess he thought I'd be judgmental. "Our firm works on other stuff too. This is just a big deal at the moment."

We talk about some other topics. Lilly mentions a movie she wants to see. Brad awkwardly asks me out. Thankfully, Lilly saves the day. "Oh, Hope's got a big, scary biker boyfriend, Brad. Sorry."

Brad's definitely shocked. I'm a little shocked myself because I'm close to bawling at the table. I'm not actually sure I still have a boyfriend anymore, scary or otherwise. I keep this to myself, though.

"You don't seem like a biker babe," Brad says without apology.

Heat creeps over my cheeks. "I wasn't."

"He's not just a regular badass, he's an MC President," Lilly brags.

Brad quirks an eyebrow at me. "I hope it's the Wolf Knights or the Lost Kings. The Vipers don't have the best reputation where women are concerned."

What the—

The question must be visible all over my face. "Our firm lobbies for some other interests as well. I know more about this area than you can imagine, Hope. So which one is it? I hear Mr. North is a clever businessman, but someone you don't want to cross, and Mr. Hunt is a gentleman, but he's got a nasty streak if you fuck with his family."

Good grief, my boyfriend has quite a reputation. "Uh, Rochlan North."

"Please don't tell him I asked you out," he says with an absolutely straight face.

Lilly bursts out laughing. Brad and I do not.

CHAPTER TWENTY-FOUR

ROCK

I'M NOT THRILLED WITH THE REPORT I GET FROM HOOT.

Yeah, I'm risking pissing Hope off for good by still having her followed, but I'm fucking worried about her. Greybell finally made bail, and I'm not taking a chance he will come back to finish what he started. From what I've been able to figure out, his family shuttled him away to a mental hospital.

He best fucking stay put.

I don't know if Hope is aware of his release. It's not like she would change her routine even if she did.

She's stubborn that way.

However, I'm annoyed with today's report from Hoot for different reasons.

She's having lunch with Lilly and some guy Hoot doesn't recognize. Although I know Lilly enjoys playing the field, I'm concerned she might have taken it upon herself to set Hope up on a date.

The idea kicks my fuckin' ass into gear.

When Hoot tells me it looks like she left the office for the night, I ask him to tail her until the turn off for her house. He gives me the call that she's almost here, and I steel myself for what's about to go down.

This has to go right. Fucking up isn't an option.

Headlights wash over me, and I squint into the light, relieved when I recognize Hope's car. She barely has the key out before she opens her door.

"Rock?"

"It's me." Shit, I didn't want to scare her.

The soft slam of her car door, gentle clicking of her heels over the pavement are just background noise compared to her voice. "Why are you here?"

"To talk."

"Oh."

She's close enough for me to see the corners of her mouth turn down. Without inviting me inside, she opens the door. I follow in right behind her, just in case.

After setting her things down, she leans against the kitchen counter. She folds her arms over her chest and nods at me.

Fuck, this is hard. "I wanted to give you this," I say, while digging into my pocket for the small rectangular box.

Her eyes fill with confusion as she stretches out one hand to take it. She slides the box open and stares at what's inside for a beat before speaking. "A phone?"

"Uh, yeah. I can have your number switched over to it later if you want." This is awkward enough without getting bogged down in the technicalities.

"Okay."

"Turn it on."

She fiddles around with it for a minute or so before the screen lights up.

"Now what?"

I hold out my hand, and she moves closer to give me the phone. Standing side by side, when I haven't been near Hope in what feels like forever, momentarily distracts me. Finally, I manage to call up the screen I need. There's a small blue heart steadily blinking at the center. I hand the phone back to her, and when her fingers brush against mine, it's a fight not to crush her against me for a scorching kiss.

"What is that?" She takes the phone from me, studying the screen. "Is that a…map? That's my house." Her questioning eyes meet mine.

I pull out my phone to show her the same screen, mine with a pink heart blinking—her.

"You…You're giving me the same thing?" My chest tightens at the sound of her low, velvety voice.

"Yes. I trust you more than any woman I've ever known." I grab both phones in one hand and tip her chin up. "But. You have to promise me you will never come looking for me if I'm out on club business. Ever. If you're worried, you tell one of the guys, give them the location and let them handle it. Promise."

She blinks a few times before answering. "Okay, I won't. Promise."

I nod, but I don't let her go yet. I want her to understand how serious this is. "The shit I was in the middle of the other night, sweetheart, if you'd come rolling in…it would have been very bad. For everyone. Especially you."

"You scare me, Rock."

My pulse jumps—how can she say that?

The heavy frown I'm wearing must nudge her into explaining. "I'm not afraid of *you*. I'm afraid *for* you. Can you understand that? My husband was very cautious and safe, and yet I still lost him. You're non-stop danger, and I'm so scared of you…dying," she finally whispers.

A number of emotions run through me, hearing her admit something so deep. I land on guilt. I need her to hear the absolute truth from me.

"I'm so sorry that I make you worry. But can I tell you something?" She nods for me to go on. "Only three things in this world keep me up at night. The thought of losing you. Losing one of my brothers. Going back to prison. That's it. I'm not afraid of dying, babe."

Admitting that to her didn't feel as bad as I thought it would.

"Prison," she whispers, as if the thought had never occurred to her.

"Yes, babe. You know I've been inside. Long time ago. Don't ever want to go back."

I watch her face as she absorbs my worst fears. Even though we've never talked about it, I know she knows.

"Prison," she mumbles again as if reality is finally dawning on her. "Then why do you—"

I stop her before she even gets the thought out. "It's all I know, babe. It's why I keep so many secrets, and don't trust anyone outside the MC. It's why I insulate myself with people who have the juice to keep us out of trouble—like Tony Cain."

She nods, but I can already see the tears filling her eyes. This is a little too much raw honesty.

"I'm sorry I didn't tell you about tracking your phone. It's not because I don't respect you, I just worry—"

I don't get to finish, because she pulls away from me.

"My life is only ever in danger because you put it there."

Almost true. "So Adam's client who attacked you, that's my fault too?"

She's got nothing. She sputters. Fuck me, did I finally outsmart my mouthy lawyer woman?

One corner of her mouth quirks up, and she shakes her head. "What am I going to do?"

I'm not really sure what she means, but I take her hand anyway. "Love me. Let me love you."

"That's not enough."

Oh shit. No, no, no.

"I need you to not get hurt. Can you promise me you'll do your best to keep yourself safe?"

I expected her to say the risks were too high and she needs to be with someone safer, or to ask me to quit, leave the club. But she demands none of that. No, she's asking me to keep myself safe.

My throat is so tight, it's hard to speak. "Of course."

"I mean from…other things too. I don't ever want to have to come visit you behind bars."

After spending the day visiting Grinder and all the bad memories that dredged up, her words are like a knife in my gut. "I'd never ask you to do that, baby."

Hurt flashes in her eyes. "I wouldn't desert you."

What did I do to deserve this woman's loyalty?

"Besides, I'd wait for you, so I could kick your ass when you got out."

That's my girl.

Taking a few steps to the side, I set the phones on the counter, then hold out my hand. She places her hand in mine, and I tug her against me.

"Remember how I told you once I'd let you go, if you wanted me to? I can't do it now, Hope. I can't. I love you too much."

Her wide, green eyes blink up at me. "I don't want you to let me go. I love you too."

Thank fuck.

"I need you." And it's true. I need Hope more than fucking air right now.

"I need you too," she echoes with a sweet smile.

She's incredible, but at the moment she's not getting me. I walk her gently backwards until she's pressed up against the wall. Lifting her legs so they're wrapped around my hips, I lean in and bury my face against her neck. My lips slide over her soft skin, licking and sucking until her breath comes out in jerky little pants.

Now she understands.

Her arms lock around my neck, pulling me close. My hands find their way to her waistband, where I pull and tug her blouse free. Sliding my fingers over her bare skin, I can't get enough. I don't think my big, clumsy hands can work the tiny, delicate buttons of her blouse.

So I tear it off. Creamy lace covers her heavy breasts, but not so much that I can't spot light freckles and perfect rosy nipples peeking out.

Hope gasps as she looks down at the ruins of her pretty blouse hanging from her. As she shrugs out of it, she pins me with a stern stare. "That was expensive."

There's no anger behind her words. She's working hard to keep her mouth from curving into a smile.

"I guess I owe you a blouse then," I tease.

Her thighs squeeze me tighter, and she reaches for me again, pulling me close. I can't get enough of her breasts—they fill my hands perfectly. I draw the lace cups of her bra down, placing her on display. Slowly, I skim one hand up her side, smoothing it over her breast, stopping to pinch and roll the stiff tips of her nipples and take in her responses. She whimpers and pushes her hips against me.

My dick is so fucking hard.

"I need to be inside you, Hope," I murmur against her neck.

Her body tenses a bit, and I pull back. Suddenly she's wearing a shy, hesitant look that I'm not liking very much.

"It's been a while."

"I know—that's why I need to be inside you so bad."

She meets my eyes, bites her lip a little, and it hits me upside the head what she's worried about.

"Baby, if you think I've even thought about another woman, you're out of your mind."

Yeah, that's what was bothering my girl. Her body relaxes a notch. She lowers her gaze and a shiver works over her. "I said we were done," she whispers with aching sweetness.

"I'm well aware. Thing is, I don't listen so well."

"I'm sorry," she whispers.

I knead my hands into her hips a little harder until she's staring at me. "You have nothing to be sorry for, baby. I'm the one who fucked up. I'm sure it won't be the last time, so I hope you'll be patient with me."

A half smile pulls her mouth to the side. "Try harder."

"No trying about it—I'm hard as steel," I tease, then grind my hips against her pussy through her perfectly tailored dress pants to emphasize my point. Meeting her sultry gaze, the words I need her to hear come pouring out. "You're it for me, Hope. I don't even see other women any more. Only you." I wish I was better with words. Even so, I think she gets it.

"Rochlan," she sighs. "You're it for me too. You know that, right? There could never be—it's why I need you to keep yourself safe."

Breathing? What the fuck is that? I don't even know, because I'm so fucking lost in her words.

I ease off her enough to slide my hand over her front, then hook a finger into her belt, tugging it free. Her clothes aren't coming off fast enough—I have to set her down so I can work everything off her body. Our hands and arms tangle together while she dives for my belt and jeans, but finally, I have her standing almost naked in front of me. Beautiful.

She looks up at me through her lashes, and it hits me hard how much I want Hope and no one else. Every single word I told her was true. I grip her hips, lifting her slightly, and she hooks her legs around me again, using me as leverage to work her slick pussy over me. Tease. I reach down and guide my dick into her. Her fingers dig into my shoulders, eyes going wide, mouth open as I keep sinking into her, deep as possible.

Those short, breathy nonsense sounds she makes drive me crazy. So crazy that, while I'm using my arms to cushion the parts of her jammed up against the wall, I can't stop myself from ramming into her.

"Yes, Rock. Just like that. Right there," she gasps. Her legs tighten around me, fingers digging into my skin. My girl is completely with me, loving every brutal thrust.

"I need...I need you, Rock." I doubt she's aware of what she said, but it pushes me right over the edge. That's what I needed to hear. She's tight and trembling in my arms, her pussy locking down on me. Her soft moaning and panting fills my ear. Her face is flushed—a stunning light pink, lips parted, face tense as she concentrates on coming. So beautiful. I'm done. Crushed under the weight of her beauty and trust. I keep pounding into her until I've got nothing left to give.

Hope

My legs are still trembling as I straddle Rock's bike on the way to his house. No matter how chilly the night air whipping around us is, there's a warmth in my chest that can't be extinguished. Rock's love and faith in me mean everything. The makeup sex is great, don't get me wrong, but those two things are priceless. I think I can put up with all the other demands of the club as long as I have his respect and trust.

Once we get to his house, Rock silently leads me inside.

"Are you hungry, Baby Doll?" he asks in a hoarse voice that makes my heart clench.

"A little."

He sits me down at the table and goes to work making something simple. Before he sits down to eat with me, he sets two wineglasses and a bottle of red on the table. I quirk an eyebrow at him, and he shrugs.

"Surprised the biker has fancy stemware?" he teases.

"A little," I answer honestly.

He nods, a small smile playing at the corners of his mouth as he pours the wine.

After dinner, I help him clear the table, and he leads me upstairs.

Butterflies flutter around in my belly. I can't believe I'm ready to jump him again so soon.

Just outside his bedroom, he pauses. Suddenly his demeanor radiates a certain significance that makes my tummy quiver for different reasons. My plans to race him to the bed and be naked in his arms within the next five seconds are suddenly put on hold.

He takes my hand and pulls me into the bedroom.

"Baby doll, I want to have a talk with you."

"Uh-oh."

Rock

Hope's wariness made me feel like an asshole. There's no reason for me to be so fucking dramatic, except I'm nervous. Very few things in life get my heart racing. But this conversation I'm about to have with Hope? Yeah, my pulse is easily going one hundred and twenty miles an hour.

But I opened my big mouth. Shutting down now would only make things weirder.

Curving my hands over her hips, I nudge her to the bed. Maybe this conversation would be better naked?

But no, I've dicked around too long as it is.

Pulling a chair over, I sit in front of her and take her hands in mine.

Even though I've gone over this conversation in my head dozens of times, it still takes me a minute to line up the words the way I want them to come out.

"Hope, baby. You know how the guys keep referring to you as my ol' lady?"

She lifts one shoulder and nods. "I used to get annoyed when people thought I was younger, but I can't say I'm thrilled about being called 'old.'"

Instantly, I'm thrown back to the day we met. I'd originally pegged her at about six years younger than her age. I chuckle at the memory of the first time we had lunch together and I mistakenly told her she'd make a fine stripper. Man, I was an asshole.

"Fair enough. But it's not about age in my world. It's about respect."

She doesn't snort or roll her eyes. She's listening intently.

Reaching up, I draw one finger down her arm and take her hand again. "It means our relationship is permanent. Stable. It's a way to warn my brothers to stay the fuck away from you."

Her lush lips curve into a wicked smile. "I'd say you've done an admirable job of that."

I want to smile at her teasing words, but she also needs to understand how serious I am. How serious what I'm about to explain is.

She meets my eyes with her soft green ones and flutters her lashes at me.

I won't let her pretty owl-eyed expression distract me from my mission. "Ol' ladies are the most important females associated with MCs."

Now she's wearing this cute baffled expression.

"Calling you that lets my brothers know I'll throw down for you. It means I trust you to never talk about club business. It earns you their respect and loyalty."

She snorts at that. "Please. Wrath has been mean to me since day one."

The corner of my mouth twitches, but I stop it from becoming a full-blown smile. "Yes. While ol' ladies are important, they're also a threat to the club in a way."

Her eyebrows draw down in confusion.

"I don't want to get off track here, but that patch Wrath wears—sergeant at arms—it's not just decorative. It means he's responsible for the safety and security of the entire club. His job is to protect and defend the members. But his loyalty is to me. And with you being a civilian with no experience in our world and being a lawyer, he had valid concerns that you could harm the club—even unintentionally." She goes to speak, and I hold my hand up. "I'm not saying I approve of his methods, but you've always managed to hold your own, yeah?"

"I guess," she grumbles. Good, I don't feel like giving her a lesson on the structure of the whole damn club. We've got much more important things to get to.

"So by being my ol' lady, that makes you my property—"

"Excuse me?"

"Again, it's about respect and commitment, Hope."

"Doesn't sound very respectful," she mumbles loud enough for me to catch each word.

I give her a hard stare. "In my world, it is. We've already talked about the differences, remember?"

She grinds her teeth and huffs, then finally nods.

"Property just means you're under my protection and under the protection of all my brothers. Remember the night of the fight when Z said he'd kill anyone who fucked with you?"

"Yeah, but people say stuff like over my dead body all the time."

I shake my head. "Yes, but again. In *my* world, it actually means something. Z wasn't talking out of his ass. He's the one who went with me to take care of those two assholes that ran us off the road, by the way."

Resembling an unruly five-year-old, she slaps her hands over her ears and yelps, "Don't. Want. Details!"

I snatch her hands back. "Okay, okay. But, you get what I'm saying? That goes for all of them. Bricks, Teller, Murphy, and especially Wrath."

"But they would do that for Trinity too, and she doesn't belong to anyone."

"She belongs to the whole club, Hope." I circle a finger in the air, then press it over her heart. "You belong to me."

Her eyes flutter shut and then open. I see her turning my words over in her head, and I can tell she's got a bunch of questions. For now, she keeps them to herself.

"You're protected by the club, but you're not available to the club," I clarify.

Her face pinches.

"I know for a fact Trinity has explained to you that she is fine with that arrangement, so do not get offended on her behalf. That's her choice."

A quick chin lift tells me that although she agrees with what I said, she's not happy about it.

"As the president's ol' lady, you rank higher than her. That's why she gets so freaked out when you offer to help her in the kitchen and stuff."

"That's ridiculous. She's been here for years and knows way more than me."

"Doesn't matter, doll. That's how it is. But I want to tell you something. You've earned her respect and the guys' respect by never rubbing that in her face."

"How could I, when I didn't even know?"

I cock my head to the side. "Come on, Hope. You've never treated any of the girls badly unless you were forced to. Ol' ladies usually straight up ignore club girls."

"Why?"

Yeah, we've veered off topic and I'm eager to get us back on track, so I'm going to let that question slide.

"Anyway—"

"Don't 'anyway' me."

Fine. "You know how you felt that night when Cookie got in your face?"

"Yeah, but Teller said that's not normal."

"It's not, which is why I banned her. But remember Roxy and her crew? Clubs girls are only around for sex. Imagine being around girls who've been with your man or you know still are with your man when you're not around. It gets uncomfortable sometimes."

The battle goes out of her, and she deflates like a balloon. Not what I wanted. "Doll, I cannot do anything about my past. We talked about that. But you're my future. Some guys still fuck around on their ol' ladies, I won't deny it. You don't ever have to worry. I waited my whole life for you. I'm not gonna fuck it up by tapping every bitch who looks at me sideways. Been there, done that."

All at once, the fire is back. My girl really hates when I use the "b" word.

"Normally ol' ladies segregate themselves from club girls altogether. Unfortunately, you don't have that luxury since you're the only ol' lady." I give her a smirk, which thankfully she returns.

Time to wrap this up and get to the point. "So, you understand that in any crowd of bikers, whether Lost Kings or some other tribe, an ol' lady being LOKI property is not a derogatory thing. It's a respect thing. If we had a visiting club here, none of them would approach you unless I okayed it."

"That's just weird."

"Look at it this way—no one is going to hit on you." She should appreciate that. Girls usually hate unwanted attention, right?

"Great. Put me out to pasture. Call me old and have me thinking every man in the world thinks I'm an ugly hag?"

"What?"

"Sometimes girls like to be hit on. It reaffirms we still look good. You're taking that away from me."

Is she fucking with me?

"Babe. In my world, hitting on another man's ol' lady is absolutely not tolerated. It is grounds for a beat down."

She leans over and kisses me softly. "Then you better compliment me often."

My desire for her is slowly strangling my balls. "In about five minutes, I'm going to have you bent over that bed showing you how fucking hot I think you are."

Her cheeks flush red, and she gestures for me to hurry up.

"Trust me, I've had to threaten every one of my brothers with physical violence at one time or another because they've affirmed how good you look."

A slow smirk spreads across her lips, and a little too late it occurs to me I should have kept that tidbit to myself.

"Even Wrath?" She scrunches her nose in disbelief.

"Especially him," I growl. "Especially after that incident in the garage," I remind her. She turns a nice shade of pink at the memory.

Raking my fingers through my hair, I grit out, "Can I please finish?"

"I'm all ears." She sits back, crosses her legs, and gives me her best attentive student stare.

Shaking my head, I continue. "So, sometimes when a woman has been taken as an ol' lady, her man gives her a vest with her own patch."

Reality seems to crash into her with the force of a freight train. "Are you saying you want to give me that?" she asks softly.

Finally. Christ, it took a fucking hour to get to the good part.

"Yes."

"Is this the biker equivalent of an engagement ring?"

"Sort of. It's more than that, really. Will you wear it for me?"

"Where?"

I almost snap, but then I rein it in and realize she's worried about wearing it in her world. "Only when you're in my world, babe. I'm not asking you to wear it to court or something."

"Hmmm...so I'll kinda be like a superhero with a secret identity?" she asks with a sweet lilt in her voice.

Fuck, I love this woman.

She's going to be the best ol' lady ever.

Hope

Completely overwhelmed with everything Rock has explained to me, one thought burns brighter than everything else. Whatever this is, it's a big commitment. Waves of anxiety are rolling off him.

Too stunned to give him the answer he wants, I bust out the superhero quip.

He seems to appreciate it, though, and some of his tension fades.

I hold my breath, then jump. "Of course I'll wear it."

He blows out a relieved breath, and it hits me how nervous Rock was about this conversation. A shiver of warmth spreads through my chest at the glimpse of vulnerability.

I really love this man.

It's starting to sink in that I'm in way deep. Not only with Rock. But with all of his brothers too.

And I'm okay with that.

As an only child, I never had anyone to look out for me. After my father died and my mother turned into a negligent train wreck, I spent a lot of time fending for myself. My mother didn't get her act together until I was in my twenties. By then, I'd been taking care of myself for a long time, and she seemed pleased to be relieved of any parental obligations. My husband came through the foster care system with his bitchy sister as his only family. Clay and I formed our own small family, and I never desired anything more.

Until now.

Rock is offering me a true family.

A bloodthirsty family with a bit of chauvinistic bent. But family.

Although I still can't comprehend the emotional strength it takes to be available to all the brothers, I understand why Trinity feels safe with the club.

"Baby doll, you make me so fucking happy." He stands and pulls me up with him. The way he drags his gaze down my body raises my temperature by at least five degrees. On the way up he lingers on my breasts, then finally locks eyes with me. Those deep, gray depths with flecks of blue turn almost black. Smoldering for me.

His jaw ticks. "You're mine, Baby Doll."

"Yes, I am."

"Going to fuck you now." He squeezes the words out through gritted teeth.

The words are harsh, but his touch is gentle. I hold my breath as he traces his knuckles over my breasts. My nipples harden under his attention, straining through my shirt. He flattens his palms over both breasts, his thumbs drawing tight circles over the peaks. Through my clothes, I still feel the heat and respond instantly.

One hand drops to my hip, and I'm yanked against him as he kisses me hard.

In between kisses, I breathe out, "Yes."

I've got to get my hands on his skin, slide them over the hard muscles. He's hard everywhere, and I don't know which of his perfectly sculpted parts I want to fondle first.

I break our kiss to tug his shirt up and over his head, then my own. I shimmy out of my pants next and kick them away.

Down we tumble to the bed. I put my whole body into kissing him. I want him to feel how much everything he said means to me. And that even if I don't exactly comprehend everything, I get the intent behind his words. I want him to understand I feel the same way.

I honestly think if someone threatened to take him from me, I would kill them.

CHAPTER TWENTY-FIVE

HOPE

It's time for another club birthday party.

This one better be a lot tamer than the last one I attended with Rock.

It's for Heidi's seventeenth birthday. She's been through a lot in the last few months, and everyone wants to make sure she has a nice afternoon. When her brother asked what she wanted, she said something simple with her two girlfriends, Axel, and her club family around her, so that's what we're doing.

Except we're doing it at Rock's house. More specifically his backyard, because he did not want a trio of underage girls up at the clubhouse. Teller and I both agreed that seemed best. For now, Teller is sharing custody of Heidi with their grandmother. Most days it doesn't go well. He tried to set their differences aside and invited his grandmother here today for the party, but she turned him down. Eventually, this stuff will have to be addressed in family court again, but I'm not going to worry about it now.

Instead, I'm thinking about the beautiful cake Trinity brought with her. I'm thinking that it's a perfect fall day for an outdoor party.

Z took charge of the massive stainless steel grill Rock has nestled into the stone patio out back. The guys wanted to do a pig roast today, but Heidi shrieked when they told her, so it's hot dogs, hamburgers, and chicken that Z is cooking up.

"You okay, Baby Doll?" Rock's arms wrap around my waist, pulling me tight to his front. His lips move against my ear, sending a shiver through me.

"Yup."

I turn so I'm looking up at him, and a thrill goes through me. He's one big, sexy man, and he's all mine.

"You're sticking around, right?" he asks.

"Of course."

He breathes a sigh of relief. "I'll feel better with a female chaperon."

A quick glance around the party, and I understand why. I trust these guys, but I can see how from the outside it might not look so good. Especially since the girls plan to have a slumber party here afterward. Especially after some of the nasty accusations Heidi's grandmother made toward the end of the custody dispute.

"That seems prudent," I say.

Rock quirks an eyebrow at me.

"It seems like the cautious thing to do," I explain.

He takes his arms from around my waist, plants them at his side, and gives me a sharp glare. "I know what prudent means, Hope."

I'm blushing furiously. Why do I do things like that?

"I'm sorry, I didn't mean it that way."

"Honey, just because I didn't go on to college doesn't mean I don't know all sorts of five-cent words." His mouth kicks up in a devilish grin, but I sense he's still annoyed with me. "Had a very hot English teacher," he elaborates.

I roll my eyes at him. Of course he did. "Seems like that would have detracted from your learning instead of enhancing it," I tease.

"Oh, on the contrary, I aimed to impress, so maybe if I ran into her after graduation, I'd have a shot at her."

"And how did that work out?"

He only smirks at me.

I pop him in the gut with my fist. "Jackass." Not my smartest move. His abs are like punching a brick wall, and I shake off the sting.

"Can't you two take it upstairs?" Wrath grumbles as he makes his way over on his crutches.

"You're mistaken, bro. She's fixing to kick my ass, not jump my bones."

Wrath runs his gaze over me. "I don't think so, brother."

"Jerk," I grumble.

"You know it." He twists to observe the backyard. "Where's the birthday girl?"

"Inside watching movies with her friends," I answer.

Wrath rolls his eyes skyward. "It's a beautiful day. They should be outside."

Laughter bubbles out of me. "Okay, Dad. I'll let them know." I'm still giggling as I stroll up to the house, and I hear Wrath grumbling behind me.

Trinity is in the kitchen prepping trays of food to bring outside.

"Do you need help?"

She throws me a harried look but shakes her head. "I got it. Maybe, go hang with the girls?" Trinity says as she jerks her head toward the living room. Girlish giggles seep out into the kitchen.

"You sure you don't want to hang with them? You're closer to their age."

Trinity seems stunned I would even suggest such a thing. "Heidi's not a big fan of mine."

This is news to me, but it's not the time to go digging for information.

Feeling more than a little awkward, I creep into the living room. Mean Girls is on, but they seem more intent on gossip than the movie.

"Is your brother here yet? He's sooo hot," Skye giggles.

Heidi's clearly not thrilled by her friend's assessment of Teller. "Ewww, he's a disgusting manwhore."

A laugh escapes me, and the girls glance up, startled and guilty expressions all around. "Hi, Hope. Come to watch movies with us?" Heidi asks while making room for me on the couch.

Surprised by the invitation, I mumble, "Sure."

Skye and Penny seem less thrilled by my presence, but they murmur polite hellos at me.

From the corner, Axel startles me with a greeting. He's on the floor, between Heidi's feet, while she's running her hands through his hair. Together, they're a cute picture of teenage romance.

"Hey, Axel."

"Does prez need me?" he asks. I can't tell if he's looking for a way out or he's really worried Rock might need him for something.

"He didn't say so, but he's right outside."

Unfolding himself from the floor, he plants a kiss on Heidi's cheek and steps out. His big, booted feet haven't even cleared the room before the girls burst into giggles.

"You're so lucky," Penny sighs.

"Who's prez that he's so worried about?" Skye asks.

"My Uncle Rock," Heidi answers with a whole lot of pride in her voice. "Hope's his girlfriend," she says while pointing at me.

The girls seem less than impressed.

"They're all so old. Aren't there any other guys in your brother's club, like Axel's age?" Penny asks.

I tamp down a giggle at that.

"Yeah, there's two other prospects, but they're older than Axel too."

"High school boys not very interesting these days?" I ask.

Skye gives me a cool glance before answering. "We're seniors now. We can't date high school boys."

Oh dear.

"Food will be ready soon, if you girls want to come out."

Heidi nods. "We'll be there."

On my way back outside, I intercept Bricks. He gives me a quick hug. "Where's the birthday girl?"

"Inside watching movies with her friends."

He chuckles. "I brought Lisa and Deacon with me, but she's probably not gonna wanna hang with them in front of her friends."

I'm not so sure about that. Heidi seems to do whatever she wants.

"Winter brought Caleb too," he continues.

"Cool. Rock set up some games in the backyard for the little guys."

He's tapping a big, pink envelope in his hands. When I glance at it, he shrugs. "For Heidi," he explains while handing it to me.

"I'll stick it on the table."

He goes inside, and I drop the envelope in a box Trinity set up outside for people to deliver their cards and gifts to Heidi. It seems most people brought gift cards, although there is one big box wrapped in green and silver paper on the table. Idly, I flip over the card and see it's from Murphy.

That should be interesting.

"Let's eat!" Z shouts.

Trinity races out of the kitchen to find Wrath. I watch them for a minute, until Rock wraps an arm around my waist. "Hungry?"

"Actually, yes."

His lips find my ear, and he gently sinks his teeth into me, sending shivers through my body.

"Not here," I groan.

His deep, rumbling chuckle races right through me.

We're interrupted by the girls flying out of the house. Z teases them, makes them say please and thank you about a hundred times before finally feeding them.

They're not amused.

After everyone's eaten, Heidi goes through her presents. She's collected enough gift cards to fill the closets of three teenage girls. One by one, she reads the cards and thanks everyone. Only Wrath, Teller, Murphy, Axel, Rock and I are standing around when she gets to the last present.

"It's from me, Heidi-bug," Murphy says with a grin.

"I figured." Heidi rips into it and beams at the helmet inside. "Oh, I love it! Thank you, Blake."

It's a big, shiny black one with a full face mask, decorated with pink skulls and butterflies. Very Heidi.

"We'll take our ride in a few, okay?"

"Yeah." She smiles shyly. "I didn't know if we were still doing that."

"Of course, Bug. It's your birthday."

She bounces on her toes a few more times, then races over to show her girlfriends and Axel the helmet.

I quirk an eyebrow at Murphy, which he doesn't see, because he's watching Heidi.

Teller's got an uncertain look on his face, but he answers my unspoken question. "They've been doing that every year on her birthday since she was like eight."

Wrath shifts and shakes his head.

We're interrupted by Heidi racing back. "Can we go now? Please?"

Murphy sets his drink down. A corner of his mouth twists up. "Yeah."

"We haven't done cake yet," Wrath advises.

Murphy slaps Wrath on the arm. "We won't be gone long, bro."

We watch them walk down the driveway for a second before Teller walks into the house.

Turning back to Wrath and Rock, I sigh. "Aw, that's sweet that they have a birthday ritual."

Wrath gives me his "are you nuts" face.

"What?"

"He needs to knock that shit off. It ain't okay anymore." He throws a glance at where Axel is hanging out with Skye and Penny.

Wow. Okay. "Wait, I thought you were team Murphy?"

Wrath shrugs his massive shoulders. "Axel's a good kid. He cares about her."

Now I'm utterly confused. "Murphy cares about her."

Wrath looks at me like he's surprised to find himself in the middle of this conversation. "It's not about that. It ain't cool to have another brother's girl on the back of your bike."

Rock taps Wrath on the shoulder. "We'll worry about it another day. Axel's fine. Teller's fine with it. Let it go."

"Yeah, okay." All at once, the tension seems to drain out of him. "You seen Trin? She was ripping your kitchen apart looking for a lighter earlier," he says with a smirk.

Rock chuckles. "Yeah, she found it."

"Cool. The cake she made is pretty kick-ass. She's real excited about it too. Those two better not be gone too long." He throws a glare down the driveway as the sound of Murphy's bike starting up fills the air.

A giggle bubbles out of me. "You're so cute," I say without thinking.

Wrath's blue eyes flare in surprise. "Cute? Sugar, there's absolutely nothing 'cute' about me."

Rock's staring at me like I just stood up and announced my intention to take up stock-car racing.

My mouth opens and closes a few times before I frame what I want to say. "Well, I think it's cute you're all worried about Trinity being disappointed if Heidi doesn't get to see the cake she made for her." I manage to babble out while sounding very much like a petulant child.

Rock and Wrath share a glance. Wrath settles back into a pose of indifference. "She spent a lot of time on it, that's all, Hope."

"Sure. Okay, Wrath." I give Rock's hand a squeeze and then head inside to see if I can help Trinity out.

Rock

As soon as Hope's out of earshot, I burst out laughing. "She so has your number, brother."

"Shut the fuck up."

Wrath loves his lethal image, so I enjoy poking at this one. "Aw, I think it's nice. She thinks you're cute. Like a fuzzy puppy or something."

"Jealous?"

"Nope. She's referred to me as sexy, sexual crack, big and scary, but never cute."

"You want her to find me sexy? Cause I'll charm the pants right off her if you want."

This whole conversation just stopped being funny.

"Thought so," Wrath says with a grin.

"Fuck you."

I'm still watching Hope's sexy ass swaying away from me. I wish I'd taken her in the garage when I'd had the chance. It might have helped ease some of the leftover tension from earlier. I realize I'd been a bit of a dick, but something about my girl thinking she' needed to explain a two-syllable word to me rankled.

"Seriously, you think we need to have a talk with Murphy?"

I can't even deal with that situation right now. "Dude, she's known him since she was a kid. It's their thing. Let it go. If Axel has an issue, he can bring it up."

"Whatever."

We wander back and rejoin the party. The girls are busy teaching Bricks's kids one of the games we set up outside. It's a cute picture, and I take a second to appreciate my Lost Kings family all in one place. I'm not related to a single person here by blood, but it doesn't matter. They're family.

Familiar arms snake around my middle and squeeze. Her scent drifts to me, but I'd recognize her by feel alone.

"Hey, baby," I rasp, placing my hand over hers. I tug her around until she's facing me and slip my arms around her.

"Having fun yet?" she teases.

I'm not sure if I would call this afternoon "fun," but I am content and I tell her so.

With everyone else occupied, I nudge Hope into the garage. "Got a project I want to show you."

She rolls her eyes because she knows I'm full of shit. Can't lie to my girl worth a damn.

"Rock," she whines, "there's children out—"

I cut her off with a kiss and behind her flip the lock on the door. "No windows, baby." Well, there are windows, but they are high up enough to keep out prying eyes.

Warm breath skates over my neck as she lets out a husky laugh. "You're so bad."

"What? I just wanna show you my latest project."

She smiles and kisses me back until we're both frantic. Then she ducks to the right, out of my grasp.

I shift restlessly, aching from the loss of her body against mine.

"Show me your project," she purrs in a teasing way that surprises me.

I look up and catch her watching me with a heavy-lidded, sexy gaze. She slides her tongue along the seam of her lips and I swear I feel it in my cock.

"You're so fucking hot, Hope, but you're begging for me to spank your ass right now."

"You wouldn't dare."

Oh, game on.

The whoop, whoop of a police siren interrupts the filthy plans I have for my girl.

"What the fuck?" I grumble.

Hope's posture straightens, and she grabs for the door.

"Christ, give me a second," I grind out, pointing to the erection tenting my jeans.

She giggles.

"Thanks, babe. Laughing at it will definitely help." Of course, that only makes her laugh harder. "That's enough. Let's go see what the problem is."

Of course, Wrath is the one standing closest to the garage and doubles over laughing when he spots us walking out.

"Shut up, dick."

Hope's blushing ten shades of red as she stalks past us and down the driveway in the direction of the glowing red and blue lights.

"The fuck?"

Wrath shrugs. "Your house, was waiting for you to go deal with it."

Of course.

Except it looks like Hope's got it covered.

Hope

"Can I help you, officers?" I call out as I stride over the lawn.

"We're looking for Marcel Whelan. He here?"

I whip around and find Rock almost right behind me. "Go find Teller."

He nods and takes off.

"What's the problem?"

"You a family member?"

"Sort of. I'm also Mr. Whelan's attorney, so what's the issue?"

He jerks his thumb toward the back of his car, and through the window I spot a tear-streaked, red-faced Heidi.

"Oh my God! Heidi?" My gaze shoots to the officer. "What's going on?"

"Caught her out with—"

"With Blake? We know. So what? Where is he?" I ask. I need to calm down and compose myself. Put my lawyer game face on. Act like a professional.

The officer cocks his head at me and motions me closer. "We got a call about an underage girl out with Mr. O'Callaghan, spotted them, pulled them over. She told us her family was here, so we brought her here. Her brother is her guardian?"

"Yes. He shares custody with their grandmother."

"Okay, so why's she out with this older guy?"

I really don't care for his tone. "He's a family friend. You're interrupting the birthday party we were having for Heidi. Mr. O'Callaghan has known her since she was a kid and takes her out for a ride every year on her birthday. Nothing more, officer."

He nods and finally looks a little embarrassed. "That's the same story she gave us."

I finally spot Murphy sitting in the back of the car with Heidi.

"Then why are they in the back of your patrol car? I'm sure you've run Mr. O'Callaghan's license by now and discovered his record is clean. They weren't doing anything wrong, so this seems a bit... excessive, don't you think?"

The officer frowns, and I tell myself to tone down the attitude. Except I'm seriously pissed. Who do these guys think they are, scaring the shit out of a seventeen-year-old girl?

He looks behind me, and I can tell that Rock and a bunch of other people are standing there now.

"Officer, what's the problem?"

"And you are?"

"Rochlan North. This is my house. Heidi is my goddaughter. Why is she in the back of your car?"

"Heidi! What the fuck?" Teller shouts from behind me.

"Easy, brother," Rock mumbles under his breath, and I sense he must be holding Teller back.

"You the brother?"

"Yes."

Finally, the cop opens the door and lets Heidi out. Thankfully, they didn't cuff her. She's red-faced and sobbing. Ignoring all of us, she runs over the lawn into the house.

Crossing my arms over my chest, I eye the officer coolly. "Mr. O'Callaghan? You've got no reason to hold him. And I hope to God you didn't cuff him."

Rock's gentle touch grazes my arm. Whether he's telling me to calm down or encouraging me, I'm not sure. I just know that I'm livid right now.

Another officer who'd remained quiet this entire time lets Murphy out and uncuffs him. You've got to be kidding.

"Where's his bike?" I ask in my sharpest courtroom tone.

"On its way to impound."

"You can't be serious," I argue. "He hasn't done anything wrong."

Murphy's busy flexing his arms and rubbing his wrists. "It's okay, Hope. I'll take care of it."

Rock

NEVER A DULL MOMENT AROUND HERE. Not even for a seventeen-year-old's birthday party.

Unreal.

Watching my woman get all fired up and take on two of Empire's finest over the way they treated one of my brothers?

Un-fucking-real.

Christ, after all the shit we've gone through, that she's ready to tear into two cops like that? I fucking love her.

What a night. And it's not even over yet.

First, we need to go inside.

Hope finds Heidi and calms her down. After a lot of reassuring, she convinces Heidi to join us in the kitchen where we're all waiting to sing happy birthday to her and cut into her birthday cake.

Poor Heidi bursts into tears when she gets a look at the giant pink and leopard spotted cake Trinity made for her. She gives Trinity a big, sloppy hug, which seems to shock Trin, but she handles it well.

Everyone applauds Heidi for handling her first ride in a cop car like a pro.

Axel and Heidi disappear into the backyard right after cake.

Trinity drives Murphy down to impound to pick up his bike. Wrath paces around the house like a gimpy, caged animal waiting for them to return.

Axel walks Heidi back inside and then takes off for the night. Hope sets the girls up in the living room with more cake, sodas, and the scary movie they picked out.

After she's done with the girls, she pads into the kitchen. Her gaze darts around the room as if she's trying to figure out what to do next. "Wow. What a night," she says at last.

Wrath's finally sitting down. He's busy shredding the label off his beer. Hope settles her hand on his shoulder.

"Need anything, big guy?"

He glances up, and I see several asshole-ish answers flash across his face, but he just shakes his head. "I'm fine. Thanks, babe."

She squeezes his arm and he captures her hand. "You did good tonight, Hope."

Obvious surprise crosses her face. "What do you mean?"

"With the cops. Sticking up for Murphy. Taking care of Heidi."

An uncertain smile curves her lips. "Thanks, Wrath," she says before making her way to me.

Wrapping her up in my arms, I press a kiss against her ear.

"You done?"

She lets out a soft snort. "Hardly. I'm going to make them some popcorn. Then I'll probably sit up with them for a while. You can head to bed if you want?"

Not likely.

I hold onto her for a minute longer, resting my chin on the crown of her head. My gaze lands on Wrath and he nods at me.

Hope pulls away and plants a kiss on my cheek. "Are you okay, Rock?"

"I'm good, baby."

She rubs her hands over my back for a minute, then wriggles out of my embrace.

I sit with Wrath and watch Hope prep more snacks for the girls.

"Hey, did I ever get to tell you I had lunch with Lilly the other day?" she asks over her shoulder.

"No," I answer honestly. She didn't tell me, but I know because I had Hoot watching her. "How is she?"

"Well, it was weird seeing her in professional mode. But she brought a friend of hers along. He works for this lobbying firm and was telling us how all these tech firms are throwing a lot of money into marijuana reform in New York. Isn't that crazy?"

Across from me, Wrath almost chokes on his beer. I shoot a glare at him before answering Hope.

"Yeah. It's interesting."

Hope hums an affirmative noise and continues working at the counter, giving me a chance to reflect on things.

A bunch of bullshit has gotten in the way of what's important to me lately.

A handful of stupid secrets and lies almost threatened to blow us apart.

And yet, there's still a few things I'm hiding.

One very major thing. After this conversation, I wonder if Hope already suspects the big, green elephant hiding in the clubhouse basement.

In time, it will all be out in the open and I'll deal with the fallout then.

Until then, there's the whole issue of getting Hope's property patch. Can't think of a woman who's ever deserved it more.

I'm glad I finally explained the significance of the patch to her. Now, there's nothing holding me back from bringing it to the table the next time we sit down for church.

As I'm sitting here watching Hope's every move, she turns and flashes a sweet smile at me.

I love her so damn much.

The club needs to vote her in.

Now.

Yeah, we've got a lot of things to take care of.

Very soon.

The End.

The journey continues for Hope and Rock in *Strength From Loyalty*, available here. You can read an excerpt from *Strength From Loyalty* on the following page.

The next book in the series is a collection of short stories called *Three Kings, One Night (Lost Kings MC #2.5)*

Links to my social media and my author notes are after the excerpt. Enjoy and thank you for reading!

AUTHOR NOTES

These are the original author notes that were published with Corrupting Cinderella on December 2, 2014. The novella I mentioned is now known as **White Heat (Lost Kings Mc #5)**.

I HAD A LOT OF ANXIETY ABOUT INCLUDING A "NOTES FROM THE AUTHOR" in Slow Burn, but since most people seemed to respond favorably to it, here's another one.

Thank you for returning for the second installment of Rock and Hope's story. Corrupting Cinderella was originally all about Rock drawing Hope into his shady world, but it ended up being so much more. I hope you loved reading it as much as I loved writing it! Their story continues in *Strength From Loyalty (Lost Kings MC #3)* and possibly some sort of novella after Wrath's book—*Tattered on my Sleeve (Lost Kings MC #4).*

I RECEIVED a number of interesting responses to the end of Slow Burn that I didn't expect. I ended it on what is known as a "Happy for Now Ending" but I had a lot of…criticisms about it that. By the way, I took this as a compliment, because it just meant people had a lot of love for

Rock and Hope. But it got me thinking—what constitutes a Happily Ever After anyway? Marriage? Babies? My own parents were married for eight years and divorced three years after having me, so I've never really thought of marriage and babies as a HEA. But I consider myself a romance writer and one of the things I love so much about reading romantic fiction is that you are always guaranteed a happy ending of sorts.

Although I'm crafting romantic fiction, I also like to strive for some realism. Relationships are hard work. Happy endings don't magically happen. You still need to work at them after you ride off into the sunset together. To me, exploring the reality of a lawyer and an unapologetic-yet-somehow-honorable criminal getting together was going to have a lot of twists, turns and compromise. Especially if I was going to keep both characters true to themselves. Honestly, Hope wouldn't be very likeable if she just accepted every single thing about Rock's strange world without some resistance. And no one would like Rock if he ditched his club to become an upstanding citizen in order to be with Hope. So, they both needed to work out some middle ground. I found their muddling through that thorny clashing of their very different worlds interesting and fun to write, and I hope you find it fun to read.

Once again, I strived for accuracy in any medical, legal and law enforcement scenes. But once again, I also bent things to suit my needs when required.

When I started writing this in January 2014, I only expected it to be one book about Rock and Hope. But as I kept writing, the other characters (Wrath especially-I had to take a good three weeks in July 2014 to get a chunk of his story down because he just won't shut up!) became much clearer and demanding. People who read it kept telling me it needed to be a series because they wanted to know more about Wrath, Trinity, Z, Murphy and Sophie.

With Corrupting Cinderella, I tied up some loose ends from Slow Burn. I also intentionally (and probably unintentionally) created some new ones that I plan to tie up in later books. Those little threads are what make it fun for me to read a series, and I hope you feel that way about my series.

What made me happiest about the responses to Slow Burn was how many people embraced my version of an MC Romance that was heavier on the romance and lighter in grit than most. I heard from a lot of people who agreed that they too were tired of the abusive treatment of women in fiction these days. The wonderful response to Rock's special brand of loving alpha hero has been amazing.

Thank you for reading!

Autumn

ALSO BY AUTUMN JONES LAKE

THE LOST KINGS MC SERIES

SLOW BURN (LOST KINGS MC #1)

PRESIDENT OF THE LOST KINGS MC, ROCHLAN "ROCK" NORTH, HASN'T managed to find a woman capable of making him want to curb his wild ways—until he meets sweet, innocent, married lawyer Hope Kendall.

Forced to represent the outlaw biker, Hope is rattled by her immediate attraction to Rock. Hope is a good girl in a good marriage. Rock thrills her, but she's not going to throw away everything she's built on a fling with her criminal client.

Rock respects Hope enough to leave her alone, even as he realizes he's become a little obsessed with her. When their connection endangers her life, he'll have to destroy her in order to save her.

After tragedy strikes, Rock is determined to earn Hope's forgiveness and convince her that even with their staggering differences, they're meant to be together.

CORRUPTING CINDERELLA

(LOST KINGS MC #2)

Although widowed attorney Hope Kendall cares deeply for President of the Lost Kings MC, Rochlan "Rock" North, the truth is they come from completely different worlds. Add to that the fact that they are also both headstrong people, and they have a very rough road ahead of them.

Real love isn't a fairy tale.

For Rock that means introducing Hope to what it really means to be part of his brutal and shady world, where the Lost Kings Motorcycle Club is his main focus. For Hope it means accepting the things she can't change, and understanding that Rock is a man who will do anything to keep her safe.

Love doesn't follow any rules.

As Rock continues to draw Hope deeper into his world, painful misunderstandings, past relationships, and opposition from the members of his club will threaten to drive them apart.

How do a lawyer and a badass biker with a heart of gold keep their love alive while their opposing worlds collide?

THREE KINGS, ONE NIGHT
(LOST KINGS MC #2.5)

Three short holiday stories featuring Murphy, Wrath, and Zero.

STRENGTH FROM LOYALTY
(LOST KINGS MC #3)

As a dark cloud descends over Hope and Rock's already precarious future, will a long-hidden secret push them both past the point of no return?

Struggling attorney Hope Kendall loves her outlaw biker boyfriend Rochlan "Rock" North with all her heart, but the questionable activities his motorcycle club is involved in threaten her legal career.

But does she even want this career anymore?

As a near-death situation makes their professional differences seem insignificant, a cloud descends over their personal relationship's already unsteady future.

Even though Hope seems to have finally found her niche in the club as Rock's ol' lady, can she mingle in politics with neighboring clubs as well? A trip to the Lost Kings MC downstate charter will put her to the test.

While Rock works hard to give Hope the honesty she craves without betraying his loyalty to his brothers, tension from outside forces threatens to push him to the brink. But it's the one secret Hope has hidden all along that may finally drive them apart for good.

TATTERED ON MY SLEEVE
(LOST KINGS MC #4)

TATTERED *on my Sleeve isn't a "typical" romance. It's not even a typical MC Romance. Prepare yourself for Wrath and Trinity's long, tattered tale of lust, fury, and ultimately forgiveness.*

Lust.

Eight years ago, the Lost Kings, MC was recovering from turmoil within the club Wrath and Trinity met. Their connection was instant and explosive.

Fury.

After three perfect nights, Wrath knew she was the one. But Trinity's dark past was about to catch up to her and the Lost Kings MC was her only hope for protection. One misunderstanding leads to a mistake that locks both of them into a war to see who can hurt who the most.

Forgiveness.

Once Wrath learns the dark secret that's been fueling Trinity all this time, he'll stop at nothing to prove they're meant to be together and that she's worthy of the love she keeps denying. Can they move past their horrible pasts to become better people and ultimately forgive each other?

WHITE HEAT (LOST KINGS MC #5)

THE QUEEN ALWAYS PROTECTS HER KING.

For straight-laced attorney, Hope Kendall, loving an outlaw has never been easy. New challenges test her loyalty as she discovers how far she's willing to go to protect her man.

IF YOU HAVE HOPE, YOU HAVE EVERYTHING.

MC President, Rochlan "Rock" North finally has everything he's ever wanted. Hope as his ol' lady and his MC earning money while staying out of trouble. The only thing left is to make Hope his wife. But as their wedding day nears, an old adversary threatens Rock's freedom, the wedding, and throws the Lost Kings MC into chaos.

LOVE MAKES THE RIDE WORTHWHILE.

While the club waits for Rock's fate to be decided, Wrath has to balance solidifying his new relationship with Trinity and fulfilling his president's orders.

LOYALTY GIVES AN OUTLAW STRENGTH.

Threats from unexpected places will challenge every member, but in the Lost Kings MC, brotherhood isn't about the blood you share. It's about those who are willing to bleed for you.

BETWEEN EMBERS (LOST KINGS MC #5.5)

A companion to White Heat. Three short stories featuring Murphy, Teller, and Zero.

MORE THAN MILES (LOST KINGS MC #6)

Forbidden love is the hardest to forget...

Blake "Murphy" O'Callaghan, Road Captain of the Lost Kings MC, has the world by the balls. Money. Women. The wide-open road. It's all his, everything he wants...except the one girl he loves, the one girl who's off limits. His best friend's little sister, Heidi.

Abandoned by her mother when she was little, Heidi Whelan's familiar with heartbreak. Especially the heartbreak of falling in love with her big brother's best friend. When Murphy pushed her away, it broke her heart. Now, on her eighteenth birthday, he claims he loves her? Growing up around the Lost Kings MC, Heidi's witnessed his manwhoring ways. He'll never give that up for her. Besides, he's too late: Heidi's in love with her high-school boyfriend Axel.

Axel Ryan loves two things—motorcycles and Heidi. He signed up to be a prospect for the Lost Kings MC because it seemed like a fun way to get closer to her. Now that he's gotten a taste of MC life, he's not so sure this is where he belongs. He's confident Heidi shares his dreams for the future, so even if he chooses another road, their relationship will survive the detour.

With more than miles between them, will the deceptions they've lived with for so long be too much to overcome? Can Murphy convince Heidi that the hard roads they've traveled will lead to the most beautiful destination of all, or is he destined to ride the open road alone?

WHITE KNUCKLES (LOST KINGS MC #7)

TWO TATTERED SOULS
After countless detours, Wrath and Trinity's wedding is only ten days away. Together they've battled their demons and are ready to declare their commitment to each other in front of their entire Lost Kings MC family.

ONE BITTER ENEMY
No one is prepared for the threat that crawls out of the shadows and issues an evil ultimatum. One that places Trinity's future in danger and jeopardizes the entire club. Trinity's more than ready to put her life on the line to save the club. For her it's not a question.

AN IMPOSSIBLE CHOICE
Wrath's role as protector of the club forces him to choose between the safety of his angel or the future of the Lost Kings MC and all they've built together. But Trinity won't relent. A queen always fights for her king. She'll risk everything to hold on to the peace she shares with Wrath.

FAITH IS STRONGER THAN FEAR

When evil takes her for a ride, will Trinity's faith in Wrath and her faith in the Lost Kings MC be stronger than her fear?

BEYOND RECKLESS:
TELLER'S STORY, PART ONE
(LOST KINGS MC #8)

Blood doesn't make you family, loyalty does.

Marcel "Teller" Whelan, Treasurer of the Lost Kings MC, has always been two things—honest and responsible. At ten years old, he was already taking care of his baby sister. At eighteen, he patched into the Lost Kings MC and took a major role in shaping the club's future.

Three years ago, he thought he'd met the perfect woman, only to have her reject everything he is—a Lost King.

One bullet is a lifetime supply.

Now, after an accident that left a girl dead and Teller almost crippled, he's struggling through the darkest time in his life. His niece, sister, and Lost Kings MC family are the only things holding him together, but his reckless actions are bound to drive everyone away.

Then, in the most unlikely place, he crosses paths with her again. The woman he once thought might be his perfect match.

Love soothes our inner demons.

Sparks fly for both of them. She's the ride-or-die woman he needs, able to calm his many demons, and bring the light back into his life. But she has a secret—one that forces him to lie to his brothers.

In chaos we trust.

When Teller's brothers find out who he's falling in love with, it will create a storm of chaos for the Lost Kings MC. But if there's one thing Teller's turbulent life has taught him, it's that sometimes love is worth the chaos.

BEYOND REASON:
TELLER'S STORY, PART TWO
(LOST KINGS MC #9)

When the most toxic people come disguised as family, who can you trust?

BETRAYAL BY BLOOD *cuts the deepest.*

Teller's found his ride or die girl. The light Charlotte brings to his life has touched the darkest parts of his soul. But a devastating secret from her past resurfaces to threaten their future.

Every truth can be erased with one lie.

When a sinister truth is exposed, it forces Charlotte to question everything about herself. Even whether she's worthy of Teller's love.

The darkest betrayals never come from your enemies.

With Teller's love roaring louder than the lies, Charlotte can finally put her demons to rest. But has too much damage been done for her to prove her loyalty to the Lost Kings?

One Empire Night (Lost Kings MC #9.5)

Holiday novella featuring your favorite Lost Kings MC couples.

AFTER BURN (LOST KINGS MC #10)

One spilled secret shines a light on the throne of lies I've been sitting on for years.

A revelation with the power to test the bonds of brotherhood like never before.

Promises I've made to my brothers I burn to keep.

Vows made to my wife I swear to honor.

Through the web of tangled loyalties, one thing remains clear.

Hope is embedded in my soul.

A love so rare I've spilled blood to protect it.

Each painful piece of our pasts brought us to this moment.

Together, we've built something beautiful, significant, and ours.

And one uncovered truth could burn it all to the ground.

STAND ALONES
BULLETS & BONFIRES
Set in the same world as the Lost Kings MC
Murphy and Teller appear here.

The one man she's always wanted is now the sexy sheriff of their hometown.

Battered but not broken, grad student Brianna Avery returns to the childhood home she abandoned four years ago. With her abusive ex behind bars, Bree needs the summer to relax and recover before returning to school. But her overprotective brother decides she needs someone to babysit her in his absence, and he picks the one person guaranteed to drive her nuts.

She's the one woman he can't have.

Telling Bree no has never been easy. Four years ago, Liam Hollister did it to preserve his friendship with his best friend--Brianna's brother. Now, no matter how she tempts him, he's determined to do the right thing. As deputy sheriff of their rural area, Liam is torn between protecting Brianna and wanting her for himself.

Take a risk or lose the chance.

Spending so much time alone together challenges them both. Old feelings and hurts resurface immediately. With each hot, sweaty day, it's harder to deny their attraction.

It's going to be a long, hot summer.

WARNINGS & WILDFIRES
Wrath and Murphy appear here.

It's a hot summer morning and I'm already running late.

I'm no one's white knight, but when I see a damsel in distress, I have to rescue her.

I didn't know it would be Aubrey Dorado, the girl I swore was off-limits.

Now she's under my skin and I can't get her out of my head.

So, I did the worst thing possible and hired her to work in my gym.

Lusting after my new employee breaks my number one rule.

But each day she tempts me with her sweet personality and clever mind.

I've been burned by love before.

Romance is a risk I can't afford.

But how much longer can I resist the attraction simmering between us?

LOST KINGS MC COMING SOON
Zero Tolerance (Lost Kings MC #11)
White Lies (Lost Kings MC #12)

SOCIAL MEDIA

FIND ME ON:
BookBub
Goodreads
Instagram
Facebook
Pinterest
Spotify
Book & Main Bites
Website: autumnjoneslake.com
AutumnJLake@gmail.com

If you loved spending time with the Lost Kings MC, please, do me a favor and leave a review at your favorite retailer, Goodreads, or on BookBub. As a independent author, I rely on reviews to help get the word out about my books. A few quick words can mean so much!
Thank you!

The End

74661592R00178

Made in the USA
Columbia, SC
13 September 2019